Praise for *Dream City: A Novel*

"Doug Unger's *Dream City* is a splendorous example of Borges's dictum that stories are about situations and novels are about characters. *Dream City* is also about Las Vegas, the traps of uncontrolled greed, and the futile attempts of one C.D. Reinhart to try to make things right. Carefully written, brilliantly structured, *Dream City* is hard to put down."

—Pablo Medina, author of *The Cuban Comedy: A Novel*

"Doug Unger goes behind the scenes in the real Las Vegas to find the Machiavellian intrigue lurking beneath the glittering surface. *Dream City* is to twenty-first century Las Vegas what *Bonfire of the Vanities* was to twentieth century New York—a marvel and a cautionary tale. This is the quintessential novel about America's most fascinating and archetypal city, where greed and ambition also make room for love and redemption."

—Sally Denton, author of *The Colony: Faith and Blood in a Promised Land*

"Doug Unger's *Dream City* captures that most American place, Las Vegas, in a most American period of growth and excess. Unger plunges his readers into a fictional account of a real transformation, in which a sleepy gambling town first becomes the brightest place on earth and then the hardest-hit metropolis in the country. Through his main character, a somehow naïve yet fully complicit hotel executive, the narrator deftly creates two realities: the anything-goes, win-at-all-costs giddy world of those raking in the cash, and the soullessness of a success measured only by wealth. Is this cautionary tale—an insider's account of the rise and fall of Sin City—the canary in the coal mine for twenty-first century America?"

—Laura McBride, author of *We Are Called To Rise: A Novel* and *The Midnight Room: A Novel*

"I don't think anybody has ever written about Vegas with this kind of depth and understanding and heart. Doug Unger knows its history and sees its future. *Dream City* reads as something important in our understanding of the lives and hearts of the new West. What a deep pleasure this book is."

—Charles Bock, author of *Beautiful Children: A Novel* and *Alice & Oliver: A Novel*

"I was worried about the subject. Everyone is bored with Vegas as mobster playground—and *Grand Theft Auto* makes a book in that genre quaint and passé. Unger's book is something else entirely. It's just stunning. By putting mid-life middle class malaise into a planet of G-strings, 24–hour entertainment and con-artist "entrepreneurs," it's simply a book I couldn't stop reading—it's real estate fever and busloads of desperate seekers of happiness on a budget hoping that 'three coins can change their lives.' The Great American Casino."

—Greg Palast, author of *The Best Democracy Money Can Buy* and *A Tale of Billionaires & Ballot Bandits*, broadcaster for the BBC, and frequent contributor to *The Guardian*

"Scholars and historians of Vegas will avidly read *Dream City*. Unger is a novelist of the highest order—in ambition as well as craft."

—Christopher Coake, English professor and program director of the University of Nevada, Reno MFA program, author of *You Came Back: A Novel*

DREAM CITY

Western Literature and Fiction Series

Like the iconic physical landscape and diverse cultures that inspire it, the literature of the American West is imbued with power and beauty. The Western Literature and Fiction Series invites scholarship reflecting on the authors and works that define the creative expression of the past and present while championing the literary fiction that propels us forward.

Drowning in the Desert
Bernard Schopen

The Ghost Dancers
Adrian C. Louis

This Here is Devil's Work
Curtis Bradley Vickers

The Brightest Place in the World
David Philip Mullins

The Desert Between Us
Phyllis Barber

The Saints of Rattlesnake Mountain
Don Waters

The Gambler's Apprentice
H. Lee Barnes

The Goodbye House
Lawrence Coates

Sunland: A Novel
Don Waters

Cold Deck
H. Lee Barnes

Dream City
Douglas Unger

Dream City

A Novel

DOUGLAS UNGER

UNIVERSITY OF NEVADA PRESS | *Reno & Las Vegas*

University of Nevada Press | Reno, Nevada 89557 USA
www.unpress.nevada.edu

Portions of this novel have appeared in very different form in *Narrative, Boulevard,* the *Southwest Review* and the anthologies *West of 98: Living and Writing in the New American West* and *Getting Better All the Time: Las Vegas Writers Explore Progress.*

Manufactured in the United States of America

FIRST PRINTING

Cover design by David Ter-Avanesyan/Ter33Design
Cover photographs © by Shutterstock

Library of Congress Cataloging-in-Publication Data

Names: Unger, Douglas, author.
Title: Dream city / Douglas Unger.
Other titles: Western literature and fiction series.
Description: Reno, Nevada : University of Nevada Press, [2024] | Series: Western literature and fiction series | Summary: "*Dream City* is a portrait of Las Vegas in its boom years before the bust that came with the Great Recession, told through the experiences of Curtis "C. D." Reinhart, a failed actor who launches a new career in hotel marketing in corporate Las Vegas during the years when it became the fastest growing city in the United States. Unger's novel becomes a *Bonfire of the Vanities* story of Las Vegas with less parody, more politics, and a psycho-history that sets it apart from anything ever written about this iconic city and global entertainment attraction that in many ways represents postmodern America." —Provided by publisher.
Subjects: LCSH: Las Vegas (Nev.)—Fiction. | LCGFT: Novels.
Classification: LCC PS3571.N45 D74 2024 | DDC 813/.54—dc23/eng/20240304
LC record available at https://lccn.loc.gov/2024003736

ISBN 978-1-64779-165-0 (cloth)
ISBN 978-1-64779-166-7 (ebook)
LCCN: 2024003736

The paper used in this book meets the requirements of American National Standard for Information Sciences—Permanence of Paper for Printed Library Materials, ANSI/NISO Z39.48–1992 (R2002).

For Carola

Postmodern, post-industrial capitalism is about consuming experience, not goods, about creating insatiable desire that must be fulfilled in front of an approving audience. Las Vegas is geared to meet this challenge, to provide the audience, to deliver more than anywhere else and hold out the possibility of still more. The ability to quench desire brings people; the chance to dream of more brings them back again and again.

—Hal Rothman, *Neon Metropolis*

O God, I could be bounded in a nutshell and
count myself the king of infinite space were it not
that I had bad dreams.

—William Shakespeare, *Hamlet*

Acting is believing.

—Common advice for student actors

DREAM CITY

Pyramid World

– 1 –

This is the way it must have happened: just before noon, apprentice ironworker Lester "Red" Stahl delivered a box of bolts for his crew on the twenty-first floor of the rising pyramid. The lower floors were busy with work gangs already setting the gold glass windows into place, the rising levels of the construction beginning to look like a finished hotel. Red Stahl's foreman sent him off on an early lunch break while the rest of his crew finished setting up forms for pouring concrete that afternoon. On his way past the crew lift, Red grabbed his lunchbox from a heap of gear in a metal tub. He stepped gingerly in his steel-toed boots along a narrow walkway toward a corner of the vast skeletal I-beam structure to where a half wall of plywood sheeting was set up. He meant to sit and rest his back against it to eat his lunch—a chicken-fried steak hero with mustard and mayo topped off with a lettuce leaf, made that morning by his wife. He could wash it down with a chocolate drink Wilma had heated up for his thermos. He was looking forward to its warmth and to a little shelter from the chilly February winds.

Red Stahl had been working as a runner for his crew all morning, balancing on the walkways and beams in his safety harness as he hefted lengths of steel rebar and spools of wire. He would be glad when they finished laying out the forms, double-checking that the corners were tied off right, all done and ready for the concrete crews. He hoped they might be sent home early today. Red found the plywood half wall where it should be, set up around one of four big air shafts. He squatted down and flipped open his dented lunchbox. On top he found a piece of his daughter's purple construction paper cut into the shape of a heart, folded in the middle. He opened it and saw that it was a note from his wife, written in her girlish, looping penmanship: *Be Mine, Valentine! Love Forever, Your Baby, Wilma—XXXXOOOOO.*

And maybe that was how it happened—the distraction of reading this sweet little note—as he swung around, still in a squat, plopping himself on his butt, then leaned his weight against the plywood.

Maybe it was this one lapse in his usually cautious nature that caused him not to test the things around him and notice that this time, this morning, the workers who usually set up the plywood had been rushing so much that they had failed to do more than pump in two lone screws on each side of the safety barrier to bolt it down. On any other day Red would have tested it first, would have pushed against it to make sure. He would have been more careful. Savoring his wife's valentine, no doubt thinking of the happy evening waiting for him at home, he relaxed and leaned back. The plywood twisted loose off its screws, tipped over, and fell away. Red Stahl's leaning carried him right along with it. He flipped violently back and over into the open air shaft, too late to catch himself, too late to grab onto anything. . . then the fast accelerating slide into the long falling.

Glass workers busy on the fourteenth floor heard three loud echoing booms as Red Stahl's body banged against the air shaft walls, then not another sound as he fell the rest of the twenty-one stories in a long straight shot all the way down. He crashed through at the bottom with what sounded like a bomb going off—enough impact that his weight ripped loose off its bolts a sheet metal intake vent that crumpled around his body like a piece of paper squeezed in a fist. A section broke free and fell in a heap of wreckage on top of what was left of him, his body buried under a tangle of twisted steel deep in the subbasement foundations. High above, at the edge of the gaping air shaft, the dented lunchbox still sat open, the purple valentine fluttering inside it in the winds.

—

Eighteen months into his job, the rush gone mad to complete the new Pyramid World hotel casino made Curtis "C. D." Reinhart feel like he'd been dropped into a whirligig carnival ride that whipped him up and back through the air then slammed him side to side until his teeth hurt. Up before dawn to gulp down coffee, scrape his face, shake out then squirm into his suit and snap a rag across his shoes, and at the breakfast table only time for a quick kiss on the cheek for Grace and a one-armed embrace around little Catherine's shoulders. It was the Friday before Valentine's Day. He noted the construction-paper hearts Catherine was cutting out with blunted scissors for her friends at school. He pressed his lips to the top knob of her spine so he could deliver a loud raspberry kiss that made her giggle and squeal. He broke off, singing, "A hug and a peck and a kiss around the neck!"

He danced out the side door, hefting his Tumi shoulder bag, a piece of toast gripped in his teeth as he shook out his keys, got in the car, and backed out of the garage. He cruised at least ten miles an hour over the legal speed along Piñon Way, racing out of the new suburbs ever expanding into the desert. Rays of sun broke over Sunrise Mountain, which shimmered in the distance like a huge stress-washed block of stone. His tires burned rubber at the turn onto Green Valley Parkway, then it was a hard left onto Sunset Boulevard, right onto Pecos down to Flamingo then the home stretch toward looming resort towers glimmering through a haze over The Las Vegas Strip and his office, dodging traffic on his way, the old joke proving true: you can always tell a Vegas driver; he's the third car through the red light.

After checking in on his "war room" staff getting a start on entering data from yesterday's new batch of Big Top and Camelot customer surveys, he settled down to the phone work. He kept busy researching and writing up recommendations for a new PMS software system for Pyramid World, setting up the consultancy visits. His team was also taking bids on what kind of hardware to invest in that could help effect the leap into a unified network for a new reservations, pricing, and accounts management system for all three Pyramid Resorts hotels. Out with the old and in with the new, money no object, according to CFO Lance Sheperd. The only real issue would be getting it all purchased and installed and all the bugs worked out in time to meet J. B. Roland's ridiculously advancing deadlines to beat to the finish line his rival, Steve Wynn, racing to open the new Treasure Island. All this crazy rush to finish, and for what? A pissing contest between the moguls? Wasn't it more important to build it right?

"Just get it done," Lance Sheperd insisted. Almost impossible on the timeline—still, it wasn't his place to question. He understood his role to be the loyal trouper: he would follow directions, do what he was told. Everywhere at Pyramid Resorts one mandate ruled: *Just get it done*. His boss worked ever closer to nervous extremes, his thin lips sucking quirkily rapid little sips from an imported bottle of some exotic water in between bursts of his one-liner commands. A meeting with Sheperd meant being interrupted by urgent phone calls every few minutes, to which he shot off curt replies: "Yes" or "Right" or "No" or "No way" or "Forget it" or "Table that" or his most common reply, "Just get it done."

At the building site itself, the unusual challenging construction of the pyramid-shaped hotel rose under a high skeletal crane. Rushing to meet the ever-advancing completion date was causing problems. C. D. saw this up close on site inspections for visiting representatives of investors and PR tours with the press. Contractors and subcontractors took dangerous short cuts: no proper safety cage was yet installed on the upper construction elevator that shakily lifted the workers up through a jungle of I-beams and mammoth concrete forms before they stepped out under the tall crane swinging a dangerous hook and massive hunks of steel overhead. No cables were yet strung on any of the top floors, as per OSHA regulations, onto which the workers could anchor safety harnesses, so half the time laborers did their jobs while hooked to the very same piece of steel they were standing on, or worse, they left themselves unhooked. Safety nets that should have been strung out every two floors or no more than thirty feet below the highest levels had been left balled up somewhere on the crowded site. All around and above, a hundred iron workers seemed to C. D. like a company of hard-hatted trapeze artists dancing and swinging in the sky, relying on balance and luck alone to get them through. He gripped onto whatever pipe or beam or anything he could reach, the noise up there like a huge stereo speaker with the volume set to the max on a hammering concert of crashes and clangs, the ceaseless, whistling desert wind causing a painful pressure in his ears.

Up and down The Strip, the same scene repeated itself, with more new mammoth hotels being built than anywhere else on the planet: the Oz Resort a shimmering city of emerald green; the tower at Caesars like a Roman monument; a half dozen smaller off-Strip "locals'" casino hotels in various stages of completion, two alone by the Station Casinos Group; Steve Wynn's Treasure Island—their main competition—like a Caribbean fantasy; and Pyramid World rising like a glass and steel replica of the famous tombs of the ancient pharaohs. In less than two years, Las Vegas had transformed into one immense construction site stretching off in all directions, crowded with machinery at the edges of deep excavations and tons of materials piled on top of each other in precarious stacks. Twenty thousand workers labored under pressure, hundreds high in the air putting in exhausting overtime to build and build and build at record speed. And at his own less hazardous job in the junior executive ranks, the mandate from "up at corporate" to *just get it done* required C. D. Reinhart to put in twelve- and fourteen-hour days until he too felt like he flew through the air on his own very high, very risky trapeze.

– 2 –

News of the fatal accident hit the Project Development offices around 12:30. Most of the staff had finished early and left for the long weekend—Sunday was Valentine's Day, Presidents' Day on Monday. Lance Sheperd had awarded his overstressed team a rare holiday, their first day off since Christmas. According to what little information they could get from Nate Provenzano, construction manager on the site, an apprentice iron worker, one Lester "Red" Stahl, had fallen into an air shaft, no one knew just how. All work had shut down. Emergency crews were on site, assessing the situation and trying to recover the man's body.

C. D. took Tim Slocum's call from up at corporate for an emergency meeting.

"Where's Greta?" Slocum asked. "Why doesn't she answer her phone?"

"Probably in the air," C. D. said. Greta Olsson, who handled most press and PR, had taken the day off. Following her difficult divorce and several disappointments with other men, lately she had bucked herself up by dating a way-too-young-for-her Washington staffer for Senator Richard Bryan, a kid rumored to be barely twenty-one, flying back and forth on weekends like she no longer cared what people said, or maybe she thought dating a much younger guy might cause the senior executives to pay her some attention. Still, that left C. D. responsible, though for what, he wasn't sure. "It's just me," C. D. said. "Me and a few guys from development."

"Round 'em up then," Slocum said. "Lance and I are on our way."

C. D. tried Greta's mobile telephone, that big brick of a thing with an antenna poking out she carried in an oversized purse—nothing. In that era just before the spread of cell phones, it was hard to find coverage that reached more than fifty miles. C. D. started pulling guys into the conference room, the few team members left in the office. Rick Rickstein first, a procurement specialist and purchasing guy, an Israeli who kept his head shaved like a bullet and who preferred high-collared suit jackets, like Nehru jackets or Marine dress blues that he ordered from a shop in Paris to make himself stand out among the junior executives and because he hated wearing ties. Rickstein shook his bullet head miserably, baffled to be included. He said in his accented English, "Why must we make any statement? We are not responsible. Won't a press release make it look like we are?"

Rickstein was right, as usual—management at most casino hotels would have said little or nothing aside from an internal note of sympathy, leaving the official statement to the construction firm. Press inquiries would have been left to team members like Greta Olsson.

"Who knows? Must be some reason," C. D. said.

He found Gary Luongo stuffed into his cramped, windowless space in the strip mall office suite amid his three telephones, his file boxes, and his multiple rolodexes—"Customer Relations Planning" was his ad hoc department, but nobody really knew just what job Luongo did on the team, except maybe advance sales to his exclusive list of the Whales and High Rollers he guarded like a family inheritance, which it probably was. Besides this, J. B. Roland, the Big Boss, showed an inexplicable fondness for Luongo dating back to the notorious "Black Book" era of wise guys and mobsters into which Luongo, the only native Las Vegan among them, had been born. J. B. had insisted he be put on their team. At meetings Luongo would say little or nothing. He usually leaned his big head of black curly hair into his hand in a bored-looking way while taking notes—always the notes with Luongo, written in a schoolboy's spiral notebook. "Tough break," Luongo said, with a touch of inherited New York accent. He settled himself not at the table but into a leather chair in one corner of the conference room.

Last, C. D. found Mark Kinkaid, the project accountant, as ever at his desk, sleeves rolled, an oily sheen of perspiration on his high forehead, a guy who gobbled antacid tablets by the roll, just waiting for the next "change order" to skew his calculations and push his staff into overtime. While waiting for Slocum and Sheperd to show up, Kinkaid wondered how much delay the accident could cause. "Jeez, it might be the only upside to this, if things can shut down for a few days? Time to catch up?"

"That's *cold,*" Luongo said, smirking.

"A man died," Rickstein said. "Maybe we can show respect?"

"Sorry," Kinkaid said. J. B. had promised a generous completion bonus to Mancini Construction, to be calculated based on how many days ahead of schedule the building could be finished. Kinkaid needed a steady supply of chewable antacid tablets as he kept trying to divine how much—and even *if*—to accord such a bonus in his balance sheets.

Slocum and Sheperd strode in hurriedly, without any greeting. Tim Slocum, VP of Legal and Business Affairs, took yellow legal pads and pens from a leather briefcase and daintily circled the table, laying them out. Sheperd would usually run their meetings with the brusque manner of a military officer giving orders, any finer points he wanted discussed gone over ahead of time with his staff by phone. He always spoke first, then would bluster and talk, fast, leaving little room for questions or replies. His fast-talking made Kinkaid joke that he always felt like he needed a Valium after their meetings. This meeting felt different, though, as Slocum circled the table, Sheperd standing by in silence. When Sheperd finally spoke, he seemed shaken, his voice subdued as he rattled off a quick summary of what he knew. Sheperd's cheeks puffed, the way they did when he was under pressure. Then he let slip, "J. B. didn't say a word. He just phoned Mancini and asked how long this would delay the schedule."

"None of us heard that, right?" Slocum checked out each of them around the table. "Let's be careful. I'm sure we're in the clear on this. Legally, this is Mancini Construction's problem, or one of their subcontractor's. Still, we don't want to *hint* at anything we wouldn't like to hear repeated in front of a judge. Are we agreed?"

The guys all nodded, agreed. C. D. sensed there might be something else going on up at corporate they didn't know about, maybe some other courtroom Slocum might be warning them against, one different from any civil action possibly arising from the workplace death. An increasing tension had infected the office in recent weeks that wasn't only about the rush to completion: whispers about J. B. Roland's pill-popping, erratic behavior, how the Old Man kept blowing up at his top executives in front of board members, plus other signs of uncertainty, like Rickstein suddenly having his budget to purchase such essentials as half a million yards of carpet and a hundred thousand light bulbs cut by 20 percent one day then abruptly restored three days later. Sheperd had moved up C. D.'s deadline twice on the new IT system and software, then in their last phone call he had said, "Forget the deadline. Just get it done. Now."

Battle lines were being drawn up at corporate. A war would soon begin, anybody's guess who among them would be left standing.

In the conference room, Sheperd remained on his feet at the head of the table, leaning against it with both arms supporting his weight, his attention uncharacteristically drifting from the issue in the room, as if he might be thinking about something personal, C. D. guessed, maybe even of his own father, a union carpenter who must have worked on unsafe construction sites. But he could never be sure exactly what Sheperd was thinking underneath his many loud authoritarian poses he meant to come off as brilliant surfaces he had carefully cut and faceted so that, any which way he turned, he intended to shed light. Grace lately preferred to avoid that assertive brilliance, not wanting to attend obligatory dinners and cocktail hours hosted by the company. "Where's *his* wife?" she asked. "Don't you think it's odd he's almost never with his wife? So why do *I* have to be dragged along?" Sheperd's wife seemed to be living full-time in a beach house in Corona del Mar, rarely seen at company functions, although all the other wives were expected to attend. Grace thought Lance Sheperd brash and boorish. "Listen," she had said, pressing closer to C. D.'s ear at a recent benefit dinner at the old Desert Inn. "When he talks, his voice is so loud you can't hear anyone else in the room!"

Today, at the head of the table, Sheperd asked in a subdued voice, "What shows we care and won't get us in any trouble?" He puffed his cheeks, letting out a breath.

For the next hour they tossed out and tested lines and phrases, Tim Slocum writing their words on the white board. C. D. had offered to do this—Greta Olsson would have taken charge at the board if she had been there—but Slocum insisted. He wrote out a sentence, they talked it through, then he erased it and they started again. Slocum argued against any direct statement of sympathy, favoring a brief but strong assertion of the company's commitment to the health and safety of its subcontracted workers. Sheperd overruled him, insisting on leading with some compassionate words. "Close with those words too then," C. D. said. He recalled an old saying from acting classes in his youth: "Ring a bell once, then ring it again, that's the rule."

Sheperd and Slocum argued about whether or not to name the deceased, Slocum citing a statistic that companies that named their dead employees in press statements were more likely to get sued.

"Name him," Sheperd insisted. "The man has a name."

In trade for this, Sheperd gave in to Slocum's demand for language reasserting the company's commitment to workplace safety. Rickstein backed him up. C. D. said, "Ring that bell twice too. Like a rhyming couplet. Like Shakespeare."

Slocum aimed a baffled look at him—a look he might give a turnip that had showed up in his groceries by mistake.

"That's what Greta would do with this," C. D. said, too softly, then he shut up.

Kinkaid added a thought about an injury the year before during a remodel job at The Big Top Hotel. Slocum wrote a phrase vaguely alluding to this. Luongo, as ever, said little or nothing. He nodded like he agreed when asked and took his notes, too many notes. Why did Luongo take so many notes? C. D. often felt a queasy contraction just below his diaphragm whenever he got close to Luongo or fell under the scrutiny of his steady gaze. He wondered what Luongo was actually doing on this project. Other than his little black book of contacts with club managers and call girls, his willingness to put in nights as a host to visiting High Rollers and Whales, why was he even here?

Their last revised draft inserted the word *prayers* in a final "ring the bell twice" sentence C. D. suggested—the religious note Slocum's idea, his experience was that a company offering prayers would be less likely to be perceived as liable. Finally they came up with a finished press release, C. D. printing the statement out by hand on lined legal-size paper. He delivered it to the head administrative assistant, Susan Wheeler, left abandoned at her desk by the other office staff, impatient to get done and home. She quickly typed it up to send to their usual list of two dozen fax contacts in the local press along with an alert that the executives were on their way. Susan would also format it with dark borders to be posted on employee bulletin boards by Tuesday.

C. D. proofed the text, then waited as the Xerox machine pushed out thirty copies. He grabbed them up along with three white company hard hats from his office closet and followed Sheperd and

Slocum out of the building. In his hurry, he forgot the blue cardigan he wore on wintry days under his suit jacket, regretting that oversight instantly as he felt the chilly wind in the parking lot. He trotted along behind the two bosses. He tossed the hard hats into the back seat of Slocum's big gold boat of a Cadillac Seville. The two executives didn't glance back once to see if he were following, knowing he would be there, as faithful as a good golf caddy, one of the regulars who accompanied site visits, relying on his memorized pitch, riding on his smile and a shoe shine. The three drove along in silence as Slocum negotiated his Cadillac through heavy traffic up Paradise to Tropicana and turned toward The Strip. C. D. glanced out the back window at Luongo and Rickstein following in a company car, a white Ford Crown Victoria, Luongo at the wheel. He wondered how Luongo had rated a company car, no doubt awarded to him directly by J. B. Roland.

At the construction site the crane had stopped. Most workers had been sent home, though a gang of Lester "Red" Stahl's fellow top-men had already unfurled a makeshift banner, a crudely painted drop cloth by the entrance to the site: *We loved you, Red!,* and under that, *Ironworkers Union Local 433*. The flashing lights of Clark County Fire Department trucks and an ambulance shone in the distance by a dark entrance leading into the unfinished building, a high triangular arch under a partly glassed-in slope at the base of the pyramid. Some distance inside, a police tape barrier had been set up, behind which TV crews, reporters, and photographers already waited. Slocum showed his ID at the guard trailer then pulled in to park the car amid the two-story-high heaps of glass, steel beams, and construction materials piled everywhere. Dust blew up. Bits of debris drummed against the car. Slocum and Sheperd pulled off their ties, unbuttoned their collars, and put on hard hats. C. D. did the same.

"Showtime," Slocum said.

They got out of the car. Nate Provenzano, project construction manager, milled around the main trailer with a small troop of assistants. Sheperd joined them, and they followed Provenzano along a rutted path through the house-high heaps of building materials. Somewhere behind them, Luongo and Rickstein trotted to catch up. This would be a statement and photo op for the press: Lance Sheperd, the public face of Pyramid World, would be photographed along with

Provenzano on the inspection tour, leaning over yellow police tape. The two men would gaze downward into an eerie, arc-lit darkness in the subbasement at the firefighters and Mancini crews still laboring at the wreckage with cutting torches. It would take hours to extract what was left of Lester Stahl from the mangled steel that wrapped his body. C. D. enlisted Rickstein to help him pass out copies of the press release to the reporters. Quick flashes from cameras lit up the spooky underworld of skeletal steel and concrete pillars that rose all around and above them into a dusty haze.

The photo that eventually ran in the newspapers was of Lance Sheperd gazing off alongside Nate Provenzano at the recovery work going on below, their faces lit by an orange glow of showering sparks from cutting torches, Sheperd's expression tight and drawn, like he was chewing on a piece of bitter root, his posture as though making ready to step off into the mouth of an inferno so he could personally attempt a rescue. Cameras flashed. Then Sheperd, Slocum, and Provenzano arranged themselves into a trio in front of the press barrier for the TV news crews, Sheperd at their center stepping forward to the microphones. C. D. positioned himself twenty feet from these principals, shivering in the cold, Rickstein beside him holding the high collar of his jacket closed, Luongo a few feet further to one side, his notebook out, as ever writing things down.

Before he spoke, Lance Sheperd paused, masterfully removing his hard hat in a reverent gesture, letting it slowly drop to his side as if it weighed fifty pounds. He stared straight into the cameras, bowed his head a little, then recited their press release from memory: *Pyramid Resorts is deeply saddened by the accidental death of Lester "Red" Stahl, who worked for the Mancini Construction Company building Pyramid World. Pyramid Resorts is concerned about safety in everything we do, whether it's a room remodel or a project as complex and enormous as building Pyramid World. Given the large number of workers on the site and the scale of activity going on, we are proud that Pyramid Resorts consistently maintains the safest possible work environment. We offer our condolences and prayers to Mr. Stahl's family and friends.*

Sheperd nodded just once and replaced the hard hat on his head. He waved off the shouted questions. As if in a small funeral procession, the junior executives joined in a slow march behind him. Nate

Provenzano led them solemnly out through the triangular mouth of the pyramid entrance to one of the construction company trailers. They mounted the steps and trooped inside. The trailer felt crowded by a long table on which blueprints were already spread out, showing details of the twenty-first floor. They clustered around the table as Provenzano briefed them and pointed out in the complex maze of a blueprint where the accident had occurred.

"He wasn't using his safety harness, bottom line," Provenzano said. "Somehow, and we'll find out how, he fell through a plywood barrier around the air shaft. We've put the shift foreman on suspension. The subcontractor's sending in a team. The OSHA reps will do an inspection Tuesday morning."

Neither Sheperd nor Slocum said anything in answer to this.

Some of the dead man's things were laid out on Provenzano's desk: a ball of sweat-darkened leather work gloves, a frayed red scarf, a thermos bottle, an opened lunchbox with an untouched lunch inside, and a purple construction-paper heart. Sheperd inspected these items, picked up the paper heart, and read the note. His neck and shoulders visibly tightened, then he passed the note to Slocum to read. Slocum shook his head grimly.

"Should be no problem," Provenzano said, his voice quickening, his expression as if he wanted to push them physically away from the desk but didn't dare. "We're still way ahead of schedule," he said. "Glass work starts again on Monday. We're giving the top crew Monday off, then it's back up to speed just as soon as we get the OSHA reps out of the way. No problem."

He gazed around, expecting some reply, then with growing urgency glanced toward C. D. as if looking for help, though he must have understood that Reinhart wasn't in any such position. A long, heavy moment passed. "Anybody see a problem here?" Provenzano asked.

Nobody answered. Sheperd turned to the table and leaned in closer over the blueprints, lost in thought, his finger tracing over a small square marked by a red x on the building plans. Over Provenzano's table, Slocum stared out through the grimy window into a heap of steel beams dumped as crazily as a spilled box of huge toothpicks. Everywhere out the windows, the view looked more like a junkyard than a construction site.

"Not to worry, there shouldn't be any problem," Provenzano

said. "We'll fly the Safety and Compliance guy in from Houston. He'll work with the OSHA reps and the union team."

Slocum asked to see all drafts of reports in writing before Mancini finalized them.

"Sure thing," Provenzano said.

"Do it," Sheperd said, and the briefing ended.

As they trooped out, C. D. noted how a grit of pebbles and dirt clods on the floor scuffed his shoe shine, as if the trailer hadn't been swept in weeks. At the top of the steps, Provenzano called out after them, "We'll come through clean on this one! Trust me!"

At Slocum's car, Sheperd tossed his hard hat in with such force that it bounced off the back window. "*Fuck!*" he let loose. He slammed the car door. "I don't give a good goddamn what J. B. says, or anybody else! Get down to Houston and put the fear of God into Mancini to clean up this *mess!* And *fuck* the holiday! Make 'em cancel their plans. Do it Monday. Make 'em sweat. We want safety reviews on every part of this site before we let them start up again."

"It's a goddamn miracle we don't have ten funerals to go to instead of one," said Slocum. "Provenzano should be fired, but that might screw up the schedule. Jesus." He shook his head as he made the turn into the weekend traffic jam on Tropicana. "I've seen accidents, but *this* one, Jesus . . ."

"*You.*" Sheperd turned in his seat. He leveled a look at C. D. that felt like a punch to his chest. "Meet me at my office, tomorrow morning, 8:30. I've got an assignment for you."

"Sure thing. I'll see you there," C. D. said.

"Good job on that press release," Sheperd added.

C. D. swallowed, tasting a dry metallic dust at the back of his throat. He wondered how Greta might have handled the situation differently, anticipating how pissed she would be at him for not running it by her, no matter that he couldn't have done anything else.

"I think it hits the right note," C. D. said finally.

"We'll see," Slocum said. "You never know with a mess like this. So much for the long weekend. The Old Man didn't want us to take it anyway, not one day off until we get her done."

Sheperd didn't answer. He gazed off moodily into the dust-blowing traffic jam. A raft of cars, several out of their lanes, floated in closer, honking horns. They were locked in, no way out. Up ahead, a double-mixer concrete truck had jack-knifed at the corner of Tropicana and Las Vegas Boulevard, all blocked off by emergency vehicles with flashing lights. The only way that could have happened, C. D. thought, was if the driver had attempted the turn going too fast, way above any safe or legal speed.

– 3 –

The Saturday edition of the *Las Vegas Review Journal* ran a small headline and brief story about the accident at Pyramid World below the fold, the press release boxed off and reprinted verbatim in the continuation of the story in the Business section. The fat Sunday paper—a special edition with an insert of Valentine's Day features, its pages bordered by hearts pierced by Cupid's arrows—would run an expanded story buried six pages deep into the Locals section. Both printed Lester "Red" Stahl's smiling picture, hard hat tipped slightly up and back over a fringe of wooly sun-orange hair. Under one of his thick muscular arms, he cradled a red-and-white-painted Runnin' Rebels basketball—he had been a big fan of UNLV, so the story said. The photo ran flanked by a stark picture of Lance Sheperd and Nate Provenzano lit up by a glow of cutting torch sparks, gazing into a mangled heap of metal below.

C. D. took in the photos, surprised to find that Red Stahl was African American—he hadn't thought of the man as black until then. The grinning photograph and the fact that he had two children made his death more personal, more real. C. D. reassured himself about their press release, thinking that it contrasted favorably and should be a lot more comforting for the Stahl family than the cold disclaimer issued by Mancini Construction. The difference between the two should instantly create an impression of which company, if any, should be the one to blame: *Mancini Construction is proud that its safety record is consistently better than the national average for a company of its size. On every job site, we make every effort to follow strict safety practices and we require our numerous subcontractors to do the same.*

That Saturday morning, Grace barely hid her disappointment that C. D. would have to suit up and go off to work again on a planned day off. He should have slept in an hour longer, then lingered over breakfast, done a few chores around the house, and gone off on errands together with Grace and little Catherine: the grocery shopping, the garden store, then a lunch out, a rare day with the family.

Instead he rose almost as early as he usually did, polished his shoes, and threw on his suit so he could make the meeting on time.

As he negotiated his way across the crowded Big Top casino floor to the corporate office suite to meet with his boss, C. D. recalled his first day on the job, almost two years ago, and his first orientation. Lance Sheperd had fast-talked, barking sidewise over his shoulder as C. D. hurried to keep up with his executive power walk through the milling crowds and gaudy décor of The Big Top's casino floor. "Almost nothing anybody needs to be ashamed of in Vegas," Sheperd said. "You toss a chip out on the table, you're treated the same as anyone else. Nobody gives a damn where you come from, where you're going is all that counts."

In a spectacle overhead, trapeze artists soared, swinging and letting go through the air over a spider web of nets strung out over the casino floor. It was hard to hear Sheperd through the noise of ringing bells, of coins *chunk-a-chunk-chunking* into metal trays deep into the labyrinths of slot machines, over shouts and cheers rising up in roiling waves from craps and card tables that stretched off into the buzzing distance like islands of fertile green fields. Dealers costumed in shirts with puffed sleeves and tight black pants like sword swallowers or fire breathers leaned over the games, their fingers flipping machine-like through stacks of chips as roving pit bosses, like *capos* in sharkskin suits, watched over them. Cocktail waitresses in black net stockings and stiff tutus cut low for maximum décolletage glided through the crowd with heavy trays held high, balancing on their spike heels. The crowd seemed like ones he'd seen at county fairs, dressed in a colorful motley of polo shirts, T-shirts, baseball caps, everywhere gripping popcorn boxes, cotton candy, drinks in plastic cups. Row upon row of people in trances bent over slot machines, pumping in the coins. In a roped-off line for the all-you-can-eat buffet, bellies swung over waists like sacks of meal. He followed Sheperd past the buffet line on their way to a discreet elevator to the corporate offices.

"Don't judge by what you see here," Sheperd said. He punched the elevator button. It was uncanny again how he seemed to read C. D.'s thoughts—his *second* thoughts after taking the new job. "This is all past history, the low-end market, built for rubes and open-mouth breathers hoping the next three coins will change their lives. That's over," he said. "We're scaling it up. We're on our way to a new future on the higher end."

Whenever C. D. was near Lance Sheperd, his thoughts and questions broke up and scrambled into a scratchy static like a radio signal in a strong magnetic field. His first year on the job he would keep note cards in his pockets, writing down what he wished to say or ask before their meetings. Sheperd had grown up the son of a semi-employed carpenter, crammed with three sisters into a saltbox house in Escondido, California, so in part he was powered by his ambitions to escape the confines of that youth spent fighting off poverty. Like C. D., in college he had at first thrown himself obsessively into pursuing an art and had failed—sculpture, in Sheperd's case, with scholarships at Cal Arts, even managing a few critically successful but financially disappointing post-student exhibitions before, as he put it, "My first wife and I found ourselves living in a walk-in closet rented from a friend. All that sculpture I'd spent years welding together rusted away in a vacant lot in Long Beach. Wasn't long before she up and left me. So I took a job cold-calling, selling stocks, and enrolled in night school for an MBA. Then I landed a gig with a firm selling those new beautiful things called *junk bonds*—lucked into that, learning everything I could from Michael Milken, what a genius that guy is, his whole jail thing never should have happened. I left that job and moved here to join Big Top, working the other side of junk bonds for them. And here I am now, ten years later, the CFO of a whole new company. Things happen fast in Vegas, if you've got ambition."

Sheperd rattled off all of this in response to a query by C. D. about how he had landed in Las Vegas, asking as a break-the-ice courtesy but really acting on that salesman's basic rule to put the prospect at ease with a personal question: *How's the wife and kids?* He followed him through and down the austere hallways of The Big Top corporate offices. Sheperd stopped at a black metal door at the end of a hall and pulled out a key. Before unlocking the door, he turned and placed a hand on C. D.'s shoulder in such a way that his thumb poked into the hollow under his clavicle with just enough pressure to hurt. "Some people would pay money for what you're about to see," Sheperd said. "But you're a stand-up guy, right?"

He looked C. D. directly in the eyes, his gaze filled with a powerful appraisal and an implied menace, too—this was Vegas, after all. C. D. doubted what he was about to see would be much of a secret to most industry insiders; still, he sensed the importance of this moment—that mysterious exchange of signals between a boss and an employee that might determine their relationship, maybe even how long the job would last. Later, the best example of this he would learn from Vegas lore was how Howard Hughes, during his aircraft company days, would take a job prospect to lunch at which a bland soup would be served. If the potential employee tasted the soup before shaking salt into it, he would be hired; if he reached for the salt or pepper shaker before tasting it, that would be the end of the interview. With Sheperd, a physical exchange factored into his judgments. He moved in closer, often putting a hand on the other guy with a challenging eye contact, like a wrestler staring his opponent down before the whistle. C. D. knew enough not to blink. He absorbed the thumb's force and returned some pressure of his own, rising up against it just long enough not to come off as a wimp but not too long before he nodded, just once—sure, boss, he could be trusted.

"Great," Sheperd said. He unlocked the door. "Welcome to Pyramid World."

A room-size architectural model spread out before them of a spectacular golden-windowed pyramid looming over the painted double boulevard of The Las Vegas Strip. It was an Egyptian-themed luxury resort built to a meticulously detailed scale, set in a garden oasis with islands of palm groves and reed-thatched cabañas with rows of lounge chairs, beach umbrellas, and elaborate fountains. The oasis wound along the edges of a gently curving pool and spa complex suggesting the flowing waters of the Nile. Slowly, C. D. circled around the model, appreciating its mammoth scale and the nuances of its design down to each painted block marking the squared-off entrances, the graceful sloping ramps, and the switchback walkways. The skeletal structure of a sleek monorail hung suspended in the air at its south end. A tall white obelisk decorated with traces of hieroglyphs marked the north end near a gilded parking garage. Before the entrance to the casino, between driveways on either side, majestically gazing east over the boulevard, lay a huge supine lion's body with the regal human godhead of the Sphinx. Lance Sheperd observed him taking it all in, inspecting every detail.

"Wow," C. D. said, finally. "The Sphinx looks like it's smiling."

"All our monsters smile," Sheperd said. "We're selling pure fantasy, the concept of experiencing luxury like the ancient kings of empires. The key here, and think about it, because it really is key and everybody on my team has got to know it, is that Las Vegas presents fantasies in ways that make people believe their lives are more real. You get that? What it is? That's what we're selling. The bigger and more fantastic the fantasies are, the more profits we'll make. In the next ten years, Las Vegas is going to beat Disney World as the number one tourist destination on the planet," he said. "Learn the concept. Learn the industry."

Sheperd walked him through various departments at Big Top—Finance, Food and Beverage, Retail, Human Resources, Hotel Operations, Casino Operations, and all the rest—showing him the organization. He led him into the dark bunker-like complex of Casino Security. They sat together in the big monitor chairs in front of dozens of video screens switching back and forth among hundreds of fracturing images of the action on the casino floor beamed from eyes-in-the-sky into that control room, packed with so many color-coded buttons and blinking lights that it seemed like a combination of the starship *Enterprise* and the Defense Intelligence Agency. Nothing in the house could go unwatched except what happened in the privacy of the hotel rooms. Even some of the managerial offices could be dialed up on the screens.

"This is our city," Sheperd said. "It's got everything a city has—streets, police patrols, water mains, sewers, schools and public works, parks and recreation. Different from a city, it's run for profit. Think of it as a city that makes profits from its citizens, who are the players and the guests. Get to know it. Learn the street map. Observe how people move, where the traffic wants to go. You're in the city planning department. Your job is to take the best new ideas, most of them *my* ideas, and help us to build and sell a new city."

C. D. would report directly to Lance Sheperd. He joined Sheperd's team, set up in a minimally furnished strip mall office building just off Flamingo Boulevard near the parklike grounds of the Hughes Tower complex, where many of the major banks and brokerage firms were housed. He joined a roster of about twelve other junior executives backed by a platoon of secretaries and assistants, his first gilt-lettered business card showing his position as within the very unspecific "Project Development."

Other team members helped him settle in, with Mark Kinkaid, a generous, pot-bellied numbers guy on the project helping him the most to learn the industry, and he sensed they would become friends. Greta Olsson in PR took an interest in him too, C. D. never quite sure if her interest was strictly limited to work. She was an aggressively perky, girl-next-door blonde who knew just how and when to bat her eyes and pump up her voice as she reached like a pickpocket into the suits of investors and closed their deals. Greta had at first contracted as an operative from an outside PR firm but gradually transitioned into a full-time position. Mark Kinkaid, Greta Olsson, and the design consultant Brick Rico were the team members C. D. worked with most. They helped him learn who was who and what was what in Las Vegas. They eased him onto Sheperd's crew, continually dreaming up, revising, and refining all over again the details of the mega-resort proposal, recrunching the numbers on it each time, too, distilling it into a flowing sales pitch topped off by a five-minute video animation of a visitor's exotic journey through the many luxuries and Egyptian fantasy of Pyramid World.

He sat in on meeting after meeting, and gradually C. D. began to contribute his own ideas. When important visitors were sent over in one of The Big Top stretch limos, he became one of the guys who greeted them. Sometimes they were accompanied by Lance Sheperd or the chief architect, Daniel Grayson, but not often. He would call in Kinkaid, Brick Rico, and Greta Olsson, and as a team they would show off the concept with ever-changing slide shows and mock-ups. C. D. would ride over with the visitors to the fifty acres of prime desert real estate at the south end of The Strip where Pyramid World would begin construction. Greta would act as the "closer" to seal the deal. He learned what he could with the patient help of Kinkaid, a worker bee in the industry, still mastering its many intricate accounting methods; and he fed off insider tips from Greta *that's spelled with two s's* Olsson, as everyone called her as an office joke, since she often added this phrase when introduced. Something about her aggressiveness, and her often potty language too, demanded that she be treated like one of the guys. But there were times when he and Greta worked together, side by side in close offices, close enough he breathed in her mixture of perfume and stale cigarette smoke, that he sensed something else too, an edgy urgency in her that felt physical somehow and that cut through her usual attitude that she was technically his immediate boss. He had felt this before, in his most hedonistic days, with a dancer or actress in a cast—that charged sense that all it would take would be for one of them to say the word. Neither of them did. Still, his work with Greta fed off this repressed erotic energy. New guys turned up, too, added to their team—a muscular, crude-talking youngster and native Las Vegan named Gary Luongo, who had family ties to the Riviera casino; and Rick Rickstein, an Israeli American and graduate of the Hotel College at UNLV who had learned purchasing with the Marriott chain. Like C. D., both handed out cards with only "Project Development" on them, and in vague ways he sensed they might be his competition in his drive to rise in the company.

Sheperd's new team tried out versions of colorful print prospectuses with air-brushed conceptual paintings of the new hotel casino set against the desert night. Inside its pages would be mock-ups of a few posh, highly designed spaces: The Isis Lounge and Night Club with revealingly clad waitresses in costumes like royal slave girls; the Nefertiti spa with Jacuzzis and fountains spouting from great golden disks; the hotel suites with luxury king beds shaped like barges on the Nile; and a family attraction aimed at kids they argued over endlessly, the Allan Quatermain and the Mysteries of the Pyramid Virtual Reality Ride, meant to trump any of the thrills at Universal Studios. All these ideas were laid out among pages of graphs, charts, and statistical summaries promising great fortunes just waiting to be made. Their pitches were aimed at an insider group of investment bankers, fund managers, and speculative investors, a market not all that different from the one C. D. knew from his days in Seattle, working with Grace, selling the VisionQuest start-up, the main difference being that the dress code in the tech industry trended toward blue jeans with wrinkled shirts seemingly pulled out of laundry bags, while the guys who invested in Las Vegas hotel casinos wore expensive suits. The big-money mentality seemed the same.

C. D. helped to develop the Pyramid Resorts logo in the first weeks. After many intense meetings spent drawing up different versions to send off to graphic design, Lance Sheperd finally set and approved their logo: a gilded pyramid topped off by the all-seeing Eye of Horus, that falcon eye believed to ward off all evil, like the Coptic eye on the dollar bill. The eye directed sunray light beams printed in holographic textured inks meant to create the illusion of bursting off the page with the comforting slogan at its base: *The pyramid watches out for you.*

C. D. Reinhart came up with this slogan. Not that he took credit for it. As he had learned from Greta, he "suggested" the phrase after a particularly intense hothouse-like team meeting the boss had attended, writing it up in an interoffice memo as though it had been Sheperd's idea in the first place. Still, the others high-fived him when the boss approved.

Part of learning the industry also meant divining the winds of what went on far over his head, or "up at corporate," as they referred to the higher-ups. The Big Top Hotel Casino had been acquired and its new resort built by entrepreneur Jim Roland, known as "J. B." down below, or just "the Old Man" in some circles. He had learned the business during the transition from the old-time Mob days, at smaller casinos, then Caesars Palace, one among a wave of big real estate developers expanding into gaming. J. B. had survived, then thrived, untainted by organized crime, so everyone said. He had proved a visionary, seeing the opportunity to capture a low-end market of quarter- and nickel-playing weekenders looking to drink, eat, and gamble on the cheap, and who of necessity had to drag their kids along with them. He attracted them to The Big Top with third-rate trapeze artists, clown shows, and pinball arcades along with stripped-down rooms that rivaled the most minimal at any Motel 6. Moguls of mega-resort glitter like Steve Wynn and William Hilton mocked J. B. for "sparing all expense" for his "Wal-Mart casino." They choked on their words when The Big Top started paying up to 20 percent profits on investments.

For years J. B. had been known for his fraternal open-door management style, welcoming his employees in his Spartan windowless office—even a hotel maid with a problem was free to drop by to consult with him. He had assembled his executive team with the attitude of a father adopting then educating a growing family of favorite sons. Lately, though, the Old Man had turned erratic, lashing out in sudden rages, rumored to be popping prescription pain pills. Also he had hired an outside PR firm to plant glowing press stories meant to cover over any possible alleged bad news from his former life as a real estate developer (union pension funds involved, including Teamsters') that echoed into the fallout from the S&L scandal during the Reagan era. In truth, J. B. Roland was among the most honest and straight dealing of any of the major players in the city. Why he felt a need to promote a clean image now was a mystery, as though he never fully got it that none of this mattered in Vegas, as Sheperd had said. These planted stories had the opposite effect, setting off suspicions he might be something of a crook, which not only wasn't true, but really, even if it were, no one would have thought it unusual—which of the big casino moguls had *not* been something of a crook at one time? This shouldn't have mattered, especially not after the Old Man had invented a whole new market for the industry.

By trying to polish his image, J. B. ended up feeding his own red meat to the press, which dug even harder into his past associations. This then drew attention from financiers on Wall Street, making them skittish during that crucial time when fresh capital was being sought to fuel The Big Top's transition into Pyramid Resorts. The goings-on "up at corporate" became a war for control. Teams of "new hires" were put together, C. D. among them, each following different top executives: Lance Sheperd, Big Jim Chevron, Tim "Paper King" Slocum. All the top guys up at corporate assembled crews, making ready to step in to run the whole show just as soon as Jim Roland could be forced into retirement. Everybody held his breath, hoping the Old Man would see the light, pass the torch, go winging off on his private jet to wherever the *Forbes* list of ousted CEOs go when they're put out to pasture. But not yet: J. B. was still fighting for control while losing his grip, the only question how much blood would be spilled before someone would be appointed to recite his eulogy.

C. D. sensed that the best strategy for someone at his level would be to keep his head down and not ask questions. He saw J. B. Roland about once a month, at big meetings. He had talked to him only a few times, the first time on a quick pass into his office during his orientation, when Lance Sheperd introduced him as "the guy who'll help take us into the computer age." To which the Old Man simply nodded, sitting behind a weirdly empty desk except for a blotter with nothing on it but a cheap ballpoint pen. C. D. shook J. B.'s limp hand over that spooky desk. "We pay a year-end bonus based on performance," J. B. said. "What kind of car do you drive?"

"To be honest, right now I'm driving my wife's Plymouth," C. D. said, recalling with a pang how they had dumped his old reliable Honda Civic in preparation for the move. He added, too quickly, "That's going to change, of course."

"We like our employees to drive American," the Old Man said.

A secretary knocked on the door frame and Lance Sheperd led C. D. out of the office, the meeting over without further ceremony. C. D. didn't think he'd be taking advantage of the Old Man's "open-door" policy anytime soon.

Over the next few months, he observed J. B. in action about a dozen times, at team presentations of Pyramid World in various planning stages. He saw the Big Boss as a tormented, overweight, older man wrapped too tightly in his suit, his mouth shaped into a permanent grimace. His heavy-lidded eyes gazed as though perpetually wounded through his horn-rimmed glasses at his assembled executives like he couldn't comprehend where they had all come from—all these young sharks circling him, fast-talking at him when they should have been sitting at his knee, listening to him as to a wise and demanding grandfather. It was as though, without his realizing how or when, his company had grown too big to fit into his paternal vision. He had no way of dealing with this other than to treat his employees like misbehaving children. He didn't really hear their presentations, still, nothing satisfied the Old Man. "Not right," he'd snap. "How much will *that* set us back?" he'd grumble. "Do it again," he'd say.

C. D. witnessed Big Jim Chevron, president and chief of Operations, lose it in the elevator in an exchange with Tim Slocum, VP of Legal and Business Affairs after a meeting at which J. B. announced he would require monthly drug tests of his top executives. "He wants piss tests? Like *we're* the ones on drugs? I'll put a cup of piss on his desk every goddamn day!" Chevron groused.

"The Old Man's doing it just to show us he can," Slocum said.

"He can fucking blow me," Chevron said.

Big Jim Chevron was the most aloof of the top executives. As Greta had put it, Chevron disliked most direct communications from employees "not at his level." And never, ever use his name in a press release. "Big Jim doesn't give interviews or answer calls from the press. He doesn't like phone calls from the junior executives either, so if you have to communicate, do it in a memo copied to Sheperd and Slocum."

As far as C. D. could figure out, Chevron preferred to wall himself off behind heavy trophy cases in his office stuffed with photos of himself shaking hands or playing golf with county commissioners, state legislators, governors, members of Congress, and three presidents—Ford, Reagan, and Bush. Chevron was known as the force behind the scenes, the executive who stewarded the gaming licenses and the special tax breaks for the company, known also as a power player who helped to pick who ran for office in the state. Big Jim didn't want to hear from anybody less than important enough, so C. D. planned to avoid any direct communication with him except at the rare meetings when he might be called on to say something.

Tim Slocum behaved just the opposite. Slocum wanted to sit down for drinks with the junior executives at least once a month, to check in with them, sure, but more to join their gang. Over drinks, his talk turned to almost anything *but* business. Slocum had a reputation for philandering, notorious for keeping a more or less permanent room over at Caesars for lunch-hour liaisons. Fastidious, even effeminately so, he also had this annoying habit of straightening a junior executive's necktie or pulling out a lint brush from his briefcase for a quick pass over a guy's shoulders. C. D. soon learned that nothing should be out of place around Slocum, not even papers at a conference table, which Slocum would go around straightening before a meeting, his thumb snapping the edges of thick reports perfectly straight like a croupier arranges stacks of casino chips. Slocum passed out business cards for the salon that did his clear-polished manicures, an old-time Vegas tradition required of dealers, as if everyone on his team should at all times be ready to sit down at a casino table to shuffle up and deal. Paper was Slocum's specialty. His office processed truckloads of it every month, everything that had to be read, passed by legal scrutiny, signed, and sealed. Slocum worked closest to Lance Sheperd, running all the paper for the company's complex contracts and financing.

C. D. gathered from the behavior of the top executives that corporate wars in some form were soon to begin. That meant nothing was certain at his new job, nothing was secure. Still, he sensed that Pyramid World would get built one way or another. Even though he reported to Sheperd and his own fate might be tied tightly to his, if he could make himself useful enough to the success of the project, he would keep his job no matter which of the top executives took control after the wars ended. It wasn't his place to ask questions about the corporate wars. He did what he was told. And he learned everything he could about the industry.

Whenever he had free time, he strolled around the busy casino floors and all over The Big Top and Camelot hotels. He breathed in that hyper-circulated air blowing down from above, stirring the ever-present stew of cigarette smoke that made his eyes tear up as he mixed in among all those partying, budget-conscious guests and players. He observed how they moved through the vast public spaces; and he absorbed some of their thrill at just being there in that sharp, adrenaline-charged atmosphere, all sense of time ceasing to exist in the casino except for the next bet, the next play. He studied the corporate and hotel casino organizational charts, and he dropped in on the management offices, astonished at how many vice presidents abounded—from Operations to Finance, Food and Beverage to Casino Operations, to HR, responsible for thousands of workers down through the various levels of the pyramid to the crucial managers for slots, table games, and the "cage," with its hard and soft counts for all that cold hard cash from this cash-making factory. He spent two days following the Facilities guys around, watching them fixing problems in the rooms with their tools. He leaned over the shoulders of clerks at the Front Desk, in Reservations, in the Call Center, and he studied work schedules in Housekeeping and Security. He looked in on other departments, too: Retail, Purchasing, Hotel Marketing, Casino Marketing, Convention Sales, on and on—just count all the VPs! What an organizational feat to keep track of them all, so no wonder J. B. Roland might be a bit overwhelmed by how big his company had grown.

In addition to dropping in on the managers and VPs, he also tested the mood of the workers in the employee cafeterias, free (or nearly free) meals for casino workers a tradition dating back to the old Mob days. Though it was generally frowned upon for executives to mix and mingle in there, the employee cafeteria was *the* place where he could sit anonymously over lunch and ask questions. The mood he picked up on over these lunches felt universally upbeat, charged, and happy, the shift workers all buzzing about their chances to be moved over to Pyramid World when it was built, money always better at the prime property. Las Vegas was booming, and everyone sensed an opportunity. Even the dealers—the workers who most had to fight off a factory-like boredom at shuffling and counting and poking out with the croupier stick over and over again and keep right on smiling no matter what at the too-often rude players who were losing, as about five out of nine usually did—even the dealers seemed pretty happy.

Gradually, C. D. formed the idea that a casino hotel in many ways resembled a gigantic Broadway musical production, one with thousands of performers all putting on a show. And he began to comprehend the full implications of the decisions he would make at his new job. Even a minor shift in a detail of the concept for Pyramid World would affect those thousands of future employees, his fellow members of the cast. This cast of thousands would need to move in and out and around all the public and private spaces with maximum efficiency. All would have to be well rehearsed in their roles. All had to learn their cues, stepping onstage and offstage smoothly. They would all have to play their parts in one seamless, continuous performance that would keep cycling through the same actions and lines and songs day after night after day, never stopping, no curtain call, for a show that never closed. And the guests and gamblers must be more than any mere audience, more than merely gamblers and guests. They must be drawn willingly into the living spectacle of Pyramid World. They must be seduced into performing too, playing their own most essential roles—the consuming and consumed—as happy citizens of its fantasy.

– 4 –

Early that Saturday morning, he parked and went in through a back entrance into the gaudy casino with its candy-striped décor, then picked his way through the milling crowd, not surprised at how busy the place was on a holiday weekend. He looped and circled around the slower-moving heavier folks in his way, noting how adept he had become at the slip-slide movement across the crowded floor that marked the professional casino worker, turning sidewise here and there, pushing in between and past the random clumps of popcorn eaters and coin bucket carriers, the limping senior citizens clutching their buffet coupons. He found the discreet elevator up to the corporate offices. That early on a Saturday the executive corridor felt strangely deserted, only a few lights on in the dim, austere hallway.

Lance Sheperd waited for him in his windowless office, oddly informal in old sweat pants and a polo shirt, clean white sneakers propped up on his desk. Always nervous around Sheperd in any case, C. D. felt overdressed in his gray Brooksease suit. He knocked on the door frame. He stepped back as if out of hearing distance as Sheperd finished talking on the phone: something about a boat. . . was he giving the go-ahead to his wife almost no one ever saw to buy a boat? Sheperd hung up without any phrase of endearment, waving a hand at him to come in. With his sixth sense like mind reading, aware that C. D. must have overheard bits of his call, Sheperd asked, "You know anything about boats?"

"A hole in the water into which you throw money."

"Right," Sheperd said. "We've got a place on the coast. My wife wants a boat parked behind it, the biggest yacht possible that'll still fit into the lagoon."

"Must be nice."

"Nice for her," he said, the implication being that buying a boat had nothing to do with him other than paying for it, but C. D. let that one slide. He had the sense that the less he knew of Sheperd's personal life, the better. "You know the difference between a forty-eight- and a fifty-two-foot yacht?" Sheperd asked, then added quickly, like a punch line, "About $50,000 a foot." His thin lips twisted into a self-satisfied smile at the man he was showing himself to be now—one just settling into the comfort of his expensive tastes. "We've been selling our stock," he said, the "we" implying the executive threesome of Sheperd, Slocum, and Jim Chevron. "You must have heard."

"Whispers. Not even rumors yet," C. D. said.

"It's going to be every man for himself around here," Sheperd said. "You should be all right, though. And if you get a call from Wynn or the guys at Oz, turn them down. Stick with the project that brought you here, even when it all turns to shit. We'll need our people on the inside when it's time to clean up the mess. Are we clear?"

"Clear enough," C. D. said. "You won't tell me more even if I asked."

"Right." Sheperd glanced impatiently at the phone. "How's your wife?"

"Grace misses the rain in Seattle," C. D. said. "But we're settled in all right. She's on the hunt for a job now, actually. Part-time. Not so much for the money but to get her out of the house while Catherine's in school . . ."

As he was saying this, Sheperd had already stopped listening, his busy eyes searching his desk for a plain white envelope. He picked it up.

"Thanks," C. D. said. "I'll let Grace know you asked."

Sheperd gazed at the envelope as if weighing its contents for a moment before he reached across the desk and handed it to C. D. The envelope was sealed, with only "Mrs. Lester Stahl" typed across the front, no return address or name. Through the envelope, C. D. felt the weight of a business-sized check slip then settle inside as he slid it into an inner jacket pocket.

"This is *not* from me," Sheperd said. "Anybody says it is, I'll deny it. This isn't from you, either, or anyone by name who works for Pyramid, you got that? When you deliver it to Stahl's widow, tell her it's from a voluntary collection from the employees. Don't say more."

"I understand," C. D. said.

"Nobody else should know about this. If anybody asks, you don't know anything about it. If she wants to write a thank-you note, have her write it to you, then shred it."

"It's good of you to do this," C. D. said.

"I didn't hear that," Sheperd said.

"Right," C. D. said. "I never said it then."

Sheperd picked up the phone—back to his boat purchase—and the meeting ended.

This was a new one, not sure how it fit into his job description, this task to figure out how best to deliver the envelope to Lester Stahl's widow. Options ran through his head: after finding out where she lived, he could just drop it in the mailbox, but that was too unsure and too unsettling—any widow receiving such an envelope anonymously would start asking questions, and questions were just what Sheperd wanted to avoid. Could he get it to her through a union contact, one of the crew guys he knew from site visits? That would bring in an outsider and start talk, and he'd be forced to lie. No. Sheperd meant for him to handle this in person. And what could that really mean? On the slow drive off The Strip back to Green Valley and home, he kept going over in his mind the topsy-turvy ethics of the situation. Here he was, presumably sent on a mission to do a good deed for a family in grief, no strings attached save for anonymity. Still, the grim nature of the errand and its source made him feel like a lowlife bag man in a capital crime. He shook off that thought. But how good really *was* this deed? What was its scale?

At a traffic light he pulled out the envelope, holding it up into the sun's glare through the windshield. He strained to read through the paper, felt with his thumb for any textures of the check inside so he might divine how much it was made out for—no way. Cars honked when the light turned green. He drove on, deciding he didn't want to know the amount, better that he didn't—if Sheperd had wanted him to know he would have told him. Not knowing was better. That way, no matter his role, he could resolve not to lie.

At home he worked the phone in his home office, calling around. One of his union contacts from the site, Rubén López, understood right away. What he told Rubén was true enough: he had "something from work" he wanted to give to Lester Stahl's widow. Rubén gave up the address and phone number without asking any more. The address sounded familiar: Juniper Circle, not all that far away, in the same Desert Forest development he lived in, in fact. He fought off an unsettling shock that the Stahl family were his neighbors, so close that he could walk to their house, what must be his unconscious prejudices about race and class mixing in his head. But of course the Stahls would have a nice enough home, and why not, when union iron workers, counting overtime, could make almost as much as he did? What had he expected, some neighborhood in North Las Vegas? He fought off an impulse to walk over and knock on Mrs. Stahl's door, unannounced, the way a concerned neighbor might, and just pass her the envelope to get it over with. He thought better of that and telephoned.

Mrs. Stahl answered in a measured, careful tone, no obvious note of grief. "Who *is* this again?" she asked.

He repeated his name. He said he had led company tours of the building site, quickly adding that he had not known Lester personally. "Still, I have something from work," he said. "I've been asked to deliver this to you as . . . well . . . as something like a token of our condolences for your loss, Mrs. Stahl, which affects us all. Would that be all right?"

"You're not one of those lawyers?"

"God, no, Mrs. Stahl. Nothing like that. This is personal," he said.

"You won't ask me to sign anything?"

"No. That's not what this is." He paused and added, "It's a gesture of sympathy."

"We haven't set the day of the funeral service yet," she said.

"It's an envelope, do you understand? I'd like to see that it gets to you as soon as possible," he said, then he caught himself and softened his tone. "I'm sorry, Mrs. Stahl. What I mean is that I'd like to deliver it to you as soon as it's convenient for you."

"I'd say come over now but my kids are a mess."

"Let me give you my number. Call me whenever the time is right. Or really, Mrs. Stahl, call me for anything else. I mean it. We're practically neighbors."

"That won't be necessary, thank you." A long moment passed. He heard her steady, measured breaths. "I'm having a few people over tomorrow after church," she said. "You'd be welcome to join us. Around noon?"

He recalled that Grace had designs on tomorrow. Always big on celebrating Valentine's Day, she had planned for the three of them to start at breakfast with cards and little gifts for each other, drinking out of special heart-decorated mugs. Then they would bundle up and take a family hike along one of the gorgeous, brushy desert trails at Red Rock Canyon, eat lunch out afterward, then head home to a movie and popcorn in front of the VCR, all three cuddling together on the couch. They would finish with a pink-frosted cake from Freed's bakery, best in the valley. He thought how much he appreciated Grace's attention to keeping holidays, and lately, her taking charge of nurturing their romance—what else were holidays for but family and romance?—even as his job kept encroaching on all other normalcy. He had been looking forward to the special day and to the evening, after they had tucked Catherine into bed early, when they could exchange intimate gifts in candlelight and privacy.

Still, in a heartbeat, he cancelled their plans. "Sure thing, Mrs. Stahl," he said. "See you then."

When Grace felt frustrated, she held it in, save that her hand raked more often through her thick, naturally red hair, messing it up in a way that usually charmed him but now gave her a pressed, harried appearance. Lines on both sides of her full lips deepened, as if she were biting the inside of her cheeks to keep from saying what she was thinking. She had said it before, times when he had had to miss one of Catherine's junior Bluebirds or school events because of a sudden demand at work; or when Grace had to quickly arrange a babysitter because of some unplanned company or fundraising dinner they had been asked to attend: "When did you sign on to be Lance Sheperd's errand boy? Or maybe you actually enjoy being a sycophant?"

And of course that word stung, because that's what he was, at least partly—the servant-in-waiting who agreed with and praised princes and kings. Still, *fuck* that, he answered in his head. What else was being in middle management all about?

She didn't say it today, under the unusual sad circumstances of his current errand—an errand they were all three involved in now—and he was grateful for that, though he could tell Grace was thinking just this as she started to make a shopping list and develop new plans. "We'll all go," she said. "Let's just do this right. How many times did Mom do this for neighbors we hardly knew? What means something is food," she said. "No-fuss food. Food that can sit out without spoiling. Food people can pick at for a week," she added in the tone she used when teaching Catherine important lessons.

They spent the rest of the day shopping and in the kitchen, preparing a big bone-in ham baked with cloves and pineapple rings, both he and Catherine in aprons, chopping celery and onions for the potato salad. They rolled out pie crusts, then watched Grace spread and pinch them into the pans, cutting dough into strips to make a neat hatchwork over her peach and cherry fillings. She showed Catherine how to set the timer and put the pies in the oven. The girls went off to dig black dresses from their closets and get out the iron.

C. D. worked in the backyard, dragging the skimmer through the pool, his Saturday chore to clean out the winter leaves. It was well into evening by the time they finished off the pizza they ordered for dinner, leaving the baked ham and jumbo potato salad in the refrigerator wrapped in foil and ready, three pies cooling on the kitchen counter. The sealed envelope for Mrs. Stahl waited, locked in a drawer of his desk in his home office den.

That night when C. D. tried to take her in his arms, Grace apologized, saying she was "just a little tired." She wrapped her arms around her big feather pillow and turned her back. C. D. reached for the remote and turned on the TV, lighting up the bedroom with CNN, the volume turned low. He caught up on the week's headlines, perhaps not so wise before trying to sleep: footage just in of a department store inferno in China, the body count mounting, people still trapped in the shoddily constructed building; then a report with disturbing images from a bombing in Sarajevo, the war in Bosnia heating up, fueled by religious hate, the images of a woman wailing with grief and tearing her hair out amid the ruins. In business news, a follow-up on the lawsuit by General Motors against NBC for allegedly rigging "staged" crashes, "faking" the news to get spectacular video to show off the recently uncovered scandal of defects in GM pickup trucks, about which top executives were allegedly aware: the gas tanks prone to explode in accidents. In politics, newly inaugurated president Bill Clinton unwrapped a speech in his Arkansas drawl about boosting the economy, followed by footage of his meeting two days before with Janet Reno, the first woman to be picked for attorney general. How unexpected that Clinton had been elected president, C. D. thought, recalling how unlikely that had seemed this same time last year, when "the comeback kid" was doing all he could to pump up energy for the Super Tuesday primaries with his loyal wife, Hillary, clinging to his side amid his vehement denials of extramarital affairs. What the hell, C. D. had finally voted for him. Doesn't every guy deserve a second chance? So it goes: down one day and on top of the heap the next, what a country. He switched off the TV and the room went dark. He wrapped a pillow around his ears.

– 5 –

The Stahl house on Juniper Circle had exactly the same single-story floor plan as their own and was painted the same light-sand beige with white trim. Also like their home, the front lawn was planted with a two-phase combo of rye and Bermuda grasses, still mostly green in February, and two Italian cypress trees reached up from planter boxes on either side of the garage. Cars were pulling to the curb in front, a few clusters of black people in Sunday suits and dark dresses just arriving. They regarded the Reinharts with what seemed an only partly veiled suspicion until they noted their arms were loaded down with food, then they granted accepting, if still wary, nods, even standing back politely from the opened door to allow them to take their offerings in first before following them inside.

This was an after-church gathering, and the Reinharts were the only white people there. The Stahl daughter stood at the door in a pink dress, welcoming arriving guests. She was about the same age and size as Catherine, clear she was making a coached effort to put on a brave face. The two girls paused for a moment, taking note of each other. Catherine said, just like that, as only a child could, "I'm sorry your dad died."

The girl bit her lip. "He didn't die. He got killed," she said.

"You got that right," said a big man who had earlier stepped aside to let them pass.

Grace got to work, joining the other ladies in the kitchen, organizing the food. Wilma Stahl, a tall, elegant woman, waited in the living room, extending her hand and opening her arms to embraces, her face shaped with effort into a polite mask that covered deep lines of trouble, fighting back grief by taking prolonged reinforcing breaths through her nose. Behind her, over the gas faux fireplace, hung the same photograph of Lester "Red" Stahl as the one in the newspapers, Red cradling the UNLV basketball, hard hat tipped back, showing his curly red hair, the photo blown up to small poster size and hastily inserted into a glassless black frame. A minister in a white collar and black suit stood at Mrs. Stahl's shoulder, the big man reaching out from time to time to steady her arm.

"Mrs. Stahl," C. D. said, taking her extended hand. He pressed it between both of his. "Thank you so much for inviting us to your home."

"Us?" She glanced quickly over his shoulder.

"We all wanted to come," he said. "I hope that's all right. We're neighbors, live just six blocks away. . . My wife, Grace, she's in the kitchen. And Catherine, our daughter. . ."

Mrs. Stahl had already fastened on the sight of the two girls side by side at the door, immersed in their own chattering conversation. They were allied by their age, of course. Still, he felt instantly proud of Catherine's instinct to act as a friend.

"Your daughter," she said. "You didn't tell me you had a daughter. Does she go to Mack Elementary too?"

"The Meadows," he said, then added, too quickly, "We thought a private school best for the first couple of years after the move. Seattle's a long way, and it was. . . quite different up there. They'll probably attend the same middle school, though," he said. "What grade is. . . she in?"

"Leticia. Leticia's in the first grade."

"Same grade!" he said too effusively.

An awkward moment passed. For some reason he couldn't move from the spot he stood on. C. D. found himself leaning in too close to Mrs. Stahl as they observed their children, a mysterious warmth flooding between them. Why should *this* happen, right now, like this? In his previous life, before he became a salesman, he had worked for years on playing just this role as an actor, cultivating a deep sensitivity in his mountain lake–blue eyes and a quality of masculine compassion in his voice, believing this might be what directors were looking for in a leading man. He had failed as an actor, didn't have that mysterious talent or whatever it took. He went broke. He gave up acting, resolved to change his life. He moved to Seattle, turned to sales, met and married Grace. Still, no matter how hard he tried to *keep it real* in his new life, sometimes, when nervous or unsure of his surroundings or of the person he faced, he couldn't help it—slick, practiced behaviors came out and there he was again, as fake as can be, performing a role. On the other hand, what role should he be playing?

And of course Mrs. Stahl would be spinning through a perplexing emotional tempest following her husband's death, her sensations alternately sharpened and dulled by grief. He searched into her deeply wounded eyes. He breathed in an electric scent that drew him in even closer, until he invaded the boundaries of any polite social space. At best, he might come off to her as sensitive; at worst, as some creepy sleazebag. He stammered, "You're a . . . a beautiful, charming woman, Mrs. Stahl. Your husband was a very lucky man."

"Well!" she said, flushing. "Thank you!" She placed a hand at her heart with an overplayed gesture of accepting his flattery, a southern girl coquettishness she must have learned somewhere—did her accent carry traces of Arkansas? She added, "I'm *so pleased* you brought your family!"

Churchgoers began pressing in behind him. C. D. bucket-stepped to one side to shake hands with the minister, who had observed everything. "Reverend Stubblefield," the man intoned with a dark resonance of his disapproval. "First Desert Baptist Church."

"C. D. Reinhart," he said. "Pyramid Resorts. I'm . . . ah . . . one of the company guys who leads visits to the construction site." He let this explanation hang in the air a moment. "We're all very much affected by Mr. Stahl's death. More than I can say."

"He was a fine man," the reverend said. "A fine, God-loving man."

The women got to work, Mrs. Stahl soon excusing herself to supervise. They fitted several portable tables together in the backyard, arranging them into one long table covered with red plastic cloths; then they loaded it with a bounty of food. The weather had turned, a sunny warm front moving in over the weekend to bring on one of those balmy, springlike February days that gave Las Vegas a breath of paradise. Today, even here, under these sad circumstances, a heart-shaped cake with pink icing and red rose decorations appeared at one end of the table. People lined up with paper plates. More people kept arriving—one other white family and a big Hispanic family, too, with a half dozen kids—Red Stahl's ironworker friends.

C. D. avoided the food. As he roamed the rooms and stepped briefly into the yard, then back inside, he thought he sensed a tension of racial defensiveness, the way a cluster of black men in their Sunday best would break off exchanges in their own slangy coded language, self-consciously straightening out their diction when he approached. He explained his presence in the Stahl home as, "We're neighbors, from just down the street." Beers and wine coolers appeared out of ice chests, and it wasn't long before the atmosphere inside and outside turned up the volume and shifted moods from a funeral dirge to something else. A happy-sounding chatter of a real party began to cover over solemnity and grief. Blues sounded from big speakers in the living room. At one point Mrs. Stahl knelt on the living room carpet, her gorgeous long legs spread out behind her, sorting through a tower of CDs and cassette tapes, Red Stahl's collection of blues: B. B. King, John Lee Hooker, Buddy Guy, John Mayall, all the greats, even Eric Clapton. She said brightly to the crowded room, "How Lester would have loved this! He *loved* a party!"

On instinct, C. D. knelt beside her to help sort through the discs and tapes, spotting a Paul Butterfield among them—clearly this was Lester Stahl's domain in the house. She let him take over. He slammed the Butterfield cassette into the player and turned up the volume. "Blues should be loud. I'll bet Lester played these *way* loud," he said, nearly shouting.

And there it was—he made her smile and shake her head. A tension eased between them. He felt that uncomfortable electric charge again, not sure where it was coming from. He glanced around quickly for Grace, hoping she was nowhere close enough to see this. His wife had blended into a circle of church women sitting in lawn chairs set up in the yard. Out the sliding glass doors he saw Catherine and Leticia already messing up their dresses by chasing the Stahl dog into a hedge of thorny bushes trying to get a doll out of its mouth. By midafternoon, only the Reverend Stubblefield maintained anything like an appropriate solemn gravity, holding court in the den with a few other men who kept glancing at the L.A. Lakers dropping a game to the Phoenix Suns on a big-screen TV with the volume muted. C. D. recognized a face or two from the building site, guessing they were Red Stahl's union buddies telling versions of what had happened.

In a little while, as the blues played loudly through the house, he suggested gently to Mrs. Stahl that they should "maybe talk now?"

Mrs. Stahl led C. D. toward the den where the Reverend Stubblefield presided. She carried her two-year-old, Lester Jr., who apparently had been napping in a bedroom but now had started to fuss. Lester Jr. made the deep, throaty sounds deaf children make when he tried to speak. His eyes rolled unusually, too, independently of each other, almost all the way white in their sockets. As C. D. followed them down the hallway, any lighter mood from the party shifted inside into a gripping knot, and he thought, *Oh, no, not this too,* with a terrible, heavy sorrow.

As if he were in his parish office, Reverend Stubblefield ushered the other men out of the den. C. D. noted the room had the same layout as the den in his own house, the same bay window looking out at an uninspiring view of a cinderblock wall. The reverend seated Mrs. Stahl in a recliner next to him. C. D. took a straight-backed chair facing them both. Mrs. Stahl set Lester Jr. loose to crawl around on the floor, where he found a plastic dinosaur toy he began scraping on the carpet then up across the big TV screen in a way that might leave a scratch on it, its T-Rex claws raking across the Lakers loping dispiritedly through the closing minutes of a losing game. Mrs. Stahl noted his anxiety, watching Lester Jr. with the toy. A sad recognition passed between them. C. D. reached into his inner jacket pocket for the envelope and handed it to her. She passed it over to the reverend, who expertly used his thumbnail to slice it open.

The reverend read the check—a cashier's check, no receipt attached. "Well, hmmmph," he said. "Somebody must have a guilty conscience."

He passed the check to Mrs. Stahl. She glanced blankly at the amount, showing no reaction C. D. could read. C. D. made an effort to address her and her only, wishing this injustice-collecting minister would disappear. "It's meant to help," he said. "That's all I know."

"Who is this check from?" the reverend asked.

"I can't say," he said. "It's part of my job not to say."

"You understand that this check might imply certain liabilities. That perhaps legal claims can be . . . supported . . . or reinforced . . . by the very fact of its existence?"

"It is what it is," C. D. said. "What I *can* say is that I believe the intentions are . . . are good ones. Whatever it is, however much it is . . . and I don't know that and don't want to know . . . I believe that it's a . . . a *sincere* gesture. No strings attached."

"Reverend Stubblefield wants me to go to court," said Mrs. Stahl.

She took a moment to let this sink in, gazing across the room at C. D. thoughtfully, as if trying to measure his reaction. "Lester was scared at that job site every day. He didn't tell me too much about it, but a wife knows how worried her man can be by all the little things. It was worse than the other buildings he worked on. Lawyers have been calling. Yesterday one came to the door and pushed a paper at me, but of course I didn't sign. I'm not signing anything. But I just don't know," she said. She leaned her forehead tiredly into her hand, from which the blue check unfurled in the air, gripped between two long red fingernails. "There's this unpaid-for house. And Leticia's lessons. And the special school for Lester Jr. to think about . . ."

C. D. glanced down at Lester Jr., still rubbing the dinosaur toy back and forth across the TV screen. Mrs. Stahl noted his gaze but misread his concern. "Don't worry, he can't hear us. He isn't even aware yet his daddy's gone," she said. A weight in the room settled more heavily over them, and for a moment, it was as if they all held their breaths. "What would *you* advise me to do?"

C. D. took his time. He sounded out the words in his head before he spoke them. "Mrs. Stahl, you must know that these people have every kind of tricky statute on the books to protect them, plus every hot-shot lawyer in the state is on their payrolls," he said. "These things can drag on, and if they do, it takes a toll. So you probably don't have a prayer, not one prayer of winning a lawsuit . . ."

"You see what I told you, Wilma?" the reverend interrupted. "You give these people an inch and they'll take it all, like we were saying just yesterday how they can take you and push you around like this and then you end up with nothing . . ."

"I'm speaking as your neighbor here, Mrs. Stahl." C. D. kept talking over the reverend, stepping on the line, as actors call it, and the reverend's voice trailed off. Mrs. Stahl's attention fixed only on him, listening. C. D. continued, "My family to your family, we live just down the street . . . Whatever you decide to do, or the good reverend persuades you to do . . ." and he instantly regretted the double edge he had put into the word *good*. "Whatever Reverend Stubblefield and an attorney you might consult believe is *right* for you to do . . . whatever that is, whatever you decide . . . please know you can count on my help."

An uncomfortable moment passed, Mrs. Stahl taking this in,

weighing his sincerity. The reverend gripped his thighs with both big hands, holding back expressing his contempt with an effort he made obvious pained him. Outside, high, chattering voices echoed from the yard. On the carpet, little Lester Jr. pushed the plastic dinosaur with too much force, cutting deep lines into the carpet pile. The child gurgled with odd, throaty humming sounds.

"You know . . ." Mrs. Stahl started. She had to swallow, breathe through her nose. "That morning. . . hard to think it was only day before *yesterday*. . . that morning, I got up extra early to make Lester's favorite lunch. A chicken-fried steak hero, then I heated up a chocolate drink for his thermos." A quick smile crossed her features. "I don't usually do that. We're both much too busy. But something *moved* me, you understand? Now that's the one comfort that I have. . . the one thing I'm holding *on* to here. . . that, and how the last thing Lester must have seen in this world is the valentine I put in with his lunch, saying how much I loved him. What's important here is *him*." She had to catch her breath again, and her body straightened, too stiffly. "What I've got to do now is what Lester would want me to do," she said. "So that's what I'm going to do."

She folded the check in half and tossed it into a mess of papers on top of a case of movie tapes like she would just as soon forget it had ever existed. C. D. started to lean a little closer as if to reassure her of something, but what? What could he tell her? That he meant well? That none of this was his doing? As he was thinking what to say next, she looked away and shook her head bitterly. "I think we're done with this now."

He nodded, agreeing he was no longer welcome. He would round up Grace and Catherine and leave. "We're very sorry for your loss," he said. He stood up, straightening his suit jacket. "Reverend," he said. The reverend offered no reply. C. D.'s instincts urged him to say something more. In the doorway he paused a moment, searching for words. "It's strange, Mrs. Stahl," he said. "Yours is the only house in this neighborhood we've ever been invited into. We've lived here two years, and you're the first neighbors that we know."

— 6 —

Back home that evening, he and Grace and little Catherine struggled to resume their natural rhythms and settle, somehow, into their own family embrace. Catherine had left the gathering fussy and bratty, not wanting to leave—to flee at his insistence, really. She had enjoyed the wake at the Stahl home, spent playing with Leticia and her terror of a dog, a beagle that had chewed up the garden hose and lifted its leg on the lawn furniture. She whined about wanting a dog of her own. "Why *not! Why* can't we have one?"

On the short drive through the neighborhood, she repeated this cry over and over, her bad habit that such an irritating soprano of complaint might make them promise anything. After telling her firmly to stop it, Grace glared through the windshield, ignoring her. Back home, Catherine slammed the car door and banged her way into the house in tears. She ran off to her room and slammed that door too. Paint had chipped off the door frame from so many petulant slams. Under other circumstances, Grace might even have spanked her, but she let this tantrum go. The day had been hard on her—hard on everyone.

They tried a family movie, *Aladdin,* meant to be a real treat since it hadn't yet been released in video; it was an early "Academy Members Only" VHS tape that Greta Olsson had managed to get for them, but Catherine continued her tantrum by sitting in the armchair, not with her mom and C. D. on the couch. She fell asleep in about thirty minutes. He bundled her in his arms and carried her to her room, a ritual by now. Grace had encouraged him to hold Catherine and be physically close from early on in their relationship. And he loved that little warm package of his stepdaughter: he loved her pretty, freckled face, the flow of her chestnut hair spreading over his forearm, her mouth wide, breathing easily, the way her eyes would twitch open, struggling out of sleep, then see who was holding her and close again. She felt heavier in his arms lately, and he understood that soon she would grow too big to carry, noting with a twinge how much he would miss this. He transferred her weight gently down onto her bed. He rearranged the lumps of stuffed animals and shamrock pillows, then pulled the comforter over her and kissed her forehead. Before he turned out the light, he whispered, "I'll work on your mom about a dog, Sweetpea." He wouldn't succeed, he knew—Grace was allergic to most dogs. Still, he thought he saw the trace of a smile pass through her dreams.

In their bedroom, he and Grace did the best they could to carry on through the sadness that had settled over them. They exchanged Valentine's gifts on the bed—for him, a bottle of lemony crisp Spanish cologne and a blue velour robe, hand-stitched in England, to replace the spa robe he padded around in that had frayed at the hems. For her, gold earrings with green jade hoops and a gauzy, peach-colored peignoir he envisioned would be part of his continuing challenge to her self-consciousness about her body, the little extra weight she carried here and there that Grace would never quite believe actually turned him on—more of her to sink himself into, to have and to hold. But it hardly seemed the kind of evening now for this kind of play. He watched Grace shake out the sheer peach robe with a little discomfort at what it implied. She kissed his cheek. She tried on the earrings, checking them out in her dressing mirror, noting how they set off her rich auburn hair and hazel eyes. "Wow. You must have shopped hard for these," she said.

Grace turned her head in the mirror to show off the glowing green jade, one profile then the other, pleased. He recalled how they had been an impulse buy, picked out in two minutes at a jewelry counter in Sea-Tac airport while on the run to catch a flight, but he said nothing.

They made slow, familiar love but without much energy in it—both distracted, doing their best to give to one another but only halfway present in themselves. He lay afterward with his arm under her shoulders, her head resting on his chest, sensing her disappointment, not with their routine sex or the loss of the holiday but more deeply with him, at what he had felt forced to do today. But what else was he supposed to do? He wished he had shoved Lance Sheperd's check in the Stahl mailbox and been done with it, not saying one word to his widow.

"I'm really sorry you and Catherine got dragged into that today," he said.

"Don't be," she said. "I'm glad we could be there."

"You were great. You were *both* wonderful."

"She's a remarkable woman, don't you think?"

"What do you mean?"

"The way you *were* to her. . . hard not to notice."

"Don't be ridiculous," he said. "I was doing my job."

"When are you *not* doing your job?"

"I don't know what else to do. I'm still getting on my feet, Grace, really." He lifted his head off the pillow, straining his neck so he could see her face. She stared off toward the dark window, her distance growing. "What are you saying here? Grace?"

"That wasn't like you," she said. "Only do it long enough, and it will be you."

"It's not like I didn't tell the truth," he said. "What did you expect?"

"I just. . . I just don't like what I see you becoming."

"Jesus. Cut me some slack, can you?" She didn't answer. "Look. I'm sorry about today. I'm not sorry about anything else."

He let out a frustrated breath and shifted positions, pulling his arm out from under her body. After a moment he rose in the near darkness and felt his way to the closet. He stepped into his pajamas and found his old frayed spa robe and pulled it on. Suddenly he felt very tired. He thought about going straight back to bed. In the bed Grace had turned away from his side, hugging her pillow. He fit his feet into slippers and kept on going, on his way out stepping over their abandoned gifts, open boxes blooming with rumpled tissue paper and a mess of red ribbons. He padded into the dining room to the liquor cabinet and the bottle of good Scotch. He almost never drank this late at night, but tonight he would have to drink himself to sleep.

He sat down and poured himself a short one, feeling its warming brace as he swallowed. He closed his eyes and rubbed his eyelids, meaning to rest them and relax a moment. A sudden vision overwhelmed him: high skeletal beams of the unfinished pyramid, Lester "Red" Stahl picking his way gingerly in his heavy boots toward a temporary half wall of plywood, where he squatted and flipped open his lunchbox. He discovered the purple construction paper cut into the shape of a heart, the valentine from his wife. Reading it, he leaned back. The plywood twisted loose off its screws and fell away, his body going right along with it, flipping back and over into the open air shaft, then the long slide, the long falling. . .

C. D. gasped. He opened his eyes. He shook his head like a swimmer sheds water and forced himself to focus, hard, recalling his actor's training to empty out his mind, erasing it into blankness. *Let it be,* he thought. *That's over and done now.*

On the dining room table, the cake from Freed's bakery still sat out, minus only one small pink wedge Grace had cut out, for herself, before the movie. He poured his glass three-quarters full of Laphroaig, that single malt he could taste the peat in, and cut a piece of cake. He couldn't finish the cake. The too-sweet frosting made the whisky taste bitter, like medicine.

– 7 –

On Tuesday, an absurdly abundant arrangement of yellow roses waited in his office, on the carpet, so big he couldn't get to his chair, the attached florist's note card saying only *Greta* in what didn't look like Greta's handwriting. Workplace rituals should interpret yellow roses as a way to say thanks, but the fact that they were delivered with only her name and no other message made C. D. pause, suspecting Greta intended something else. Greta well knew how cramped his office was, his desk crowded with an oversized monitor, file organizers, stacks of papers. The arrangement she had sent was so effusive, so over the top, with baby's breath sprays and greenery and curly tendrils of glittery spirals on spikes topped with gold glitter stars, the glitzy jungle of the thing so absurdly huge and gaudy there wasn't any place to put it, not even on top of his file cabinets without it tilting dangerously over the edge.

All right then, he *got it,* and clever girl: Greta meant for him to have to carry this ridiculous star-filled thing at arm's length out of his office and down the long hallway to reception past the open doors of his coworkers—past Rickstein, Kinkaid, Rico, even Luongo and the office girls, bearing it before him in an awkward march, a target for their snickering for the rest of the week. Still, he shouldn't take it personally. He suspected Greta meant the message as much for them as for him, her way to say don't even dream about stepping on her turf, not ever, no way.

Greta Olsson hadn't fully changed jobs yet, still dividing her time between her agency office at S & S Partners and her corner suite at the strip mall complex with the rest of the team. Her schedule put her at the agency that day. If she had been in her team office, C. D. would have dropped in to clear the air, explaining how he had backed her up at the meeting for the press release, how he had reinforced her role even though she hadn't been there. All that busy Tuesday, he tried to think of some way to answer back in between his dozens of catch-up calls to confirm appointments and fees. Early in the afternoon, he drove over to The Big Top to make a presentation up at corporate to the HR team to go over how to organize and recruit the PMS training crew he was charged with setting up. After his presentation, doing that sidewise slip-and-slide through the gambling crowd on the casino floor, he happened to glance through the gift shop window. He spotted just the thing—a glass slipper, real crystal, set up near a fairy tale Cinderella display for kids.

Were he and Greta close enough coworkers for this? He didn't know. Still, he wrote out a card that said only, *Almost midnight,* had the glass slipper gift-wrapped in gold foil paper, then called for one of the company messengers. An hour later, back at the office, his phone rang.

"You *bastard!*" Greta said.

"So how was D. C., Pumpkin?" he sang too brightly.

"*Touché,*" she said. "*Haa*-hah!" she laughed. "*Touché,* okay?"

"Right," he said. "As long as we're . . . all right? Are we? All right?"

"Of course we are," she said. "Next time just don't do such a good job, okay? Talk to you," she said, the way she usually hung up so brusquely on their calls.

He let out a breath he had been holding, and he understood—in the power relationships of the company, Greta outranked him. Anything he could do to reassure her of her position helped, doubly so because of her natural insecurities as the only woman in the men's club of Project Development. For a moment he mulled over what a mess Greta's life with men seemed to be, and what a mystery that such a smart, attractive woman could never hang onto any relationship. He felt satisfied that he had taken the risk to answer her back the way he did, as a joke between friends, then he settled in to finish out his day. He did the same for the rest of the week, hoping no other fallout would rain down, and no other tragedy.

Construction resumed at Pyramid World. A month passed, filled with twelve- and fourteen-hour work days and Lance Sheperd's mandate, *Just get it done*. Mancini Construction announced a quarterly earnings report in a boxed feature in the *Wall Street Journal*—gross revenues topped $2 billion from high-rise construction projects all over the country. The company made sure its report circulated well before any news broke that it would be cited and possibly liable for safety violations from the initial OSHA investigation of the fatal accident at Pyramid World. After a series of meetings between

Mancini and OSHA officials—after the first two, meetings were no longer attended by any Ironworkers Union official—four citations for safety violations were issued that might have resulted in six-figure fines that, months later, after an appeal, would be reduced to one infraction only, for an improperly fastened plywood barrier to the air shaft. The final OSHA report would place all other blame on Lester Stahl for not wearing a safety harness. The amount of the fine against Mancini Construction for the one infraction eventually would be reduced to a mere $13K and change, and even this paltry sum would languish through a further appeals process and remain unpaid for years.

As for Mrs. Stahl and her allies from the First Desert Baptist Church taking the case to court, after a few pro bono papers were filed in hopes of a quick settlement, which Mancini Construction refused, no lawyer agreed to continue the case. Nevada workers' compensation law mandates that employers pay dependents of killed workers some portion of their salaries—about $1.5K per month in Red Stahl's case, barely enough to cover a house payment, and only for as long as his widow chose not to remarry. In trade for these payments, Nevada law shields most employers from further liability. Up and down The Las Vegas Strip, the same hard tale repeated itself, with five fatalities at construction sites during those early 1990s boom years. This was why no union representative had sat in on further OSHA reviews. As one local shop steward put it, quoted in a feature on high-rise construction deaths in the *Las Vegas Sun*: "Why waste our time if the game's already rigged?"

At the offices of Pyramid Resorts, Tim Slocum gave C. D. informal updates of the legal proceedings, a gradual relief descending on the company that, as Slocum had predicted, any potential fallout from Red Stahl's death might just blow away. Las Vegas high-rise construction fatalities had become accepted by the legal system and the public as part of the price for growth and progress, beliefs powered also by a frontier attitude dating back to the Great Depression and the hundreds of deaths suffered during the building of Hoover Dam: workers took their chances in exchange for higher wages. At least a half dozen of their remains were encased in the huge blocks of the dam's foundations, where they had fallen before the concrete had set. The matter of the check from Lance Sheperd came up once, in

April, in a letter from the pro bono attorney representing Mrs. Stahl requesting facts, also asking C. D. Reinhart if he would agree to give a deposition.

"Don't answer that," Slocum said. "It's a fishing expedition. Nothing to tie the check to the company anyway."

Slocum didn't volunteer anything more about it, and C. D. assumed that Sheperd had kept him informed from the beginning. The letter and its request sat on his desk for a few hours as he rushed through other work. Clearly, this was his choice—he could do or not do what he had said he would do, he could help or not help Mrs. Stahl with her hopeless case. Only years later would he come to understand that this marked one of those crucial life moments when he could have reached for the ethical over pragmatism and convenience, even at the risk of his job, but how much was his job really worth? For years, the story he would tell himself was that he really *had* thought this choice over, had carefully weighed the options and examined his conscience. But he didn't think about this choice more than five minutes. He quickly pushed the attorney's letter to the side and dove deeper into his tasks: mapping out schedules, reviewing applications to hire system trainers, making phone calls, attending meetings. He would be the good trouper. He would do what he was told. After all, he had his own family's security and well-being to worry about. Before the end of the day, he turned the letter over to Slocum's office, presumably to be filed for a required time period and then eventually destroyed.

Saturday, two weeks after this, he was rushing around the new Home Depot on Pecos Road, stocking up on the usual items: light bulbs, water softener salt, replacement sprinkler heads the lawn guys kept breaking off in the front yard. He pushed out past the paint display toward the cash register lanes, and there she was—Mrs. Stahl, with her daughter. She glanced up and saw him. Her face, so striking and elegant, instantly registered her revulsion. Her upper lip twisted into a defensive snarl like she had seen a monster—a vampire or a zombie. She jerked back and shivered, physically repelled. Before he could think of what to say, she had grabbed her daughter's hand and roughly pulled her closer, wheeled her cart around, and vanished down the next aisle over, fleeing him.

This bothered him, sure, but what else should he have expected?

He had been the messenger, no more, not the one responsible. He shook off the incident, doing his best to forget it. By midsummer, when the whole Las Vegas Valley became an insufferable cauldron, the temperature hitting 111 degrees, all legal actions against Mancini Construction had been dropped. Little Catherine reported from neighborhood chatter among the kids that the Stahls were busy packing and would soon move to Arkansas. Briefly, C. D. considered braving the punishing heat to walk over to their house and try at least to explain himself, then he shook off the thought—seeing him again would only make Mrs. Stahl feel worse. When he heard news that the Stahls really had moved away, he felt more than relieved.

By then he had other worries. That spring, the corporate wars had broken out into full battle. J. B. Roland stripped the ranks of his top executives—Sheperd, Slocum, and Chevron—getting rid of them in a day. The Big Boss fired all three chiefs along with most of their staffs on grounds of insubordination and disloyalty, presenting proof to the board based partly on Gary Luongo's abundant notes. After this, it was all the junior executives left in Project Development could do to take cover—C. D., Kinkaid, Rico, Rickstein, Greta, and all the others. They would keep their heads down, their mouths shut, and wait for the smoke to clear enough to see where they stood.

In the meantime, all their complex tasks and preparations to open Pyramid World were put "on hold" until the Old Man could install a new executive team, the only sure word coming down was that they would have to look more closely now at cutting costs. C. D. flew to Seattle for a grim meeting with CEO Tim Chin of Chin Solutions, the software company he had talked Sheperd into contracting with, so he could put off rather than cancel purchasing the whole new property management system meant to pull Pyramid Resorts together into a digital future. That caused a crisis, as payments on the contract would be indefinitely delayed. C. D. had to do his best tap-dancing apologies and sing a song of possibly false reassurances to convince Tim Chin not to sue.

On top of that, when the Old Man took over and cut all budgets, C. D. had to furlough his office staff "kids" processing daily survey data—those glossy paper check-off brochures for "two drinks free" tediously compiled by hand, at keyboards—so if he wanted to complete that project, he would have to put in extra hours deep into the evenings entering the data himself, so crucial to the marketing plans he and Greta had put together. He did this, evening after evening, as unsure as he was about what might happen to the results, not sure if all the hundreds of hours his team had put into collecting information about and profiling customers would ever be used or would be impulsively deemed irrelevant by the Old Man and so end up wasted, trashed. Based on a few feeler calls, C. D. even considered jumping ship over to the Wynn hotels, to The Mirage or the new Treasure Island that had nearly completed construction. But in the end he stayed on board, remembering Sheperd's words about needing *people on the inside when it's time to clean up the mess.* All this trouble had landed on him and more would be coming.

During the worst of these upheavals, as the company kept speeding toward completion of the new casino hotel—J. B. Roland in a mad rush to open Pyramid World in whatever condition, no matter what, during those stressful, difficult months—C. D. would at times think back on Lester "Red" Stahl's death with a sickening sense about his own role. He would recall how quick had been his self-protective reaction to remain loyal to his company and his job. And for what now? Loyalty to what? Who—and what—was he allowing himself to become?

He would recall that letter from Mrs. Stahl's attorney, its specific language, and how in it, he had learned the amount of Lance Sheperd's check: $50,000. He was not glad to know. It made him think differently about Sheperd and what he had believed until then had been a caring gesture made from sincere, even altruistic, motives. He realized it had been nothing like this, sure now that Sheperd had done it so as not to have to face his own conscience, and that to Sheperd, as with his fellow major players in the industry, his workers were expendable. Amid the pressure and rush to complete Pyramid World, the executives had presided over a negligent risk to worker safety and had bartered with their lives. Or if Sheperd didn't think of it that way, to his mind—and C. D. only thought this when he believed the very worst about Sheperd—the check was not so unlike a tip, or *toke,* as they call it in Strip lingo, for services rendered. On the other hand, any check at all might be thought of as generous. Who was he to judge?

He guessed the amount of the check had been determined impulsively too, that same week Sheperd sold off $20 million of his Big Top stock. He recalled Sheperd banging out the phone calls, no doubt finely tuning the gaming stock market in conspiracy with his broker to milk the most from every share in a major defensive maneuver in the corporate wars. Interspersed with these calls Sheperd made frequent calls to his wife and to her yacht salesman on the coast, call after call after call. . .

Lester "Red" Stahl's death was just a chop in the seas, a minor distraction among more pressing matters Lance Sheperd handled in such a polished, brilliant way with his subordinates and the press. Soon after, his cheeks didn't puff so much when he spoke. His voice rose again until no one could hear anyone else in a room. He settled back into his usual rhythms and self-confidence, his customary strides with those pumping, rowing arms, his executive power walks across the casino floor. Amid all the high-pressure crisis that weekend in February, on impulse Sheperd had arranged a cashier's check to Mrs. Stahl through his personal accountant so that its source would be difficult if not impossible to know. He had ordered it made out for a sum only by chance swimming in his head—the price per extra foot of the yacht he had purchased as a Valentine's gift for his wife.

– 8 –

Pyramid World was built in less than two years, a record even during the Las Vegas boom. But in the crazy rush to beat out the competition, the new resort wasn't nearly ready to open, not at all running smoothly in dress rehearsals. And thanks to the way it was completed, after Chevron, Sheperd, and Slocum had been sacked for spurious reasons (some gleaned from Gary Luongo's notes), the hotel didn't in any sense live up to the standards of luxury Lance Sheperd had once envisioned and they had all worked so hard to achieve. Their elaborate plans were wrecked by the corporate wars. Seven months before completion, J. B. Roland pulled off his power play with the board. As for Gary Luongo, the Old Man planned to jump-promote him to be the new assistant VP of Hotel Operations at Pyramid World, a job for which Luongo had no experience or qualifications. C. D. stewed over what life might be like with Luongo possibly giving him orders, having to work under that sleazy thumb. He considered quitting, now or soon.

Lance Sheperd called him on his home phone several times, his tone blustering: "Hang in there. Won't be long before we're back in charge," he said. "I don't want to come back to an empty house." And: "Do your job. Just don't do it *too* well, you get what I'm saying?" Then: "In this town, at this level, it's all about loyalty. Give yourself a gut check. Who are you loyal to? And why?"

"You," C. D. answered. "Because you'll take care of me."

"Right. When have I not taken care of you?"

When *had* Sheperd taken care of him? He thought this but didn't say it.

"Don't take too long," C. D. said finally, then he lied, "I've got another offer, selling software start-ups again. In Palo Alto, a first-rate place to live."

"Bullshit," Sheperd said. "Vegas is the future. We want you on the team."

C. D. understood that Sheperd phoned him or took his calls only when he wanted something, and that, in his mind—in the new ideology of Wall Street–powered Vegas—loyalty was a concept meant for chumps, for suckers, for customers lured into casino players' clubs by promises of complimentary cheap buffets and a stack of "free" gaming chips or "bonus points" meant to fuel even more their capacity to lose. As with so many new banking offers, investment firm ads, and credit card come-ons filling the air during that optimistic era, big rewards were promised in the boldest of fonts if people would just *sign here*—then the offers were taken back in the unreadable fine print. Still, C. D. trusted Sheperd, even though he couldn't have articulated on just *what* his trust and loyalty were based other than on some fuzzily developing image of himself as becoming, somehow, *like* him—or *with* him, though on a far lesser scale—filthy rich. Money was the implicit promise. But why hadn't he put a hard dollar figure to Sheperd that defined what his loyalty was worth?

He didn't know why, save that every time he was about to do this—ask for a better than handsome salary plus a bigger year-end bonus and stock options if and when Sheperd and his executive team could mount a comeback and take charge—a strange sensation stopped him, like a huge fist squeezing inside, so that he froze in place, a sensation not unlike stage fright, and he lost his nerve. Sheperd must have understood this about their relationship, how C. D. believed loyalty was a virtue with an inherent value all its own. He had pulled Grace and little Catherine along and made the move here, then began maneuvering through corporate Las Vegas, believing Sheperd would see his virtues and properly reward him. In return, he would play his role as a faithful supporter through court intrigue, and even more so now, as a loyal former employee. No matter what, he would remain loyal to the end.

After Chevron, Sheperd, and Slocum were muscled out by the Old Man, stock prices started to fall. The new management J. B. Roland brought in, most from Phoenix shopping mall development and so new to hotels, scrambled ineptly to catch up to completing construction and at the same time follow the Old Man's orders to cut back drastically on such a high-end design. Luxury went out the window. The result would be a hodgepodge mishmash of the expensive ruined by the cheap.

Pyramid World turned into a catastrophe. The complicated inclined elevators inside the pyramid-shaped hotel would get stuck in midair in their inner angular spaces due to last-minute shoddy replacement hardware to cut costs. The same would happen with the Allan Quatermain and the Mysteries of the Pyramid Virtual Reality Ride, an aspiring rival to the Back to the Future attraction at Universal Studios, which, because of the Old Man's cutbacks, would never work right: the hydraulically mounted, pitching coal cars on which customers would ride deep into an underground Egyptian fantasy often got stuck at oddly tilted angles on the tracks, thrill-seekers and their kids forced to climb down ladders, helped out of that spooky pit by hotel security with flashlights. J. B. Roland personally reviewed all budgets, cutting, changing, and crossing out features with his cheap ballpoint pen: as previous contracts were cancelled, luxury furnishings were downgraded to the kind of ersatz wood veneer one might expect at a Motel 6; carpet and fixtures were similarly cheapened; six-hundred-thread count or double-layered Turkish terry sheets and towels were replaced with two-hundred-count polyester blend and one-ply towels; even the beds were stripped of value as designer Brick Rico's carefully planned investment in super-comfortable Stearns & Foster mattresses with memory-foam pillowtops, meant to appeal to higher-end guests, were replaced by the most basic off-brand mattresses—a kind with blue prison stripes—and creaky box springs. "Jesus," Brick said when Rickstein unhappily informed him of this move. "You ought to deliver one to his house, let his wife tell him how it feels to *fuck* on one of those things!"

Add to this the deliveries and setups barely completed in the rush to finish. Some guests checked into rooms with five TV sets and no bed. In the lobby, the "ferry crossing" went awry: some ersatz reed boats would sail almost empty across the fake Nile while others foundered in the shallow waters, packed as full as cattle cars with baffled, irritated guests gripping their bags. And somehow, in the confusion of J. B. Roland's rush to beat Steve Wynn's opening of the Treasure Island and still do it on the cheap, some idiot on the Old Man's new executive team cut out the service elevators from the architectural plans at the last minute. No service elevators? The result would be that dozens of maids, room service waiters, and maintenance crews would have to wheel carts full of dirty laundry, trays holding ketchup-smeared dishes, and ladders and supplies in a continually trooping display across one side of the casino floor to the other, inconveniencing an astonished crowd. Workers then loaded themselves and their gear into the same malfunctioning, oddly sized elevators used by the guests so they could rise to their room floors, packed in all together up the inclined angle of the pyramid walls. And as if all that weren't enough to doom the property, the $10 million laser meant to beam like a bright beacon from the peak of the pyramid to the wonder of all who beheld The Las Vegas Strip turned out so intensely bright that it blinded pilots on critical approaches at nearby McCarran Airport, a real safety hazard, so legal challenges from the FAA would result in an emergency court order shutting it off until it could be fixed or replaced. On and on, a total mess. Pyramid World was dying under J. B. Roland's command. The insider joke became: "What do you expect? Pyramids are supposed to be tombs!"

The rise and fall of companies proceeds like what happens to civilizations. Tyranny takes over, progress stops. All suddenly gets fixed in place, frozen due to fear, then darkness descends. At Pyramid World, executive tyranny caused a crisis at the top. Fear ruled mid-level management: fear of being the guy who gets something wrong; fear of looking like an idiot; fear of being fired, which could happen at the whim of the Big Boss or even the likes of Gary Luongo; above all, the fear of taking chances. Lance Sheperd had always encouraged speaking out and risk-taking on his team, never punishing anyone for an honest mistake or a wrong idea—he even praised wrong ideas, as long as they were new ideas, before he discarded them—his philosophy being that no business can succeed without taking risks. In the last rushing months before the grand opening, a culture of fear took over Pyramid World. Junior executives practiced ducking and covering, like children in Clark County in the 1950s cowering under their desks during that Cold War–era of the Nevada test site, the county emblem showing off a mushroom cloud while girls in bikinis sunned themselves under the hyperbrilliance of A-bomb explosions lighting up the desert skies. The junior executives and middle managers did their best to duck and cover from the fallout of corporate dysfunction. Mostly, they kept out of J. B. Roland's sight, freezing in place when they had to make decisions. They perfected the art of writing a kind of memo that took credit for what the Big Boss might praise while shifting blame to others for whatever he might dislike, interoffice memos written in a vague, arcane language hard to decipher without knowing the insider code. In the meantime, everybody updated their résumé and started looking for a new job.

C. D. Reinhart tried to do the same—duck and cover—but he couldn't quite. The day came when the Old Man almost completely wiped out the IT development budget at the last minute, all of C. D.'s song-and-dance efforts to keep the project going on delay now cancelled. He flew to Seattle at his own expense to give Timmy Chin the news that the contract with Chin Solutions would be terminated, no matter any legal issues and the considerable money already paid—almost $4 million so far, only $3 million to go and they could have the new integrated PMS system by opening day! C. D. made the distressing drive up from Sea-Tac airport through misty, contemplative Seattle weather, mulling over options if he quit his job, no matter his assurances to Sheperd, because, really, what was this *fuck*ing job now anyway?

At the southern reaches of the city, he passed by the drab, yellow apartment complex overlooking the I-5 traffic and its whooshing noise where he had once lived—once existed is the better word—after he had quit acting and moved to Seattle, his first job going from business to business selling deals with discount coupon books. He found a good position marketing the VisionQuest start-up, where he had met Grace and they had been so happy, for a time. Then they had been defrauded on their partnership shares by CEO David Schmelling when he had sold the company and walked away with millions, and they were both unemployed. Just before that happened, he had met and talked with Lance Sheperd at the Comdex convention in Las Vegas, resulting in the opportunity at Pyramid Resorts. He had launched into this new job as a delirious adventure, but now, what was it really worth?

So okay then, he thought, what about coming back here, starting all over again in Seattle? Despite opportunities in the tech industry and the natural beauty of the Emerald City, except for the settled happiness he had discovered with Grace and Catherine, Seattle reminded him mostly of his failures. Would he want to live here again? He wasn't sure. Grace still missed life in the Pacific Northwest, her family roots, their weekend escapes into the forested parks in the crisp, renewing air of the Cascades. She always held fast to the idea that another life waited for them here if all else failed, repeating a phrase they had sworn to each other like a promise when they had made the move to Las Vegas: *It's not like we're going to live here forever*. So he wasn't only on his way to see Tim Chin and give him the bad news. He also had to deal with a catastrophe at Grace's old house on Queen Anne Hill, that money pit she should have sold but held onto like an exorbitant insurance policy. Her latest family of low-rent tenants had just vacated the place, leaving it trashed with crayon tornado scrawls by their kids and a plumbing flood that had ruined the floor—again!—in the downstairs bathroom. They would have to take out a new loan for the thousands this would cost on top of their other expenses—Catherine's private school, the mortgage, the home equity loan, two car payments, their nearly maxed-out credit cards and all the rest—how could he manage all that if he quit his job?

No matter the hell his job had become, at least he still had his salary.

C. D. sat with Timmy Chin in his U-district office under the faint gray light of a rainy day showing through the high windows. All around them, spread out in crowded, tiny cubicles with ropes of taped-together wires hanging from the ceiling and running across the floor, forty or so diligent young nerds on the Chin Solutions programming teams worked away at building a new brilliant property management system made up of colorful click-through logos and hieroglyphic symbols, those streams of numbers and words and oddball characters in bright lines of code like a musical score singing away across their glowing screens. Though Chin Solutions had other clients—a contract with a mid-sized airline to build a website and software; the same for a Seattle-based Alaska cruise line; a dozen small business clients, too; and Tim hoped to land a contract with a chain of hotels being built in a rush by the Peoples' Liberation Army in China, for which he was developing a version of his PMS system translated into Mandarin—at least half his company's gross revenue would be wiped out if Pyramid Resorts pulled its contract with him. Tim Chin had put everything he had into building his company, barely even paying himself a salary, his wife, two babies, and his harsh, old-country mother-in-law still packed into the same crumbling, three-room flat on the downhill side of Chinatown where they had lived since he was a student. Still, he took the bad news impassively, as was his nature, understanding this wasn't Reinhart's doing. He assured C. D. that Chin Solutions could still make it somehow, only letting on how upset he was by gazing out grimly over his beehive of workers still typing away at their keyboards, shaking his head. "Have to let half of them go. Tough to get them back. Programmers can call their own shots these days," he said.

The Old Man terminating the contract with Chin Solutions left Tim Chin with little choice but to file initial papers to sue for whatever he could get. When he got back home, C. D. heard for the first time the Vegas answer for when casino hotels broke contracts, which they were doing more and more, straight from J. B. Roland at their first and last one-on-one confrontation: "Let him go ahead and sue. We'll see how long he lasts."

Later, C. D. and Tim Chin went out to a nearby student dive and got drunk. What else could they do? C. D. narrowly avoided getting stopped for a DUI on his way to spend the night sleeping on the floor of that disaster of Grace's rental house so he could be there in the morning to get estimates from contractors. He wished Grace would come to her senses and sell that wreck, get out from under all the hassle and repairs. But only lately she had reminded him how easily they could find themselves living in it again. He hoped not. Yet who knew what would happen? He recalled the quote Greta Olsson had dug up somewhere, joking how they might use it in a new marketing campaign for the mess at Pyramid World: *Nothing goes as planned; even Pharaoh turns to sand.*

After he returned to Las Vegas, he learned of more deep cuts J. B. Roland had made to what remained of the IT budget. Instead of the big purchase order for three hundred new IBM 486 machines for Pyramid World and to replace obsolete hardware at the Camelot and Big Top hotels, the Old Man had ordered Rick Rickstein to scour the market for bargain machines. Rickstein found a deal at one-fifth cost for government-surplus, obsolete Zenith PCs to use as work stations, the cheapest possible clones with already outdated, measly 286 processors—they would work, sure, but only barely without upgraded RAM. The IT techs, Ron and Roberto, took one apart, holding up the cheap components with incredulous whistles.

Roberto likened it to a Ford Pinto. "Better jump clear of any crashes," he joked. "Might catch fire and explode."

At their one and only confrontation, C. D. did his best to explain to J. B. Roland the necessity and efficiencies of new information systems, repeating an oft-used phrase in the software industry: "Information will be the currency of the future." The Old Man looked at him like he was a deadbeat trying to pass a bad check. He then described to J. B. what "the internet" was likely to do for the hotel industry once it took off, using the "will replace telephones with space age communications" example he had heard used in pitches to neophyte tech investors. The Big Boss regarded him as though he had just confessed to an alien abduction. In sum: he got nowhere.

All the Old Man thought about were immediate costs. Instead of any new system, his plan was to keep on using an obsolete version of the DOS-based "Check In" program The Big Top hotels had been slowpoking along with for years, one-twentieth the cost of a new system, sure, but software only just barely maintained by a subcontractor outfit down in Georgia doomed to go out of business soon. And Check In still required keeping hard copies, using a partial version of the old-fashioned hotel "rack" system, with all that paper and tedious labor of desk clerks filing records by hand. He tried to point this out to the Big Boss, gently challenging him by suggesting future extra labor expenses and guest inconvenience, but the Old Man wouldn't budge. J. B. didn't trust anything he couldn't see on paper. He didn't believe in survey data, either, having relied on his own instincts and intuitions about customers all his life. He saw only the market segment he already knew—Wal-Mart shoppers, the family crowd who traveled with their kids in RVs, retirees on Social Security on the hunt for cheap buffets, the nickel and penny slot players, the low-rent rubes. He slapped his empty desk blotter with his open hand and snapped, "No extra costs!"

That was that, their meeting was over. C. D. kept thinking but not saying: *The problem is mistaking cost for value.* He later kicked himself that he didn't have the guts to say this to the Old Man's face, since he left him feeling sure that, right after the grand opening, he would end up fired anyway. In the weeks that followed, as Pyramid World turned more and more into a mess, C. D. found himself demoted to an unspecified position in Hotel Marketing. He mainly worked with Greta Olsson on the grand opening, also on doing ad buys in travel magazines and talking on the phone with direct-mail jobbers and travel agents cooking up discounted junkets for advance sales. The logo with the one-liner he had dreamed up, *The pyramid watches out for you*, felt insincere and fake, like it should be rephrased now into a warning.

– 9 –

For the grand opening, the original plan had been for Lance Sheperd to address dignitaries and the press triumphantly as the public face and spokesperson for Pyramid World. He would welcome the VIP crowd onto the casino floor and invite them into the restaurants and lounges, all decked out with a sumptuous feast and drinks for a rousing celebration. Not to be: the Old Man insisted on a more subdued cocktail party gala, personally hosting the more important politicians and VIPs inside the casino in the Nefertiti Lounge, while outside, more muted ceremonies would greet the less important guests, then Gary Luongo and the junior executive team would lead these groups inside to a modest first-drink-free then cash-bar reception. In the weeks leading up to the opening, Luongo, followed around by a buxom assistant whose main role seemed to be showing off her cleavage, kept assigning and reassigning the same tasks to different people, as if he had forgotten just who he had ordered to do what the day before, so even the scaled-back plans for the grand opening fell into chaos. Finally, their team met on the side without telling Luongo, Greta taking the initiative to do this. They pieced the event together as best they could.

The big day arrived. C. D. Reinhart stood in a crisply pressed khaki linen suit and a chocolate-colored tie, and he wore a pith helmet. He gripped a microphone, using what he recalled from his acting-for-television training as he smiled for the cameras and at dozens of reporters from the press corps. Before them clustered a big gang of smartly dressed dignitaries, including the mayor of Las Vegas and the governor of the state along with members of the city council and county commission, half the Nevada legislature, and all the rest—the power elite who had turned out to celebrate under the fireworks and also to snatch at their share of the publicity. Another, larger crowd of the general public gathered along Las Vegas Boulevard, gazing at the mesmerizing glass surface of the impressive twenty-five-hundred-room hotel that reached up at a breathtaking 41.5 degree angle—only 10 degrees gentler than the slope of the great pyramids of Egypt—the smooth glass planes like brilliant gilded mirrors reflecting the last rays of the setting sun.

The plan: C. D. and Greta, costumed in their khaki and pith helmets like adventurers on safari, would work as a team out in the entrance, leading the elite visitors, stopping from time to time to explain various attractions and read from the walls of hieroglyphs. They would invite the VIPs and press to follow them on a journey into the incomparable luxuries of Pyramid World. They would start under the tall square arches of the casino entrance, set off by columns painted with hieroglyphs depicting the journey of awakening by the god Ra, symbolic bridge god into the afterlife. Then they would lead the visitors past the snake symbol of Apophis and then the ostrich plume hieroglyphs of the god Thoth, he who guarded the gates of paradise, using a feather to weigh their hearts as they transitioned from the burdens of mortal life to a spiritual journey into the heavens.

A blue-toned theme shimmered under the arches of the main entry, suggesting a mystical water crossing, a boundary between two worlds. C. D. and Greta would lead the VIPs across the inner driveway onto a wide, reed-carpeted walk near the main casino doors where a chorus of soothing flute music at the threshold was meant to suggest their arrival into the paradise of Osiris. Guests would step into the vast interior of the casino spreading out before them like into a cool flowing garden with its acres of slot machines and gaming tables. Scantily clad Egyptian slave girls and slave boys waited for them with trays of drinks and exotic foods. Dealers wearing Egyptian headdress costumes stood at attention at the green felt tables, ready for the first rolls of dice and shuffles of cards. As the elite crowd progressed further inside, bands and other show people on strategically placed stages would start belting out songs of joy. Timing was important. As J. B. Roland welcomed them inside, just as the sun fully set, he would give the signal to set off a spectacular fireworks display.

Waiting to begin, C. D. stood beside Greta, microphone in hand. He repeated a few chanted lines as the elite group finished milling around, still assembling, his voice sounding distorted, too artificial through the cheap portable speakers: "Welcome to Pyramid World, the most spectacular new luxury attraction on The Las Vegas Strip . . ." He fought squeals of feedback no technician seemed able to fix. He repeated his lines as security guards herded the VIPs and reporters behind a barrier of golden ropes. "Welcome to Pyramid World. . ."

A short distance behind him, only partly included in the frame shot by the cameras, lay the Sphinx. He turned his head and looked out over its huge rounded back as it gazed east over the traffic-jammed boulevard and sidewalks crowded with public spectators, his view from the entrance directly over its tail and across the full length of its mammoth lion's body to the back of its regal blue and gold headdress. The sheer scale of the structural foam statue of the Sphinx truly was impressive—this mythical creature, steeped in ancient mystery, protector of tombs yet also archetypical nemesis of humankind and primal source of their terrors, threatening to tear at their throats with its claws, *the strangler* in ancient Greek—and there it was, this replica of the Sphinx of Giza lying there so passively, as if fully tamed, welcoming all comers with its human-seeming eyes and its monstrous smile.

Greta made a chopping motion with her hand to begin. Behind gold ropes, the elite crowd pressed into a tighter group. Cameras zoomed in for a closer focus on C. D. and Greta. Swimming through his head were bits of an inscription from one of the columns in the Valley of the Kings, hieroglyphs that his team and most new employees of Pyramid World were originally supposed to have taken special training classes to learn to read or to memorize phrases as actors would lines from a script until J. B. Roland had cut that budget too, so who knew how many employees had actually learned the meaning of the language on the walls? C. D. had completed the classes. The phrase on the column he stood under read: *We see the outward as relevant, when the spiraling in is what determines our lives.*

One of the reporters gestured at the hieroglyphs rising in vertical graphs above him and asked, "Do these mean anything? Or are they just decoration?"

"Our design team traveled for months back and forth to Egypt," C. D. announced. His voice echoed with fuzzy vibrations through the cheap speakers. "The hieroglyphs at Pyramid World are painstakingly transcribed, many from sacred sites in the Temple of Man. Hieroglyphs aren't only pictures, or ideographs. Some are characters, but most represent a kind of phonetic language. . ." He sounded like a tour guide as he raised an open hand and gestured toward the large symbols and pictographs and sounded them out, "Ptah-Seker-Osiris," he read. "We are herewith entering the kingdom of Osiris. The inscriptions as we enter Pyramid World are meant to evoke a pleasant journey into the luxuries of paradise. . . ."

As Greta stepped closer to his side, he thought he detected some urgency in her body language. He read her gestures and strained expression as telling him he was going too far, that he should *keep it simple, stupid, you're losing them*. He led the group past a second column, reporters following. He had gone over these wall paintings with the training team—five graduate student Egyptologists flown in from the famous Oriental Institute at the University of Chicago before the Big Boss cut even that minimal budget, so they had to substitute training classes with crudely printed scripts. A rough translation of the hieroglyphs he stood under should read: *Man denies the magic of harmony, loving only his habits, therefore he suffers.*

He was about to recite just these phrases when Greta pinched him. She reached over to grab the microphone. He tightened his grip on it, and for a second or two, they tugged back and forth. He sensed a confusion among the press as they tried to follow what he had been saying about the hieroglyphs, realizing he must be talking too fast and trying to say too much, but how else should he explain? Panic shone in Greta's eyes, her urgent message to him again: *Keep it simple, idiot!*

He smiled more tightly at the cameras. Another reporter asked about the hieroglyphs, "So you're saying these inscriptions are real? They're copies from Egypt?"

What to say? He thought of the weeks designer Brick Rico and his team had spent in the Valley of the Kings, researching and appraising, coming up with these precise hieroglyphs, all decorations, yes, but all chosen, too, for fortuitous meanings. Finally, he raised his arm in a broad gesture meant to include all the columns of inscriptions that surrounded them. "Some are copies, but some are not," he said. "These are all *like* the real thing, chosen or composed for Pyramid World." Then he added: "This stuff means stuff!"

And that ended up being the quote of the day, followed by or accompanying the vertical panning by the cameras of the tall columns of hieroglyphs. This would be the sound bite that made it into most promos and news documentaries from that era, too—that quick little scene, with his four words, before the evening news features went to edited jump cuts of the lights, ringing bells, and music from the launch shows inside the casino, then ended their segments with colorful starbursts of fireworks over the golden pyramid in the night sky.

So there he was, and there he would be, a part of Las Vegas history now—C. D. Reinhart, junior executive, in his linen suit and pith helmet, fixed forever in that moment as an ebullient spokesperson summing it all up, his bright white teeth smiling falsely at the cameras as he waves an arm at the cheap-looking copies of hieroglyphs on the ersatz columns, ushering the VIPs of Las Vegas on with his microphone like the ringmaster of a circus waves a bamboo cane over so many freaks and animals parading by for the newest attraction under The Big Top. And years later, he would recall all the millions of hours of labor and toil that had gone into building this dream city of gambling and excess, the fortunes made and squandered, the tears and blood that had been shed, and the men, like Lester "Red" Stahl, who had lost their lives. To what end? And what about all the tens of thousands of others who had given the best years of their lives? *This stuff means stuff*. What did it mean? What was it all really worth?

Thirty years later, these questions would still fill his head, after Pyramid World had been bought and sold two times over and the Las Vegas press announced plans for its demolition. The columns of hieroglyphs had long ago been painted over with a dull pale yellow. The lion-hued body of the Sphinx had been bleached by the sun into a patchy, indeterminate color faded to almost white. He would read about plans for yet another nighttime implosion, the whole angular structure collapsing into a tangled heap under dust clouds roiling into the dark desert skies. He would be reminded how little here intended to be permanent, nothing meant to last, nothing for the ages. The scrap and rubble would be cleared away. In its place would rise something new. And he would recall that day how he had summed up his general if imprecise sense of this place—this dream city, Las Vegas—and had weighed his own heart and existence too: "This stuff means stuff." Right. But what? What did any of them really know of Egypt? A civilization and society for thousands of years almost forgotten, left for later ages to piece together from its monuments and tombs. And what about here? What, here, would remain under the desert sands?

Second Chances

– 1 –

Las Vegas boomed. Everybody worked who wanted to work, and almost everyone worked. Still, most people rarely stayed at one job or in the same place for very long. Little else seemed permanent, either—wipe out the past, blow it up when it's done. Monumental landmarks with storied histories were regularly imploded in great echoing explosions that quaked the earth and sent mushroom dust clouds swirling into the nights: the Sands, the El Rancho, The Landmark, the Dunes, the old Desert Inn, all in just a few years. People kept moving up at their jobs and from one house into another in the ever more sprawling new housing tracts, seeding in the grass, planting the palm trees, digging the swimming pools, laying the brick barbecues—then, just when a neighborhood would be shedding its dust-blown newness with green lawns and streets full of kids, they sold their houses for a third more than what they had paid so they could "buy up" and move again. On and on, level to level, climbing the pyramid in an accelerating rise.

The dream city grew. Four thousand, then six thousand, then even more people arrived every month—the number reached eighteen thousand in the month following the Northridge, California earthquake in 1994—a migration that powered the construction industry building the new strip malls, office complexes, and housing tracts, laying out the new pavement, utilities, and drainage systems spreading out in all directions. At the heart of this unprecedented growth, the new mega-resorts were hiring dealers, bartenders, servers, maids, salespeople by the thousands with no end in sight, or so it seemed. Steel and concrete skeletons of hotel towers under construction kept rising in all directions, topped by the tall trees of cranes that stood out like the masts of great sailing ships against the pastel desert skies.

Those years marked a transition period between the "old" and "new" Las Vegas. The town left behind its former era of sprawling garden motel complexes laid out behind the one-story neon storefronts of the casinos. The desert oasis concept transitioned into a new era of themed resorts and supercasinos offering complete fantasy worlds. The plate tectonic shift of this transformation also marked a sea change in who ran the city, a move away from the wealthy individual financiers—men like Howard Hughes, Kirk Kerkorian, and William Hilton, men like developer Del Webb, Jay Sarno, and old Sam Boyd, the men who had been replacing the healthy sums of Mob-controlled and union money, plus money from the Mormon-run banks tossed into the mix, that had laid the original foundations. These men were in turn replaced by the far more lucrative and seemingly limitless bankrolls of Wall Street just beginning to flow out into the desert like an ever-rising tide that would wash away the city's previous financial history.

A lot of "old" Las Vegas history C. D. Reinhart picked up from the blunt talk of his barber, Dominick Bodolotto, who worked out of an old-fashioned shop complete with red-striped pole Downtown, just off 5th and Carson. Dominick served a lot of Vegas business people with his no-nonsense cuts, men he kept perfectly snipped at least twice a month. His wife, Angie, worked with him, filing and polishing away at guys who still needed the obligatory card dealer's manicure. The Bodolottos had moved to Vegas in 1960, "In da days a da Rat Pack," as he put it, his *dees, dems and dohs* accent straight out of Chicago. "Ya see, Vegas was different den. No bullshit," Dominick said. "Not dat different from Chicago, ya get what I'm saying? Da Mob, dey knew how to take care o' people. Any guy who work for dem, dey took care o' dem, dat's da difference. Dems were da days," he'd say.

"You can say dat again," Angie would echo, filing away at the back of the shop.

Both were nostalgic for the era before the famous Vegas Black Book banned Mob figures from gaming, those years when tough guy and Lucky Luciano associate Moe Dalitz brought in all that Teamster money to bankroll the Desert Inn and Stardust (and he had a major hand in the Convention Center); when Johnny Roselli ran the "skim" for the Chicago Mob and reputedly just about controlled the whole town (until the FBI found him suffocated to death and dumped in a Miami bay, long overdue for recall testimony to Congress about J.F.K.'s assassination); the days when Frank "Lefty" Rosenthal, with notorious leg-breaker and hit man Tony "the Ant" Spilotro at his side, raked in millions off the top of the cash flowing into the casino cages at the Hacienda, Fremont, and Stardust. Other old-time locals figured in this history—Bennie Binion, Jackie Gaughan, Bob Stupak. Dominick and Angie told colorful stories about them all. They lamented the day when Howard Hughes started buying up the town with his billions. This happened about the same time federal law enforcement finally focused some attention on all the bodies that had been turning up in the desert year after year like seasonal fruits.

"Lemme tell ya, not one guy ended up out dere dat didn't deserve it," Dominick said. "It ain't like in duh movies. Nobody got popped dat didn't ask for it, ya get what I'm saying? And da rest a da town? Believe me, ya never saw a more wide open place. It was like one big party, everybody making money. And now? What do dey dink dey's doing? Buildin' all dese skyscrapers here? No way dis craziness can last!"

Dominick kept saying that the real trouble was *care* for the people, and by people, he meant not only the solid, hard-working employees in the industry but also the tourists and their money. "Where's da 99-cent steak anymore? Where's da free lounge show? How's a tourist suppos'd to feel when he gotta pay 10 dollahs for a lousy burger after he drops at least a t'ousand at craps? Deese new guys are all set to ruin a good ding, 'cause dey don't know to take care o' da people. Present company excluded," he added. "Smart guy," he'd say, whipping the barber's cloth off C. D.'s lap.

He called almost every customer who sat in his chair a "smart guy." On the way out of his shop, Dominick would shout after him, "Good luck, smart guy!" Angie's voice—she never forgot a name—would echo, "So long, C. D.! See ya in a few!"

By the time C. D. and Grace moved to Las Vegas, the "old" era was on its way out. But some of the old Vegas fun and adventure still remained. He and Grace discovered the lounge at the old Desert Inn before it was imploded and forgotten, arranging babysitting for Catherine so they could escape into the nights to sip cocktails and dance in their seats to the lively sounds of Keely Smith and Sam Butera belting out their classic Louis Prima numbers. They took little Catherine to some of the headliner shows too, outings that recharged their optimism about making the big move to Las Vegas: Liza Minnelli performing torch songs from *Cabaret*; Shirley MacLaine in a top hat and sequins proving once again she was one of the best all-time hoofers there ever was or will be; Siegfried and Roy doing their truly magical magic show with those magnificent white tigers springing through clouds of stage smoke at The Mirage. Fridays once a month, C. D. and Grace joined the Kinkaids to go out dancing to whatever band headlined at the Gold Coast. Over drinks, Mark and Grace—both CPAs—would talk straight-line accounting, deferred taxation, and cost controls while C. D. and Pam rolled their eyes.

Some Saturday nights, they went out for intimate dinners at the old Di Martino's on Maryland Parkway, one of the best Italian restaurants in the city. Once they spotted the octogenarian Milton Berle with his old flame, Marie Lillo, in a corner booth. And nights when they really splurged, they booked a table at Piero's, where the established Vegas elite dined when they weren't co-conspiring on insider real estate deals at the old Las Vegas Country Club. Either there or at Piero's, the Las Vegas elite used to gather like an incestuous society of ancient kings: the Greenspuns, the Molaskys, the Rogers, the Joneses, the Barricks, the Rieds, the Ruvos, the Hiltons, the Kerkorians, on and on, many already or soon to be counted among the wealthiest families in the country. A visiting star or famous athlete always roamed through the crowd at Piero's. B-ball stars Charles Barkley or Michael Jordan dropped in after blowing fat rolls at the casinos. Don King with his gangsta entourage dragged beat-up boxers and semi-clad escort girls behind them. Jerry Lewis and Frank Sinatra Jr. were regulars, as were Wayne Newton and Robert Goulet. Celebrities filled out this scene of the wealthy and elite, drawn to the dining room at Piero's as to a temple of power and influence.

Added to this mix, Jerry "Tark the Shark" Tarkanian might be tottering through the Piero's crowd, the towel-chomping coach famous for putting UNLV and its Runnin' Rebels basketball team on the map by winning the NCAA championship. Tark often would be leading a very awkward, physically towering new recruit fresh out of a community college or rescued from a second-rate urban school. The kid would be so tall he would have to duck his head not to bump into low-hanging light fixtures. When the big kid's shadow fell over their tables, the perfectly coiffed ladies of the Las Vegas elite would freeze their smiles while gripping tightly to purse straps hanging from their chairs. Tark delighted in stirring up this race-based discomfort in that crowd, showing off his young prospects around the city.

Lance Sheperd, too, might be dining at Piero's among this ruling elite, conspicuously *not* with his wife, as Grace kept pointing out. Sometimes Sheperd's busy eyes would spot C. D. and Grace. Gesturing regally like a local *don,* Sheperd waved them over to introduce them around, billing C. D. as "one of my new talents." C. D. and Grace would stand there and join the table conversation for a few minutes, a lot of the talk politically angled but not much about Republicans or Democrats—party affiliations casually irrelevant in that crowd—their politics more about the latest tax breaks and land swaps with government agencies and how best to grease the wheels of the Clark County Commission to get it all fixed up just right, the politicians and the wealthy working together to grow their fortunes during the boom. The state had no income tax. And Nevada collected among the lowest gambling and mining taxes on planet Earth, both big issues that had fueled the rise from local offices for first-term senator Harry "Pinky" Reid. When he was in town, Senator Reid could be seen regularly at Piero's working the room, taking the pulse of the Vegas elite, Lance Sheperd among them.

After Sheperd finished introductions, he would raise his voice in that irritating way he did at dinners until it was hard to hear anyone else at the table. Grace would give C. D. a wink and squint that said *bor-ing* in their married code, anxious to get away. Sheperd made clear by his effusive introductions that being shown off like this was a part of Reinhart's job. Unlike Grace, he felt exhilarated by this heady crowd and wanted to stay longer. At Piero's and at community and company functions they attended for Pyramid Resorts, in little more than two years, he and Grace met and shook hands with almost every member of the power elite in Vegas, C. D. on a first-name basis with many of them. Where else in the country could this have happened?

"All they ever talk about is real estate, money, and each other," Grace complained, back at their own table. "How can that be anybody's idea of fun? And Lance Sheperd? What a blowhard! Definite case of overcompensation." She raised a hand and curled her pinky finger, letting it dangle there limply. C. D. quickly reached out and lowered her hand to the table.

Out in the new housing developments off into the mesquite and sagebrush wastes, thousands of lots were laid out, hills terraced, washes and arroyos filled in. Ever-growing brigades of construction crews kept busy knocking out stick frames one after another like stapling big cardboard boxes together, then bolting them down to concrete slab after slab after slab, the workers laboring away in their thousands in the dizzying heat through the summer months when their bodies sweated out more water than they could drink; then they pushed on through the sudden dust storms and flash floods of the winters. Before the big drainage systems could be laid out and dug all over the Las Vegas Valley with any kind of sensible engineering, whenever it rained, crews of county workers trucked sandbags around to block off mouths of streets that ran with riverlike rapids bobbing with debris. Always some car would be trapped under the Charleston underpass at the I-15 in a rushing flood, its driver standing on the roof and frantically waving for helicopter rescue.

Las Vegas would more than double in size in less than ten years. Season after season, construction crews kept spitting out their millions of nails like a huge moving assembly line of strenuous labor and knuckle-scraping toil, a noise everywhere in the air of work-truck back-up sirens and the *clap-a-clap-a-clap-a* of nail guns echoing in the distance, all tossing up what amounted to the same basic designs of ranch or two-story stucco boxes sprouting up in monotonous ranks of beige or brown or sunset pink developments across the big bowl of the Las Vegas Valley. Tract homes grew off in all directions, south into Green Valley and Sun City then on into the Southwest; out even further into The Lakes and far north into Summerlin; up the terraced slopes into the more luxurious tracts that grew even further north until they slammed against the mountains of Red Rock; and newer developments of ever more expensive homes spiraled steadily upward into the southern hills with their magnificent views, on the other side of which craggy slopes ran down into Boulder City and the sapphire blue of Lake Mead.

Who *were* all these people? In watering holes like Paddy's Pub just off Flamingo, where he dropped in sometimes on his way home from work, C. D. got to know some of the new people who were moving here, not so unlike the way he and Grace had moved here "on a wing and a prayer," as her mother might say. He knew them by the expressions on their faces, something like the expression on his own face not long ago—that darkly troubled tiredness of a guy just barely making it here, knowing he had less than a quarter tank of gas left in his car, an expression that also said he meant to climb up out of defeat by grasping, fast, at the new opportunity Las Vegas offered for a second chance. He had failed at a first life, so he had changed his life. In making the move to Las Vegas, he had placed the same bet as more than a million other newcomers, gambling on a second chance. His marriage, too, was a second chance. C. D. came to believe that what Lance Sheperd had said about the alluring fantasies of Las Vegas might be true enough for the tens of millions of tourists increasingly drawn to its attractions—that the ever more elaborate resort concept illusions had a paradoxical capacity to make people believe their lives were more real. But a different truth powered the people who were coming to live here, a truth much closer to reality: Las Vegas was the city of second chances. No other city in America offered so much at that time.

America sorely needed such a place. Losers were welcome here. Through the '80s and '90s, workers were laid off from factories by the tens of thousands; three out of five small businesses went belly up; one out of four farmers left or lost their farms and rural America lost as much as 20 percent of its population; almost three out of every twenty professionals failed at their practices or lost their licenses in other states. Add to this the fact that half of all married couples split up in financially taxing divorces. Living paycheck to paycheck, only one catastrophe away from losing it all, people were going bankrupt or getting stripped of everything they owned with tragic frequency. An untold truth of America was that for every story of success, it was possible to find threefold testimonies from people who had failed. Anyone who had failed elsewhere and could just *get* here could find a job in construction, the hotel and service industries, or in the professions. The city promised that if you were careful, steady, and willing to work, you could recover some success in life, even if modestly defined as a stucco tract home in the desert and a kid in college. During that era in America, if Las Vegas hadn't existed already, the country would have had to invent it all over again just to relieve the pressure. Lance Sheperd had been right when he said that in Vegas, it didn't matter so much where you came from as where you were going, simple casino logic that with each new bet placed, the past ceased to exist, only the future counted. Las Vegas kept reinventing itself by this vision for the future.

That future for Las Vegas counted on ever more attractive fantasies than mere hotel casinos and sin pits in the desert—the city aimed at a more compelling goal that its visitors perceive themselves at the center of a thrilling experience. C. D. learned the Vegas hospitality industry. He understood it more in depth from local columnists, journalists, and historians, such as Jane Ann Morrison, John L. Smith, Jon Ralston, Jack Shoemaker, and the great Hal Rothman who summed it up: the postindustrial economy was about consuming services and experiences, an economy more about people than goods. The tourist "attraction" meant to stimulate desires that could be fulfilled before an approving audience. As Rothman put it so aptly, the new Las Vegas was being built to create desires and provide the audience. Its attractions meant to deliver more than anywhere else the kind of intense experiences that would promise even more the next time. Desires for these experiences attracted more people. Dreaming of more would bring them back over and over again.

In pursuit of this goal, the city gleefully destroyed much of its recent history, the hotel casinos of old Las Vegas brought down in spectacular implosions. In their places rose multibillion-dollar resorts designed to perform as *experiences*. The Bellagio and the Venetian brought a faux Italy to the desert. In front of Bellagio, an eight-and-a-half-acre "Lake Cuomo" merrily sprayed its fountain show four hundred feet high on the half hour, water spouts dancing to operatic music; and at the Venetian, a small-scale Piazza San Marco drew visitors to the center of an exotic illusion like a massive stage set of Venice, complete with indoor canals and singing gondoliers rowing along through an upscale shopping promenade. Then came more: the Paris with its faux façades of the City of Lights, a scale model Eiffel Tower and Arc de Triomphe looming over The Strip while inside, quaint boulangeries, bistros, and cafés ringed its gay casino floor. Before these had been built, Pyramid World asserted its ersatz fantasy of Egypt; Treasure Island offered shows of battling and buxom buccaneers; sprawling Emerald City boasted cartoonish movieland themes in the biggest hotel on earth. Soon, the New York-New York Hotel Casino showed off its fake Manhattan skyline, its blue-green replica of the Statue of Liberty thrusting her torch up more emphatically than the original over tourist multitudes milling along on the sidewalks below as if to say this—*right here!*—is the real promise of America. So it happened that, one after another, themed mega-resorts advertising ever more luxurious experiences grew up at an astonishing pace, their sculpted foam façades and skyscraper towers lit up with ever more dazzling, dreamlike displays.

The number of hotel rooms in Las Vegas tripled to reach 135,000 (this number would hit 150,000 in the new century). Growth projections into the future boasted of no end. The hotels kept booking up to 92 percent capacity on weekends, around 75 percent full even on weekdays, with the average daily rate—that numbers-crunched ADR in industry lingo—climbing beyond all expectations. As Lance Sheperd had predicted, Las Vegas surpassed Disney World as the most popular tourist attraction on the planet. By the turn of the millennium, Sin City would top Mecca for its annual headcount of pilgrims. These truly were boom years, an era when the whole town was powered by energy and ebullience, new people moving in by the thousands every month to take their second chances at life, brought in by the promise of plenty of time-and-a-half overtime for blue-collar workers and for everyone else at least a possibility of getting rich, or if not rich, at least they could achieve that *feeling* of being rich, which can be just as satisfying.

As the power elite of the city built their empires, C. D. Reinhart also fixed his ambitions on a future goal, one he mapped out on the complex organizational charts of Pyramid Resorts: he would work his way up to that vice presidency he knew would be there for him within a decade, maybe sooner, if he worked hard enough, stayed careful enough, played his part well, and, as the old poker saying goes, could hope for decent cards. Both he and Grace had grown up not in poverty but at its edge. No matter their past setbacks and doubts, he kept telling himself that all was in place for them both, together, as a team, to work hard enough and climb high enough to achieve those most redemptive of American dreams: money, advancement, *success*.

– 2 –

The day he accepted the job offer with Pyramid Resorts, Grace Ritchie finally said yes to one of C. D.'s many marriage proposals. That Grace was older, divorced, and had a daughter, he saw as assets, not the complications she feared. The big move to Las Vegas might be harder for Grace than agreeing to marry him—such a rooted Washington girl, despite issues with her mom. They had worked together three years at the software start-up called VisionQuest—Grace handling the accounting and C. D. the sales. They had gradually, tentatively started dating, which led to more. He fell in love first, able for the first time in his life to say and mean "I love you." Grace accepted this, and let him move into her old wreck of a house on Queen Anne Hill. He proposed marriage at least every other month. Grace wanted to wait to be sure, no room in her life for a second mistake, and so they settled into trying out a life together until he could prove his case.

They were swindled out of their fair share of the payoff for all their work at VisionQuest when the CEO, David Schmelling, sold it off then dumped them with paltry severance checks, hardly the payoff they had been promised, both left without jobs. They thought of suing him, but the up-front costs and the years it would take to reach a settlement stopped them. After C. D. met Lance Sheperd at the Comdex convention, Sheperd pitching the town and feeling him out for a job, to which C. D. had said no, Sheperd phoned him again to offer a position. In the wake of the VisionQuest betrayal, the job offer in Las Vegas felt like a godsend. Again, he asked Grace to marry him.

Grace had her doubts. They "reviewed the situation" (as they called these deliberations in their partnership). Grace disliked the ideology Las Vegas sold to the world to chase after more, without limits. They discussed the delirium of the casinos and the fleshpot buzz and neon excess of The Las Vegas Strip, its promise of luck and excitement, that life could change in a blink, how all seemed based on the existential possibility that the universe itself might after all be made up of pure chance, and who could imagine living in such a place? Still, what kind of a salesman was he if he couldn't get her to say yes? They celebrated over a bottle of wine shared in candlelight and intimacy. After that, the tougher sell might be little Catherine. How would she accept being so far away from her dad? C. D. had no idea how to pull that off, had no experience reasoning with a child, but he trusted he could find a way.

He believed he had been getting along well with Catherine, cautiously building a relationship, and as Grace had noted, her excess energy did seem to settle down with him around. For his part, he'd begun to feel an inner scrape of jealousy when Catherine called out "Daddy! Daddy!" so excitedly on the days when her mostly absent father, Frank O'Malley, a boozy deck hand from the Ballard fishing fleet, drove up in his battered truck, greasy baseball cap pulled low over his eyes, reeking of fish holds and beer, and as he watched Grace conferring with her ex-husband at the curb while handing over a bag packed with Catherine's things.

"Aren't you worried about letting her go off with him when he's like that? After he's been drinking?" C. D. had asked. "I mean, does he have a problem?"

"I worry about Frank when he's not drinking," Grace said. "He only gets mean when he's sober." C. D. also gathered that Frank O'Malley had indulged in a kinky side in their marriage that Grace abhorred. "Sex for Frank meant slapping a porn tape into the VCR first. *Boring*. Let's not talk about that, ever," she said. "Don't ask me why I ever married him. When we met, I thought I saw something in him that reminded me of my dad. *Wrong*," she said with a bite that implied something deeper she wouldn't talk about, a wound devolving all the way back to her father's death by carbon monoxide poisoning—maybe accidental, maybe not—in the garage of his mostly one-man logging company after her mom had left him for another man. "But Frank does love Catherine," she said. "He'll keep it together, and *clean,* for her, which is all I care about now."

Most of Catherine's visits with her dad were hosted by Grace's mother and her mother's husband—her fourth. Frank drove Catherine up to their "hole in the woods," as Grace called it, with many outdoor, wholesome activities set up by Catherine's grandmother because Frank rarely had money enough to do much more than pay for his booze plus the upkeep on his shabby trailer near Mount Vernon, a rust-streaked double-wide Grace swore she would never step foot in again. After their modest wedding, they sent little Catherine off to visit her dad and grandparents while C. D. and Grace did the heavy lifting for the big move. These arrangements left Catherine even more confused—how could her *real* daddy *not* be living with Mom anymore and her mom be living with this *new* man with the funny name instead, and so far away, while her Grams and Grampa kept acting like nothing had changed?

After the baffling disruption of the move to Las Vegas, Catherine grew even more concerned, straining to comprehend her new reality. They would live in a new tract home out in the desert, bought sight unseen with almost no money down amid a housing crunch so tight they were lucky they could. The house felt like a hastily built box of wallboard and stucco Grace complained had a "cheap echo" as they moved into its modest rooms. C. D. and Catherine crawled around on their hands and knees together, busy unpacking boxes piled in the dining room, hunting for her books to carry into her bedroom. Catherine insisted on doing this chore herself, arranging her books by the colors of their spines in her small red bookshelf. She pulled out an oversized green picture book with a leprechaun on the cover Frank O'Malley must have given her, and she asked: "Will Daddy come see me here? When am I going to see Daddy?"

A tremor in her voice struck him—her voice when she was about to cry.

"Soon," C. D. said. "You'll see him soon. When he's back from fishing, okay?"

From the kitchen, Grace let out a frustrated breath, loud enough she meant he should hear it. She clattered more loudly, unpacking pots and pans. C. D. poked his head around the archway at the noise. She aimed an urgent, silent signal at him, moving her lips: *We need to talk!*

"Why did you say that? Part of the attraction of moving here is to get away from his *raids*," she said. "Frank driving up unannounced, drunk, with some cheap stuffed animal. She won't forget what you said, you know . . ."

"I'll buy him a ticket. It'll make her happy. Poor kid."

"Poor kid? What about *me!*"

"I'll get him a hotel room," C. D. said.

"Fat chance that works! How *could* you!"

And so it went. They unpacked and moved into the new house—that stucco box with a red tile roof painted the same sand beige and so like all the other houses in their development that, more than once that first week, C. D. turned into the wrong driveway. A month later, in between Frank's boat work in Seattle after the big run to Alaska for the pink salmon season, C. D. did what he said—he bought him a plane ticket. He did this after another argument, the first real "issue" in their marriage. He had decided that making Frank's visits possible would be a part of what his role as a good stepfather should be, so that Catherine wouldn't grow up with any embattled or divided sense of her divorced parents. He had entered her life at an age when she knew full well who her real father was, and that she loved him. To try to replace that father would be wrong, real folly, and might give her a complex later on that could cause her to reject his own fathering. He reasoned to Grace, "How else will she see him more than once a year?"

"Don't for a second think you're doing this for Catherine," Grace said. "You're doing this for yourself. For some crackpot idea you can fix things for her, when it's really you who needs the fixing."

"You're wrong," he said. "This *is* for her, for her happiness."

"Have you thought about what it might do to us? Have you?"

"We'll be okay." He moved his body closer, pulling her to him. He stroked the back of her neck, massaging that tight spot in her muscles, then down into her shoulders.

"All right, I'll let it happen. Against my own best instincts, I will. But I'm doing this for you, not for her, just so you know," she said. "I mean, have you considered how once you get this going, how we could ever make it stop?"

He had no answer to that one. They didn't reserve a room. Grace convinced C. D. that Frank might hole up drinking and ordering adult films in a hotel room, so they'd have to toss him in the shower and drag him out to see Catherine. She didn't want them paying for "*that* kind of Vegas vacation," as she put it. "He'll keep things under control if he's stays here," she said. "In front of Catherine, he'll have the presence of mind to stay good and oiled but not get falling down. And do you know how *sad* that makes me? How sad and crazy I'm going to feel seeing him stuck on our couch, sipping at a big Slurpee-size rum and Pepsi, both of them *totally* zoning out together to old movies on TV?"

Frank O'Malley's visits went more or less just that way, only Grace hadn't told him how gratingly Frank could play up his Irish shtick with Catherine. Shamrock souvenirs, little plastic leprechaun statues, cheap green trinkets—anything Frank could pick up in the gift shops on Fremont Street after his poker games—started filling the house. A shamrock pillow, shamrock T-shirts with *Kiss me, I'm Irish!* and *Erin go bragh,* even little kitschy green stickers he helped Catherine paste all over her bedroom that peeled off layers of paint when they were removed. One night, flush from a poker game, Frank bought a color movie poster of John Wayne and Maureen O'Hara wrapped in each other's arms, that signature image from *The Quiet Man* that, along with *The Informer,* he claimed he never tired of playing on the VCR. Frank tacked up the poster on Catherine's bedroom door. He plugged in the tape and the two of them snuggled together on the couch, watching it over and over again.

"Your Daddy's really only half Irish," Grace snapped at dinner that evening. "Isn't that right, Frank? Your mom was Polish? Isn't that so? Tell her, Frank . . ."

Her ex-husband was too lit up on rum and Pepsi to pay much attention, off into a playful riff with Catherine, doing an obnoxious imitation of Barry Fitzgerald that made her giggle—their own little game. Later, he tried to sing an Irish lullaby as he tucked her into bed, his voice breaking way out of tune, rasping into a coughing jag from the many cigarettes he kept ducking into the backyard at half-hour intervals to smoke. He sang, *I'll take you home again, Kathleen, across the ocean wild and wide* . . . He stumbled through a few more lines as Catherine put her hands over her ears, shouting, "No, Daddy! Stop it! No!"

She fell into giggles as he played around at tormenting her, pretending to start singing it again, his voice rising like a dog's at the moon. When she shouted for him to stop, he tickled her, calling her in his booziest imitation Irish voice "me wee leetle Kathleen."

"To bed! Right now!" Grace interrupted. Frank O'Malley obeyed her, sobered up in an instant, ready for C. D. to drive him Downtown to the poker rooms at Binion's anyway. As Grace turned out the light, she said, "Your name is *Catherine*. Catherine spelled with a

C, not a *K*, not like the Irish spell it. You're named after your great-grandmother, Gramma's mom, who was English, and a Puritan. Nothing Irish at all about your name. Just so you know . . ."

Catherine hadn't quite put together what a divorce meant or how this worked exactly, imagining that, after she went to bed, all three of her parents would go off to Mom's bedroom and snuggle in together—she had expressed fantasies about this. Usually, Frank had been either at home planted on the couch in front of the TV or away for weeks at a stretch "gone fishing"—Catherine had a sing-songy way to say this phrase—in Alaska or Puget Sound. Why shouldn't life be the same when her dad came to visit now? That her dad slept in the little shoebox of a guest room surprised her. She asked why. "You'll understand when you grow up" was the best Grace could reply.

And Grace had been right—once this had started, how could they ever stop? For years to come, similar scenes would play out in their lives. The most difficult would be the Christmas visits from Fisherman Frank. Catherine knew her dad had nowhere to go, and she begged them—how else could she get to see him at Christmas? Grace would complain that what C. D. had started was actually cheating them out of their own family holiday, depriving them of making their own traditions, just the three of them.

"Why can't we at least have our own holidays?" Grace lamented, every time.

During Frank's visits, Grace withdrew deeply into herself, talking less to everyone. It seemed hard for her to act like she was married to either man. They would work on this issue for years. C. D. started that first Christmas, after Catherine's too excited anticipation and then Frank's arrival like a sailor set free in port had gradually calmed down. Together, they all set up and decorated the tree. C. D. took "my girls"—as he liked to call them—off to Christ Church Episcopal for the special service on Christmas Eve, which Grace, who hadn't been raised with much religion other than her mom's Depression-era New Deal beliefs, looked forward to "as a break from Frank," since whenever Catherine invited her dad to church, he shook his head no, crossing his stocky arms across his chest with a quick, automatic reaction as if from an inner defensiveness of the long ago lapsed Catholic, symptoms C. D. recognized in himself. He and Grace had made the decision to join the Episcopal Church and expose Catherine to its more tolerant ideology than the stricter, more burdened Roman Catholicism in which both C. D. and Frank had been raised. Besides, as Grace had put it, with the Episcopalians, Catherine might at least stand a chance of seeing a woman minister. C. D. and the girls stood and knelt among the congregation, reciting from the Book of Common Prayer, which seemed strangely bland and unthreatening compared to the Catholic missal he recalled from his youth. C. D. and Catherine shared a hymnal, getting lost flipping through the pages, singing. Back home, Frank boozily waited up for them by the Christmas tree until both together—the two fathers—tucked Catherine into bed.

Frank staggered off to the guest room, and in a few minutes, they heard his gruff snores. C. D. and Grace finished all the work of the gifts, spreading them out in abundant piles under the tree so Catherine could wake up to them in the morning. They set up the half-drunk glass of milk for Santa, took bites out of Santa's cookies, swept the oatmeal and glitter "reindeer food" from the walk. Then, in what soon became their own husband-and-wife yuletide ritual, they snuck off to their bedroom to exchange a nightgown and pajamas. He had always preferred sleeping in the buff, but a good stepfather learns to wear pajamas. Grace knew the kind he liked—all cotton, drawstring if possible, few buttons. And each year, he would shop carefully for a nightgown or peignoir for her in the expensive boutiques, always trying to balance what covers and what reveals, something to help with her self-image, as she always thought her body too heavy. He picked through the frilly racks, choosing one he thought might please her best when she would gaze at herself in the mirror, turning her body first one way, then the other, and try on the matching robe while he uncorked the wine and watched.

Her ex-husband's presence in the house, even boozily asleep, encouraged a greater self-consciousness in their sensual moves. Hushed and quiet, they worked through a strange tension of their awareness of him so nearby. This forced a more intense concentration on each other, until, finally, their holding back led to all the more release. They both felt but never spoke about, not once, how Frank being there made this difference—more careful attentiveness on C. D.'s part, taking more time to let the wine free their spirits, then extra care in her unwrapping, kiss by kiss, like a virginal seduction. Afterward, he held her in bed with a deeper satisfaction, a more powerful holiday joy.

So, yes: this was his doing—his insistence that they open up their home to what Grace called Frank O'Malley's "raids" that happened season after season, year after year. Frank was usually so broke that C. D. bought him a ticket for the trip. Why? For his stepdaughter's happiness. He believed this, no matter what Grace had said. And Frank wasn't at all unpleasant, the way he blustered into town so full of his upbeat Irish charm, bringing simple trinkets or gifts, not only shamrocks or cheap green things but often soapstone Eskimo carvings of fish or birds or other totems, hand-whittled cedar boxes, leather wallets and bags made by his sailor friends—gifts C. D. and Grace had little use for but would keep stored away, then set out on bookshelves and end tables before Frank arrived. And weeks before every visit, Catherine's excitement as she waited for her dad filled their home with happy energy. What could be so wrong if it made her so happy?

What C. D. didn't see, at first, was the stressful balancing act all this forced on Grace, repulsed and frustrated by her ex-husband and everything he said and did, but having to avoid letting her emotions show in front of Catherine. Grace hid out a lot in their bedroom. She cooked and served the meals, straining to keep up her end of a pleasant chatter, usually about her mom and her husband and their place in the woods, the only subject other than Catherine that she and Frank now shared. Hard to imagine how Grace and Frank had ever been married, save for those moments when Frank fell into a stupor in the living room, slurring his words with a harmless, child-like smirk, talking on about his boats and his skippers and things that had happened out at sea, full of little stories about whales and dolphins, seals lying out on rocks in the sun, his voice trailing off into a repetitive murmuring. Then Grace would soften, help him up, put her arm around his waist and guide him off to the guest room. "Okay, now, Frankie boy. . . Let's go! Oop-ah!"

She only halfway fended off his groping smooch good night at the door. And each visit, Grace would go through his oily duffel bag to do his laundry, note the holes in his ratty socks and underwear, then make a run to the mall. Nothing stirred her affections so much as that mothering role. In these brief acts of tenderness, C. D. could glimpse how Grace and Frank must have been as a couple. He saw flashes of Frank's younger, more rakish self, understood that he might once have been an attractive guy in a thick, swarthy way—the weathered sailor chasing after the naïve country girl feeling trapped up in the woods, terrified she'd turn into an old maid, so he had serenaded her with tales of the gulls, the bald eagles, the sea birds, the otters and the glaciers, the raw wild beauty of Alaska. Grace had let him carry her off to a low-rent life in his trailer near Mount Vernon. While Frank was off fishing, Grace took classes at Skagit Community College, then enrolled full-time at the University of Washington. The year Catherine was born, she earned her degree and her CPA, and she had had enough. She moved to Seattle, doing the divorce from a kit. Grace had met and married C. D. believing that her old relationship was behind her except for exchanging a few words with Frank while passing Catherine off to him for visits. So in Las Vegas, Frank's "raids" felt to her like a deliberate pillaging of her emotions, leaving her moody and frustrated. After some serious talks, C. D. understood Grace felt guilty that her ex-husband had turned into such a pathetic case, as though it were somehow her fault that he had chosen a bachelor existence and an alcoholic life—a life like a gradual, painful drowning.

Grace finally talked this through with him. She even saw a therapist about this issue and others, her dad's self-inflicted death, accidental or not, among them. Gradually, her turmoil about Catherine's father settled down. They treated Fisherman Frank like some wayward, messy uncle to the family, even Catherine picking up a bit on this—an uncle they all sent money to at times, after he called saying he had been "skunked" out fishing or had lost what stake he had left in the poker rooms. Harmless enough, Frank would turn up in December and early June, often bringing a cooler full of salmon or halibut as a gift to fill the freezer along with his little trinkets and gifts. Mostly, he would sip at his jumbo rum and Pepsi on the couch, sitting with Catherine in front of the TV, playing endless old movies. When the four of them were at dinner, he'd talk about how lucky Catherine was to have two fathers. "Two dads are better than one." He kept repeating this. He didn't ask for much else but that they all agree: "Ain't it lucky you got two fathers!"

In later years, it would be Catherine who drove him to the casinos during his visits. She became the one who would wake him up from a boozy doze and help him off to bed. In the end, they adjusted to Frank O'Malley a lot like they did to their other visitors—Grace's mom and her husband, and C. D.'s brothers and his sister, all in their families who came and went, so often on short notice, the old saying about moving to Las Vegas proving true: every relative down to second cousins will be sure to visit. They welcomed them, sure, happy enough they were here. Still, they learned how to live their lives in and around them, and at times despite them.

"Let's hope for decent cards," Frank said as C. D. dropped him off Downtown on that first visit just after the move, after they had put Catherine to bed. He sounded like a man long ago resigned to modest hopes. C. D. watched Frank slouching off down Fremont Street with his bow-legged strides of the veteran sailor, off to try his luck at the famous poker tables at Binion's. On the lonely drive back into the desert suburbs, C. D. was still smarting a bit at how father and daughter had made up their own "tickling Kathleen" game so easily, no doubt connected by the blood relationship that bonded them. He searched his memory for any similar game that he and his stepdaughter played and he couldn't recall any, except maybe once, up in Washington before the move, playing piggyback at U-pick strawberries. Catherine rode his back like a happy, chattering monkey as he crawled along between the abundant rows of vines, gathering in the berries, from time to time handing one up for her to taste. Wasn't that a kind of game? Had they played others? He couldn't recall. Why did such moments come so easily to natural fathers? And with such difficulty to stepfathers? Was this the case generally, or something about his own relationship to Catherine?

What did it really mean for him to be a good father to her, a good *step*father?

Whatever would be his role in Catherine's life, he wanted more than anything that it be positive, that he would never put his own ego or selfish desires for affection to be returned in the way of what was best for her—that was the main thing. He must learn to father her in the ways he thought right for her, and he would insist on this as strongly as he could, making known his own guiding values and concerns, no matter what conflict that might bring on with her mother or her natural father, which seemed to be what a good stepfather should do for his daughter. He would be her friend, always, even if that meant taking her side against her mom when she was right. And of course he would support her education, guide her, set an example for her, and provide the material things, those went without saying: money for college, later for her wedding day, other money when she needed it for the rest of her life. He would be sure to be there for her in these material ways.

More importantly, though, he must be there for her when her natural father failed her emotionally; and he would never bring up her father's failures as a wedge or any other issue about him to make stronger his own relationship to her, not ever, knowing that kind of paternal competitiveness could be cruel to her well-being and betray her trust. On the contrary, when the time inevitably came when Catherine would suffer disillusionment about Frank O'Malley and how he lived his life, he would find ways to defend him. He would reinforce the good in the man and remind her of his acts of love, so that she might suffer less. And no matter how this arrangement finally worked out, he saw how at least on one main count Grace had been right—once started, it would go on for the rest of their lives.

At home, before he settled in with Grace to smooth over her tense mood—by loving her in the best way he knew how, if she would let him—he looked in on little Catherine, in bed with a lime green, gaudy shamrock pillow Frank had given her hugged against her ear. Such innocent happiness glowed from her features, plain to see. He meant to tiptoe in and give her a quiet kiss but then thought better of it, not wanting to disturb her happy sleep. He left her door open just a crack, the way she liked it. She was very particular in this new house that her bedroom door not be all the way shut or left open too far. He adjusted it again, setting her door in the approximate position that she usually approved.

And there it was, yes, of course—like their own little game most nights since the move after he put her to bed. He would take a moment to open and close her door a few inches either way, teasing her just a bit with this, too, until she told him: *There. Right there.* Then they said "Night-night," all set right again in her world, at least for a time.

– 3 –

Passing that second-year milestone at working his new job in Las Vegas, C. D.'s dreams of success and the domestic life he and Grace and little Catherine had been shaping were put at risk by the corporate wars. Also, after ironworker Lester Stahl's death, not responding to the attorney's letter felt in some way complicit, and there were times when C. D. gazed around at the almost finished Pyramid World with flagging enthusiasm and increasing doubts. Pyramid World was being scaled back radically by J. B. Roland during its crucial completion phase, becoming a strange concoction that promised exotic luxury on the outside while on the inside delivering little more than a different type of cheap circus show with Egyptian costumes. On opening night, C. D. and Greta, in their linen suits and pith helmets like characters on safari, acted like carnival barkers herding the VIPs inside. C. D. recorded for posterity that lamest of lines: *This stuff means stuff.* And catastrophe followed.

Reviews and customer surveys universally panned Pyramid World for its inconvenience, lack of service, and obvious cheapness everywhere. Within a week, stock prices dropped into free-fall. Then, three weeks after the opening, a large pipe burst on the sixteenth floor inside the tilting walls of the pyramid. A massive waterfall cascaded over the edges of the interior balcony, a destructive curtain of water dropping vertically through the angled space high above, then smacking to the casino floor below with enough force to knock people out—it was like their very own Victoria Falls making rainbows and misty skies inside the pyramid, flooding out the casino below.

After the opening, amid such chaos and mismanagement, C. D. considered quitting every day. He felt sure he would be fired anyway, but the Old Man kept him on. He scrambled with Greta Olsson to craft the announcement of the sudden closing for repairs caused by the epic flood. They came up with messaging this as "a property-wide upgrade to address guest concerns" to counteract so many thumbs-down reviews. After that, he and Greta and everyone left on the junior executive team spent a week assisting the understaffed, still uncoordinated reservations crew, hour after hour phoning future guests to cancel rooms and offer them free buffets and discounted packages at Big Top or Camelot instead, to which half the customers hung up with curses. Forget about the strategic marketing campaigns they had spent two years crafting. Within the month, C. D. and Greta were writing press releases defending J. B. Roland from a barrage of accusations of incompetence even as they kept busy pumping up the ad campaign for "the grand *re*opening" of Pyramid World after the plumbing disaster got fixed. C. D. dreaded going to the office, never sure what he would face.

Still, he felt sorry for the Old Man. Not that he got to see the Big Boss much, since he attended so few meetings now, as if once the new hotel had opened, after all his obsession with cutting budgets down to each light bulb and screw until completion, he was no longer interested in anything but counting the money. Gary Luongo would come cruising by, unannounced, his buxom secretary picking up the press releases and ad mock-ups as though, since his promotion, he no longer had to touch anything directly. Luongo rode in a big white limo down to J. B.'s same old shabby, windowless office at The Big Top and ran the ad copy by him, after which Luongo phoned in a list of corrections, most of them dead wrong. C. D. revised the banner under the logo from *The pyramid watches out for you* to *Experience the Pyramid!* for new photo spreads with models scantily clad in Egyptian costumes or a generic Ken and Barbie couple holding up fistfuls of cash at the slot machines. Their jobs turned into saving J. B. Roland, if they could. Not only was he taking hits in the business press because of the falling stock price, old accusations of possible involvement in the Reagan era S & L mess were surfacing again. How could they save a man who never listened to anyone but himself?

In the Old Man's mind, he was under siege. Every defense he ordered them to write up was a negative one, J. B. pushing the story to the board that his disgruntled former executives were undermining his properties. Really, he had no PR sense at all—the trick always to turn a negative perception into a positive one, mainly by not defending or attacking, not even if the Old Man's reading of his embattlement were true. Instead, he should be asserting some new zinger of an idea to create a more appealing public perception by means of the happy lie: *Luxury comes at a price, so Pyramid World will spare no cost to ensure that touch of luxury everyone deserves.*

C. D. crafted that one, and Greta kept trying to get the message through to the Old Man. Either he wouldn't listen or Gary Luongo blocked her communications. J. B. kept insisting on attacks against Sheperd, Slocum, and Chevron, defending himself in the press and to the board. Like everything else at Pyramid World, his tactics didn't work. Rumors ran about J. B.'s health, that he might be suffering from heart problems was the public story, while in private, talk increased about his pill-popping. In sum: Pyramid World was dying, and so was J. B. Roland's command of the company. With increasing urgency, everybody, down to the level of floor managers, who hadn't already left started looking for a new job.

Rickstein would be the first from Sheperd's original team to abandon ship, after secret meetings with Sheldon Adelson. Adelson and his close executive circle had amassed a mammoth fortune by developing the Las Vegas Convention Center into an immensely efficient, profitable operation. Adelson had bought the old Sands Hotel, where the Venetian would soon be rising after the dust settled from the implosion. Within a decade, he would be billed as "the richest Jew in America" on a White House visit to President George W. Bush—for Adelson, that religious identification paired with his wealth became a source of pride. At the Las Vegas peak, Sheldon Adelson would rise to become the third richest person in America, after Bill Gates and Warren Buffet, or so the *Forbes* list said, and he would remain in the top ten for years.

"His wife is Israeli," Rickstein confided at lunch to C. D., feeling him out to determine if he also might be interested in making a move to the Sands to join Rickstein's new team. "Sheldon likes Israelis. We're fighters. We understand *price*. He'll let me take over his pricing. You could come with me, help build the IT. Revenue management is the new future," he pitched. "Why stay with a sinking ship?"

What Rickstein didn't know about were C. D.'s frequent phone calls from Lance Sheperd, who kept insisting that he stay. After his exit from Pyramid World, Sheperd, Slocum, and Chevron had bought up a crumbling casino complex over at Stateline and maneuvered through all the complex licensing process with the Nevada Gaming

Commission, positioning themselves for a comeback. Could this happen? C. D. wasn't sure, but as ever, he would remain loyal to the end.

Grace disagreed with his loyalty, the word *sycophant* appearing a few times in their late-night discussions. He knew Grace had already started contacting her old friends in Seattle, feeling them out for what jobs might be available, not telling C. D. directly, rather hinting at this while dropping bits of gossip she picked up from Marjorie Slocum and Diane Chevron at Sage Valley Spa that the venture at Stateline didn't seem to be going all that well, how their futures might include moves to La Jolla or Lake Tahoe, pastures where the Vegas rich grazed away in their golden days. C. D. countered that their negative gossip might be disinformation, a wartime tactic, his former bosses knowing anything they told their wives would turn into rumors spread around town. He intended to hang in there and see what happened.

After a grueling winter campaign, the corporate wars finally ended. Sheperd, Slocum, and Chevron co-conspired, formed groups of investors, and bought up the now underpriced stock—*all in,* as they say in poker—then they forced a vote on the Pyramid Resorts board to send J. B. Roland packing. This threesome—industry insiders called them *the junta*—power-walked into the executive suites at Pyramid World armed with a new gaming license and backed by political players in the city and state. At J. B. Roland's old office at The Big Top, security guards changed the locks and stood by as the former Big Boss carried out his few personal things. The Old Man tried getting back in the game, fighting to buy worn-out resort casinos (slated for demolition), offering up all the personal cash he could get his hands on, but few players in town, much less on Wall Street, would back him now, and the ventures barely limped along, sadly. He died of heart failure three years later, a broken man. People in Las Vegas rarely spoke of him after that, no matter the mass-market, family-oriented sea change he had pulled off for the entire industry.

At Pyramid World, happy days were here again, with Sheperd running the finances and day-to-day operations, Chevron overseeing strategic plans and working his deep political connections everywhere, and Slocum and his crew keeping it all oiled and legal, processing the truckloads of paperwork from such a huge operation.

They also made plans for new growth. Sheperd and Slocum began dealing in increasingly complex bond issues and recently developed financial instruments called CMBS—commercial mortgage-backed securities—needed for further expansion to build two new casino hotels already on the drawing boards at billions of dollars each, projects meant to carry Pyramid Resorts Group into an immensely more profitable future.

At conference tables, Sheperd pumped up his team: "Capitalism is all about getting bigger, economies of scale. The so-called *free* market is just happy bullshit to make the rubes feel better. Capital power doesn't compete with capital power. The bigger a business is, the more capital it attracts and the more powerful it becomes. The casino industry is no exception. Within ten years, we're going to see three or four big players left standing in this town, hell, in this *state,* in this whole *industry,* and we want Pyramid Resorts to be one of them."

The boss talked on about the future during that rushed, happy period that marked the reorganization of Pyramid Resorts. An executive from Caesars Palace, Ricardo Soledad, came on board to fix the mess J. B. Roland had made of Pyramid World. The first thing he did was fill in the inconvenient ersatz Nile River that ran through the lobby so guests could get where they were going without climbing into a boat—what a champion move. Old Vegas hand that he was—leader of the team that had renewed Caesars Palace with luxurious five-thousand-square-foot villas staffed with servants in togas and priced at 20K per night for Caesars' list of loyal Whales—in record time, Soledad began upgrading the rooms, starting with suites on the upper floors, so the hotel might come closer to the luxury it had once promised. He shut down the faulty Allan Quatermain and the Mysteries of the Pyramid Virtual Reality Ride that customers at best were riding only once—the pitching coal car seats frequently got stuck, guests and their kids forced to climb down ladders helped by hotel security with flashlights. He tore out the "reality ride" machinery and tossed the abysmal surround-sound adventure film into the trash. In its place, he installed a cocktail table filled theater in which he mounted a prurient show called *Nubian Girls of the Nile,* a genuine rainbow coalition of tits and ass parading by, a spectacle of topless breasts on varying shades of oiled brown bodies (only one or two token white ones) trailing gauzy jeweled scarves suggesting Egyptian costumes, a vision to behold. The new show sold out, the first Strip attraction to feature brown and black performers, shattering the previous tradition (and code) of topless showgirl whiteness. Helped by Greta Olsson's erotic ads and C. D.'s new *Experience the Pyramid!* tag line, Ricardo Soledad transformed Pyramid World into a Las Vegas experience that had always worked—the exotic sex palace for adults.

And Lance Sheperd took over, power-walking through all three hotels and casinos, reviewing the financials in every department, meeting with managers, directors, and employees down to shift supervisors and pit bosses on the casino floors to assure them that a new corporate culture now ruled. He encouraged feedback, listened to ideas, and tried out suggestions. He let everybody know that as long as they worked their honest best, they would have his support and could count on job security. What a smart manager, C. D. thought, one who successfully reenergized a demoralized workforce. Better yet, he meant what he said. Soon, the culture of fear that had taken over during the final days of J. B. Roland had washed away.

Through Sheperd and Slocum, new money taps flowed. In all the hotels, those creaky, government-surplus work stations would be pulled out and replaced by brand-new IBM 486s in three weeks by Ron and Roberto, who would now be running a growing IT crew. C. D. got word he could recover and oversee installing the new multi-property PMS system Chin Solutions had spent so long developing. Sheperd rewarded Timmy Chin with a new, more generous contract, renewable in five years, worth $2 million more than the old deal to get Chin Solutions back on board. Tim Chin took C. D. and Grace out to Piero's to celebrate, and what a high, happy time. C. D. organized and stewarded months of training in the Chin Solutions new "Orchestra" PMS program for over two thousand employees, working with Frank Rachette in HR, the trainers flying back and forth to Seattle to learn how to teach the new system. The Strip properties were soon connected by hardwired cables into a common grid, and with the new PMS system up and running, the three hotels began harmoniously playing and singing like a rousing symphony, an ode to joy.

At the Flamingo strip mall offices, C. D. renovated, knocking out walls, following a "community space" concept he had seen work well in Silicon Valley, creating one big war room with a ping-pong table and nerf ball nets plus video game stations to keep his newly hired staff and data processors happy while they sent out surveys, collected guest data, tracked the new Pyramid Club customer loyalty program, dealt with software glitches or with the occasional employee who plugged in a disk brought from home—soon a fireable offense—and froze up the work stations with a nasty virus. He called his staff simply his "kids," a crew of fifteen or sixteen or so working flexible hours. They came and went, always a steady turnover. Most were fresh out of tech schools or still computer science majors at UNLV and, like UNLV's student body, they were diverse, like most labor pools in computer fields heavy on South Asian Americans but also several Hispanics, one or two African Americans, and the rest white kids, all from varying backgrounds. He gave most of them their first entry-level jobs, paying two and a half times minimum wage, before they moved on to something more challenging that paid far more. He considered his IT shop a model for the future. And how exhilarating to be around those "kids" as they thought up so many new ideas, most cooked up while talking together in their community space or ping-ponging and Pokémon-ing away. C. D. also devoted one corner of the shop to what they called "Whale Watch"—his kids searched the globe for new potential cetacean gamblers so he could feed their contact info and profiles to the casino hosts. Soon, Pyramid World turned around, bringing in handsome profits, C. D. doing his part for the resurrection.

As for Gary Luongo, after the corporate wars, the new triumvirate kept him on board. "Don't even ask," Slocum said at the conference table, sharply, to dumbfounded looks, when they were learning the new organizational charts, meetings to which Luongo had been "cordially not invited." Greta couldn't believe it, pointing out to Slocum and Sheperd what a traitor Luongo had been, and what a creep to women too (none of the men acknowledged they heard this). So why *was* he kept on?

"He does things for us no one else can do," Sheperd said. "Work with him."

So they did. With all the information from his data-gathering crew, C. D. worked side by side with Greta preparing detailed "targeted marketing" campaigns meant to bring in a better-heeled crowd of guests—customers projected to gamble at least 3K to 5K in the casino, rent pricy cabañas around the pool, bang back $10 cocktails, fill tables at the Hathor Prime Steakhouse. And Luongo did prove his worth in this campaign, using family connections to help recruit a top-notch host from the old Desert Inn plus another seasoned pro from Caesars who began working a list of Whales they flew in to stay at the renovated Pharaoh Sky Suites—as big as townhouses, complete with half-naked valet service, girl or boy. For the Whales who brought a wife or family along, Luongo put together a special "travel book" of first-class getaways to beaches in Acapulco, Martinique, and Puerto Rico, also with pages showing off luxury shopping extravaganzas to Palm Springs and Rodeo Drive, part of an overall strategy, as he put it, "to keep the Whale at the tables while we fly his wife and family the fuck out of town."

Still, Greta remained convinced that Luongo should have been fired. That Big Jim Chevron was such an insistent backer and Sheperd and Slocum went along reinforced company lore that Luongo must have thicker "juice" than anyone had imagined, squeezed out from as deep inside the melon as the Nevada Gaming Control Board or the governor's office. So they kept Gary Luongo on board. His buxom assistant moved into Tim Slocum's suite in legal as a front desk receptionist, such talents as hers always honored in the industry.

That left C. D. Reinhart, Greta Olsson, Mark Kinkaid, Brick Rico, and others on their team back where they had started, under Lance Sheperd, now tasked with developing Pyramid Resort Group's next exponentially bigger and more luxurious hotel casino, a new $1 billion mega-resort planned for the southern reaches of The Strip: The Beach. The new resort Sheperd envisioned promised three golden hotel towers and a convention center, all linked together by high-end shopping galleries spreading out in a curvaceous, sickle moon–shaped architectural array, among its major innovations a twelve-acre complex of cabañas, lounges, and spas arranged along a spectacular white sand beach with artificial surf breaking on its shores. So C. D. expanded his IT team by two employees, computer techs who could keep ahead of the mind-bending software upgrades and tech issues the new resort would demand. He and his team also worked alongside staff from the HR Training Department to introduce all fifteen-thousand-plus Pyramid Resorts employees to the novelty of emails, soon to be standard for most company communications.

C. D. spent months assigning his staff, setting up schedules, overseeing as they trained the trainers and, as ever, putting in ten- and twelve-hour days. He and Greta turned their focus to concept marketing and "brand development" for The Beach that would include the first ever "Web presence" in the form of an artist's pastel rendering of sleek golden towers reflecting a white sand paradise that took most computers—mere three-figure megahertz desktops the norm in those days connected to creaky, dial-up modems—at least five seconds to load, colorful stripe by digital stripe, onto their graphically limited screens. When the image of The Beach finally loaded, across the bottom of the screen appeared a slick promo banner of future room rates and show titles with a phone number to make advance reservations. So C. D. Reinhart made history again, authoring the first ever "pop-up ad" for a Las Vegas hotel: *Join us for life at The Beach . . .*

– 4 –

The local saying did prove true: once you've moved to Vegas, every relative down to second cousins will want to visit. In their first two years, C. D.'s three brothers and his sister, Cathy, who always brought along her rug-crawling kids, began regularly crashing into their lives. And on Grace's side, in addition to Fisherman Frank, her mom and her mom's fourth husband dropped in for visits too, often on short notice—Janice and Dewey pulled up in their clunker pickup truck and camper that left an oil stain like a black butterfly (Grace likened it to a Rorschach test) on the new driveway.

Brothers he hadn't heard from in months called him from the airport just as they stepped off the plane, announcing, "Hey, man, I'm here!"—as if C. D.'s move to Las Vegas meant a lifestyle choice to host a continuous twenty-four-hour party. Real estate brochures for their house had boasted of "three luxurious bedrooms" but really, the third measured a very tight ten by ten feet, barely enough space for a standard double bed, nightstand, and dresser, with a tiny closet built for a monk. Okay enough for his brother Desmond, who they could just hand a spare set of keys to then try to sleep through his predawn arrivals after his blackjack marathons and his bar hopping. He sneaked in, creeping around the house like a thief doing his best to be quiet. Nothing could wake up C. D. faster than someone trying to be quiet. Still, he considered himself lucky Desmond had made it back in his rental car without a DUI, grateful not to be jangled out of sleep by that kind of late-night call. Desmond was a good-time guy, always upbeat, insisting on taking them out at least once each visit for a show and a buffet when he came up flush from the tables. That was the era when the old Vegas variety topless show standards like the Folies Bergere at the Tropicana and Jubilee at Bally's gradually began to be usurped by the Cirque du Soleil shows out of Montreal, beginning with *Mystère* at Steve Wynn's Treasure Island, hard not to be awed by those acrobatic feats and transported by the eerie live music composed by genius René Dupéré, all of it age appropriate for little Catherine. No matter Desmond's night-crawling habits, his playful, sunny manners made Grace and Catherine love having him around.

No problem, either, for visits from little Francis, called "little" all his life by his brothers even after he grew up to be as tall and sturdy as any of them. Recently discharged from the U.S. Navy, he worked at some top-secret post with the National Security Agency that brought him regularly out to Nellis Air Force Base for assignments he would never say a word about, not even a hint, his cover story to say only that he worked in "aircraft sales." C. D. guessed he must be assigned somehow to the new "pilotless" aircraft being developed out at Nellis, not that Francis would ever say. His youngest brother's visits presented no burden. He simply preferred whatever family embrace C. D. and Grace could provide instead of the Spartan motel rooms off in the desert around Nellis where his agency colleagues were staying. Spookily quiet, up and out by 6 in the morning and home by dinner, Francis would pitch in to wash the dishes then sit in the family room weirdly mute in front of the TV until his bedtime at 11. After about a week of this, Francis would pack his duffel bag and be gone just as suddenly as he'd arrived.

The only subject C. D. and his inscrutable brother Francis ever really talked about was the folks. Francis had grown closest to them, bearing news of Dad's arthritis and later of Mom's early-onset dementia and how Dad wasn't sure he had enough money set aside so he could risk retiring. C. D. felt grateful for such take-charge concern by Francis and the updates from Rockland, Illinois. Only once did a visit go wrong, when C. D. jokingly introduced him as "my brother the spy" at a Sunday barbecue at the Kinkaids'. Back home, Francis gripped him by both shoulders, finding pressure points C. D. didn't know existed, his arms going instantly numb. Francis said coldly: "For your safety and mine, you will never say that again."

"My safety? What do you mean, *my* safety?"

"Good night," Francis said. He went off to the guest room, shut and locked the door. This would not be his last visit, but he left hanging in the air that it might be when he said goodbye the next morning.

Cathy and her husband, Jake, proved entirely different, with four young kids barely spaced more than a year apart. They took over the house, the kids trailing their blankies and juice boxes and litter of used Handi Wipes through an apocalyptic-seeming wreckage of plastic toys scattered everywhere—all but impossible to walk around without stepping on something that resulted in a full-throated chorus of the three little guys and the new baby girl crying all at once. Jake billed himself as a "property manager" in the Chicago suburbs. In reality, he made a catch-as-catch-can living doing pick-up jobs as a handyman while he aspired to something better—what, he hadn't yet figured out. Cathy, even with all those kids, was still struggling to finish an AA degree in the pre-nursing program at nearby Elgin Community College. On their stressed budget, of course their family vacations would be, as Cathy *gu-gu-ed* and *ga-ga-ed* to her kids: "Special trips! To Uncle C.D.'s and Auntie Gracie's new digs in Vegas!"

Cathy was the girl in the family, and none of her brothers could say no to her, in part from a sense of residual guilt, on top of their natural brotherly affection, that she had had to grow up as Mom's "little helper" in cleaning up after four savage, messy boys. Smart and strawberry blond, like Mom, with Dad's dark brown eyes and crafty energy, Cathy could make whole wheat pasta and pesto from scratch while on the phone sweet-talking her landlord into another three weeks' extension on the rent back in Elgin and at the same time switching out a dirty Pamper for a clean one and grinding up the basil, pine nuts, and parmesan while reloading the foam rubber ammo rings into the head of a walking-talking robot toy so her two eldest boys could fire off colorful discs, zinging them all over the house. She managed to get all this triple-tasking done with quick, efficient movements at the kitchen counter, luckily for everyone never mixing up the tasks. Then she pulled on the bathing suits and blew up balloonlike floatation devices and slid them up her kids' arms so they could splash around like fat little water birds in the pool. C. D. and Grace's own little Catherine soon developed a traumatic concern that one of her toddler cousins might drown, so, like a tiny child lifeguard, only barely out of kindergarten herself, she braced herself at the pool's edge for hours at a stretch, watching over them. She started waking up at intervals in the nights to sneak out through the living room, where the babies would be tucked in messily all over the couches. She would slip into the yard to make sure the childproof pool fence gate hadn't been left unlatched, so she barely slept. Grace also had a hard time with his sister's visits: "It's like being T-boned by a day-care bus!"

C. D. gratefully, blessedly escaped to the office and his work. His new job at Pyramid Resorts, with its access to freebies at the "family-oriented" Big Top, proved a huge help for his sister's visits. Grace and Catherine could herd Cathy and Jake's chaotic brood off to The Big Top's all-you-can-eat buffet with comped coupons. After stuffing themselves, Jake and Cathy could go off to play "adult games" in the casino while Grace and Catherine wrangled the toddlers up to the mezzanine level to entertain them with carnival games like the mechanical camel-racing course, with sounds of racetrack bells and cheering crowds; the T-Rex dinosaur ring-toss contest; the Gypsy Magician lever-action machine, with its funhouse mirrors and billowing stage smoke each time it coughed out a prize—all the games super easy to "win" until the kids were loaded down with more cheap stuffed animals and plastic junk than they could carry. The Big Top arcade buzzed at all hours like a parent's vision of hell. Kids rocketed around wildly out of control on sugar highs from all that soda and cotton candy, whining at the adults to cough up more clown-face game tokens or lift them up again onto the carousel rides. Games in that "family-fun" arcade mostly required some form of bet or risk, with generous odds for a payoff. Hundreds of children worked themselves up into a sweaty, desperate frenzy, fussing, crying, demanding even more, powered by their first basic lesson in the pleasures of greed. C. D. never let on what Lance Sheperd had quipped once about this kids' arcade taking up so much valuable space inside the casino: "Early childhood training for gambling addiction."

C. D. crossed paths every once in a while with gaming executive Jim Kirby, VP of Casino Operations, nicknamed "the Vacuum Cleaner" throughout the company. From listening to Kirby and Sheperd, his occasional talks with pit bosses, and the time he spent out walking the casino floor, he had learned how gambling had been sharpened and honed into a hard science of numbers. The way The Big Top arcade for kids had been set up, he was sure that from all the research on "behavioral gaming patterns" there must be a prediction, complete with descriptive statistics and algebraic regressions of survey numbers expressed in graphs and tables, that projected the long-term results of such childhood exposure into future "gaming" revenues. This was Vegas, after all, and that's what his family came here for, as did millions of people: *to play.*

Cathy, Jake, and their kids couldn't say enough about how much fun they had playing in Vegas. They usually stayed a week, after which C. D. and Grace and Catherine loaded them up in their dented, funky old van, C. D. having slipped Jake money on the sly for the long drive back to Illinois to make up for what he had lost at craps. By the time they waved bye-bye in their driveway (the butterfly-shaped oil stain permanent now), their own little home and family felt like a bomb had gone off at its heart. The three stood huddled together, dazed, shell-shocked, mentally broken. They desired only to scurry back inside that wrecked house as fast as they could, lock the doors, and hide for at least a week. But they couldn't, because they *lived here,* so they had to get up in the morning to resume their lives—work, school, everything.

"No wonder I don't want to have more than one child," Grace said after their second visit, still waving at Jake and Cathy's van as it turned the corner and vanished off Piñon Way.

"I don't ever want kids, Mom, not ever," Catherine said, her exhausted, hollowed-out eyes squinting into the sun. She had turned six years old that spring.

C. D. draped an arm over her shoulders and gave her a squeeze.

"I'm just glad the one kid we've got is you, Sweetpea," he said.

Not that they would get much chance to rest up. Visiting season is every season, all year round in Vegas. The seasonal visitors' wheel, steady as a clock, cycled around to Janice and Dewey again in their peripatetic journeying phase to get away from all the rain up in Washington State. They pulled into the driveway so their truck could refresh the oil stain. On and on, month in, month out, not everybody staying in the guest room in their house, praise be—some checked into hotels or dropped by while on business at the busy conventions that cycled through town. On almost no notice at all, these unexpected visitors called from their rooms: "I'm here! In Vegas, baby! When can we play?"

The Las Vegas visit C. D. wished he could arrange at least once was from his parents. Hoping he could draw on some sense of the youthful adventure his father had once thrived on as a press photographer, he tried to persuade him to grab up Mom and jump on a plane just to see it—what a place to make pictures, plus the "juice" at his new job might land his dad a photo shoot that could even pay him for the trip. C. D. made that first, most energized call inviting him just after the big move from Seattle, also an effort to work out a truce with his father, who had always considered him a failure. He tried to explain over the phone his new *position* in the world, in on the ground floor of a booming hotel industry. He described his new life in the casino resort business as *solid, reliable, steady*. After listening in silence—the longest he could recall his father ever listening to him—his dad replied: "It's a casino, right?"

"Right. It's a casino, but it's also a resort, a *hotel* and a resort," C. D. said.

"So. . . you're Bugsy Siegel now?"

". . ."

"What kind of a life is that?" his father said.

And that's how his father would be to him, no matter what—disapproving of his life. Whenever he thought of his father, an image took shape—he saw his dad holding up a press proof to inspect it in better light, working late hours in his photography and printing shop, gazing through half-frame reading glasses with an unsatisfied expression, his eyes puffy and tired, his cheeks blue with heavy beard shadow, a brooding, deeply unhappy man. They did not have a good relationship, never had. Home in Rockland had become an uncomfortable place because of this.

Still, C. D. did not want give in to resentments of his father. He tried to sympathize, considering how his dad saw his life—he had never wanted to settle down and give up his promising career in news photography. In his youth, he had lived an exciting life in the press corps characterized by travel and drama, first as a war correspondent in Korea, then in Rome, where he had been posted to a major wire service bureau. His life's ambition had been to continue to travel the world as a press photographer living great adventures, making his fame. He came home on a three-week visit to attend his older sister's ordination as a Dominican nun in Chicago. After she took her vows and became Sister Mary Agnes, embraced forever into that cloistered, contemplative order, her family rarely saw her again. Dad had met Mom at the Catholic Charities event following that ceremony of solemn vows, and somehow they had let themselves go in a delirium of mutual attraction. What a way to meet! Then to sleep together just after his sister took her vows as a nun?

Hard to believe, but so went the family story. Back in Rome, Dad received Mom's letter telling him she was pregnant with their eldest, Justin. Dad's next posting was supposed to be somewhere in East Africa, covering the aftermath of civil war and rebellion. How could he risk his life like that now? So he did the right thing, or at least Mom's version put it that way: "He did the right thing."

C. D.'s father returned to the U.S., to Rockland, Mom's hometown. They married and had five kids in quick succession, their second and third only eleven months apart, so Dad's life became devoted to service for them all. With a bank loan based on a contract he talked his way into with the Rockland School District to do class pictures, Dad set up a photography studio and print shop. He condemned himself to snapping hundreds of pictures in succession followed by endless hours on his feet amid the sharp, acrid smells of his darkroom, grinding out thousands of classroom, wedding, graduation, and christening portraits every year for people he mostly didn't like, people he nevertheless put on his best smile for and whose vanity he worked hard to please with his touch-up brushes, his filters and soft-focus lenses, his ability to light and shape plain-looking faces in ways that made them as attractive as they could ever be. Dad became known as the reliable, meat-and-potatoes town photographer, with his bow ties, his Rolleiflex cameras, and his stepladder—people delighted in watching him balance on the top step of that ladder, holding up his strobe, shooting them with a downward angle that made their double chins disappear. Later his printing business took over; there was more money in press work during those years of the ever-expanding suburban economy. Still, he barely made enough to make ends meet, the bills keeping him up late at night, his migraines severe after long days spent in the grinding noise and frustration of his machines. Dad came home at all hours, hands black with ink, knuckles bloody from repairs.

All the kids worked, either with Dad or at other jobs around town. C. D. put in afternoons in the studio, working tedious, repetitive hours in the red safelight glow of the darkroom—everything for the high-volume enlarger meticulously preset by his dad. He spent hour upon hour clicking the button, advancing the roll of photo paper, sliding the strip of medium format negative ahead, clicking the button again, repeating these motions again and again as in a factory, breathing in the heavy, sickening fruit juice–like odors of the developers and toners, the sharp vinegar sting of the fixer. Bending under that big machine, he made hundreds of prints a week for Dad's jobs: faces, faces, baby, baby, couple cutting wedding cake, proud parents, faces, family in arrangement with dog, priest with family, priest with dog, girl in white christening dress like an upside-down ice-cream cone, bride with her lifted veil kissing groom, wedding party, priest with bride and groom, boy at a christening dressed like a white-jacketed headwaiter, award ceremony at Rotary Club, class picture, class picture, more class pictures, family with new baby on couch, new baby alone, more baby, cat, cat, baby with cat, reunion of old men in funny hats at the Shriner's all raising glasses, faces, faces, more faces, a big family arranged into a pyramid with kids sitting on the carpet and Mom and Dad at the peak gazing proudly over them—on and on. C. D. wandered through his teenage years in school and in the streets and shopping centers of Rockland with an alienating sense that he had seen or met almost everyone in town without their ever knowing. Years later, he understood that the insights of that experience had contributed to his instincts for marketing.

Like his brothers Justin and Desmond, he preferred to work with the big printing jobs, keeping the ink and paper supplied, making temperamental adjustments at the press under the warmer lights in the back of the shop, but a mistake at the press could cost so much more, so that was out until he was older. Still, who could really stand a job watched over all the time by his parents? His brothers took other jobs in town as soon as they could—as busboys and waiters, as caddies at the Rockland Country Club—abandoning Dad to stew and simmer at his work mostly alone except for Mom, who managed the office, piled high with bills and file boxes, keeping the books and tracking down deadbeats on the phone.

Money pressures plagued their parents. They fought, real shouting matches. Doors slammed. Glasses smashed. Mornings afterward were spent with the kids tiptoeing around them, trading urgent glances like warnings not to make a move that might disturb whatever peace was holding in the house for now, for a few days at least, until the next time, or else. Or else: Dad's belt came off his pants more frequently than any of them would like to remember. But they feared most his shouting, withering verbal assaults that scalded them with rage.

When they fought and shouted at each other, Mom would break down first, rushing upstairs in tears. Dad followed after her, and their sounds of conflict and misery would gradually die down, but sometimes they kept going all night. No matter what, the next morning Dad would be out the door early to start up the temperamental Studebaker Lark station wagon, that dull green wreck he somehow kept going with blue sticky gasket sealant and jerry-rigged wires, then Mom would pull herself together upstairs, fix her hair, make breakfast for the kids, then follow Dad to the shop in the old Ford Falcon. How could they work through a day so close to each other after nights like those?

They could. They did. Years later, the story his sons would finally tell each other about Dad was that he had always done the best he could, tough guy that he was, and what a hard, hard worker, always, typical of his generation—look at the big family he had raised. That belt and the enraged shouts were just his way, like the way his dad, old Otto Reinhart, had raised him—a habit those first immigrant Reinharts had brought with them from lower Bavaria. So it wasn't Dad's fault, and he never hit them all that hard or shouted when it wasn't deserved, bless his memory. This would become the story they told about their father.

Dad had never taken any of them fishing. He had never played catch. Not once had he attended a big game his sons were playing in at school unless he was being paid to take pictures. No picnics. No outings. No family vacations, not one. C. D. couldn't remember an evening spent together as a family at a movie or even an hour in front of the television at home. The only family activity any of his brothers could recall with Dad was when he pulled out his tools from their neat, organized boxes and one or another of his sons would help him with a home repair. All Dad ever seemed to do was work, work, work—*those Germans*. And even though none of them would ever say so, the sad truth was that his sons grew up afraid of him. In the end, his unhappiness with his life drove his children away.

C. D. went off to college, to the University of Illinois Circle Campus in Chicago. When he decided to take the chance to aspire to and major in acting, his father reacted with derision. He could only sit in stoic silence while listening to Dad's comparisons to his brother Justin, enrolled in graduate school at the University of Michigan, "He's going to be an engineer, he's going *to be something*." He compared C. D. to his next eldest brother, Desmond, who had dropped out of college to work at a rivet plant in nearby Skokie. "All he wants out of life is to smoke pot and fuck around. And you? Acting? What kind of a life is *that?* You throw away all we've worked so hard for. . . for *what?*" C. D. knew better than to answer him, which could only result in shouting. "God knows what I would have done for a chance like this. Some of us get a chance in this life and some of us don't," his father said. "You're an ungrateful son of a bitch."

So it would be from then on—*the ungrateful son of a bitch*—his assigned family role.

In Las Vegas, he kept inviting his father to visit, but "no" was always the answer. As for his mother, she offered cheerful well-wishes that barely disguised her disapproval. "Las Vegas? You're living *there?* Why would I want to go *there?*"

His mother had never done much traveling anyway. As she grew older, she wanted little more than to be able to attend Mass on Fridays and Sundays, never straying too far from Rockland and what she knew. Neither Mom nor Dad would once step foot in any of C. D.'s homes. For little Catherine, these step-grandparents would exist in the form of a Charles Schultz Snoopy calendar sent each Christmas, all Mom and Dad could afford to send their grandchildren on their tight budget. For birthdays, Mom sent a Sacred Heart card containing a crisp new dollar bill. "For Tarzan!" she wrote in her looping red ink cursive, as though going to the movies still cost a buck and little had changed since her own memories of double-feature Saturdays at the Rockland Theater, her worldview stuck in an American past of the 1950s that she held onto and idealized. C. D. took Grace and Catherine to Rockland for a holiday visit the year after their big move so they could join in Mom's last big Thanksgiving with the whole family, all five kids and seven grandkids (at that time) gathering in her home. His mother served up the turkey with the warmth and serenity of a Norman Rockwell painting. Catherine had been able to see how his parents lived and where he had come from. He hoped she might begin to feel that his family would be her family now as she rollicked around that big old drafty house with her cousins, or her *step*-cousins, at an age when biological origins made little difference to kids. C. D.'s brothers and sister accepted little Catherine like any other of the many Reinhart nieces and nephews, praise be. How Catherine would accept all of them—the whole Reinhart tribe, *those Germans*—only time would tell, as time would tell also for his aspirations to be a father to her, one very different from his own.

– 5 –

During that happy era when Sheperd, Slocum, and Chevron reorganized Pyramid World and C. D. had joined the team for The Beach, his older brother Justin turned up for a visit, brought to town by a conference of the Water Quality Association International at the Rio Hotel. Whenever Justin said to do something in a certain tone, all his brothers would do it, no questions, in deference to the many times Justin had stepped in to take the blame and sacrifice his bare butt to Dad's belt. Though C. D. knew better, he caved in to Justin's pressure to gamble with him, pretending to be coaxed by his big brother's phrase that in Vegas amounts to a form of famous last words: "Let me show you how to count cards."

As an engineer, Justin lived and breathed calculations and math. So he felt confident in his capacity to "keep a running count" at blackjack, even into a four-deck shoe. Whenever the speedy adding and subtracting of cards passing over the felt in a busy game reaches a mental calculation of plus three or better, the system calls for doubling the bet; and if the count goes higher, which it only rarely does, then triple the chips. Card counting on top of a "basic strategy" should theoretically add up to winning. Except that players who do win by card counting require a bank of several thousand dollars even for a $10 minimum game to carry them through the inevitable slumps and short shuffles. Most card counters have to spend ten to twelve hours or more sitting at a blackjack table breathing in all that smoke, straining to keep the count amid the bleeping-ringing casino noise. Very few end up making more than about $10 to $20 or so per hour, max, until the game begins to feel way too much like a tedious, mind-numbing job—real work and not play—the card counter feeling like some boring hanger-on to the players around him who are actually having fun, not to mention the one or two who might happen to get lucky. Still, math whiz Justin wanted to count cards, and who was his little brother to say no?

At least he got to show Justin around town and brag about his new job in a booming industry. As he drove his brother around the city in the brand-new Mercury Sable he and Grace had bought to conform to J. B. Roland's "buy American" demand, he noted how hard Justin tried not to show he was impressed. Parked for a moment on the heights of Sunrise Mountain to take in the expansive view of the Las Vegas light show, Justin only said, "Just imagine what will be left of this place when Lake Mead runs out of water. Projections are that it'll dry up. In the next fifty years, the whole Southwest is going to turn into a desert. As for Las Vegas, when it comes to a choice between providing water for all that agriculture to feed the world or water to feed Sin City, which will the country choose?"

C. D. only nodded, not answering that one. He had his own ideas about what the country would choose. He changed the subject, and Justin agreed to lobby their father on C. D.'s behalf to help shift Dad's conviction that his third-born son would never amount to anything. C. D. wasn't sure how much Justin could do, but at least he would try.

The new Rio Hotel Casino stood a short way off The Strip on West Flamingo, its red and blue glass tower rising up somewhat modestly compared to most resort casinos in those days. One of its main attractions was a Brazilian-style *carnival* complete with dancing party girls tossing Mardi Gras beads in the lobby. Mid-level VIPs liked to gamble there because of these party girls, and also for the minimal design of the cocktail waitress uniforms—hard to imagine how those colorful strips of spandex stayed in place on the female body, vanishing to almost nothing at the waist, revealing almost everything at the rounded derrière as the waitress glided along on her vampish spike heels. Rumor had it that an aerospace engineer from NASA had figured it all out, the same scientist who had fit all the complex gear into the space suit astronauts wore to walk on the moon. The Rio was as good a place as any for Justin to try out his "system."

C. D. should have known. Part of his learning the industry had been listening to Jim Kirby, "the Vacuum Cleaner" and Casino Operations VP for Pyramid Resorts, who reinforced the old Vegas saying: *The house never loses*. At a $10 minimum table, C. D. sat uneasily next to Justin, paying too much attention not to the cards but to his steadily growing then shrinking minibank. C. D. started with $400 in chips. He earned a good salary, no question, so why should he worry about 400 bucks? Justin's bank was at least seven times that much. Still, C. D. worried, his fingers clicking through his chips at the table cushion, a sensation like needles stabbing into his arms each time the dealer raked one away. Whenever he sensed money was being wasted, he felt needle pricks up and down his arms.

"Watch me," Justin said. "Bet the way I do."

He watched Justin wagering 40 to 80 a hand, so C. D. followed, doubling his bet to 20 a few times and twice up to 30. At first they were winning, joking in camaraderie with four other players against their common enemy—a pleasant, gay-seeming dealer in a bow tie and green vest who kept up an energetic patter like a seasoned showman. C. D. counted with his fingers as he watched the cards coming out, clicking through $1,000 in chips after an especially lucky streak. Justin's stacks of chips towered up to ten times what C. D. had won. He watched Justin sipping his third complimentary Irish coffee, his expression as sure and confident as the unwavering principles of fluid dynamics. C. D. knew they should walk away, or at least take a break, but Justin insisted, "Why quit when we're winning?"

Win and run, C. D. thought, the only way to stay ahead of the game, but he didn't want to rain on Justin's confidence. The gay-seeming dealer switched out to a hard-edged, older Thai woman—the nametags listed nationalities—as silent and stolid as a tree trunk that could deal cards. The other players sensed a massacre and cut their losses. Soon only the two brothers remained. They started losing in one torturous, no-matter-the-plus-value-defying streak, almost every single hand, to which Justin kept saying "odds are" and "the way it goes" and "statistical anomaly." Chip stacks withered away into an empty green void. It wasn't long before Justin muttered only "damn" and "shit" and finally "impossible." They picked up their last $10 chips, placed their bets. "Zero," said Justin. "Neutral. Odds are . . ."

The dealer showed an eight of spades, Justin an uncomfortable seven of hearts, and he flashed one corner of his hole card to show C. D. the queen of diamonds. C. D. looked at his jack of spades dealt up with a ten of hearts underneath—a solid twenty, odds way in his favor for a winning hand. Basic strategy. The brothers stayed. The dealer flipped over her hole card to show twin eights of spades. As the house must hit on sixteen, she took it, and just like that, the five of clubs improbably slid out of the shoe: game over. As that terrible black card turned up, C. D. found his fingers stabbing out reflexively, no longer feeling connected to his hand. As if it were acting all on its own, his palm slapped over that last $10 chip, fingers curling under the edges, gripping.

"Sir?"—the first word in what must be an hour from this wood block of a dealer. Her brown, clear-manicured fingers reached out, unsure if she should make any move actually to lift C. D.'s hand. "Sir? . . . Please?"

Needles stabbed both arms inside his elbows. Finally, he willed the hand to pinch the chip between his thumb and index finger. He lifted it up off the green felt but then suddenly he couldn't let go; he pinched the chip more tightly. The dealer reached out and gripped the chip too, with three fingers. They waged a brief tug-of-war, the Thai woman remarkably strong, blue-green veins pulsing on her ringless hand, until the chip jerked into the air an absurd little distance, now in her grip. Then it was gone.

Justin didn't seem to notice this action. He gazed off into space, lost no doubt in watching numbers racing past on like a digital calculator screen inside his mathematical mind, replaying memory tapes of the run of the cards. A river had flowed uphill. He still didn't believe it could.

"Excuse me. I've got to go," C. D. said, his mouth filling with saliva, his stomach twisting into a cramp. He leapt off his chair and stumbled off like a drunk in search of the nearest men's room, where he vomited. He rinsed out his mouth with tap water. He recovered in a few minutes, his face flushed, his shirt soaked through, then stepped back out onto the casino floor to hunt for Justin.

He wandered through the bleeping-ringing maze. Really, he knew better about casinos—these loud, gaudy expanses of slot machines and table games, the heart of profitability for the business in which he now played a role. He recalled Jim Kirby reporting on the ever-shifting layouts of slot machines, deliberately designed to create new "traps" and "lanes" and "end caps" and "labyrinths" based on hard scientific studies of traffic patterns through casino spaces, an architecture intended to "attract and distract" players, disorienting them so that, never knowing in which direction to turn, they would get lost among all the machines and keep plugging money into them.

Kirby spoke of "predictable percentages" for gaming wins based on time spent per customer on the casino floor. All the games offered some margin in favor of the house. From poker games and baccarat, pitting player against player, the casino took a small percentage as the dealer and host. Among the other games, blackjack offered closest to even odds, a slightly less than 1 percent house advantage; betting the odds on craps was next best for players, depending on where chips were placed on any run of the dice. Better than a 5 percent margin belonged to the house at the roulette wheel, with a similar percentage for Caribbean Stud and about half that edge for Pai Gao Poker and other "funny game" concoctions. Keno was the worst "sucker bet" of all, between a 25 and 40 percent house advantage. And slots? Forget about it—the house edge ranged from 5 to as much as 15 percent, so only a fool looking to be parted from his money should play them. Why did people get so addicted to playing slots? Kirby talked up research on "human response behaviors to cycles of instant gratification and reward" and how the machines could be set to give quick little five-, fifteen-, twenty- or even sixty-credit "wins," stimulating players to break into an excited sweat, then sit there mesmerized by the spinning drums until they'd go for broke, chasing the big jackpot that almost never hits—and only will long after the machine has more than paid off the house.

Tales of "beating the house" ran all over town, most of them fictions. A lucky few walked out of the casinos big winners (doubling their money or better)—"about one in nine players," according to Kirby—*one in nine*. About four or five broke even, more or less (up or down a little); and three or four ended up losers (in a descending scale toward wipeout), the players who supported the house, the company, the city. Overall, casinos raked in 6 to 8 percent of all the money bet. The trick with "winners" was "to get them back into the house" by using comped meals or show tickets and players' club points or "free play" slot promotions. For the biggest winners, send airline tickets or even a private jet to pick them up; and if they win big enough, offer them, plus anyone they care to bring with them, a High Roller suite. For high-stakes gamblers, cut them discounted play up to 97 cents on the dollar if they buy in at least $100K in chips; and for the right flush Whale, get the casino host to book one suite for the wife and the suite right next door for the mistress, but better make sure to put enough hosting staff on all three to arrange their activities 24/7 so the wife and the mistress will never even see each other while the Whale is playing. In the end, do *anything it takes* to get the big players back into the house, so gamblers can do what they were born to do, what, in truth, they really wish to do—*lose*.

"Gamblers are addicted to *action,* not winning," Lance Sheperd had explained early on, showing off the gaming on The Big Top casino floor. "The real pros in this town, the professional gamblers, will bet on anything. They'll put money on what color dress next comes through the door. Everything," he said. "For the action, not the end results."

Sheperd talked about gambling as an addictive behavior often, especially with investors, projecting casino wins as a solid profit source in his business plans. Most players lost a manageable amount and kept a brave face. They limped out of town at worst disappointed, consoling themselves that, after all, they had *played,* they had had *fun*. Only about one in a hundred ended up skinned, penniless, destitute, calling relatives to wire them gas money or bus fare, or, in the worst cases, filling out forms at Las Vegas Travelers Aid to get out of town. The unpredictable moods and dark vibrations of menacing depravity big losers could send out all over a casino floor were bad for business, so pit bosses were trained to watch closely for these dead-enders, knowing just when to step in to offer free meal tickets and try to talk some sense. With this, plus watching out for cheaters among the players and dealers, pit bosses more than earned their pay.

About twice a month at some hotel in the city, the maid opened the door to a room to discover that a tragic player who had lost everything had committed suicide—hanging most common for men, prescription pills for women. All Vegas hotels had a special "suicide squad" with highly efficient procedures to block off the room, bring in the coroner, pack up belongings, and swiftly spirit away the body down a service elevator so no other guest would be disturbed, then the room might be rented out again the next evening. Rarely (yet it still happened) some busted player who truly had lost it all would take a spectacular leap off a terrace or a balcony or through a smashed window, choosing to go out with a *bang,* landing twenty or thirty floors below, the only suicides anyone would ever read about in the local press. But soon—as happened at Pyramid World with its open-air interior design, its floors of rooms with inner balconies rising up the tilting pyramid walls over the casino floor below so easily accessible to jumpers—the PR staff, especially Greta Olsson, became expert at quashing reports in the press by a few small favors, comped show tickets or ringside seats, access to celebrities for interviews, that kind of thing, until the press hardly mentioned even the most spectacular of these suicides. And anyway: what hotel in any city didn't have its share of self-inflicted deaths?

Given the tens of millions of visitors each year to Vegas, the suicide rate wasn't all that high. Hard to say, either, if the impulse rose as a consequence of gambling, since the *leaving Las Vegas syndrome* also factored in—those hell-bent souls who came to town to *blow it all out* one last time, then say goodbye. According to Kirby's studies, most losers left Las Vegas actually happy and planning to return. Lance Sheperd would on occasion launch into a loud philosophical monologue to investors that pitched gambling behaviors as closely akin to Sigmund Freud's *death drive*—the malevolent twin of *Eros* and, Freud theorized, just as fundamental to the human psyche. According to Herr Doktor, man is the only animal that irrationally seeks out his own destruction. Jim Kirby had another way of putting this to explain gaming psychology: "Truth is, most gamblers aren't really happy until they lose. They play to lose, not win. Our job is to make them happy."

At the Rio, hunting for Justin, C. D.'s mind filled with what he had learned about gaming as he circled through its confusing labyrinth of slot machines. He lost his way, butting up against a bank of machines at the end of a "trap," cussing because he should know how to avoid them. Finally, he ran into his big brother making his way back to the same blackjack table where they had just lost their money. Justin had run a credit card at the cage to stake himself to a second bank. He seemed refreshed and even more convinced that his card-counting system would prove as valid as hard math. "You'll see how the odds *must* swing the other way, over time," he said. "The key is a big enough bank. Are you in? You game?"

C. D. didn't like to gamble. Neither did Grace. Life is enough of a gamble. And he felt he shouldn't push Lady Luck. Blowing $400 with Justin had been enough. That 400 bucks would keep him awake, fretting, cringing, imagining real things he could have bought or bills he could have paid or how he might have put that money to better use—he would see a fluttering rain of dollar bills in his head all gone now, wasted, and feel needle pricks up and down his arms. That night, he used words with Justin he soon learned to say to all visitors who asked him to join them at the tables, even insisting, without knowing how rude they were being, as if gambling were a new obligation he owed to their friendship or position in the family. "No, thanks. It makes me sick when I lose," he said. "But you go ahead. Have a good time, that's the main thing. Play. Have fun. Here's hoping you win."

He headed home, making it in time to help Grace put little Catherine to bed. She had come down with a cold and light fever, so he relieved Grace at the bedside, holding a cool washcloth to her forehead and reading her a story until she fell asleep. Then he cuddled in with Grace just in time to watch Jay Leno on *The Tonight Show,* feeling life settling back in place, set right again, like nothing amiss that evening had happened.

Justin never told him how he finally came out after his card counting. He finished his conference and left town with a quick phone call from the airport to say goodbye. C. D. guessed he must have behaved like so many gamblers in Las Vegas, caught up in their trances of death wishing, chasing their money and losing.

Years later, after nearly two decades in the industry, during the first wave of the Great Recession that crashed the tourist industry and drove almost every Las Vegas resort casino into receivership, C. D. began to think about gambling differently, not as *death wishing* or "happy to lose," as Kirby had put it, but as something else—in the end, for most people, gambling was a reach for improbable hope. People who exist with the stark certainty that their finances will never be enough to raise them above their ever-lowering expectations place risky bets so they can experience, however briefly, the luxury of hope. With so little left to lose, any day they win, that's a banner day; and days they lose, as they most often do, well, then it's really all the same. And while playing, that's oblivion, no need to think about whatever else is going on—all attention is focused on the game, for as long as it lasts, for a good long while, or so they hope.

– 6 –

Over the next four years that it took to build The Beach, C. D. believed he grew closer to Lance Sheperd. He joined the close group of informed insiders Sheperd took with him on the road. The Project Development team made manic trips on the Pyramid Resorts Gulfstream to pitch presentations to investment bankers and senior traders at conference tables full of Poole, Campagna, and Fioravanti suits, sitting high up amid the beckoning towers of Wall Street: at J. P. Morgan Chase, Merrill Lynch, Goldman Sachs, and at the ever-reliable Lehman Brothers, the cozy firm that came through with the final $200 million needed to complete construction and so saved the day. What storied times at the old Lehman's, before the big move into their new building in Midtown. Their meetings usually took place on one of the three floors Lehman's occupied at One World Trade Center, spillover office space from their traditional headquarters near Wall Street—those hallowed halls hung with priceless masterpieces by classical painters.

C. D. would remember most vividly the unique *sound* of the World Trade Center complex—an eerily hushed compression of New York street noise the moment he stepped foot onto the broad plaza between the Twin Towers reaching so dizzily toward the clouds. He became instantly aware of his own diminished scale while striding below those gigantic buildings. Crossing the plaza seemed to take an eternity as his human insignificance was drawn in and absorbed among thousands of others into the busy echoing chamber of a mammoth lobby. And he would never forget the tension blowing up from the trading floors of Wall Street like a cross between an Arab bazaar and a hospital emergency room—an atmosphere far more charged with urgency than any casino floor in Vegas. Those were glory days on Wall Street, and at the World Trade Center. No one who felt that energy can ever forget just being there.

In New York, their team met mostly with "the guys" Sheperd knew, only rarely with a woman among them—guys who had long ago developed a taste for risk and its rewards. These were confident men, men filled with a brashness that came from being paid huge sums of money for tasks that, as far as C. D. could tell, took no more brilliance than playing the odds at craps on a run with loaded dice. Still, these guys never stopped working, plugged like cyborgs into phones and monitors, and later their BlackBerrys. When the markets closed after tense hours at the Wall Street gaming tables, most showed edgy appetites to go out partying: booze and cocaine and night-crawling through the sex clubs. On these pitch trips with the team, C. D. developed a reputation for avoiding such after-meeting activities. Sheperd and Olsson would host them at times—Greta padding her reputation as "just one of the guys" by being one of the more boisterous hard drinkers at the strip clubs. Just as often, the bankers did the hosting, picking up the sky-high tabs on their expense accounts. Money fueled their world. Showing it off was part of their game.

"The first billion is easy," Sheperd used to say. "It's that second billion that's the real bitch." He strode up and down the aisle of the company's brand-new Gulfstream GV with its luxurious conversation pit seating. He cheered them on, pumping them up like a coach before the big game. "Let's get it! Come on! Let's *get some!*"

"Get some!" became their in-house cheer. "Did you get some? We *got some!*" with high fives and double martinis all around on the return flights when Tim Slocum had the signed deal contracts and MOUs tucked away in his Hartmann brief.

On a few of these pitch trips, Sheperd made clear the wives or partners could be brought along, and C. D. took Grace, who felt obligated to join the party. Sometimes, Sheperd took his daughters along—Cleo, a chatty brunette college girl, a student at Brown who clung to Greta Olsson like a role model on shopping tours up and down Fifth Avenue; and Miranda, a more brooding kind of teenager with frizzy blond hair, an awkward girl who wanted little else but to stick to her dad's hip and stay close to his power meetings, usually chaperoned by a firm's receptionist. On these New York trips, Grace and Kinkaid's wife, Pam, and even Slocum's wife, Marjorie, rode along. Grace found it odd that Sheperd never brought any partner of his own. Marjorie would rule over the wives and partners, like the pampered *grande dame* and organizer of this women's auxiliary, as ever acting blind to her husband's philandering. Grace sat with "the girls" at the back of the plane, Marjorie Slocum plotting out the shopping, show tickets, and whatever "coup" she had pulled off by snagging reservations at Daniel or Jean-Georges, among the trendiest restaurants in New York at that time. A trip for "the girls" should be like a party, while "the guys" and Greta would be stuck pounding out the meetings followed by strategy sessions in Sheperd's or Slocum's hotel suite.

After those long work days in New York, C. D. preferred to avoid parties. He would come back with "the guys" to Le Parker Meridien, Sheperd's preferred hotel in those days, mostly for the fabulous French cuisine at Maurice. After the guys left to join their wives or partners, C. D. would stay behind to put in an intense hour at the hotel fitness center, pushing his body extra hard to sweat out the bad memories and regrets brought on by just being in New York. He took a quick shower, then threw himself onto the pillow-topped king bed, all whipped out, folding his naked body into the luxurious sheets to wait for Grace to climb in with him after whatever play or musical or concert "the girls" had gone out to see. The last thing he wanted to do was see a Broadway show or sit in a theater audience. *Nubian Girls of the Nile* or Penn & Teller or Cirque du Soleil's *Mystère* felt like part of his job to keep up with Vegas entertainment. But live theater in New York? No way. The city was the scene of his failure as an actor, years ago. Sitting in a theater audience stirred up too many emotions—regret, sure, at his dark memories of that past life he hoped he had put behind him, but also, strangely, embarrassment, not only for himself but for the players on the stage.

He didn't tell Grace about his acting years, or at least not very much: not his half dozen minor showcase roles; not his pair of second-company touring shows; not his one bit part on TV. He had spent six years struggling and striving in this city—the hardest years of his life. Just being in New York could set off shocks of dissociating recall not unlike a form of PTSD at so many reminders of his failures: the hotel in Midtown within sight of his former agency, where he had sat through humiliating meetings with his agent, who he had come to call only "the Mouth," cracking her gum and dressing him down with profanities at the jobs he had missed. Or riding in the company limo that passed buildings housing studios on the West Side where he had sweated away hour after hour in workshops and classes and "at the bar" in front of mirrors; or the noisy, sooty streets on the Lower East Side where he had once barely existed in a buggy, dank basement apartment, at times so poor he begged day-old sandwiches from the corner sub shop or subsisted on brown rice; or that club up on First Avenue, JP's, where he had tended bar until he quit because he couldn't risk being around all that cocaine. It made him shiver to glance out the window at signs for the L subway line that had shunted him off to Brooklyn to slave away in boiler rooms at tedious phone banks selling cheap kitchen gadgets just to survive. But all this wasn't it, really—reminders of the hard times, the disappointments, the loneliness and self-loathing of a life spent so anxiously broke yet still so in awe of the city and all it offered, like so many young people born elsewhere. It was his sense that, gradually, the great city had stripped him of his hopes—that for those who *didn't* make it there, New York, New York is the place where dreams came to die. He wished only to erase that failure from his memory.

He also didn't want to face the kind of young man he had been. He had been (and still was) a man some women looked at a second time. In New York, he had cultivated and exploited this. He developed a hard edge to project straight back at that second look some women aimed at him—*bastard attraction,* he called it—then he would date them and have intense selfish sex, pillaging their emotions and lives, then break it off and move on to the next. He rationalized that serious relationships would violate the struggling actor's most practical rule: *Never bring anything home you have to feed, paint, or clean up after*. Toward the end of his time in New York, he lived off women, picking out the most vulnerable and getting them to pay his way until he moved on to someone new. Over and over again, turning circles on the ice, a total bastard.

Summer stock, Portsmouth, New Hampshire: a rare professional job, in the featured comedy, the romantic lead—the play doesn't matter, the play is not the thing. He had a summer fling with a student intern, a lighting technician, Claire Campbell, a naïve blond theater major from the nearby University of New Hampshire. Just nineteen, her most significant sexual experience had been the summer before, working as an au pair for a rich family in Bar Harbor, a summer spent fighting off the pawing advances of a visiting stepson until she finally succumbed and then the family had fired her. A shy, quiet girl in between her freshman and sophomore year, she landed an internship with the summer stock company.

Curtis Reinhart, the actor, stepped onto the stage of her life in his leading role. He used all he had learned about a young girl's vulnerability, expressing his "true" feelings for her while underneath, a sinister calculation grew, his goal to keep scoring an intense sexual fooling around with her that would last the summer run. He never intended to go further, no matter what he kept promising her for six intense weeks. The night following the striking of the sets, he dumped Claire with no explanation, leaving her a weeping heap in her humble schoolgirl apartment in nearby Durham, located over a grocery store, the window fan blowing in odors of rotting vegetables and tainted meat from the dumpsters below. He actually prided himself on his ability to make his heart so cold—it was best for the girl anyway not to take up with an actor, right? Lesson learned, she'll be better off for it, plus he had taught her a trick or two in bed bound to serve her well with other, more desirable guys. He left her crying in her bed.

Two months later, in New York, the stage manager phoned him with news that Claire Campbell had committed suicide. She had swallowed a bottle of pills. She'd been found the next morning by a friend.

The stage manager was soliciting contributions for flowers for the campus memorial. He contributed, of course; then he also thought it appropriate to send his own individual arrangement, a modest one all he could afford. A week later, the flowers came back in a crushed box delivered to the filthy mailbox entryway to his basement hovel, the blooms and stems torn to bits by hand, no doubt by one of her friends. Inside was a one-word note scribbled in blue highlighter pen: *Murderer*.

He recalled his powerful anger at the girl, at Claire, at what she had done to herself, rage enough that he carried the box with the note clear over to Third Avenue and stuffed it into a trash can. He turned his back and walked away, meaning to push that sad incident out of his head forever—she wasn't the first psychotic girl he had dated, right? Date around enough, it's bound to happen, isn't it? Yet he knew he was at least partly to blame, the way he had treated her. He carried a sick knot in his middle at what he had done to her, a cruelty he could never atone for or redeem. He would carry this remorse for the rest of his life.

Little happened after that in his acting career, as minor as it was, until he gradually accepted that he did not have sufficient talent to make it past that lonely broke life he was living with all its spiritual emptiness. He changed his life. Or he thought he had, the fake performer who had emerged with Mrs. Lester Stahl a kind of slip. Being in New York always raised the question, again: how much, really, *had* he changed?

So, no, he did not particularly like the trips to New York. And he hoped never again to sit in a live theater audience in that city. Grace could go off with "the girls" to see all the shows she wanted. He would welcome her back from these evenings out, grateful she accepted his aversion to theater without him needing to explain, deeply appreciative as he listened to her descriptions of her evening and changed out of her clothes. Together, they ordered late-night snacks and selected from one of the best room service wine lists on earth. They happily rumpled up the sheets making love, indulging in a brief fantasy that they were away from it all, on a nine-hour honeymoon, just the two of them—sex, food, more sex, more food, until Grace dozed off to an in-room movie while he read his book, then he fell asleep, the two of them spooning. The next morning sent him hurrying off to another pitch session with the team.

When he asked Grace what she liked most about the trip, she answered, "The room service," wiping crumbs of caviar, butter, and toast points from the corners of her mouth. She paused briefly, teasing, then added, "And being in bed with you, of course."

After two more similar manic trips on which Sheperd invited "the wives and partners" to go along, Grace decided she didn't really enjoy them much, especially as they tended to happen by last-minute invitation. She had taken a job three days a week with a public accounting firm doing taxes—which she felt was a bit beneath her, but they needed the extra money—and she didn't like to shake up the schedule. Besides that, she shied away from shopping in groups with the executive wives, appalled by the prices charged by Marjorie Slocum's choice of stores and boutiques. "We're just not in their *league*," Grace would say, showing him some small item, a scarf or a wallet or a pair of sunglasses she had felt peer-pressured to buy at a cost that made her gasp. "We'd have to take out a second mortgage to buy some rag of a dress in one of those places. That woman has no idea how the other half lives!"

He argued that she *should* buy expensive clothes on these trips, part of the game they were playing. The quickest way to join "the other half" would be showing they belonged.

"That's just not *me*," Grace said. "Can't we just be ourselves?"

Grace didn't especially like the way they traveled, either, on the company jet. When friends or family members marveled at how C. D. and Grace had been zooming around in a private jet, she told them, "I'd rather fly commercial, even coach is better. It's hard to relax on a company jet. You have to spend the whole trip talking to people."

Also, for these group trips, Marjorie Slocum would offer—would insist—that Catherine stay over at the Slocums' home with their daughter, Jane, who was one grade ahead of her at the Meadows. "I feel sorry for Jane," Grace said. "She looks so unhappy. And she's so skinny, I swear she's got an eating disorder, poor thing. How comfortable should we be that Jane and Catherine hang out together? What bad habits might Catherine pick up?"

"You should trust Catherine more," C. D. said. "I'm betting the influence goes the other way, that she'll be good for Jane, which is why Marjorie wants them to become friends."

"Who's even watching the girls in that gaudy castle? A live-in maid who can barely speak English? That hulk of a chauffeur who used to work for the Mob?"

The Slocums' ostentatious mansion in the posh Spanish Trails community looked out over a spectacular view, and they kept a full staff: maid, cook, groundskeeper, and chauffer, who also watched their daughter. When Catherine stayed over, she rode with Jane to school in the family Mercedes. And it was true what Grace had said about their driver—a pock-faced beer barrel of an old Italian guy named Elio who at one time served "in security" for Moe Dalitz, "Mr. Las Vegas" of Meyer Lansky's notorious gang, a known close associate of Lucky Luciano. No telling what the man had witnessed, or done, in his time. On the other hand, how could the girls be any safer than with a guy like him? He gave them butterscotch candies. He plugged in cassettes of operas and told their stories on the drives. What could be wrong with that?

"It's good for Catherine to see how the wealthy live," C. D. said. "*We* might have that kind of money one day. What are we in this for, anyway?"

"What *you're* in it for," Grace said.

"Aren't we in this together?"

"Of course we are," she said. "But consider us more like. . . I don't know. . . how about along for the ride? We should be careful of that much money."

Grace began to say no to these company trips, not that the wives and girlfriends were often invited. Usually, Sheperd's team traveled on their own, three or four of "the guys" along with Greta winging off through the nights on red-eye flights with meetings lined up for the next morning. And mostly, these trips were busy, tension-filled ordeals, under pressure to *get some,* Greta and the rest of the team often hung over from the obligatory late-night partying in New York, part of what sealed the deal before they returned home.

– 7 –

The Beach Resort Casino finished construction in record time from conception to completion, the hotel towers, gardens, and luxurious artificial beach materializing at the south end of The Strip in all its gold-windowed, white-sand glory. Lance Sheperd had changed general contractors after the Mancini mess at Pyramid World, with an in-house risk-management team reporting weekly to monitor safety measures for the many subcontractors. This resulted in a remarkable workplace safety score, so much so that, the year after completion, Lance Sheperd and Big Jim Chevron accepted an award from the National Safety Council for "CEOs who get it" that also earned them more influence with the unions.

Building The Beach became an intense money chase. Sheperd was so confident he could pull it all off that he ordered construction to start before they had completed the financing. Each part of the project carried different "paper" and investment deals as the building progressed, which increased pressure on his team even more. The hotel and casino complex finished first, leaving the vast Beach Convention Center still to finance and build. Before that deal was set and launched, they proceeded to stage the soft and hard openings of the casino hotel, events Greta and her team, with C. D. assisting, spent four months in a rush of plans to pull off like a grandiose Broadway production complete with an A-list roster of invited movie and sports stars, including the newly elected governor, through Chevron's influence, in a shared role of master of ceremonies with Lance Sheperd, the public face of Pyramid Resorts. Whatever complaints Grace had often voiced about Sheperd loudly dominating dinner tables and events, those qualities proved perfect for grand openings. He performed with the audience-rousing skills of a boxing announcer as he moved with his microphone from attraction to attraction addressing the crowds.

All went off almost perfectly, the only glitch a last-minute emergency caused by input from a Chinese advisor that the feng shui in the casino might not feel propitious enough for Chinese gamblers so could scare them away, China fast becoming the most lucrative market to aim at to bring in High Rollers and Whales. Designer Brick Rico consulted with Jim Kirby, who reluctantly opened up somewhat the slot machine layouts. Massive, stylized statues of white lions were hastily located and purchased, flown in from Thailand, then driven in on forklifts to be placed on either side of the colorful jungle-themed entrances to the casino floor. As an added touch, near the cash registers at the lounges and bars, gold "good luck" cat statues were imported from China and set up, with their paws reaching toward the southeast. Greta Olsson also brought in a Medicine Elder from the Nuwuvi people—one of the Southern Paiutes whose reservation covered a piece of Downtown Las Vegas and on whose unceded land the whole city had been built—who spent most of a day smudging the casino, the lobby, and some of the offices with sage smoke, beating a drum and singing sacred songs. When C. D. asked, Greta poked him in the ribs and said, "Can't be too careful, right? I tried to get a Catholic priest in too, but he refused. *Haa*-hah . . ."

Following the grand opening, the new resort was booked to 100 percent capacity as many as four days per week, the artificial white-sand beach packed shoulder to shoulder with happy sunbathers waited on by attractive beach boys and beach girls attending to their every whim, all these more upscale customers drawn into the Caribbean fantasy to *experience life at The Beach* that their team had worked so hard for and designed.

Those were glory years, as C. D. later thought of them, years when everyone from the bottom up through the many levels and ranks of the now very large company he worked for, all fifteen thousand employees—the valet parkers, the dealers, the pit bosses, the restaurant workers, the retail sales staffs, the front desk clerks, the housekeepers cleaning the rooms, the hotel sales and bookings crew, everyone in the pyramid on up to the middle managers and junior executives on up to the top—everybody *got some.* Money kept flowing in as if from everywhere. Everybody in every industry in Las Vegas *got some,* so much money it seemed impossible to imagine a time when all that money piled on top of money in thick cash bricks stacked as high as the ceilings in the casino cages would ever come to an end.

And did he *get some?* Did his years of work pay off as promised?

Yes, he *got some*—he *got his*. Without his having to ask, Lance Sheperd took care of him, as he promised he would, and with that spooky sixth sense, as if reading his mind. Shortly before The Beach opened to such rave reviews and record crowds, Sheperd rewarded C. D. Reinhart with a higher than anticipated raise and stock options, plus he added a surprise bonus, a new pearl-blue BMW 740 I—that car drove and shone like a Rolex watch. C. D. enjoyed especially the tight humming of its 4.4 liter V8 engine echoing off the concrete pavement and low ceiling of the hotel's new parking structure. The automated yellow gates sensed a coded dashboard button then lifted up and swung away, like magic, over his tinted sunroof—then he would glide that beautiful Beamer into his executive parking space with his name painted on the curb. He sat there a moment, listening to that jewel of an engine idling, breathing in that new car smell like a faint electric charge through leather and honey. He felt valued, and worth it, rewarded with what he had earned, a sense he carried with him long after he turned the engine off and climbed out, feeling the door closing behind him with a solid, secure, pneumatic *thump* of precise German engineering followed by that quick little *beep* as the locks slid home—perfect. Soon he would move into his new office overlooking the palm garden.

Not that C. D. and Greta and their team could relax and enjoy for long the triumph of the opening of The Beach with their significant raises. In addition to the daily work they did to push new marketing plans to keep the resort filled, The Beach Convention Center remained to be financed and built at a cost of $250 million. They needed to *get some,* so the team prepared new presentations and flew off on a pitch trip to get more.

C. D. could rarely sleep on airplanes. Sometimes, late into a night on a red-eye flight, he would get up to go splash water on his face in the brushed steel lavatory of the company Gulfstream. He would gaze at his reflection in the mirror and not quite recognize who he was seeing. Later, shivering in his seat under the air-conditioning, a sudden foreboding would drop over him like an icy blanket, bringing on a cold, dark mood. Maybe it was because they were on their way to New York again. Or maybe it was being up in the sky at that lonely, dark morning hour, the rush of cold recirculated air filling his ears, everyone else fast asleep. An apprehension chilled him from deep inside that, with one wrong move, maybe one wrong word, this life he and Grace had been working so hard to build could fall to pieces. He sensed a fragility in everything around him, like he was living inside a bubble of finely spun glass.

– 8 –

Never trust a friend completely, as friendship often turns to something else.

C. D. couldn't say exactly how or when he learned this golden rule of the corporate world. The higher he climbed, the more aware of this rule he became, one of the reasons, in the end, he could count on few if any friends. Grace noted this, too, in the form of a question he could never answer, so he would change the subject or just say nothing after she asked him, with an edge of accusation: "What happened to your friends?"

Grace could count dozens of friends. She discovered friendships easily and kept them up. She maintained her circle of girlfriends in Seattle, some from her college years, who she talked with on the phone and who would occasionally visit them in Las Vegas amid the regular cycles of family visits and seasonal "raids" by Fisherman Frank. In Las Vegas, Grace had made several new friends ranging down and up the social scale, including Lien Luu, called "Lu," her nail girl at Green Valley Beauty; and Samantha, called "Sam," from the checkout counter at Smith's—she would meet both for lunch or coffee at least once a month or invite them over to the house after work. She also socialized with a shifting roster of people she met from her part-time accounting jobs and dragged C. D. off to obligatory cocktail hours with them, mainly investor-owners of restaurants or other businesses around town, most recently, two young real estate agents and their wives. Out for drinks in this party of six, upbeat and pleasant with jokes and laughs, Grace and C. D. caught on they were "swingers," feeling them out to join them at the notorious Red Rooster club later that evening for an orgy. Grace took his hand under the table and squeezed with some urgency. They said no, thank you, and he could see Grace crossing them off her mental list of potential new friends.

Grace was always looking for friends. The first week after the move, she made a friend of Pam Kinkaid—wife of C. D.'s first work buddy—who shopped with her in the malls, and when Pam finally had kids (after years of trying), she would take the Kinkaids' twin boys off with Catherine to Sunrise Park so Pam could enjoy a "sanity break" from being a mother for a few hours. Grace also made friends up the social ladder, all the way up to Marjorie Slocum and Diane Chevron, power wives from the executive ranks at Pyramid Resorts, women left alone too much to while away their afternoons tippling expensive chardonnay. They invited Grace to join them for lunches at the old Las Vegas Country Club and for workouts at the Sage Valley Spa, that battleground for wives of the city's elite in their fight against the hip spread and waist roll from all the dining out. C. D. noted how Grace and her many girlfriends talked among themselves with a shared intimacy special to women that would forever remain a mystery to him. Grace could be dropped by parachute into the Brazilian jungle or Australian outback or into a teeming market street in Hong Kong and, within about half an hour, she would emerge with a new friend. He admired this quality in his wife, sometimes with a tinge of envy.

He had to admit, not sure why, he did not make many friends. Or most of his so-called "friends" came from work. Kinkaid in accounting, yes—they talked at least every other day like best buddies and socialized with their wives. About once a month, he had met Rick Rickstein for lunch, his old pal from Pyramid Resorts before Rickstein's big move and steady climb at the Sands. C. D. stood in as father of the bride at Rickstein's wedding to Josefina, a dark Jewish beauty from Buenos Aires whose father at the last minute had been denied a visa. What better friend could a man have than a guy who gave away his bride to him? What a fun occasion it had been at the new Venetian, leading Josefina down the marble steps in her wedding white to join Rickstein and their rabbi in a big white gondola decked out with the cloth canopy. They sang their marriage praises and smashed the wineglass, then were rowed off together by a singing tenor gondolier through the ersatz indoor canals of the shopping arcades. But Rickstein had gradually risen to VP of International Marketing, these days working to set up new casinos the Sands was planning to build in Macau and Singapore, so he was rarely back home in Vegas. Rickstein seldom called or emailed anymore. So it goes and so they went—the friends who drifted away as they outranked him in the corporate world.

He considered Greta Olsson his friend, his gal pal at work. Side by side, they brainstormed and labored away at all the many details of marketing plans to the public and the powerful, taking turns covering for each other too, and co-conspiring in the office and after hours, usually over a quick drink at the Camelot Steak House bar, watering hole for their team. Or Greta would join the others at the cigar bar at Del Frisco's, ever in her workplace role as *just one of the guys,* her tactic to get past the proverbial glass ceiling in the industry by behaving like it wasn't there. He had no more ambitious or capable friend than Greta Olsson. Though on the organizational charts Greta was one level above him and so a kind of boss, after nine years on the same teams, he counted on her friendship. And they were effective together. Greta proved a master at big-picture strategy, also at smart layouts and graphic designs. She was the one who took their ideas to the higher-ups, able to walk into any of their offices without an appointment. C. D. excelled at choosing the best copy, at surveys and data analysis too, and at the ever more focused targeted marketing by his growing teams of "kids" he kept working away in the exponentially developing digital universe, mostly emails and crude pop-up banners in that era, the new social media still a few years away from transforming the whole world.

They shared almost everything and could say almost anything—part of what defines friendship. Greta would try a new perfume and hold her wrist out to him to sniff, asking, "What do you think?" During the years when Grace was still working through her frustrations with visits from Fisherman Frank or with C. D.'s heavy work schedule, he would ask Greta's advice: "What can I do so she feels better? Any ideas?"

C. D. and Greta did things for each other in the way friends do. He could never forget that early frenzied trip to Australia to pitch development of The Beach. On a half day's notice, they rode the corporate jet all the way to Sydney for a three-hour presentation to an investment group Down Under; then Sheperd turned them straight around for the return flight so they could make it back to Vegas by 9 a.m. on the very same day they left, crossing back over the international dateline to present the exact same pitch to an investor group visiting from Chicago—what crazy times, what impossible schedules.

In Sydney, on the limo ride from Mascot into the ultramodern city, C. D. had turned on his laptop for a last-minute check of his PowerPoints. His lithium battery caught fire. At the first painful heat on his thighs and spurt of smoke, he tossed the laptop to the floor. In seconds, the limousine filled with choking fumes. The driver switched on his emergency blinkers and pulled over. Greta, C. D., and the driver jumped out onto the narrow shoulder, heavy traffic whooshing past them dangerously close. They managed to wrap wet towels from the limo's bar around the smoldering computer—the case partly melted, the hard drive cooked. C. D. panicked, searching through his briefcase for a crucial backup disk that he somehow in all his hurry had left on his desk—not there. Back in the limo, which still smelled of melting plastic, cruising again toward the city, trying to catch up to Sheperd, Slocum, and Rico in their separate car, he started cussing out this whole crazy trip—*Fuck!* Why did they have to work in such a *fuck*ing rush? And why way *the fuck* down here?

Greta let him finish his rant. She smiled at him, slyly, as she fished a small nylon case from the chaos inside her purse. She held out a disk, winking. She had it! How did *she* have it? How had *she* burned a copy of work he had completed only twenty hours ago?

As it turned out, Greta had sneaked a copy of everyone's presentation for the team. She'd been doing it for years as part of her nervous movements around their offices and conference rooms. Routinely, without asking permission, she plugged in disks at their meetings and burned copies of what they were working on with a sleight of hand like a magician pulling off card tricks, a habit from her early days at the PR agency when she produced TV commercials and live events, clever girl. Still, she saved his ass, so how could he complain?

"Always carry backup," Greta said. "Backup for *every*body. *Haa*-hah," she sang out in that lewd, two-toned laugh of hers that sounded like a merry ding-donging bell. She scooted closer to him on the limo seat in a mock-flirtatious way. She dropped the disk into his lap—a direct hit—then cupped a hand to his ear and whispered hotly, "No one ever needs to know!"

Greta had saved him often over the years, like a true friend. And he had done his best in return. He recalled a night in those early days after the catastrophic opening of Pyramid World, during the big shake-up from the corporate wars, when it fell on Greta to represent the company and give a speech at a major fundraising event for the Las Vegas Cancer Center attended by half the power elite in the city, including both U.S. senators in those days—Reid and Bryan. Greta's ambition was to do more of this, her goal one day to step up to VP of Community Affairs. On her way into the banquet in the big ballroom at Caesars Palace, the spike heel on one of her smart red Guccis caught on a piece of metal carpet stripping. The heel broke off, the shoe collapsing under her. She would have gone down in a spill if C. D. hadn't been right there to catch her arm. Her expression tightened with panic. She slipped out of the shoe, stuffed it in her purse, then managed a strange tilting walk with one heel on and her other stockinged foot, gripping his arm as he escorted her through the milling pre-dinner crowd to her seat at the VIP table way up front. At the table, he pulled the shoe out of her purse and said, "Don't worry, I've got this."

His plan was to beeline straight for the nearest high-end clothing store and buy her a new pair of shoes. By chance on the way, racing along corridors like through a maze toward the casino and shopping gallery, he spotted a facilities guy from the hotel on his knees working at an opened panel full of tangled wires in a corridor wall. The sight of the guy's heavy tool belt stopped him. As well as tools—pliers to straighten shoe tacks, a hammer to drive them back where they belonged—the guy also carried super glue. They knelt together on the carpet, bent over that too fragile, way too expensive shoe, and in about two minutes, presto, better than new. C. D. tipped the guy two 20s for his help. Back at the table, he found Greta already schmoozing up Senator Reid. He sneaked in behind her and knelt by her chair. Before she knew it, he had slipped the shoe back on her foot, giving it a little squeeze and two friendly taps. "Done," he said. "Now go break a leg."

He searched the ballroom for his own table, toward the back, where he had duties waiting. Greta gave a bang-up speech that evening, confident, charming, funny, putting all her girl-next-door appeal into this role on behalf of the company, announcing a $1 million donation from Pyramid Resorts that would make headlines. Cameras flashed. She glowed in the applause, rock solid on her spike heels. He didn't know how long that cobbler's errand had taken him, but for years, out with coworkers or while warming up important visitors with casual talk, Greta would tell the story of her shoe emergency with a note of astonishment at how quickly C. D. had fixed it. "Nine minutes, can you believe it? The repair has held up, too. Those Guccis are still my favorite red shoes. So I asked him to do the other one, you know, so *that* heel wouldn't break off? And he sends me to a shoemaker! Just like a guy, right? Does one thing right then a girl plays hell getting him to do it the same way again. *Haa*-hah!"

Working in such close quarters, Greta couldn't help but let slip to him small hints about her personal life, which she generally kept hidden behind her professional mask. Before turning thirty-five, she had racked up three failed marriages, all to guys she called "friends" afterward but rarely mentioned again except for the first one, Jack, when she was very drunk, the one who had left her heartbroken. He was a wealthy owner of TV and radio stations in Minneapolis, and before moving to Las Vegas, Greta had worked at an agency that did their PR. They had shared a brief professional whirl of a marriage, a star couple of the Twin Cities social scene, then Jack had dumped her for a woman Greta described, bitterly, as a "mousy, stay-at-home wife," a betrayal she could never accept or understand. More to flee the public humiliation of the breakup than to advance her career, she had jumped at a job offer in Vegas. She married quickly, two more times, both to younger men—the first to an up-and-coming minor league baseball player with the Las Vegas Stars who washed out, fell apart, then divorced her and ran off; the second to the son of the owners of a successful Toyota dealership whose pressuring parents didn't approve, meddling until Greta couldn't take it anymore. This time, Greta left first. "A girl gets tired of gold chains and white shoes, that *ilk* from sales. Present company excepted, of course, no offense. Car dealerships are the worst," she said. Sometimes, when she drank enough to get maudlin, she talked longingly about Jack and let slip how, twice a year or so, she flew off to Minneapolis just to have lunch with him, "like old friends."

What followed over the years seemed to be increasingly desperate dating, including to married guys among the executive ranks. C. D. warned Greta about these, frankly telling her she wasn't "trophy wife" material anymore, to which she only scoffed. Affairs she let slip: the too-young-for-her fling with a staffer for Senator Bryan, as if to get the attention of the higher-ups, something to let them know she was available; then to an ex-VP from The Frontier who ran for

County Commission and lost—what is it about politics that can make ethical-seeming, solidly married guys start fooling around? Next, one Ira Moscowitz, an up-and-coming junior executive at the Sands, one of Greta's relationships C. D. guessed at and Rickstein confirmed as Greta's talk became peppered with *oy vey* and *mensch* and *mazel tov* and unprompted forceful defenses of Israel. C. D. leveled her with, "You must be living on another planet! You think he's going to leave his family for a blond *shiksa* like you? His father will tear his clothes and say *kaddish*, the whole *shtick!*"

That one didn't last long. "My Jewish conversion adventure," Greta called it later. "But at least I got to have dinner with Benny Netanyahu, future prime minister of Israel, right?"

During that era, Benjamin Netanyahu made frequent trips to Las Vegas, hosted by Sands casino mogul Sheldon Adelson, presumably to refill his coffers with campaign cash, so much so that some Sands executives, including Rickstein, were soon on a first-name basis with him. Not long after that, during the months when their team was working double-time preparing to open The Beach, C. D. suspected Greta began to indulge in hushed-up "nooners" with Tim Slocum in the room he kept at Caesars. He scolded her, "How can you *not* know you'll screw up your career screwing *him*? Don't fuck where you work! Don't do it! Besides, Slocum's in the stratosphere, kiddo, *way* out of your league. And even if that weren't the case, what kind of a future's in it with a married guy who bangs cocktail servers every day?"

Greta never exactly denied this affair. She never confirmed it, either. She rarely let C. D. in on her personal life while any affair was going on, except by a few dropped hints, possibly to gauge his reaction, which, for some reason, would be disapproving or full of warnings. Like a sad joke between them, meaning to smooth over any hurt feelings at how harsh he could be and also to act as her friend, whenever she would drink too much and get weepy about her personal life, he'd put his arm around her shoulders, give her a brotherly squeeze, and say: "Why do the best women always choose the wrong men?"

Late one night, deep into the third hour of a long flight, off to New York—again!—on an *almost* final pitch trip to complete financing for The Beach Convention Center, which had not been easy, C. D., as usual, fought for sleep in his customary seat at the back of the plane. His father had told war stories about plane crashes from his experiences as a photojournalist, how the best odds of survival were for passengers sitting near the tail, so he always sat way in back. Despite this exhausting red-eye, the team would have to hit the ground bright-eyed and sharp in the morning. C. D. suffered that peak of frustration near madness when he could never sleep on airplanes, no longer afraid of the plane crashing as much as terrified that, like in some reverse version of hell, he would get stuck on this flight forever and never land. He gazed up the aisle with envy at Kinkaid and Rico, burrowed under blankets, snoring away, and toward the distant dim glow near the cockpit cabin, where Slocum and Sheperd slept in private spaces closed off by drawn curtains. Sheperd could always sleep, night flights no problem for him. He had emerged even from the twenty-hour endurance trip to Australia as fresh and speedy as ever, probably why he thought nothing of herding his team onto the company jet at any and all hours. Whatever Sheperd could do, he expected his team to do—one of his rules.

Greta usually drank her way through these deadly boring hours inside the corporate Gulfstream. On many trips, they had shivered together, wide awake under the hyper-cooled air blowing down on them. After her fifth double vodka tonic, Greta would finally pass out—it was a near miracle she was able to shake off her hangover and perform just fine after they landed. This night, though, she had more trouble sleeping. Restless, she kept getting up out of her seat, stumbling up and down the aisle in an aimless way, a camel hair blanket wrapped around her neck dragging along the cabin floor. When she had had too many drinks, Greta often made this strangely rude but weirdly sensuous gesture: one of her hands would reach out, palm open as if to wave hello or goodbye, and very gently, almost not touching, but, yes, actually *touching,* her fingertips would ever so slightly stroke someone's hair—she even did this to complete strangers, a time or two managing to touch the hair of everyone at a dinner party. C. D. had observed young children doing this, like naturally reaching out in curiosity to feel an adult's hair, the usual reaction a pleasant one to the charm of the child. When Greta, drunk, made this same gesture, most people didn't notice or pretended they didn't, but he had seen a few jerk their heads back, insulted. When this happened, Greta would pull her hand away as from a hot stove, smile cutely, as a child would, and say thickly, "Sorry."

On that endless jet ride, Greta began to do just this in the aisle. She reached out first to Kinkaid's balding head, lightly touching the fuzzy hairs up top; then she stroked Brick Rico's perfectly trimmed executive cut, his head lolling back on a neck pillow. From the near darkness toward the back of the plane, C. D. noted Greta searching in his direction. Deep in his middle, he felt a sinking sensation as Greta took several off-balance staggers toward him down the aisle, her blanket trailing like a cape.

He thought she meant to take the seat across from his, as she sometimes did, but he caught a quick flash of pure wickedness in her ice-blue eyes and a lopsided, sleazy grin. In slow motion, Greta stumbled and sank to her knees between their facing seats, tangled in her blanket. "Le-es play," she whispered thickly, then more loudly, "Shhh!"

His first thought was that she must have lost her balance. He started to reach out to grasp her under her arms and lift her into a seat. Before he could, she flipped the blanket so that it tented her head over his lap. Not realizing what she was doing, he felt his slacks unzipped. Her hands reached in, her moves so quick and unexpected that he didn't have time to squirm away before he felt her fingers slide in through the slot of his boxer shorts.

"Hey! Whoa!" he said.

He heaved his lap up, bucking her head back.

"Shhh!" she said. "Nobody can shee . . ."

"You *don't* want to do this!" he whispered loudly, trying the gentle approach first, feeling for her shoulders under the blanket so he could lift them up and push her off. He felt puffs of her hot breath. Then her nails dug in, finding home. "*Ooo-ch!* Let go!"

"Wow," she said. "Nice doggie . . ."

"Damn it!"

He tossed off the blanket. He grabbed a fistful of hair and yanked her head up. The face that swung into the dim red light from the exit sign didn't register the pain this must have caused. Her expression went blanker, drunker, her mouth slack. By the glaze in her half-closed eyes, he knew she was totally gone, in a blackout, wouldn't know or remember a thing. He relaxed his grip on her hair. Her neck went limp, her head rolling to one side, heavily, like a melon on a string.

"Uhh-ohh," she said. She tried a faint ghost of her cheery, professional smile.

"You're really a fucking bore when you're drunk," he said.

He rose to his feet and zipped up. He stepped over her into the aisle and took two long strides toward the lavatory. "Bad Greta," he heard, faintly, behind him. "Bad girl. . ."

In the plush teak and brushed steel lavatory, he splashed water on his face. For some reason, he also reached for the cologne and slapped his cheeks, like this could wake him up, help him to achieve clarity. He raked a hand through his hair, straightening it back into place. They had worked closely together for nine years. How many times had he covered for her when she got this drunk? How many parties and dinners and events had he steered her out of, calling her a cab? Sure, Greta got loose and lewd at times, like it was a part of who she was in that role she played as just one of the guys. They had played at flirtation, yes, part of the banter between them. But never—not once—had she crossed professional boundaries in this way. Her drinking was no excuse.

He sat down on the cold steel toilet lid, hoping to think through what had just happened. In the morning, if she remembered at all, Greta would no doubt want him to consider her behavior as just another work buddy having one drink too many, no big deal, no apology needed. And wasn't that the case? Why should he take this so seriously?

He must also be to blame. He knew he was a man some women looked at twice, turning heads, and sometimes, without being aware, he traded on this quality, sending out signals he didn't mean, or he reverted to that bad-boy edge he had hoped to get away from in his life, that *bastard attraction* some women rose to without knowing why. After he had fallen in love with and married Grace, this could still happen, unintentionally (or so he hoped). And in Las Vegas, a more predatory, huntress kind of woman at times could box him into a corner with an aggressive, hungry expression, as if sizing up a piece of fruit, or they would give him a hard sensual look that offered everything. Without Grace, he might have run off to a wilderness just to get away. What the women who came on to him didn't seem to get was how much *he loved his wife*. He liked marriage too, that life commitment, and he meant to keep his promises. Or maybe some women sensed this and it drew them to the challenge. When this happened, he played disinterested and oblivious. He stuck even closer to Grace, if she were with him, and if not, he turned away and went home to her as soon as possible and held her even closer as if to say, *Please, please save me from this,* though he doubted if she understood. Whenever Grace witnessed this happening, she somehow blamed him, as if such approaches from women were his fault, though he assured her he had done nothing to encourage them. And he hadn't, had he? Still, no wonder there were so many offers *to play* in a place so much about play as Vegas. What did she expect? "Never trust a man who's prettier than you are, Mom always said," she would say.

Grace directed this phrase at him as if proof it really was his fault, no matter what he said or did. But as long as he didn't act on or respond to any come-on or chance erotic impulse or encounter, as can happen, as inevitably does happen, as long as he remained *faithful* and *honest,* why take this all so seriously? So okay, then, Grace felt threatened, clearly. On the other hand, when had *he* become such a prude?

All this swimming in his head amid the rush of recirculating air and the whistling of jet engines like a monotonous drumming in his ears, C. D. sat there, examining his life, bathed in the bright white fluorescent glow from the light over the mirror in the lavatory of the corporate Gulfstream, thinking about what had happened, or almost happened, with Greta. He hoped Greta would be passed out by now, sprawled sloppily in the seat just behind Lance Sheperd's curtained-off space. He wondered: how could such a talented, smart, attractive woman, so competent and professional in so much that she did, be so messed up in her relationships with men? How? He felt sorry for Greta, for her deep unhappiness, for her escalating disastrous alcoholism, struck also by a sinking sense that he would save her if he could but she was beyond saving. A sad terrible warmth and tenderness for her suddenly rose inside, hitting him like a punch to his chest, then a pity for her that moved him to the edge of tears and caused him to lean over and squeeze his arms around his midsection with a baffling pain until it passed. And he recognized with a shock that this must be a kind of love.

They landed, and the sleepless work day followed, Greta sipping at her spiked latte with a slight trembling of her hands only C. D. noticed as they traded places showing PowerPoints while Sheperd and Slocum did most of the talking at Goldman Sachs. This was their second presentation there, aimed at representatives of Deutsche Staatsbank the guys at Goldman were bringing in to "spread the risk" on the quarter-billion-dollar financing. Executives for both banks balked at signing the MOUs, as had been agreed. They offered less favorable terms. Sheperd's cheeks puffed; it was clear they faced a co-conspiracy by the banks to keep upping by factions of points the financing and fees, their excuse the possible overbuilding of convention space in Las Vegas. This could cost $10 million more.

Their team took the slow limo ride back uptown to strategize in Slocum's suite, C. D. noting how Greta leaned her head against the window and dozed off, draping a hand across Slocum's knee. At the hotel, Sheperd worked the phone with Victoria Herrera in Convention Sales—best ever at her job, Sheperd remarked—and told Greta to assign a feature profiling her for the trade magazines. He asked Victoria to use what remained of business hours across the country then keep on pushing into evening and even "wake 'em up if you have to" to confirm as many more advance sales as she could to add to the considerable number already signed—new figures to throw at the banks so they might end up less screwed.

Unknown to the sharks at Goldman's, Sheperd had been talking for weeks to his guys at Lehman Brothers for a possible backup. He set a new meeting at Lehman's in the morning. "So fuck 'em," Sheperd said after he hung up the phone. "Imagine their faces when we dump 'em."

Slocum agreed. They would reshape their proposals. Convention Sales came through with last-minute deals. Greta made three runs down to the business center to pick up the new faxed agreement memos they could add, C. D. knowing she volunteered so she could sneak quick cigarettes on the way. Kinkaid kept busy redoing numbers with the new sales: the smaller ones an antique gun show and the annual meeting of the National Association of Campus Safety Administrators, and two big ones Victoria Herrera and her crew had been working on for months that she finally closed with added discounts—the American Veterinary Medical Association and their trade show, four years out; and the American Dental Hygienists' Association, to which Sheperd remarked: "Ten thousand attendees, 90 percent women, all pent up from cleaning teeth all year? We'll need extra security for the wild party *that's* going to be . . ."

They ordered room service dinners, talking over changes for the new presentation, Sheperd, Slocum, and Greta at the table, the rest eating out of their laps. C. D. hardly touched his food so he could take notes, his job to revise and update the PowerPoints. All day, Greta hadn't made eye contact with him, not even once. He understood by this that she was avoiding him, so unlike how she would have behaved if nothing had happened.

Sheperd sent them off to their rooms to rest up for the meeting the next morning.

What followed that night had been preparing to occur for all the nine years they had worked together, shoulder to shoulder, side by side, co-conspiring as both workmates and friends but with an ever-growing current of erotic tension between them they were less and less able to cover over through their teasing good-buddy joking to each other, peppered at times by their sincere sharing as friends. As had happened a dozen times on other pitch trips, he heard Greta's familiar three knocks at his hotel room door on the excuse of dropping off her notes for the changes he needed to add to their presentation the next morning, only this time, instead of turning with her loud lewd laugh to leave him standing there freshly showered in his robe, she stepped through the open door and past him into his room. As he turned, the door wheezed shut on its spring. Greta moved in close and leaned against him. She broke down in tears. "I'm sorry, so sorry, I'm sorry," she said, crying. "I'm such a fucking mess."

She held onto him and he held tight to her, onto that small hard package of her muscular body, no softness to her anywhere, reminded of how surprising her physicality always felt to him whenever they had hugged as friends. They held each other like this a while. Then they both let go and he could never recall just how this happened but he found his lips pressed to hers and then their tongues were suddenly moving like swimming fish in each other's mouths. She was the one who broke off, saying, "Oh, God, God, what are we doing?" as she peeled off his robe. She pulled her dress over her head. He reached around and unclasped her bra. "Just once," she said. "God, just this once," she said, pulling him over to the bed.

The sex was hard, muscular, demanding, felt to him more like sexual athletes than lovers, pushing at the edges of the physically possible. Greta in her take-charge way adjusted their positions as they fucked and fucked and fucked without stopping until they fucked each other to a first standstill, then she maneuvered them both into sitting up so she could wrap her legs tight around his waist and scoot herself onto his lap and slip him inside. He held onto her body and lifted against her weight with all his strength. She artfully drew her legs out from around his waist and stretched them, high, then even higher, extending them over his shoulders toward the ceiling. He gulped in large swallows of air, feeling how deep inside her this forced him. She took fuller charge, and he let her, no more wrestling or fighting her as she pulled away and then pressed his body hard into the sheets, riding him. He closed his eyes.

Light shows started behind his closed eyes, then he was lost in sensations that he was actually leaving his body: visions of streets, sidewalks, the tall buildings of New York and the deep canyons they made and had cruised through on limo rides transforming into visions of all cities everywhere he had ever imagined traveling through, seen from the air now and rushing by dizzyingly underneath, wildly soaring, faster and farther, his body moving up and away higher in the air until they all spread out below him with their millions of lights like the lights of The Strip at night glittering in a vivid dream, then he was off and gone even farther beyond the stratosphere into some other dimension, then the blue marble, a view looking back at planet Earth from infinite space, and then stars, he saw stars. The stars blacked out, gone into an unconscious darkness absent of sight or sound. How long this lasted, he didn't know. A sharp cry split the night—he wasn't sure if it was his or hers or theirs—and he landed back on the bed and they had finished, his eyes still closed, a voice in his head repeating over and over again, too late to save him, *I love my wife, I love my wife, I love my wife, I love my wife . . .*

No holding each other, no intimacy, no sharing in any glow, Greta jumped out of bed with a renewed cheery energy, pulling on her dress, slipping her feet into her shoes, stuffing her stockings, bra, and panties into her bag. He rolled over and buried his face in the pillow. He felt her sit down on the bed next to him and work at something on the nightstand. He raised his head and saw she was resetting the alarm on the clock radio.

"You're getting up early to make changes to the presentation," she said in answer to the question in his expression. She held up a disc and set it on the nightstand. "We have to get some tomorrow, remember?"

"What. . . What did we just do?" he asked.

"Look, this is nothing serious, okay? Nobody needs to know. Grace never needs to know. Not unless you tell her, in which case, I'll deny everything, right? *Haa*-hah," she laughed.

She stood up and slapped his bare ass hard enough that it stung.

"Thanks, kiddo," she said—using that word to him he had so often used to her—shaking out her hair and heading toward the door. "You're a good man, C. D.," she said. "Don't take life too seriously. I'm saying this as your friend, and I mean it, all right? All in fun," she said. On her way out, she blew him a kiss in that teasing, bantering way they had as though nothing at all had changed between them. "See ya!"

– 9 –

"What happened to your friends?" Grace would ask him, with an edge of accusation, when she caught him alone and brooding, especially during the harder times that were coming. As for his friendship with Greta, it would never be the same again, not because of anything coming from her—she would behave in all outward ways more or less as usual—but C. D. kept a greater distance in their dealings with each other in their daily work lives and personal exchanges as they worked shoulder to shoulder in their new executive offices. He would play along that everything was the same, but a new hesitancy, a new caution from his charged erotic awareness left incomplete affected every move. Back home, in bed next to Grace, he lay there, restless, not able to shake sense memories of his lust while at the same time cringing at his faithlessness to his marriage, to the good, trusting woman next to him he knew he deeply loved. Still, if Greta had offered, he would have done it again, would have agreed to a sordid affair that surely would have caused pain and suffering beyond what he allowed himself to imagine. This would be Greta's choice—all she needed to do was give him a look or a nod or a word, like a shared secret. That secret gave her power over him, and it changed everything. Why did sex ruin so many friendships? Why did it complicate and harm so many lives?

Three days after they returned to Las Vegas, successful after landing the financing, Greta scheduled a meeting to begin mapping out new website designs for The Beach Convention Center beginning construction—the official opening still two seasons away. Greta plopped a dry foam cappuccino on his desk as she did sometimes when she wanted a favor from him. "Time to do something about drinking so much and the little blue pills," she said, a sharp sweet odor of vodka on her breath. "I'm sorry. I'm a total mess." She told him she would be checking into a rehab on Monday, into Betty Ford, the very best, lucky they had the space. She presented him with a folder of her tasks, mostly ad copy to go over and approve, revisions to run through with the agency, plus a list of meetings he would attend and phone calls he would make in her place. "Can you cover for me? Please?"

Of course he said yes. He stood up out of his office chair and reached for her. She let him hold her, but only briefly. Before he could act on an impulse to kiss her, she squirmed out from under his arms. "I need to get my head on straight," she said. She pointed a finger and touched his nose. "You need to go home and make love to your wife."

—

After returning from her twenty-eight-day stay in rehab, Greta managed an extended period of energetic sobriety. In early spring, Big Jim Chevron loaned her out to the Nevada GOP to work election 2000, her charge to help organize an effective PR campaign that helped, along with rafts of contributions from Pyramid Resorts and other big players in the city, to bring in most of the ticket: Senator-elect John Ensign, Congressman Jim Gibbons, a half dozen state legislators plus a slate of conservative judges. Purple state Nevada turned red for George W. Bush in that first post-millennium election that made America look like a banana republic in the eyes of the world, focused on hanging chads and disputed ballots in Florida until the United States Supreme Court decided the issue once and for all in a politically motivated 5-4 vote. Years later, this would be another regret C. D. would recall—how in support of Greta, also giving in to peer pressure at work but mainly for Greta, he voted straight-ticket Republican for the first time in his life. He didn't tell Grace, who would not have forgiven him voting that way (daughter of an old Grange Hall New Dealer that she was), not exactly lying to her but implying a vague support the other way that amounted to the same thing.

What a triumph for Greta at the ebullient Election Night party as she stage-managed the winners, bringing the newly elected candidates to the podium one by one at The Beach ballroom to speak before the cameras. She ran them like programmed machines through their interviews with the national press—no smarter or more effective PR flack than Greta, when she was sober. But then the next day, she vanished, flew off on a celebratory binge that took her all the way back to Minneapolis, where she woke up a week later from a blackout drunk in bed with a stranger and not recalling how she got there. She checked herself into a rehab again, a luxury spin-dry in Malibu this time. And so her drinking went, on and off then on again, in cycles, as she lived mostly alone and "manless," as she put it with that laugh of hers.

Gradually, as they both moved up in the company, they worked less and less closely. Always he had believed they were friends, and maybe they should be closer now than ever, but he never recovered from that crazy night when she—*she,* after all—had made the first move. Friends just didn't act that way with friends. Yet he felt sure that, no matter the life-wrecking catastrophe, if she stepped into his hotel room or anywhere else as she had done in New York he would respond in the same way. There were times when he more than hoped she would, and the best he could do was keep his distance. So the ease they had established together would be muted from then on, by how much varying day by day.

He would never tell Grace. It had taken years of his reassurances for Grace to get comfortable with the idea that he worked so closely alongside a woman like Greta, and still, she had never accepted her entirely, had always sensed a threat. And that might be the worst thing about this, he thought—if not his wife, then who could he talk to about what had happened and what he felt? Not only the burden of carrying the lie with his wife but the lie he had to live with at his job now, too, which, no matter all his mental and emotional efforts to push it away, had found its way into his heart. Who could he talk to about this? Who could he sound out to in hopes of arriving at some clarity? Not to a single friend he could think of, except for the one friend he would have gone to with something like this, the only friend he had had who had ever truly listened, this one close friendship forever changed.

— 10 —

September 11, 2001: that day when the skies went so eerily silent, empty of the airliners landing every three minutes at McCarran Airport, the World Trade towers going down like two black dying blooms against the New York skyline. What a national body blow, and in Las Vegas, how spooky, so much quiet. During those days of empty skies, people realized how accustomed they had grown to the ceaseless growling of jet engines overhead. That absence of familiar noise along with the quick emptying out of the casino hotels disturbed, and the longer this quiet continued, the more apocalyptic it seemed.

C. D. and the executive team spent two days helping Lance Sheperd track down hundreds of business contacts on phone calls, not reaching most of them for at least forty-eight hours, finally relieved that no one they knew—not one of the investors or bankers or business people Pyramid Resorts depended on—were among the dead. After seeing footage on CNN of crowds of Palestinians celebrating with ululations on the West Bank, Sheperd made angry calls to his political connections, staffers for senators and congressmen and even President Bush, lobbying for a war—in his mind, any war anywhere the Middle East would do. He paced the hallways at The Beach, poking his head into their offices, saying, "Just nuke Mecca and get it over with. *Fuck* 'em all!"

Sheperd ordered special discounts and comped meal coupons for the six thousand guests who got stuck in the hotels for a week, unable to fly. Though it hadn't been a peak week, tens of thousands of visitors in Las Vegas found themselves stranded. Most people—tourists and locals—didn't know what to do or say. A strange subdued mood hung over them and throughout all the casino floors as if echoing down from the empty skies.

Overnight, in front of the New York-New York Hotel Casino, on the sidewalk and along a low wall, people lit votive candles lined up in rows ten deep along the sidewalk near the replica NYFD fireboat at the foot of the structural foam statue of Lady Liberty. Arrangements of flowers began to appear in great mounds under hand-painted banners reading: *We miss you!* and *9/11 Heroes!* Firemen's T-shirts carried from all over the country were laid out along the barrier fence like funeral wreaths. Cards and notes for the dead and missing from the Twin Towers and the Pentagon multiplied into a messy but impressive display. An impromptu memorial, entirely spontaneous, took over that whole busy corner of Las Vegas Boulevard. News stories told of folks driving in from L.A., San Francisco, Denver, Albuquerque, one from as far away as Fargo, North Dakota, to lay wreaths in honor of the first responders and others who had died, then they turned around and drove home, as if that ersatz Manhattan skyline of a casino was as close to the real New York City as they could travel to or imagine. What could this mean? Other than the deep human need to express grief, the growing memorial in front of the New York-New York, sincerely constructed by hundreds of people expressing their hearts and honored by thousands who paid their respects, confirmed how much Las Vegas had succeeded in projecting its illusion more successfully than anyone had ever dreamed: representation had become reality.

Over the next year, the skies over Las Vegas were painfully slow to fill again. Visitor numbers dropped way below maintenance levels. Sheperd called C. D. off his latest pet project, developing PyramidTravel.com—a travel website conceived to provide some healthy in-house competition to the rapacious discounters at Hotels.com, Expedia, Travelocity, Priceline, and all the other online travel agencies (or OTAs) putting pressure on the hotels and driving pricing and inventory managers crazier by the day. Sheperd's ambitions for PyramidTravel.com seemed truly promising, as side by side with Timmy Chin and his Chin Solutions team, which was adding staff to build such a complex site, C. D. began meticulously planning to hit the by then 4 million customers in his data base with customized micromarketing campaigns tailored to each income and subinterest group—the search engines AOL and Yahoo plus new revolutionary developments at Google were just figuring into this scheme—plus the new OTA could serve as a data-mining monster to anyone logging on to book a trip. Sheperd ordered PyramidTravel.com put on hold. For months after 9/11, hotel rooms in Vegas got tough even to give away. The tourist industry stalled, fell into a tailspin, crashed.

Painful announcements followed: all the executives down to the junior ranks, including C. D., Greta, and the others on their team, would take salary cuts of 20 percent. At meetings he attended with Slocum, Chevron, Olsson, and Frank Ratchette—VP of Human Resources—Sheperd presided over crafting press releases and speeches for both external and internal announcements of layoffs of some four thousand company employees. They called these "temporary staff reductions" instead of layoffs. And they designed a seniority-based "longest working, first hired back" policy to keep protests from the Culinary Union to a low grumbling. What else could they do? Surely not among the most tragic or even significant casualties of terrorism, the Las Vegas economy tanked. Share prices dropped into the basement. All over town, the same—at Oz Resorts, at Harrah's, at the Sands, the Wynn, over at Boyd, at Station and the Palms and all the rest, then add in the ripple effect and the 9/11 attacks resulted in more than forty thousand workers left idle and without pay, more employees laid off than at any time in Nevada history. Business press headlines became universally dismal, often phrased in the form of questions: "What Can Bring Back Las Vegas?" And "Is the Party Over?"

Bad news came down for C. D.'s own team. He had to lay off half of his twenty-two IT staff—his "kids"—most fresh out of college. At least most should prove mobile enough, he discovered, after putting in hours working from his electronic address book, phoning local contacts and others as far away as Palo Alto and Seattle to scare up new jobs for them. Still, what a loss to local resources, what a waste. Timmy Chin kept his contract, volunteering to reduce his monthly fees. Still, Chin Solutions would have to endure layoffs too. Lance Sheperd had grown to like Timmy Chin, often calling him on his own to ask questions, C. D. more than relieved that the boss would "take care of Chin" for as long as it might take for a recovery.

Throughout Pyramid Resorts, the situation grew more dismal, transforming into grim. For a month, C. D., Greta, and Frank Ratchette followed Sheperd through session after session with employees gathered in meeting rooms at The Beach Convention Center—that huge new echoing space left deathly empty now from cancellations. They agreed how Sheperd looked beaten, wrung out, exhausted, *not* himself. After Frank Ratchette introduced him, he would take pages of the latest version of his speech from Greta and step up to the podium, his eyes bruised looking, like he'd been losing sleep, his shoulders hunched over as he leaned his weight, wearily, against the lectern. Sheperd read out conditions for the "temporary staff reductions" with a deflated tone of genuine, even guilty apology. After his speech, he stepped away from the podium and worked the room, shaking hands, patting backs, pressing the flesh of the dismayed employees like a politician after conceding an election. These sessions ended with workers directed to tables by Ratchette and his HR staffers for assistance in filling out forms for unemployment compensation.

More weighed on Sheperd than the tanking tourist economy. C. D. learned from Greta that his second daughter, Miranda—the brooding, awkward one—had been expelled from her first year at UC Berkeley, arrested for allegedly breaking into the gross anatomy lab and "borrowing" parts of cadavers to use in some kind of grotesque anti-government "performance art" with a group of campus radicals. She faced felony charges and prison time. Sheperd was paying a small fortune to a team of defense attorneys to get her off. "Body parts, can you believe it? No wonder he's so wrecked," Greta said, still sober after her post-election rehab. "How would you feel if it were your daughter?"

All this with Sheperd's daughter was still developing as he presided over the meetings to lay off employees. C. D. learned from his talks with Rick Rickstein over at the Venetian that nothing so hands-on was standard practice with any of the other executives in the industry. The HR staffs on their own were usually assigned such dirty work, with very few courtesies. In their talks, Rickstein sounded oddly upbeat, even cheerful about the slump and its effects. "Why not use this as an opportunity to clean house? Study cutbacks we make now so we run things more efficiently afterward? Why not take advantage? Why not?" he asked. "Never waste a crisis," he said. "See what you can gain."

Only later would rumors emerge about a secret "efficiency study" that no one up at corporate would ever admit to imposing on the Housekeeping and Custodial staffs, Sheperd denying such a thing had ever happened to an outraged cohort from the Culinary Union who threatened to sue for Title VII discrimination. Allegedly, the study analyzed the performance, absenteeism, and job longevity of both documented and "undocumented" housekeepers and custodians, also collecting data (anecdotal or not) on country of origin of the workers. Las Vegas had long been known as a kind of safe zone for undocumented immigrants—the casino resorts and restaurants so reliant on their labor that the whole industry would be hard pressed to stay in business without them (or at least not at "efficient costs"). With a wink and a nod toward the city's power brokers, Las Vegas Metro police officers operated with a "hands-off" policy toward so-called "illegal" immigrants, and Nevada made driver's licenses and other paperwork easy and unthreatening. So if they could just get here (and buy fake IDs and Social Security numbers from the local cottage industry) the "undocumented" were safer from ICE than almost anywhere else. Rumor had it that "the efficiency study" revealed that "undocumented" housekeepers from El Salvador were the most cost-effective workers, closely followed by so-called "legal" El Salvadorians and others from Central America. Someone—no one would say who—then sent a mandate down to HR to prioritize rehiring (and later newly hiring) employees with these profiles.

In response to the Culinary Union's gripes and threat, Greta crafted press releases and pushed out glossy articles featuring Ricardo Soledad, president of The Pyramid World Hotel (an old, sage Vegas hand, now in his seventies), who, more than breaking color barriers with *Nubian Girls of the Nile* had been filling in the ranks of mid-level management jobs with Hispanics and two or three African Americans, a couple of Asian Americans, too, though a good many were Cuban Americans, as he was. Greta profiled him as living proof of the company's commitment to diversity (to which Big Jim Chevron reportedly quipped: "Does he really count? An anti-Castro Cuban who fled Havana fifty years ago?"). Amid all the 9/11 layoffs accompanied by a rise in national ugliness toward nationality, ethnicity, and difference fueled by anti-terrorism rhetoric and fears, Greta's well-crafted "diversity statements" emphasizing "nondiscrimination" policies felt, well, pitiful and ironic, considering that mostly brown and black employees were laid off first in the meeting rooms Sheperd presided over. Witnessing that, and with rumors of the alleged "efficiency study" no one would admit existed, C. D. understood in a new way how much he inhabited a white-dominated world. It was a world of insider connections and codes, a hieroglyphic world to which one had to be fully initiated, filled in, and, yes, white, to be able to read and respond to the signs with any advantage. Not one of the executives up at corporate nor in his own ranks of up-and-comers was a person of color, not one. It was the same up and down The Strip. Though a few executives were rising at Caesars and elsewhere, he knew of only one executive of color in the corporate meeting rooms, one Shona Singh, a new VP of Community Relations at Oz Resorts, a tall, elegant, charismatic South Asian/African American woman who came to them from the mayor's office, much touted by leadership at Oz for her diversity and obviously hired for her political clout with the city.

Thousands of workers were laid off from their jobs. In the third month of this post-9/11 dead period in the Vegas economy, with mass layoffs completed and new rollover financing in place, mainly by the boss calling in favors on Wall Street, Lance Sheperd went missing from his office suite. Calls to his executive assistant, Sharon Greene, yielded vague replies as to his whereabouts. Lance was simply "out of town" she would sing out in a cheery voice, her tone like that of a proud mother bragging about a favorite son. Sheperd began to be out of town so much that it seemed he might be fleeing the office, maybe even in trouble of some kind. He rarely left ways to reach him, not even for emergencies. Where was the boss going? What was he doing?

Not even Mark Kinkaid with all his access to company accounts could get a solid fix on Sheperd. Kinkaid speculated that he must have gone off to the two-hundred-hectare vineyard he was developing in Provence; or maybe Sheperd was at the tri-level mansion he was busy renovating in the hills overlooking Malibu; or he could be making the purchase of that historic building in Paris he had talked up on their last trip to New York—a sixteen-room mini-palace located in the posh 6th arrondissement with a view of the Luxembourg Gardens. Sometimes he would be rumored to be away on trips with his first daughter, Cleo, usually to the Caribbean; or traveling with Miranda, free on bond from her criminal case, acting as a father the way he always had by loading her up on the company Gulfstream to go wandering with him all over the globe. The only certainty was that Lance Sheperd would not be at his penthouse in Las Vegas or at his family's beach house or on his yacht, visiting his wife. He never visited his wife. Kinkaid had glimpsed complex property division papers drawn up for Sheperd and his wife that defined their "compatible separation"—only rational, Kinkaid maintained, since Sheperd by then had crossed an indefinite boundary defining superwealth such that liquidating capital assets or dividing up that much money made divorce an impractical mess. Still, where *was* he? What was the boss *doing* when he was away?

Lance Sheperd "sightings" became major events: "He was in Vegas last Tuesday, in the cigar room at Del Frisco's," Greta said. Kinkaid expressed concern that there might be a health problem, to which Slocum answered with no little irritation, "What are you talking about? He dropped a 50K donation at the St. Jude's fundraiser only yesterday, that's his health problem!" Or even more strangely: "One of the pit bosses reports he was walking the casino floor last night, checking out the lack of action at the tables," Brick Rico said. "When was the last time you heard of Lance out walking the floor?"

Maybe one week in three, Sheperd would be in town, and in his office. Could the boss be burning out or losing interest in the company? People wondered. During one of the rare weeks when he was back in his office, C. D. met with him, at his request, to catch him up on delayed project plans for PyramidTravel.com, which Sheperd hadn't asked about in weeks. C. D. explained different types of "cookies" they could use to gather data on their customers. He had to explain what a "cookie" was—like an in-house spy planted in targeted computers reporting back data every millisecond. Sheperd never used a computer, relied on his staff to use them for him. He never wrote emails, either—he communicated in person, or at meetings, like an old-time Mafia don, or in phone conversations (he used a landline only for business), then made his decisions official by ever more quaint-seeming faxes or hard copy memos. Sheperd spent a few minutes reviewing the cost projections C. D. had worked out for building, staffing, subcontracting, and maintaining the new travel site, not even blinking at the $2 million more than they had planned, and C. D. could only guess what they might be charged by the search engine companies—that new industry hadn't yet figured out any consistent policy for its revenues, so he had no idea how much Google and Yahoo and Microsoft and AOL were going to hit them up for when they fit Pyramidtravel.com into their algorithms so it might pop up whenever anyone punched in key words for "travel" or "trip" or "Las Vegas" or planned a vacation. And C. D. would need a higher-paid staff more experienced than his "kids" to help hound the hotel, airline, and rent-a-car revenue managers for advance bookings and discount deals. Finally, he presented the possible marketing concepts. Sheperd preferred minimalism, a few bold strokes for the graphics, black-and-white illustrations and ads featuring bony, drug-addict-looking models with arresting, glassy stares, what seemed an exact opposite to selling any traditional Vegas glitz. Why so much anorexia? Such starved and dangerous-seeming sensuality? But the boss was the boss, and he would get his way.

"Great work," Sheperd said, looking over the ads, his cheeks puffing. "But no go on this for some months. Don't ask me how long."

C. D. would be left unsure if the boss had really approved the plans or not, the way he closed the folder of mock-ups with such weary body language. An awkward silence passed between them. Then C. D. asked, as casually as he could, "What do you think of the stock price? At twenty-four, it seems way, way undervalued."

In the weeks before 9/11, Pyramid Resorts had traded as high as ninety-one. C. D. and Grace had a good bit of money now in mutual funds, and he couldn't help but think that placing a big bet on Pyramid Resorts to rebound might be a very smart move.

Sheperd's eyelids drooped halfway, as though bored by the question. His attention shifted toward the open double doors of his balcony, his expression like he was trying to read something blurry and far off into the drooping palm leaves. "Hard to say," he said tiredly. "These days, who can stomach the risk? Vegas is still number five on the target list. What happens if we get hit? Even without an attack, no telling how long we'll stay down."

Everyone in the city was nervously aware that at least three of the 9/11 terrorists had spent time in Las Vegas, the place where they had picked up at least $30K in hard cash to fund the final phases of the attacks. Two of the hijackers had even spent an evening out at the Olympic Gardens, a mid-level gentleman's club on Las Vegas Boulevard, the topless dancer who had provided Mohamed Atta with what must have been the last lap dance of his life saying of him, "He seemed like any regular guy except he was a really, really lousy tipper."

FBI investigations revealed that Las Vegas might be one of the next targeted cities.

"Can Grace take that kind of risk?" Sheperd asked. "Can you?"

C. D. felt a squeezing inside, a sick sensation near his diaphragm like his instincts were sending him a message. But what was the message?

"I don't know," C. D. said. When Sheperd didn't offer anything more, he said only, "Thanks," then turned the subject back to work, packing up his files. "We need a 'go' on this pretty soon or we'll have to recalculate the costs. Let me know when."

Their meeting concluded. On his way out, after thanking Sharon Greene at her desk, he passed none other than the notorious Michael Milken, major innovator of the junk bond trade, sprawled out over the couch cushions in reception. He had been an old crony of Sheperd's and involved in financing the original Big Top for J. B. Roland. Milken looked pale and too thin, even sickly. He was dressed like an over-the-hill pool boy in faded jeans, a wrinkled polo shirt, and sneakers, and he wasn't covering over his emphatic baldness, not wearing a toupee since he had been let out of federal prison early after serving two years on a plea deal after being charged for securities fraud, conspiracy, and market manipulation, crimes of which he claimed he was innocent and always would. As the story went, Milken had beaten prostate cancer and turned his life around. After prison, he kept busy knocking on doors all over the country on behalf of his medical charities supporting cancer research. The fact that Milken was here, now, during the slump—a multibillionaire even after his prison time and paying hundreds of millions in fines, then forever banned from the securities industry—looking so laid back and relaxed, too, in the executive reception room at The Beach, raised questions: what was Milken *doing* here? Or Lance Sheperd *with* him?

It wasn't C. D.'s place to ask. And what, exactly, *would* he ask? He nodded at Michael Milken as he passed the reception couch. Milken returned his greeting with a boyish smile and a quick opening up of his fingers like they knew each other, a familiar-seeming, schoolboy waggle of his hand so familiar that C. D. wondered if he might have met Milken somewhere else without remembering. Or was this just his way, behaving toward anyone in Sheperd's inner circle like a senior classman at the same prep school? Or members of the same club?

According to Kinkaid, Milken was rumored to visit The Beach several times that year, each visit coinciding with a "Sheperd sighting" in Las Vegas. Sheperd and Milken allegedly dined together at Del Frisco's or Postrio, just the two of them. Kinkaid speculated about Sheperd and what might be going on, "testing rescues" for the downturn, repeating rumors about Milken, and about Jack Welch, Angelo Mozilo, Dick Fuld, and other top-ranked business moguls of the era who regularly cruised through town and took Sheperd's meetings.

They played that frequent office game "How much is the boss's net worth?"

Kinkaid knew casually Sheperd's personal accountant. Through that dismal winter and depressing spring following 9/11, he started to suspect Sheperd might be losing, and big, maybe even close to going broke. "He's put his L.A. mini-mansion on the market," Kinkaid said. "And he pulled his offer on the big house in Paris. Why else would he do that?"

Sheperd was selling off most of his collection of expensive cars too. At one point, Kinkaid and C. D. could count at least twenty-three different cars they knew of that Sheperd owned and drove, several costing in the six figures. Before 9/11, Kinkaid had calculated the net worth of the boss to be around one hundred million, "give or take 10 mil." Something was going on, that was clear. "Why else would he need so much cash right now?"

That May, they were sitting together under the umbrella in Kinkaid's backyard, at their first family barbecue of the new swimming season. They sipped bourbon-spiked iced teas and watched Kinkaid's twin boys splash around happily in the pool, watched over, as ever, by Catherine in her role as life guard, while Pam and Grace kept busy with the food. C. D. gazed at Catherine—tall now, with that awkward self-consciousness of not yet knowing how to carry the new shape her body was taking on, her womanly growth spurt coming late for her age, but now her breasts were filling in so fast that Grace took her into her bedroom every night in a ritual filled with shyness and charged secrecy to lather her chest with cocoa butter to prevent her from getting stretch marks. She would grow past her mother's size, he saw, and might have trouble with gaining weight all her life. Still, Catherine would be taller, with really great legs. Observing her in a one-piece orange suit already too small for her, as she half played with and half mothered Kinkaid's two boys kicking around in the pool, he noted how attractive Catherine was growing up to be, how striking, in a tall-girl way, and this thought pleased him.

"Slocum won't say one word. He should know what Sheperd's up to, if anyone does," Kinkaid said as they were tucking into their fillets, prime beef ordered from Village Meats, so tender they could cut into them with the edges of their forks. "Every time I hint at asking, Slocum shuts me down. And Shelly"—Sheperd's personal accountant—"Shelly says Sheperd's cut in half his monthly transfers to his wife. Why would his wife let him get away with that?"

"*Jesus!*" Grace slammed a bowl of coleslaw on the table. "Can't you two *ever* talk about anything but Lance Sheperd and money? It's boring! *Boring!*" she said. "What movies have you seen? Have you read any books? Which one of you has read a *book* lately instead of a balance sheet! *Jesus!*"

Grace got up, slid the patio door open with a bang, and strode off into the house.

"Sorry," C. D. said. "She's right. I've been talking too much about money."

Catherine aimed her attention at her plate. It was clear she would not take sides, though hanging in her thoughts must have been her persistent appeals to switch to public high school next year—*Green Valley High, Home of the Gators!*—so she could be with most of her friends, part of her pitch how they could save the whopping sum her tuition at the Meadows was costing, plus she could join one of the best swimming teams in the valley. Pam shrugged, busying herself with wiping up after Tommy and Sammy, who had made a mess of their slaw. How great it was to have such close friends as the Kinkaids, C. D. thought—how nice that both couples could be themselves, no matter what. How many tantrums had they witnessed from Pam when she had thrust those two crying boys at Kinkaid and then stalked off in a snit?

"So-o-o," Kinkaid said. "Anybody up for seeing that new cult film at the Suncoast, what's it called? *My Big Fat Greek Wedding? Hoop-ah!*"

Grace slid back onto the patio in time to hear this, and they all laughed. Still, her irritation about his obsession with money was no joke: *money, money, money*—the song from *Cabaret* rang through his head—what else makes the world go 'round?

The only subject he and Grace argued about these days was money. The longer he had earned his new salary, the less he had felt content with it, and with the 9/11 salary cut, he was borrowing more. They argued. Usually, it would be Grace accusing him, shocked at how thoughtlessly he launched into new spending, opening up new credit lines, putting up his cards for everything. In reply, he used the money Grace was shelling out as a defensive weapon, bringing up the thousand a month or so she sent to her struggling parents on their five-acre mini-farm in Washington State to help cover costs, mostly for expensive prescriptions. He also sent money to his family from time to time, mainly to his sister and her husband to tide them through the latest crisis. And how about the hundreds they sent to Frank O'Malley whenever he landed in trouble with his latest DUI or in between deck hand jobs up in Alaska? Before his seasonal visits to see Catherine, C. D. sent a check to Fisherman Frank so he might have enough to play his proper role as a father. Money sent to Frank was kept secret from Catherine, reserved as a verbal knife edge for each other behind closed doors. Still, whose fault was it when they *both* supported her ex-husband?

And for the visits from family, of course he shelled out for tickets to headliner shows: mostly for Cirque du Soleil spectacles with such breathtaking acrobats and rousing discordant live music—*Mystère* and *O*—plus first-rate magic shows Penn & Teller and Siegfried & Roy plus the Blue Man Group and every kind of show in between, Uncle C. D. springing for $300 to $400 per family visit on shows, and why not? What else should he do to play his part in "the entertainment capital of the world?"

Money. Grace added up the increasing monthly outlays for Catherine's private school tuition, then more for her college fund. Add to these their two mortgages, the home equity loans, the rising utility costs, plus what they were making up in added retirement set-asides into the 401K—Grace's insistence—to catch up from the sums they had lost in the .com craze when they had both read the market so dead wrong. And Grace just couldn't understand how being *who he was* at Pyramid Resorts cost money, like dues to an exclusive club—thousands each year in obligatory donations to charities the company supported, also checks to candidates from both parties that Big Jim Chevron roved around the offices collecting during election season, these days mostly for GOP politicians, which gave Grace plenty of ammo to fire at him, as in, *For those shameless idiots and liars? Really?* What he almost answered back but didn't: contributing to liars from both parties was part of his job.

Let's face it: they were bleeding money. As much as he earned, even despite the salary cut, they should be getting rich by now. Grace also earned money from her part-time accounting business specializing in restaurants, but that seemed a dribble in the bath compared to such an outflowing river of money they shelled out every month. Lately, Grace was having some trouble with her restaurant accounting, too. She had discovered that the chef-owner's wife of a mid-scale bistro called Beverly Hills Place had been raking cash off the top, defrauding its investors, and now the chef husband expected Grace to hide these late-night fistfuls of bills from the cash register straight into his wife's purse. Grace would have to quit—yet another job she walked out on for ethical reasons, that cliché phrase "cooking the books" originating in the restaurant industry and all too common in Las Vegas.

Now add on the fat payments for Grace's new Volvo V70, billed as the "safest car in America" in this accident-prone town, so they wouldn't worry so much about all the driving she was doing through ever-crazier Vegas traffic, chauffeuring Catherine around to her expensive flute lessons, her swimming meets, her schoolgirl parties, whole wagonloads full of her friends to U2 at the Thomas & Mack and Mötley Crüe and other rock concerts at the Hard Rock Hotel and elsewhere that C. D. of course put up the money to buy the tickets for—like a magic trick, he shuffled his credit cards, pick a card, any card, and guess how much they owed. As Grace pulled out of the garage in that stocky new car packed with kids, C. D. often repeated a new war-era joke: "There's nothing so much like an M-1 tank as an American mother in her Volvo."

Now add on everything else for Catherine. Everything she pestered them for, she got in the end, even her whacky demand that they buy her a pair of "sea green" contact lenses that cost nearly $1K, not because she needed glasses—her vision was fine—but so she could keep up with the latest "cool" fashion fad to change the color of her eyes to impress the kids at school. Lately, Catherine was going through a religious phase, too, so Sundays, she and C. D. rode off together for services at Christ Church, where, from a sense of misplaced Catholic guilt or maybe to prove they somehow really did belong with those well-heeled Episcopalians, he was way too generous to the collection plate. Everything Catherine wanted she would get except a dog because of Grace's allergies, which kept her going to the best allergist in town for shots two times a month, so add in that expensive bill not fully covered by their insurance. Grace's mantra to him when it came to money for Catherine: "I was deprived as a kid. My kid will *not* be deprived."

C. D. agreed, Catherine would never be deprived. Still, Grace lay awake with the debited figures swimming in her head. Both stewed and fretted about the damages bad tenants kept doing plus the maintenance expenses on Grace's deteriorating rental house in Seattle, too, always, it seemed, on the wrong side of making a profit, more ammo for him in their "discussions" about money.

But let's not leave out the two of them—how they spent a small fortune on themselves indulging in dinners out: Le Bouchon, Post Rio, Bradley Ogden's, Michael Mina's, Spago's, the brand-new Alizé at the Top of the Palms, the best restaurant with a view in the whole U.S.A., and on and on. Grace loved dining out, her favorite thing to do. Las Vegas was fast becoming a first-rate restaurant town. "We never got to eat out when I was growing up," she would say, as if this gave them permission. C. D. could hardly remember eating out, either, with his big family. "It's been a hard week," he would agree, already picking out which card to use that carried the lowest balance. "Let's not even think about it. I'll buy . . ."

So money for fine dining became accepted, like a mutual sin, an expense Grace couldn't resist despite her instinctive caution about most of their expenses and her grilling him about his credit card statements followed by her astonishment at all the money flowing out. Still, after a memorable dinner, Grace would run up grocery bills for all the ingredients and wine pairings to duplicate some of the tastes and textures offered by the fabulous chefs now cooking in the city: Thomas Keller, Wolfgang Puck, Bradley Ogden, Michael Mina, Eric Klein, André Rochat, Saipin Chutima, and on and on. "We're actually *saving* money if I can learn to cook this at home," she would explain, as if he had asked. At restaurants, C. D. showed off his platinum AmEx card, sometimes hitting it for as much as 500 bucks for a dinner for two. Nothing made her happier, it seemed, than a first-rate dinner out, along with what followed later, after they had boated home in his gas-guzzling Beamer to complete their "dinner-date nights" in bed, an ever more distant clutch of guilt at what had happened with Greta making him more attentive to his wife's desires. C. D. joked: "Sex is always better after a duck *confít* and truffles, right?"

Grace laughed. All seemed right again, at least until morning. She knew she was letting him prey on her weakness, using his salesman's instincts, the way he could read people and play to their imagined needs. Still, the morning after, she worried about money again. On the other hand, everywhere she went in those days, even during the 9/11 slump, maybe even especially then, her friends and the people she worked with were all chasing after money, living beyond their salaries by borrowing as much as they could. Lien Luu, who now co-owned Green Valley Beauty, was caught up in buying and selling houses in the older neighborhoods, "flipping" through ever bigger mortgages, convinced she was actually making a profit on "the investment." Sam, cashier at Smith's, and her partner, Rita, were constantly upping their home equity credit lines to get by, mainly to keep up payments on Rita's chemo for breast cancer (successful so far, praise be). Not to mention the executive wives who were her friends, Marjorie Slocum and Diane Chevron, who spent inconceivable fortunes redecorating their mansions in Spanish Trails then flew off on ever more exotic shopping trips all over the globe. But even at their level, Grace wondered how it could all be sustained. Finally, she felt comfortable enough, among friends, to ask, and Marjorie put it this way: "Being this rich isn't so much about *having* money, darling. It's about how much the banks are willing to keep giving you so you can spend even more."

Everywhere she looked in the city, it was like a race, with increasing speed and danger, as though no one could focus on the things that are here and present and consider them enough even when they were—people kept reaching for a delirious fantasy that promised more. She saw C. D. getting caught up in this same race, chasing after money for its own sake. She didn't like this in him, not at all, that look that came over him, a particular glisten in his deep blue eyes, not unlike lust, she thought, only hungrier, more intense. When she confronted him, he responded with quick little cliché quotes: "It's like being a shark. You stop swimming, you die." Or Oscar Wilde: "When I was young, I thought money was the most important thing. Now that I'm old, I know it is," and Grace could only shake her head.

What did she expect? He worked in a world in which the measure of a man's success was money. And wasn't "to make money" the one life goal he had been most sincere about when they first met? "What about you?" he countered. "You're an accountant, for God's sake. By definition, that means you should be more obsessed with money than I am." She parried back: "I'm an accountant because I love numbers. Saying it's about money is more proof you know nothing about accounting, as if we didn't already know."

He laughed at this, and said, "It's not like it's going to be forever . . ."

Grace had grown up close to poor, her logger dad barely scraping a living together among her earliest memories; and later, after his death, her schoolteacher mom often scrimped on meals the last week of the month until payday—she recalled oatmeal with powdered milk for breakfast, spaghetti with ketchup for dinner, so no wonder her weakness for food. When she was stressed out, nervous, or just plain bored, food became her way to let go, her tonic for forgetting. She loved to cook, gleefully lost in the chopping and prepping, in reading through recipes, trying out new dishes. "Creative procrastination," she called it. "I don't need to think about anything else."

Not only because it pleased her but also to justify his own spending, C. D. encouraged her passion for food, not confined to the small fortune she spent on fresh ingredients but including the herbs and oils and condiments tough to find at times way out in the desert. He backed up her impulses to buy every new appliance and gizmo: the Cuisinart processors, the KitchenAid blenders, the miniature pasta factories, the juicers, the espresso machines, the jumbo Jenn-Air subzero fridge they had to knock part of a kitchen wall out to make fit, appliance after appliance, large and small, until all that chromed and stainless steel machinery stood parked under the cabinets like high-tech military hardware stockpiled for a futuristic war. Soon, it became like a test of spatial organization abilities just to find room on the kitchen counter to butter a piece of toast. So Grace renovated the kitchen, spending 40K before she was done: granite countertops, recessed lighting, Kohler double sink and fixtures, a professional chef's Wolf range complete with hood exhaust fan that sounded like a jet engine taking off. When it came to food, her discipline melted. Renewed energy filled her as she slaved for hours cooking up some special French sauce or elaborate main course from *Food and Wine* or *Bon Appétit,* then served it up in candlelit intimacy with exactly the right pairing of a bold Malbec or rare Bordeaux. She loved to spend whole days devoted to a spectacular meal: first the shopping, like a scavenger hunt, then the meticulous prepping and attentive slow cooking, especially during the three or four weeks a year when Catherine went to stay with Janice and Dewey up in Washington to visit her dad. Grace "dropped off" her diet that she had made a show of keeping up like an athletic discipline and as an example for Catherine.

When Catherine was away, they had the whole house to themselves. They could sit at the dining room table deliciously naked under their robes while savoring her special arts, because afterward what else should they do to finish off such a splendid meal? Many peak experiences as a couple happened after food. Also before the meal, as Grace prepared. More than once C. D. read her arousal as she cooked so they ended up rolling around in flour and butter and lemon zest on the kitchen tiles, bodies slick with peanut oil, minty from marinated lamb, spiced with curry, sweetened by exotic fruits. How important was it to their marriage that they feed each other this way, so did it really matter how much it cost?

Face it: they led busy, *expensive* lives—and why not? Vacations: two weeks every year, encouraged by Diane Chevron and Marjorie Slocum, too, who helped Grace plan them, to Paris, Rome, Barcelona, Buenos Aires, then it was on to Hong Kong-Shanghai-Beijing. Grace started budgeting $25K per year on family sprees overseas, she and C. D. both agreeing they were really doing this "for Catherine's education." Besides, neither of them had traveled anywhere growing up. As for everything else, C. D. signed on: full cable with premium channels plus, book clubs, vitamin clubs, CD clubs, stacks of magazines that sat fresh all over the house, unread, because who in this world had the *time?*

And clothes—he was the guilty party for clothes. Yes, he *did* put out $3K for that chalk-stripe, cobalt-blue Zegna suit, and every guy in his position needed a black Armani like a Vegas uniform for hosting VIPs, and, hey, he just *felt* better wearing fabrics by Loro Piana. And with all those trips to New York, he couldn't help but drop in at William Fioravanti in Midtown to get measured then pick out a first-shearing, Belgian gray wool flannel that felt like a buttery miracle, the famed Fioravanti "power look" a gift to himself for his hard work, no matter that it cost as much as some families fork over for a high-mileage used car. And their budget went off the charts twice a year for Brooks Brothers' semi-annual sale, "slim fit" the only shirts in Christendom that hung on his body just right—look, he explained, half of what he did could be completely *fucked up* if he showed a frayed collar or cuff. Face it: with the life they were leading, they weren't getting behind, not that, not yet; on the other hand, they weren't saving a dime. Grace worried. More than concern about their own financial security, she felt a growing uneasiness about the *morality* of spending as much as they did, given the deprivations and poverty of so many people in this world. She especially felt this during calls to her mother, listening to her litany of struggles to get by on little more than Social Security amid news of Dewey's truck breaking down again, on and on, until before she hung up, she was already writing out a check. C. D. didn't worry so much, though he brought up money issues more than Grace did, always scheming about how to make more. Still, with his better than good salary even with the 9/11 cut plus what Grace was earning, too, shouldn't they be satisfied? What more could they want?

A new house, one fitting his place in this world. C. D. became fixated on this idea, and the "forced savings" that a big new expensive home—a house that would surely be a showplace—would compel them to make by the monthly payments. Kinkaid predicted a 7 percent pop on the equity every year if the town ever picked up to where it had left off during the boom. Not to mention Grace could finally get the kind of kitchen she deserved. They started looking, at first casually, spending Saturdays as a family cruising around in Grace's new Volvo into the new neighborhoods spreading up and out to the southeast: Green Valley Ranch, Anthem, McDonald Highlands, Southern Hills; then further off, deep into the northeast, into the community of $3 million mini-mansions growing up near Summerlin around the new Red Rock Country Club. They would have to put off such a big purchase for a time, he knew, Grace's good sense telling them to marshal together the right size down payment first. They would have to wait for Las Vegas to recover from that tragic 9/11 year and the sharp downturn, from his salary cut and year-end bonus check reduced to next to nothing—one quarter its usual amount, Lance Sheperd counting, as ever, on C. D.'s loyalty to "the team" to stay on board and not put out feelers for another job. As if in apology for that measly check, the boss let slip a few hints that he would more than make up for it when the town turned around, whenever that would be.

When would that be? "Sooner or later," Sheperd said, as though an assurance, but no assurance at all, really, accented by his sagging body language at the subdued company Christmas party, his tone like crying poor himself, after which he limped off like a beaten man to his vineyard in Provence to pass a grim holiday season among his leafless, wintry vines.

– 11 –

Years later, thinking back on the post-9/11 slump, the way Lance Sheperd had behaved for months so pessimistically—especially at that Christmas party, where he appeared so miserable and broke—C. D. would still slap his hand against his forehead. He should have known. He should have recognized an act when he saw one. All shifted into focus about two years after 9/11, as the hotels began filling up again, reaching a prosperous near 90 percent occupancy rate. The business press ran stories about "recession-proof Las Vegas" and "boom town U.S.A." once more. Amid rumors of a big buyout offer for Pyramid Resorts, the stock price recovered and rose, by midsummer reaching an all-time high of 121. And what Sheperd had been doing all along became clear to everyone.

In the months immediately following 9/11, day after day, one purchase at a time, all made in small, incremental bits so as not to push up the stock price, Sheperd had sold out almost everything else he owned so he could go *all in* on Pyramid Resorts. He ended up owning close to 8 percent of the company, snapped up at rock-bottom prices. The whole time he was buying—that first year of the tourist economy crisis—he had been traveling all over the financial world spreading bad news, creating an impression for investment bankers, brokers, traders, and the media that Pyramid Resorts might be doomed by its debt load and by the shock of terrorism sure to depress the economy in Las Vegas as far any insider like him could see into its bearish future. Not even Big Jim Chevron or Tim Slocum knew. Sheperd had managed to keep his bad-news buying strategy secret even from them.

"How did he do it?" C. D. kept asking Kinkaid when all was revealed, about the same time America began sending one hundred thousand troops across the border to invade Iraq—the whole world fixated by "imbedded correspondents" filing stories for the twenty-four-hour news cycles about "the hunt for weapons of mass destruction" and "the road to Baghdad" and all the rest, much of the nation totally believing in the expertly staged performances of Vice President Cheney and President Bush pushing a quick victorious war, neither of them mentioning the grim possibility that hundreds of thousands of innocent people would die and millions would become refugees. Not that guys in C. D.'s orbit were thinking much about the war, the swift rise in stock prices more on their minds. "How could Sheperd have kept it such a secret?"

Kinkaid described the smaller shell companies and holding partners Sheperd had set up, many overseas to escape SEC and IRS scrutiny, then how he had folded his stock holdings back into his control. "A work of genius," Kinkaid said. "This is one they ought to be teaching in the MBA programs, course title: Making a Killing."

"Is it even legal?" C. D. asked. "Self-dealing like that? Insider trading?"

"Gray areas at worst," Kinkaid said. "The SEC is incompetent or asleep anyway."

"*Shit!* I had an instinct to buy!" C. D. turned a little circle in Kinkaid's office crowded with paperwork and files. "He talked me out of it! He looked me in the eye!"

"Imagine how pissed Slocum and Chevron must be," Kinkaid mused.

No matter if Slocum and Chevron were pissed. Why should Sheperd care, especially if a big buyout of the company came down? And they had to give him credit: Lance Sheperd had pulled it off, fooling everyone. He had tripled his wealth. Playing the "how much is the net worth of the boss" game now, Kinkaid calculated around $300 million. "Look at it this way," he said. "Our stock options are in the stratosphere, so how can we complain?"

"It's like high society," C. D. scowled, quoting Oscar Wilde. "The only people who complain about it are the ones who can't get into it. *Fuck!*"

Still, by mid-2003 and into 2004, the "boom town" days were coming back again, gradually, with more boom than ever before, more money flowing in than anyone anywhere had ever dreamed, and without end, or so it seemed. Thinking back on it all, C. D. would recall that banner day when he had finished supervising the installation of PyramidTravel.com, three years in the planning and building. He and his staff had completed the pricing deals with the airlines, car companies, and hotels. All tests were successful to "go live" the next morning (Saturdays best for this kind of launch) with striking minimalist graphics ready to start popping up and flashing across tens of millions of computer screens all over the globe, tailored for the upscale traveler looking for a blowout vacation with a jungle-beat music track and arresting images of semi-clad female and male models a bit on the anorectic side, as Sheperd preferred, a marketing theme promising the experience of an erotic paradise.

Sheperd seemed more than a happy man these days. He was in the office more, spreading energy and optimism everywhere. Word from Greta was that he had found a steady woman to share his life, a former ballet dancer turned aspiring actress from Venezuela named Esperanza Milonga. He had started commuting most weekends and taking odd days off to be with her in his house in Malibu. As ever, Sheperd kept his private and business lives separate, but Greta had met this ex-ballerina a few times on quick trips to California when she had worked on speeches with Sheperd that he gave at Los Angeles galas and at Cal Arts, Sheperd busy making an impression for philanthropy in the L.A. social scene as a measure of his new superwealth. Greta was a more than attractive woman and she knew it, still, as she put it to C. D. on a recent call, "Standing next to her, I feel like a total shipwreck."

This new woman in Sheperd's life clearly made for part of his happiness. But more, every move the man had made for two decades had turned into a success. He had been featured twice with his hand-penned portrait in the *Wall Street Journal* as a star of the industry. The executive secretaries reported he had been whistling in his big office lately, shreds of little tunes with a samba beat—who had ever heard of the boss whistling before?

That Friday afternoon, Lance Sheperd summoned him to a private meeting.

"Congratulations," Sheperd said. "We're moving you up to corporate."

He reached out his hand, and C. D. shook it—an effusive, firm grip. On the table in his office, they went over C. D.'s new contract for a mind-popping raise of three times what he had been making before the 9/11 cut, more stock, a new office in the corporate wing, and his new title: *vice president*. His contract would be ready to sign on Monday. Sheperd explained his new duties: "Except for the resort marketing side and the travel site, you'll let go of most other IT operations. We're going to outsource those to a new company we're launching. It's called Las Vegas Data Solutions. Every resort in the city is going to move its data-collecting and tech departments there. We're building one central resource with service for everybody, all the hotels pooled together, at one shared cost. . ."

Sheperd pitched. C. D. learned that Timmy Chin and Sheperd had been meeting, usually up in Seattle or at Sheperd's big house in Malibu, building this new business that would spin off the data services C. D. had worked on for a decade to develop at Pyramid Resorts and reported weekly to marketing directors at all the company hotels. Sheperd had pitched the new venture to his fellow CFOs and CEOs and top executives in the industry—at Oz Resorts, at Harrah's, at Wynn, at the Sands, at Station Casinos and all the rest. He had brought many of them on board so they could share in the profits, not only parceling out percentages to the parent companies but also giving lucrative shares to the key players, including, of course, himself and Tim Chin, who would own the biggest slice of the shares. Las Vegas Data Solutions would cram new-blade technology hardware and racked high-speed servers plus some eighty employees into a new super-cooled building over by McCarran Airport, so provide a local "cloud" for the Las Vegas resort industry, complete with new data-mining software and complex algorithms to track consumer behaviors (and pool revenue management to set prices), all fed back in a never-ending information stream to the marketing teams overseeing more than thirty individual casino hotels, with C. D.—in his new role as a VP—on the receiving end of one of these streams. Most of what C. D. had built for the past ten years at Pyramid Resorts would be handed over to the new company. And neither Sheperd nor Chin had so much as warned him.

C. D. would never know for sure if this had been Tim Chin's or Sheperd's brilliant idea, and he would kick himself ever afterward that it hadn't been his own. Instantly, he understood why—the efficiencies of a central data collection, analysis, and processing center selling services to all the hotel casinos in Las Vegas (and beyond) could save millions. It would be a localized outsourcing of technologies capable of massive inflows and outflows of customer information not even conceivable a few years before, plus the hotel casinos could save on the salaries of IT employees as well as other costs, and on information services no longer duplicated "in house" or by subcontractor companies. Soon, such outsourcing would become an industry trend.

Also, by forming this new business on the side, Sheperd had figured out a way to rake in extra income by means of lucrative no-bid contracts for fees paid by Pyramid Resorts to a subcontractor he now partly owned. It could work much in the same way mogul Steve Wynn took an extra Vegas rake from his shareholders by co-owning the design firm that regularly renovated Wynn hotel rooms, and this along with pocketing considerable income from his Fine Art Gallery of multimillion-dollar paintings that he kept moving around to and leasing to his hotels, most recently the Bellagio (with jaw-dropping tax breaks from the state). Just the way business was done now, the top executives profiting on the side from their companies and shareholders as much as possible. As Sheperd pitched on about Las Vegas Data Solutions, C. D. felt a spinning sensation under his diaphragm, sure his face expressed his discomfort no matter how much he tried not to let it show. A calculator in his head added up the estimated value of the more than 4 million customer profiles and data on them—the guys at Google he had been meeting with at their sprawling red brick campus in Palo Alto had speculated as to what hard dollar value to assign per head for such customer data, the first time he had ever thought of his work that way. The figure in his head ticked up to $30 million. All this would be handed over now. The same would happen at the other resort hotels (way behind what he had been doing, but still) and his mental calculator added on those numbers, too, ticking up to, what, $120 million? More? And when the new company launched, Sheperd would add to his considerable net worth something like 10 percent of this?

Sheperd knew he knew it was likely no one on the board—or on any of the other corporate boards, either—would comprehend the scope, attentive only to his pitch about costs and efficiencies. Or if any of them did, they had been invited to join the new company.

"Let's celebrate," Sheperd said. He invited C. D. out to his private balcony overlooking the executive palm garden. He snipped a cigar—a nearly black, handmade Padrón, his own custom maduro blend—then snipped another and offered it to C. D. He accepted it, his first thought how Grace would make him strip off his suit to air out in the garage before letting him in the house—what a silly thought at such a moment. But he needed the collegial pause, the chance to absorb what was happening—was this really a promotion? Or was he being moved up the ladder and rewarded to get him out of the way?

"Look. What are you good at?" Sheperd asked. They lit up. A cloud of fragrant smoke drifted over them. C. D.s lips curled around that bitter little log of primo tobacco, his tongue recoiling. "Talk. Sales. The *pitch,*" Sheperd said, his cheeks puffing. The blue waters of the fountains sparkled at the base of the palm trees below. "That's what you're good at, am I right? That's your *talent,* and I want to see you *thrive*. . . Computers, sure, you've spent years building our system. But it won't be long before all that goes like the call centers, some outfit in India or China can do it cheaper and just as well. So. . . Think now. Are you thinking?"

"I'm thinking," C. D. said, his throat burning, his eyes tearing up with smoke.

"You know *customers.* That's what's important. And we want you focused on them. Full-time. Just down the hall from me. Take all you know, all you've learned, and keep bringing them into the house. You'll have your own budget, your own staff, anything you need. I'm counting on you to keep us ahead of the rest, with *your* expertise, *your* ideas, and just get it done. And I want you to be happy. Isn't this what you've been working for? Reinhart? Are you happy?"

"It's a milestone for me, that's for sure," C. D. said.

He puffed, still thinking. From Sheperd, he should have expected as much. But Chin? Timmy Chin? They had worked together fourteen years. And he had contributed a great deal to Chin's success, pushing Chin Solutions at no little risk to himself. How many hundreds of hours had they spent co-conspiring, sweating projects through to completion? How many miles had they trudged side by side in the busy corridors of the trade shows and the Consumer Electronics Show in Vegas that had replaced the old Comdex, pitching Chin's company? On the other hand, he had to admit Sheperd was right: it wouldn't be long before a lot of what Chin Solutions did could be outsourced. And the bigger players like the MICROS folks and their "Opera" PMS system now running half the industry would outcompete Chin's Orchestra system; or a new company called Agilysys would outpace Chin Solutions with advanced features and innovations that could make him obsolete. Tim Chin would be a fool not to *get some,* when everybody else was getting theirs. Grace would never speak to Chin again. She would probably cry when she found out, tears of outrage followed by a profound sadness at his betrayal—she had known Tim Chin since before she had met C. D., during the early VisionQuest days. Whatever friendship he and Grace had shared with him would be finished. From then on, it would be just business. C. D. would no doubt try to soften the blow, could already hear himself talking to Grace in his head, telling her it was really all about the money, and how, in that sense, Timmy Chin was right to do this—what else should he have done? And just look at *us* now, with the promotion and all that comes with it? A lot less work than he had been doing, and think about *the money!* They wouldn't have to worry about money anymore.

And what was it Grace had always said—how you decide to be happy or you're not?

"I'm happy," C. D. said, drawing on the cigar and feeling its dizzying, stimulating effects as he breathed out a contemplative cloud. "I get it. I get it all, Lance. And of course I'm happy."

"Glad to hear it. Never say I didn't take care of you," Sheperd said. He reached into the inner pocket of his suit jacket—teal blue, a borderline garish color, C. D. thought, wrong for the season. Sheperd pulled out an envelope and passed it to C. D. across the ashtray table. He held the envelope for a long moment, sensing its contents, not sure if his best move should be to slip it into his own inner pocket, unopened, as a gesture of his loyalty. But Sheperd was looking him directly in the eyes, his gaze filled with a powerful appraisal, and C. D. sensed the importance of the moment—Sheperd wanted him to open the envelope, and when he did, it would seal their deal. C. D. pulled out a key and slit it neatly open. The check inside spooked him, showing again that sixth sense of Sheperd's that was like reading his thoughts, the signing bonus exactly enough for the down payment on the jumbo mortgage that he and Grace had discussed they needed to build their new house. Paper-clipped to the check was a business card with the gold Pyramid Resorts logo and his new title: *C. D. Reinhart, Vice President of IT Marketing.*

"You've earned this. Be happy." Sheperd reached over and cuffed C. D. on the shoulder in that way he had when he was pleased. "Let me walk you out," he said.

They left their cigars half smoked in the big ashtray, and Sheperd walked with him to the parking garage. And he couldn't help himself—he power-walked like Sheperd, matching his pace, past Sharon Greene and through the reception area, picking up the same rhythmic, rowing movements of his arms. They nodded cursorily at the two secretaries behind the big desk. They rode down together in the executive elevator, then stepped out to continue striding across the casino floor, packed that day with throngs of happy, energized guests—all up-scale customers, well-dressed and turned out, overflowing with extra income in that era of incomparable American prosperity. What Sheperd had said was true, he really *did* know these customers: median age thirty-five to forty; median income $100K and up; average home value $500K or more; car value $30K+ for at least two; shopping preferences Nordstrom's, Neiman Marcus, Bloomingdale's, Saks, Brooks Brothers, and Orvis; frequency dining out two times per week at $30 average cost per person during work weeks and willing to double or triple that check on vacations; preferred political affiliation the Grand Old Party, of course. On a Vegas vacation at The Beach, they would spend up to $2K per head at the tables or slot machines without blinking. More crucially (and a major factor his team had identified), this upscale crowd would match or exceed the $2K they gambled on shopping, dining out, and entertainment. These were the kind of customers attracted not so much by discounts as by upgrades. These urban professionals and DINKS—double income, no kids—constituted the ideal customer base to keep building for The Beach, and C. D. more than anyone had brought them here. At the same time, casino hosts were seeing to every fickle need and strange desire of at least a dozen Whales in the house dropping millions a day (and several in from China thanks to the hiring of a Chinese host to bring them in, Jason Wang, a banner new achievement since Sheperd had walked away from a chance to invest in Macau as "too corrupt"). There was always a steady cetacean action in the High Limit gaming salons now. What a busy store! How it all rang and beeped and buzzed!

As Sheperd and C. D. power-walked across the casino floor, happy shouts rang out from a craps table off in the distance, that Vegas celebration as the player made a point, rolling through the air in waves. C. D. absorbed that sense of hope and excitement, breathing in a deep lungful of its super-cooled air with added faint citrus scent from the high-speed air exchangers blowing down from above. Always, he felt the thrill of the hotel casino, feeding on the electric charge in its atmosphere, astonished as ever by its vastness and complexity, even after all the years he had worked in the industry.

They rowed along together through the acres of slot machines and gaming tables toward the parking garage. And C. D. convinced himself that he really was happy with his new title, his whopping new salary, and more—the sense that he was being invited into Sheperd's inner orbit. Even though friendship didn't exist in his world, what passed between them, whatever it was, felt closer than before (all clear, all understood), a show of friendship in a world without true friends. They strode shoulder to shoulder past the Jungle Nightclub, which had become such a lucrative youth attraction, its disc jockeys flown in from Europe and table service starting at $1,500 a bottle at one bottle minimum per person—a guy could spend at least $5K in a night (and more) just trying to get laid. Though the club was still dark, C. D. sensed its promise of a thrilling *experience* waiting to begin. He and Sheperd power-walked together past the nightclub and through the doors into the parking garage, then split off for their own named spaces.

"Catch you Monday," Sheperd called out, like a friend. "Congratulations!"

—

C. D. started his car and checked his watch. He had to push his BMW through and around heavy Friday traffic way past legal speed and play dangerous with a red light to make it to Whitney Ranch Pool on time. He ditched his tie and raced into the building. He spotted Grace in the bleachers impatiently waiting, her face showing relief as he joined her, out of breath, just in time for the whistle for Catherine's main event—a four-hundred-meter medley for the regional finals for the swim and dive team at Green Valley High. Grace gripped his arm and leaned in close. She wrinkled her nose at the cigar smell and gave him a questioning look, to which he said he would tell her later, saving his big life-changing news that, wherever it was he had thought he was going, he had finally arrived. As things turned out, he wouldn't tell Grace and Catherine until the next morning—this would be Catherine's time, Catherine's day.

Together, they watched Catherine, tense and wet from her warm-ups, stretch her fingers to her toes, loosening up, her body glistening in her tight green bathing suit. She glanced up into the bleachers and saw him, quickly waved and smiled. Then she stepped up to her place, third lane, all the swimmers lined up in the multi-colors of their schools. Her body froze for an instant like a statue, then came the whistle and her perfect gliding launch into the water. He shouted with encouragement and anticipation through her always very fast backstroke, her long legs and arms like a graceful dance propelling her out ahead of all the other swimmers, two laps adding time. She transitioned into her confident breaststroke that kept her there, gliding through the water like a second skin, propelled by her rhythmic arms and gently kicking legs. Her laps with the butterfly churned a little too much and she kicked too hard, losing time. Then how he raised his voice, cheering her on, *Go! Go! Go!* and calling out her name through her chopping freestyle which she had struggled with for years and had so often caused a heartbreaking fade to finish third or fourth—only this time, in this race, she had built up enough seconds and split seconds, she had enough of an early lead that she touched the edge of the pool before the others, breathless and surprised. C. D. and Grace embraced and cheered, hopping in their seats. They watched her teammates swim over and hug her around the neck, her coach leaning over the water, applauding. Catherine looked up at them in the bleachers.

He had never seen a happier expression on her face.

Rise and Fall

– 1 –

Six years into the new century, C. D. Reinhart felt lucky. He had achieved the promotion and salary he felt he deserved, and he and Grace had just finished building a splendid new house in the heights above Green Valley. What a house it was, with modernist geometry and wall-sized windows, no doubt too big and impractical, still, it was the house he believed fit his new position in the world. He and Grace moved in after two years of planning and construction. They were completing final touches, choosing furniture for vacant corners, picking out tasteful art for so much space that needed to be filled.

To do just this—also expected of him in his role of vice president—they attended a gala for the Vegas Valley Art Museum. Arm in arm, they mixed among a growing crowd of the city's elite in a ballroom at the Bellagio Resort. Set up in the magnificent foyer were donated high-ticket paintings on easels, sculptures of varying sizes and kinds, displays for hotel and spa "getaway" packages, fine-dining certificates, baskets of vintage wines, expensive jewelry, and other luxuries, each with a form on a clipboard for writing bids for the "silent auction" before the dinner and the speeches. C. D. and Grace roamed among the Las Vegas elite, not quite sure they belonged. He had to keep reminding himself that he had earned his place in their stratosphere; they deserved now to sail along through this wealthy blue sky.

In the teeming ballroom foyer, it felt like he was swimming through a royal lagoon. The A-list of Vegas mega-millionaires plus two or three billionaires and several politicians were holding court, decked out in their finest in this tribal ritual of charitable giving. Among these superrich, C. D.'s own crowd milled—executives and management from the casino hotels, from Oz Resorts, from Caesars, from the Sands and Boyd, and from Pyramid Resorts. Lance Sheperd cruised through and among them, talking loudly. C. D. observed how the executives schooled and flowed, swishing, dipping, swiftly changing directions. The VPs and managers especially showed off their fins, swimming just a little bit swifter than the rest, darting here and there, meaning to glad-hand as many of the rich and influential as they could sniff out, after which they swam back over to the paintings, sculptures, and first-class getaways at auction, competing to write out bids in a feeding frenzy of predatory bites at what they could sink their teeth into here—what deals, what steals.

C. D. showed himself off, too, careful to seek out and shake as many influential hands as he could without seeming too pushy. Every few minutes, he had to convince himself all over again that he belonged here, dressed in his pencil-stripe, first-shearing gray flannel suit from William Fioravanti that he felt he glowed in with the radiance of his new position. Grace trailed just a bit beside and behind him, dressed in a long violet gown with embroidered bolero jacket she felt hid her hips just right that she had discovered at a half-price sale at Talbot's, as ever the price-conscious wife. Her pearls glowed, a double strand with matching earrings he had given her for their fifteenth anniversary. He wanted to kiss her inside the neat circle the necklace made, in the hollow depression at the base of her throat.

At no time in their lives had they ever appeared so elegant together. He had remarked this to her as they were dressing, taking her hand and drawing her close beside him, posing as a couple before the full-length mirror of her immense walk-in closet in the new house. Noise from the television rattled sharply from the bedroom—small arms and machine-gun fire, a live report from the battle of Ramadi. He liked to dress while listening to the news, but this was too much. That winter, the war in Iraq had reached a high pitch—troops battling deep into the Baathist heartland with mounting casualties. He ducked into the bedroom just in time to catch gruesome images: the body of an insurgent dragged like a sack of heavy trash across the floor by a Marine from Alpha Company. The Marines took positions and started firing out a window.

Luck: the same week C. D. and Grace moved into their new house, his brother Francis had all but lost his left leg, blown apart in an IED explosion. Francis called it "bad luck." C. D. didn't know why Francis had been sent over there for the NSA. It must have been important, because he carried the equivalent status of a military officer, enough to be evacuated and treated at the Landstuhl Regional Medical Center in Germany. Their mother had asked C. D. to visit him there. He was the brother able to take time off and afford the trip.

When he told him he would be away and why, Lance Sheperd had reacted with a slight jolt in his tall leather desk chair. At first C. D. thought Sheperd's reaction was one of sympathy, then he realized it came from another of his big ideas—a promotional scheme to offer returning war veterans discounts at Pyramid Resorts: "Good for the country," he said. "Good for us too, because think about it—guys like that? No telling how much casino play we'll get out of guys who feel that lucky to be alive."

Sheperd set in motion all that would be needed to get this done.

After the uneventful flight and the hour-and-a-half drive in a rented car down the autobahn from Frankfurt past wintry bare fields and evergreen-covered hills dotted with well-kept German villages, C. D. arrived at the immense American medical complex run by the military. At the guard house, he showed his passport and a copy of the official email about Francis. Guards let him through into a labyrinth of what looked to be numerous two- and three-story concrete structures laid out in an interconnected rectangular web. The gray sprawling hospital struck him as resembling grainy black-and-white photographs of warehouse-like auto-assembly lines in Detroit at their manufacturing peak in the 1950s—like acres and acres of the historic Ford plant, long ago abandoned, rusting away. His impression of the hospital as being like a factory wasn't wrong—during World War II, the vast complex had been built by the Nazis to manufacture parts for their V-2 rockets. When Landstuhl ran at peak capacity, as many as nine hundred fresh casualties arrived every month.

Lost, C. D. wandered down corridor after corridor until he found building G, Ward 4, or "Golf 4," which struck him as cruel, as he couldn't imagine the maimed young soldiers he passed would be swinging a golf club anytime soon, some surely never again. The close corridors smelled sharply of Lysol and iodine, of stale urine, and something else, too, that he couldn't identify—a faint, acrid odor of something burnt, like a taint of burning rubber. He tried not to glimpse through open doors into the rooms. He didn't wish to intrude, still, he couldn't help but note the mangled heaps of wounded soldiers under sheets that looked too gray in the dismal light from the factory-size windows. A flickering glow from muted TVs reflected off the drugged-looking eyes of young men lying helpless in their beds, all missing pieces of themselves. The charged quiet throughout the ward struck him, how even the nurses and medical personnel stepped lightly and talked in hushed voices, as in a church, as in the presence of the sacred. He found his little brother Francis at the end of the corridor, in a private room assigned to officers.

"Bad luck, that's all," Francis said, groggy from fentanyl in a pump beside his bed. "Thanks for making the trip."

C. D. unloaded the bag of token gifts for Francis from the family: a Chicago Cubs sweatshirt, a spring-loaded hula girl toy that bobbed and swung its grass-skirted hips, a container of his favorite Rice Krispie bars Mom had made for him, and from Grace and him, an open-dated, first-class airline ticket from Washington, DC, to Las Vegas for whenever Francis could visit, though judging by the propped-up mummy contraption with tubes and steel pins sticking out—what remained of his left leg—he wouldn't be taking a trip for a while. Along its puffy length, red and yellow streaks had soaked through that package of wires and bandages, drips and swirls like messy brushstrokes.

C. D. sat by the bedside most of the day. The blue fentanyl pump attached to the IV line beeped. Like a reflex, Francis shot his hand out to it, pressed a button to release more painkiller and it beeped again, its digital clock resetting. C. D. talked, forcing cheer into his voice, pitching how excited Grace would be to have him visit, the sooner the better. He told Francis about the big new house, its spectacular views of Las Vegas, especially at night, and the luxurious guest room they would make ready for him (he reminded himself to get helper rails installed and a shower seat for the guest bathroom). As he described these new luxuries, he wasn't sure if Francis was registering much through the effects of the drug. Mostly, he sat there quietly while Francis dozed, in and out of awareness, escaping pain. C. D. held his hand a while, the hand not tied by tubes to the IV tree. Francis let him do this, squeezing back. C. D. couldn't recall when he had ever held hands with any of his brothers. Before leaving, he did something else he had never done before—he kissed his brother's forehead in his sleep.

—

In their new bedroom, C. D. switched off CNN. No sense in mulling over any of that now—the war, the casualties, the battles in Anbar province, the bad luck for Francis. This wasn't the time for ugly reminders, not tonight, dressing up for such a high-profile occasion. Tonight should be a celebration, another acknowledgment of the success he had achieved. He rejoined Grace in front of the mirror.

As he straightened his red with blue sunburst-pattern Carlucci tie just a fraction, Grace frowned at her profile in the new dress. She jabbed a hand out playfully and mussed his hair.

"Hey!" he said, jumping away.

"Never marry a man who's prettier than you are, Mom always said."

"Your mother should see us now." He spread out his arms. "Look, Mom!"

"Don't forget Mom's an old Wobbly, a die-hard Socialist. She'd never approve."

Eat your heart out, you old Socialist, he thought but didn't say. This had become a routine between them—this give-and-take about their proper place in the larger scheme of being rich they were still feeling out. Often, whenever he cheered on their new wealth, Grace invoked her mom's Grange Hall beliefs. All right, then, he admitted it—pursuing money had been his chosen path to escape the near poverty they had both grown up in and had worked so hard to put behind them. But for Grace, the richer they grew, the more she spoke nostalgically of her backwoods life growing up, hard as it must have been. More money in their lives made her increasingly nervous, conversely insecure. The costs of building the new house plus all they were still spending on it especially caused her concern despite his insistence that a house was an investment, not an expense. She should face it: they were rich now, richer than they had ever imagined. Tonight, he would show Grace and show them all—no looking back—just how rich they were, and how far they had put hard times behind them.

In the ballroom foyer of the Bellagio, as in a dream, money rained down, greenbacks sifting and whispering through the air over that wealthy crowd like snowflakes, cold cash piling up thickly at their feet at least knee high, or so it seemed. He imagined them kicking through drifts of green bills everywhere they moved. Not a word or thought about the war, Iraq, the bloody battles, not here, not for these people. The diamond-like glitter from crystal chandeliers cast an icy gleam over that sea of money. Cold cash rained down so persistently that the Vegas elite seemed to brush it off their shoulders as though it were a mere nuisance and as if there could be no end to their prosperity.

That feeling of wealth could be contagious. C. D. gazed at a painting of a gorgeous, fanned-out spectrum of rainbow colors by Charles Ellsworth. The canvas glowed as with an inner light. He calculated where he stood now on the scales of wealth, and he knew instantly that he wanted it—that vibrating image of pure brilliance, like a painted rainbow he could already envision hanging over the mantle of the new house, measuring five feet by eight feet, just the right size. Its striking lines and colors would announce to all who beheld it something of his new unflinching prosperity. Grace saw what he was about to do. She took his arm. "Oh, no," she said. "You're not. . . really?"

"Watch me," he said.

He reached for the pen. He noted three other bids in the spaces, all in six figures. The last one he recognized from the signature as Lance Sheperd's. Seeing his boss's name there powered C. D.'s hand even more as he upped the bid by $5,000.

"Where's Lance?" he asked.

Sheperd hovered over by the wine basket display table, his radar out, already excusing himself to Danny Greenspun—that upbeat younger brother of the storied newspaper and real estate clan who had assumed, it seemed, the role of the family's culture dog. Danny held up a kind of electronic instrument, showing off the latest gizmo for the purchase and downloading of digital books. Sheperd swiftly finned away from the younger Greenspun, moving toward C. D. and Grace with an aggressive, swimming gait.

"Oh, *shit,*" Grace whispered. She smiled tightly as she greeted Sheperd, then stepped out of his way.

C. D. stood shoulder to shoulder with his boss, an energy between them now like the times they had discovered themselves working out at adjacent trainers at the old Las Vegas Athletic Club. Each had started pumping away all the harder to outdo the other. In that arena, C. D. always won. He resolved to win here, too, however he could.

Sheperd nodded once, firmly, all business. He scribbled in a bid that upped the price of the painting by $20,000. The boss stepped back, observing C. D. closely, daring him. C. D. shook his arms out a little, getting rid of faint sensations like needle pricks inside his elbows. He picked up the pen and matched Sheperd's ante—20 for 20, then he raised it by $10,000. Grace paled under the blush of her careful makeup. Over Sheperd's shoulder, she silently formed words with her lips and teeth aimed at C. D.: *Stop this.*

Too late now. Sheperd leaned over the table and wrote in another bid—$40,000 more—then he stepped in closer with a fraternal smirk. "You ever seen the art at my place?" His flat tone sounded more like a statement than a question. "The penthouse?"

"I've never been to your place, Lance," C. D. said. With a carefree flourish, he signed off for the topping bid, this time by 5 over Sheperd's 40. "You've never invited me. Or any of our team, as far as I know, except for maybe Greta."

"Is that right?" Sheperd asked. "I guess maybe not. . ."

Sheperd glanced over the bids. C. D. sensed a mental calculator flipping through a series of numbers, the same set to his jaw as when he decided terms of a financing deal, an indication that he might have drawn a line at some final amount. Observing his boss, C. D. sensed he would end up owning the painting, but at what price?

"Come on, Lance, don't do this to me," he said. "I've got a kid in college."

"I didn't know you were interested in buying art," Sheperd said. "This is a good piece. Not the best of Ellsworth but very much *like* his best, which could be good enough, only you gotta be careful not to pay too much for it. In buying art these days, you should go for work below 10 grand by artists who are up and coming or else lay out at least ten times that much for more established painters. The trick with them is to know how high to go." He took in a shallow breath. He held it about two seconds, his thick neck pushing what must be uncomfortably against the white collar of his custom, two-toned shirt, long out of fashion. For all his hundreds of millions in net worth, the boss still didn't know how to dress, C. D. thought, or whoever dressed him had little taste. "What the hell," Sheperd said. "It's for a good cause, right?"

"Son of a bitch," C. D. said.

Sheperd flashed a jerky, lopsided grin that came as close as he ever did to admitting defeat, or was there something else going on? C. D. tried to read his real intentions but drew a blank. Sheperd leaned over and wrote in a bid for $20,000 more. Judging by the careless way he tossed down the pen, that would be it for him. Grace turned her back, not able to watch, standing there tensely. Whichever way this went, how could they get through dinner at the same table with Sheperd? Then it struck C. D. that the only way *not* to cost his boss money, which would irritate him more than anything else, maybe even enough to make his life miserable as only a boss could, would be if he topped that final bid. Sheperd knew this as he cuffed C. D. on his shoulder, playing the good sport. Before he aimed a parting glance at the painting as if erasing it forever from his universe, he said, "You and Grace drop over tonight. I'll show you my collection."

C. D. swallowed, hard. He gazed at the Charles Ellsworth once more, a confirming voice in his head saying, *All right, you want it, so you're all in now*. He picked up the pen and wrote in a sum $1,000 over Sheperd's final bid. In the end, he would purchase the painting for more than it cost to put his daughter through college and grad school; enough to cover his mother's senior assisted-living expenses for however long she had left to live; and to support his brother Francis, if it came down to it, if his government disability wasn't enough—these and other comparisons came to mind. A bell rang in the distance, the smart young benefit staffers collecting the auction lists. When C. D. saw the clipboard with his final bid on it carried off, he could hardly contain himself from jumping up and down, shouting, *I did it! This is ours!*

"Wow," Grace said, taking his arm. "Should I say congratulations? Or should we start pawning my few jewels?" She laughed nervously, then gave in to his excitement. They stood together, stunned by those radiant, spectral colors—that piece of true genius that had just entered their lives. "I'll learn to appreciate it," Grace said. "I promise. I will."

—

Later, at almost midnight, they followed Sheperd's black company SUV to his penthouse in the exclusive Flamingo Towers. The twin, green-glassed buildings of the posh condominium rose about three blocks away from The Las Vegas Strip. Greta—now vice president of Marketing & Community Affairs, having earned her dream job, too—caravanned behind them in her silver BMW. At the close of that benefit dinner at which they all had one glass of wine too many, Greta had inserted herself into their expedition, saying, "I'll make the coffee"—as if the boss weren't capable of doing this for himself. Sheperd nodded just once, agreed.

The liveried staff at the Flamingo Towers must outnumber the occupants, so the joke ran. Two valets dressed in green vests and caps like postmodern Peter Pans jumped at their car doors. Three night clerks checked in their names after they had passed through a tropical atrium lined everywhere with marble and polished brass. The echoes of their footsteps washed away in the rushing sounds of a gilded lobby fountain that stood two stories high, a landmark of opulence as impressive and imposing as for royalty.

Rumored to keep Vegas quarters in the same towers were three famous movie stars under assumed names to avoid paparazzi, at least two top-ranked players from the NBA, the ex-president of El Salvador, four mistresses of the city's elite, and one U.S. senator *not* from Nevada—one of the prime perks of the Flamingo Towers its guaranteed discretion. Sheperd had been one of the original investor-owners, setting up in his new condo after moving out of a tidy mansion he owned with his wife as part of a separation agreement, though she had mainly raised their daughters at her place on the California coast with a fifty-two-foot yacht parked in a nearby lagoon. As far as anyone knew, Sheperd stayed alone at his penthouse when he worked in Las Vegas. He held court in his office at The Beach four days a week for about three weeks each month. He divided the rest of his time into flying off to the house in Malibu he shared with the exiled ballet dancer turned aspiring starlet from Venezuela who Sheperd seemed to keep as though a private secret, never one to mix business and personal affairs; or for a week or two at a stretch, he might be visiting his vineyard in Provence; or else the boss flew off on globe-trotting business ventures to New York, Paris, Barcelona, and lately, he had been spotted in Osaka, as ever on the hunt for new deals. Really, few people could say for sure just where Lance Sheperd lived. Or, like so many of the superrich, he lived everywhere.

After the late dinner, Grace would just as soon have gone straight home to celebrate their purchase and share some intimacy. But this would be the first time in sixteen years that Sheperd had invited them to any of his many residences. That Greta had followed them, adding herself to their party in such a passive-aggressive way, caused Grace to ask on the ride over, "Is anything going on between Greta and Lance?"

"Naw," C. D. said. "She's done meetings at his place, that's all. And at his house in Malibu, helping with PR for Sheperd's new girl. The ex-ballerina? Remember?"

"Greta's giving us a message," Grace said. "She's making a move, wait and see."

"Impossible," he said, uneasy at Grace's question for a moment, fighting off a jolt that she might know or sense more than she had ever let on. Still, Greta and Sheperd? Not a chance. Sheperd would never stoop to messing with his best Gal Friday. Besides, Greta made a point of acting with him like she was just another of his guys, and he had always treated her that way, sharing off-color jokes, exchanging little manly jabs with her too, like he did with the guys to establish an ease of masculine physicality. Sheperd and Greta?

"No way," C. D. said. "Never happen."

Lance Sheperd's luxury penthouse seemed the kind of place meant to be decked out like an opulent sky palace. From the topmost fifteenth floor, the neon spectacle of the city rose up all around them through green-tinted, ceiling-high windows, Las Vegas showing itself off in all its lit-up splendor. With its three thousand square feet encased in glass, this condo must feel like living inside an aquarium, C. D. thought, so no wonder how oddly it struck him that, rather than decorated for luxury, the interior of Sheperd's penthouse had been renovated instead to show off his obsessive minimalism. Sheperd led them on a quick tour. The living room held almost no furniture, just one lone sofa with a brushed-steel coffee table and matching end table, the empty space all around lit by recessed lighting aimed not to illuminate areas of the room but instead at the flat-white, art-filled walls. He had decorated his condo into what amounted to a postmodern art gallery, even down to the floors, which must once have been covered in rich stone or polished woods. Sheperd had had them stripped to rough concrete, then painted with a clear varnish—all gray cement floors, like an unfinished loft. The only spaces that appeared lived in at all were the double-bench nook off the kitchen, a slate table in there messily piled with magazines and newspapers, and a large master bedroom in which a neatly made king bed stood stark and alone facing a smallish LCD-TV mounted to the wall, a glass bedside table the only other furniture aside from that lonely-looking bed. Several books lay stacked at bedside, opened and face down, as if Lance had started to read each one then stopped a quarter of the way through. The walk-in closet door stood half open, the suit and shirt the boss had worn to work that day carelessly tossed over a standing rack, hangers and shelves mostly empty. Everywhere, his penthouse appeared barely used and minimal except for the art on its walls.

After a quick glance into the nearly bare closet, C. D. recalled how Sheperd rarely took any luggage when he traveled with his executive team, never more than a briefcase and small carry-on bag. He must stock closets wherever he went, or maybe he ordered ahead or sent someone out to buy things he needed and had them delivered to his destination. More than once, C. D. remembered the boss on the company Gulfstream carrying nothing but the slacks and polo shirt he wore. The next day, he would be in a new-looking suit and tie. On return trips, he rarely took anything back with him, either. Why hadn't he noticed this before? Come to think of it, he couldn't recall Sheperd traveling in or wearing to the office the same clothes twice. No matter his questionable fashion sense, his expensive clothes always seemed new.

Sheperd had spent most of the past five years living in the Flamingo Towers whenever he worked in Vegas. As weirdly bare as he had made it, no question this was a spectacular penthouse, one that in every respect might have been outrageously appointed, interior-designed and made beautiful. The right furniture and lamps, or even a nice rug or two spread out over the bare concrete floors, could have made a big difference. Yet here he was, hemmed in everywhere by flat-white walls with his art collection staring down. Through the surrounding high windows, the lights of the city blinked and glowed like the view from deep inside a Christmas tree. Outside, on a broad terrace that seemed to hang in midair without visible support, stood a lone glass patio table and one padded chair, as forlorn looking as if they'd been set up in an empty tennis court. Along a hall leading past Sheperd's stripped-down master bedroom, a door opened on a cavernous, eerily unfurnished second room, at one time either a guest room or an office. This room had been left entirely empty, even the walls, but in contrast to the other rooms, everything—walls, ceiling, floor—glowed with a rich yellow wood. "My bamboo room," Lance called it, proudly. He flicked on the lights just long enough for a quick peek. How spooky it felt in there, like the interior of a bamboo coffin. "This is where I'll hang pieces from my Japanese collection. I'm still working on that one. It's still in storage in L.A.," he said.

"Nice," C. D. said. Grace mumbled something about the warm grain of the bamboo. As Sheperd led them back toward the living room, he talked up each piece of art with a youthful eagerness, like an echo of what must have powered him during his student days. Sheperd had majored in art at a small college in California, C. D. recalled. With the envious appreciation of the onetime art student, Sheperd led them around on his gallery tour. "This is my Judd box over here. You know Donald Judd?"

He pointed toward an orange and white construction at waist level on the wall, a box about the size of a desktop computer tower turned on its side, polished to a plastic-like gleam. "This used to hang in the office of the CFO of Citibank. One of his VPs set a coffee mug on it, mistaking it for a shelf. Needless to say, that was the end of that VP at Citi. I picked it up for one hell of a price plus the cost of restoration, which, you wouldn't think it. . . for a fucking coffee ring. . . cost 5,000 bucks."

"What about Windex and a paper towel?" Grace said.

"You'd think," Sheperd said. "Way it goes with these things."

For every piece in his collection, Sheperd had a story. "This is a Michael Heizer over here, very few like it"—he gestured toward the abstract swirls of ochre, reds, and browns on an unframed canvas, the images barely suggesting a landscape. "Heizer quit doing paintings like this years ago so he could spend the rest of his life moving tons of earth around. *City*? You know it? Like some futuristic Aztec or Maya metropolis way out in the desert?" C. D. shook his head. "He's spent thirty years building it so far, a fantastic thing, earth art at its best. Heizer's a mad genius. The guy lives out there like a hermit, hardly lets anybody see what he's doing. He nearly shot at me when I drove out to take a look, and hell, *he* was the one who invited *me* after I made a considerable donation through the Zia Foundation. Crazy guy. . ."

Sheperd went on, describing each piece. His voice rose energetically at his Robert Irwin, a white-on-white construction of a round shape that, under the lights, cast gray shadows like flower petals all around it. The tones of white and gray caused an optical illusion that made the work appear to be not mounted to the wall but hovering, weirdly, in some ethereal space all its own. Sheperd told how he had consulted on an L.A. real estate trade with a gallery owner and bought the piece "at a price close to a steal," he said. "At this level, art is investment. This Judy Chicago painting of these potholder-like thingies, and over here, that pair of classic gas pump images by Ed Ruscha . . ." Sheperd led them past these too quickly to absorb the images, impatient with Grace as she stopped to gaze into a grid of glowing green lines lit up with a humming fluorescence Sheperd informed her was a work by Dan Flavin. "That one's worth quite a bit more since he died. But put it this way, I'd hate to let anybody know what I paid for *that* before I knew how to buy," he said. "Even with my degree from Cal Arts, I didn't know how to buy. That Ron Davis over there," he gestured toward glowing segments of color by the entry, "and this mirror-glass box by Larry Bell. And oh, yeah. . . that Peter Alexander in the corner? You see that spire? Polished resin. On those, I could triple what I paid. Those make up for the others, before I knew how to buy . . ."

"What you see here isn't one tenth of what I own. Most of what's here is strictly minimalist, from the L.A. school. At the house in Malibu, it's a different style. I've got a couple of good Lichtensteins and Rauschenbergs, and an early Eric Fischl. And a Frank Stella I picked up that looks like a pencil poked through a protractor. Strange deal on that one. Years ago, some idiot Whale didn't pay his markers, welshed out on us at The Big Top, so we went after him. When the Stella turned up on a seized property inventory, management had no idea what it was worth, not a clue. Not that I lied to them," Sheperd said. "But let's just say I convinced them to just about give it away."

"Over here," he went on, leading them to one end of the living room, "This one's a gift from the artist, Richard Serra, after I donated about a third of the cost of one of his sculptures for the Cancer Center." Sheperd positioned them before a strange dividing wall at one end of the room. The wall wasn't attached to anything but the floor, not rising to meet the ceiling, a three-quarters wall built as extra space to hang art. C. D. and Grace gazed at a large work on paper by Richard Serra that covered most of it—a huge, heavy paper sheet with a great swipe of thick black ink on it pressed into a striking abstract pattern. The image struck C. D. like the curving tail of some immense calligraphy. Despite the heaviness of the ink, like a layer of asphalt, and its texture, as if made by a single sweeping stroke from a gigantic brush, the work still felt spontaneous, quickly drawn, a thick curving line surrounded by crisp white space left waiting to be filled.

"You know Serra's work?" Sheperd asked. "His sculptures?"

"Sure do," C. D. said. "From museums. . ."

He felt Grace's hand reach for his. She squeezed it very tightly as they gazed together at Serra's work on paper. Really, he didn't know much about this art, though he had read books and had spent time in museums. He remembered a few years ago, when they took a madcap "cultural vacation" to Europe for Catherine's education, two hurried weeks dragging her through the great museums and cathedrals so swiftly that her aesthetic sense and innocent love for art threatened to shut down with sensory overload. Toward the end of that exhausting tour, they found themselves in Spain, in that huge, vault-like space located in the belowground level of the Guggenheim Bilbao. Part of that vast underworld displayed gargantuan, darkly brooding paintings by Anselm Kiefer—each at least two stories high, like apocalyptic renditions of postindustrial wreckage mixed with spilled brains. On the floor before these, a monumental steel sculpture by Richard Serra stood in the way—a massive, unsettling thing, set there off-center and jaggedly diagonal, meant to disturb natural movement through the space.

The three of them had stopped in the sculpture's rusty shadows, confused and quieted, looking up uncertainly at the heavy, curving steel blocks rising like a wall. They felt dwarfed, awed by their own smallness and fragility. Instinctively, they huddled closer together, reacting as they would if an ocean liner were coming straight at them with no time to get out of its way. The blocks controlled them, as they had no choice but to follow their winding direction across the floor, then in and around and even *under* them—what could be holding them up?—into the dark shadows they cast, their movements directed by those heavy tons of sheer leaning mass until they could find a way out of that frightening underworld. How relieved they were when they finally emerged onto a rampway leading outside onto a plaza and into sunny, open air...

"No way to go wrong with a Richard Serra," Sheperd said. "Best work here."

To C. D., this Serra on paper meant to express some abstract variation on the arc of a curving shape. But it seemed to him much more than this, as if intending a similar threatening effect as his sculptures. If in the beginning was the word, one trailing brush stroke of the calligraphy that made that word might actually look like this, might weigh as much as this, and this much of the word would be all mere humans could possibly see, much less comprehend. Still, even to attempt such an expression disturbed. For him, it crossed a superstitious boundary, like a blasphemy. He decided he didn't like it, not at all. He stepped back, repelled.

"I'd like to commission a Serra sculpture for the lobby of a new casino," Sheperd said. "It would cost millions. Only who would even catch on to what it's doing there?"

"I don't know, Lance," C. D. said, turning away from that menacing black thing. Grace wandered off, nearer to the windows, taking in the lights of the city.

Sheperd strode a few paces from his superlit walls to the center of his living room. He stood there on his bare concrete floor, the lighting there dim in contrast to his walls, his figure in shadows becoming almost like a dim silhouette. He spread his arms as if to embrace the whole gallery where he lived. "Well... What do you think?"

"It's... overwhelming," Grace murmured.

A long moment passed. C. D. hoped his boss wouldn't be able to read his thoughts—how this penthouse art gallery felt way too busy, the walls too cluttered with too many images, creating a discordant effect of cancelling each other out. Sheperd by his excess in hanging minimalist art had managed to defeat what must be the intentions of minimalism. The walls were almost baroque in their excess.

"Coffee's on!" Greta called out from the kitchen.

Years later, C. D. would think back on that night, recalling not so much the specific words Sheperd talked on with over coffee, the four of them bunched shoulder to shoulder on his kitchen nook benches, as he would the happy, empowered enthusiasm in the rhythm of the man's voice. He talked that night about some preposterous scheme to start a Wall Street hedge fund in art futures, selling bundled paper tied to investments in art, contracts that would enable bets to be placed on the rise and fall in the prices of works by selected lists of artists both living and dead. "We could even sell insurance swaps on the artists. You know, hedge the big pop in prices when the artist dies," he said. "Nobody's thought about that one. Could really work in a hot market, and art's never been hotter than it is now."

As ever, Sheperd peaked in enthusiasm when talking up his moneymaking ideas, powered by that same huckster brilliance C. D. had heard him use with reps from the banks and funds when he presented concepts for a new hotel. He and Grace sat across from him in his kitchen, sipping their coffee, listening to Sheperd talking on in this way. At a certain point, his eyes no longer appeared to see any of them. He kept looking over their heads, as if at a covey of birds flitting through the air, messengers from an astonishing future no one but Sheperd could see. Greta served, seeming all too at home in that kitchen that appeared almost never used—a white inspection sticker never removed from one corner of the stovetop range. Greta wiped down the tiger eye granite counter with a sponge she knew just where to put back in a bin under the sink. She kept getting up and down from the nook, refilling their cups, hovering with a barely concealed erotic charge at playing house, clear in her moves she was laying claim to this kitchen. Sheperd hardly seemed to notice. He kept talking on about the fortune to be made by investing in art, acting as though no one else were in the room, like he might fast-talk this way only to himself, sitting there alone. He must do this, C. D. thought—sit in this kitchen all alone, talking to the air, cooking up his schemes.

Grace scooted off the bench and insisted on rinsing cups and saucers. While she and Greta worked briefly at the sink, Sheperd leaned in close over the table and said quickly, his voice lowered with conspiracy, "You bought a pretty good painting tonight. Ellsworth's really something. He just never quite fit into my collection."

"What?"

"I'm the guy who donated it to the auction," Sheperd said. "You took it off my hands."

C. D. felt a sick flip in his middle. Needle pricks extended down his arms.

"Don't worry. Even at that price, you'll still make out, just wait a few years. You still got a deal. And it was for a good cause, right?"

Sheperd cuffed him on the shoulder in that way of his, more than pleased. C. D. felt a pressure growing in his ears that muffled sounds. He grinned tightly through the leave-taking chatter. A bit of awkwardness then followed as Grace and he put on their coats, Greta obviously making herself available to stay behind, "to go over some marketing ideas" her excuse. Lance brusquely turned her down. He took her coat off the hanger and draped it over her shoulders, then he aimed her toward the door. Saying goodnight, he kissed her on the cheek. Sheperd also kissed Grace on her cheek, something he had never done before. The two men exchanged a quick fraternal embrace, a fast gripping of their shoulders and bumping of their chests. C. D. couldn't recall them ever doing that before, either. Usually, their physicality had been confined to those little arm punches, competitive pokes and jabs in a masculine co-conspiracy. This felt different—almost warm, or as warm as Lance could allow himself to be.

They rode down in the elevator in an atmosphere of Greta's embarrassment, the two women rigidly quiet with each other, saying nothing, C. D. still too distracted and stung to notice the tension between them. After the duets of uniformed valets had hopped to and retrieved their cars, on the ride home, C. D. drove along in silence, a dry, metallic taste in his mouth. In his mind, he tried to balance his joy at buying the painting against his dismay at how Sheperd had played him. He would say nothing about this to Grace—why deflate her willingness to appreciate it? And in the end, he reasoned, no matter how much he had paid, the Charles Ellsworth was exactly the right art to hang in the new house, a radiant masterstroke that would complete their new home. He loved that painting, no question, and wasn't that worth far more?

Grace wasn't thinking about the painting. She kept going on and on about Lance Sheperd. "There he is, with all the money he could ever need, really, with *all the money in the world,*" she said. "And he's living up there like *that,* confined to a kitchen nook and a bed, strutting around worshiping the expensive objects he owns. Sad, sad, *sad,*" she said. "Did you see that empty guest room? Can his daughters even visit him there?"

C. D. didn't answer, driving on into the darkly lit hills that looked out over the city, up into the exclusive highlands where they now lived. Since Catherine had gone off to college, it was just the two of them occupying the big sprawling space of their new house.

"Don't you think it's sad?" Grace insisted. "I mean, is *that* what all his money is about?"

In reply, he reached across the car seat, put his hand on her knee and squeezed.

"Can you tell me? Can you?" she asked. "What kind of a *life* is that?"

—

At 3 a.m., long after Grace had gone to bed, C. D. wandered, restless in the new house. Checking his email, he found a group mail with the header *Urgent* sent by his brother Justin about Francis, news that he had suffered a complication, an infection of some kind. Justin had copied Francis's description that it was just "more bad luck" because it would delay his return from Germany, the doctors didn't know by how long. C. D. understood that it must be serious or Francis wouldn't have mentioned it at all, and he might lose his leg. He mentally reviewed his busy schedule in case he needed to make another trip.

Trying to take his mind off this news—what could he do?—C. D. found himself gazing up at the blank expanse of Florentine marble over the new fireplace. He tried to envision how the veins and textures of the stone would be set off by the vivid painting when it was hung—that brilliant spectrum, such ingenious innovations at the edges of visible light. He measured in his mind just how it would fit there, first sure, then not so sure. He thought of Sheperd, what a son of a bitch he had been—how many tens of thousands had he cost him? On the other hand, wouldn't he have done the same in his place?

No. He wouldn't have. He wasn't capable of that level of competitive deceit, not even as an expensive game between guys. A foreboding struck him then, a sensation that hit him physically, near the center of his diaphragm, causing him to force in a deeper breath. In Las Vegas, the first thing people learned about luck was how it could change. How long would it last? Francis might not make it, if the worst happened. What else could go wrong? His new job, his new house, the spectacular city below, felt somehow transient and temporary, like a hot run of cards. He shook off that feeling, wishing he could sleep.

In the still unfamiliar kitchen, heating milk and honey, he picked up the remote and switched on the TV. In the great room, images and sounds came to life on the big LCD screen, still tuned to CNN. Before he could reach for the remote and turn off the TV, he saw and heard Baghdad: a marketplace after a bombing, locals pulling wounded and dead out of wreckage. A crowd of men carried bodies aloft, wrapped in bloody shrouds—blots and smears of vivid red. Voices shrill with pain and rage, they called out the greatness of their God. Then a scene of the women, wailing, before he switched it off and the screen went dark.

– 2 –

Luck: he believed luck had smiled on him for most of this new life. Still, he had to keep reminding himself to be grateful to luck, as the surest way to lose one's luck is by not expressing enough thanks to Lady Luck for her attentions, until, like any fickle, capricious beauty, she turns her back and showers her favors on others. People cultivated luck in Las Vegas. They stroked special objects and talismans in their pockets, wore the same "lucky" hat or worn-out shirt or shoes. Players turned three times counterclockwise in doorways to ward off bad luck; or they woke up mornings to take stock of themselves and determine if they felt lucky that day. Some gamblers took regular, often circuitous, routes around the city that they thought brought good luck; or they believed that a precise time of day or certain days of the week were especially lucky. Many folks insisted on playing the same slot machine or taking the same seat at the same table with the same dealer or they wouldn't play; others never played the same machine or dealer twice, especially once they had won, or worse, had lost enough they kept chasing their luck, convinced they could hang in there and get lucky again. Smart players know the odds before they play. Still, luck just *happens,* and it can change. Lady Luck appears in different costumes, shows altered faces, picks out new people at her whim to blow them kisses from the moon. And often, it's hard to say if any kind of luck is all that good or all that bad, because how luck works can shift in its effects. The times in his life when he had felt most unlucky, hadn't what he believed to be misfortune later changed, even turning, as though miraculously, around?

That long-anticipated season arrived marking the big payoff from the sale of Pyramid Resorts to Oz Resorts—that lucrative corporate buyout Lance Sheperd had been preparing for with all his shrewdness, negotiating for over three years. Chevron, Slocum, all the vice presidents and directors, and on down the organizational pyramid to the mid-level managers *got some,* in varying amounts according to their stations. C. D. and Grace's take from their stock plus his piece from the spin-off of PyramidTravel.com would total more money than he had ever dreamed he would earn in a lifetime—a number of millions it took an extra edge of a thumbnail more to count than the fingers on one hand—enough money so that he might even hang it all up and call it a career and be proud of his achievements, as a lot of guys would if given the chance. What luck, without question, that this should happen.

Grace pointed this out to him, "reviewing the situation" after their payoff from the sale. The sum turned out to be almost exactly what she had calculated would be enough so they could "get the hell out of this madhouse city" and never worry about money again. She insisted that she had never really liked Las Vegas much and these days even less, the town becoming more and more "all dreck and glitz," she said. "It's a small miracle Catherine came out even *close* to a whole person growing up here."

"That's not true. This town's been great to us. We've spent the best years of our lives here. Really, where else could we have done so well?"

"Okay, I'll give you that," she said. "But it's not like it was going to be forever, right?"

All that week of the big payoff, C. D.'s mind had started spinning like a white lab mouse on an exercise wheel inside his head—*creak, creak, creak*—as he counted up his millions, ticking them off on his fingertips. He added in what seemed a skyrocketing appreciation on their big new house, and any way he figured it, their net worth astonished him. Mark Kinkaid had started sharing what he had heard about Sheperd's plans to build a new mega-resort: *Biscayne Bay*. The project would follow the latest Vegas rule—condo towers would be built alongside the new resort hotel, their sales would wipe out construction costs, then the condos could be spun off from the mother company. Biscayne Bay would emerge with minimal debt, owned entirely by its investors, after which Sheperd would take the whole shebang public. Anyone lucky enough to get in at the beginning might double his money or more, and what could be sweeter than that?

Sheperd hadn't yet formed his new company or Project Development team, but C. D., Kinkaid, Greta, and his other former executives surely would be asked. But this time, more than hanging in there for the solid jobs, how could they *get in on it from the beginning?* How could they take seats at the table to play?

They must insist this time to be included, Kinkaid kept saying. Inside the cage of C. D.'s head, the white lab mouse began racing again, *creak, creak, creak,* the exercise wheel spinning, spinning. He couldn't help but envision the flashing digital readouts of all that money they would make on his imaginary calculator, how he could double or even triple his new wealth. Or...

Take the money and run. Get the hell out of Vegas. Get out and...then what? Go where? Back to Grace's crumbling old house in Seattle that they had spent a small fortune maintaining, barely covered by renting it out to a succession of pain-in-the-ass tenants?

"At least there's a culture there," Grace said. "In Seattle, they don't just blow it up every decade." She half seriously suggested they build a modest house near her mom's double-wide trailer on their scruffy acres up in the woods. "They'll need me to help take care of them soon. At least there, I could grow a decent garden. Everything I plant won't curl up and die in this ungodly heat," she said, sniffling miserably from another bout with her seasonal allergies.

That might be true, C. D. admitted—Grace might be happy enough—but what would *he* do? Not even close to his idea of the good life to have to muck around in knee-high rubber boots when the blue clay soil of western Washington turned to tapioca pudding under incessant rains. On the other hand, in Las Vegas, the mid-June temperature was set to break 109 degrees for the second day. And forget the old saw that "it's a dry heat"—anyone who didn't guzzle bottle after bottle of water all day long felt dizzy, in danger of passing out. If folks didn't tent off the dashboards of their cars, putting hands on steering wheels could nearly blister them. Homeless shelters were packed to bursting—the homeless in Vegas died of heat exhaustion, not freezing. In the paper that morning, Grace read how students at UNLV had placed a thermometer at the center point of a crosswalk across six lanes of the broiling asphalt of Flamingo Boulevard and the temperature had hit 143 degrees! Whenever it hit over 105, Grace swore she couldn't breathe. So back and forth, they argued.

"Well, if Washington's out for you, then pick a place. *Any*place else," she said. "San Diego. Miami. Santa Fe. Or Maui...How about Hawaii? Why not? Why not give some island paradise a try? We can sell out here and go almost anywhere else."

"Don't you love our house?" he argued. "We *love* this house!"

"Life's a hell of a lot more than owning a house."

They lay awake in bed, the curtains drawn back from the glass door to the balcony, the lights of the city spreading out in all their arousing spectacle across the valley. Turning his gaze to this view always lifted his spirits, though he understood, rationally, that it was all just a transitory architecture, the hotel towers with their windows lit tonight emptying out in the morning, the still unfinished condo towers rising in a frenzy of rushed construction of the latest "Miami phase" of the city's growth standing like a line of soldiers in their underwear waiting to be shot. All right then: it was a city made of neon announcing temples of consumerism, a city of gaudy billboards that signified little about who its people actually were. There was no center, if Las Vegas ever *had* a center, and little sense of community. Even when its citizens did gather together in parks or in plazas or for public events, they moved through the public spaces as though encased in their own fierce individuality, powered by self-interest, and proud of it, too, like the purest incarnations of Libertarians. They traveled back and forth to attend the teeming attractions of The Strip as if transforming in their passage into but another number among the transient tens of millions of tourists. They cruised through the streets straight past each other feeling safe behind the tinted windows of their cars—inside each car a separate citizen with a separate thought, anonymous dark shapes passing each other by. Who even knew who their neighbors were? Grace discovered more connection to their future and growing old together in her sewing kit, in her gardening tools, in her personalized stationery, even in writing out checks each month to pay the bills than in all this glitzy show. She claimed she'd feel more joined with her true identity and with their place in "the flow of human history" anywhere else in the world.

"But this *is* history," he said, sweeping his arm toward the impressive view through the balcony doors. And no matter how much he understood rationally that it all sprang up from the madness of a real estate boom ready to boil over and douse its own flames, and that out there in the suburban streets of their neighborhood curving past $2 million, minimum, houses still going up on lot after stony lot, there just *had* to be an end to it sometime—but who in hell knew when?—he kept going back to this view, these magnificent lights, this show of hope the city represented. Still: did he truly want all this—Las Vegas and everything it implied—for their future?

Yes. He did.

"It's all about image for you," Grace said. "All about how things *look*, not what they are. You're vain, really. The most vain man I've ever known."

"Vanity, vanity, all is vanity . . ." he sang in the dark.

"Don't do that," she said, punching his arm. "We've got the chance to be comfortable. Happy and comfortable, in a place where we can be proud to live."

"But we can get really, really rich," he said. "Not just comfortable. Rich. Rich enough to make Catherine comfortable. Rich enough to make life easy for your mom."

"We're rich enough. And Catherine's better off making her own way."

"Think about it. How many people even *get* this chance?"

A long moment passed, Grace thinking this over, turned away from him on her darker side of the king bed. C. D. scooted closer, wrapping his arms around her body. He kissed the back of her neck. Slowly, he moved his hands further down.

"Don't," she said. "You always do this."

"Don't you like me doing this?"

"Of course I do, you know that. But not now. Not to win an argument."

He held her, drawing in the scent of her fragrant hair. He slipped his left hand under the strap of her satiny gown then over a big soft breast, stroking her nipple, his body pressing closer into their spooning, and she wasn't resisting.

"What I want to say . . . what I'm trying to tell you . . . is I'm lonely in this house."

The new house: that had become her issue now. As proud as they were of such a home—and Grace had been proud, or said she was—they saw less of each other in a house so big. He recalled his little brother Francis's first visit to the new house, finally using that ticket C. D. had given him, staying a week, showing off his first prosthetic leg with its high-tech knee that he could walk on pretty well, praise be, though he couldn't last more than about an hour at a stretch without having to push through discomfort and pain. His leg wasn't done yet. He would need at least one, maybe two more surgeries "to fix it right," as he put it. How proudly C. D. had set him up in their new guest suite downstairs, showing off the helper rails he had installed in the green marble walls of the shower plus the other gleaming fixtures, the designer drapes, the Blu-Ray system for the plasma TV. They celebrated, inviting the Kinkaids and some of Grace's friends over, and Grace cooked gourmet dinners every night. In the evenings, the brothers drank beers out on the balcony so they could take in the spectacular view. Still, the day Francis left, he said, "It's nice. Really nice. But your other house was more . . . well . . . cozy."

If it weren't for his brother's missing leg, C. D. might have said what he thought: the U.S. intelligence community flies drones all over the Middle East from Nellis and Indian Springs where they blast God only knows how many people to hell and smithereens, and here, my brother-the-spy misses feeling *cozy*?

His sister Cathy, with two of her kids (teenagers now) enjoyed the new house. It had plenty of room for them all to spread out, use the PebbleTec pool, mess up the kitchen, and he and Grace could escape to their master bedroom and hardly hear them. Desmond, too, liked the new house a lot; he'd visited three times, each time with a different girlfriend, C. D. getting the idea that bragging about "my brother's mansion in Vegas" was part of what helped him score. Janice and Dewey hadn't driven down more than once, during Catherine's spring break, health issues making it hard. No one else in the family had visited yet, but he assumed they would. They were hosting fewer visits from family and friends than in the old house, he didn't know why.

Grace had started complaining of loneliness, how some afternoons, she felt she was "just knocking around" in the big new house. Only natural, as he kept telling her, blaming it on "the empty-nest syndrome"—her response to Catherine having gone off to UCLA. She had put in year after year of motherly devotion making their old cracker-box house on Piñon Way into something like a teen center with "structured activities." He recalled the health food club Grace had pushed, and the Green Valley High "Students for Amnesty

International" group—entirely Catherine's idea during a sophomore altruism phase. Grace had chauffeured Catherine and her friends all over the southeast suburbs. She would sit in the parked Volvo, watching out for the girls as they walked the Henderson neighborhoods knocking on doors for donations. And Grace opened up their living room to let the girls "just hang out" in their increasingly contemptuous postures of existential teenage languor, their slackly sensual bodies draped all over the furniture, volume turned up way too loudly on his new quad speaker system to the latest Spice Girls, Atomic Kitten, or Eminem. This was during those high-pressure years when C. D. had to travel a lot to complete development of PyramidTravel.com. He would get home late after spending hours packed into the heated gym-locker smell of the airline shuttle, mindful of how much he had missed—so many peak moments of Catherine's growing up. He would step through the door into a lingering fragrance of clashing sweet perfumes mixed with a faint acidic aroma of sexual frustrations like a trace of bitter orange, and instantly, he felt at home.

One of the regrets Grace expressed about the new house was how they had waited so long to make their decision, moving into it just after Catherine went off to college—too late for her to feel like the new house was her home. She visited, yes, for the occasional weekend and for holidays. She went out a lot, catching up with her friends. And this past winter, Catherine had carried on the yuletide ritual sitting with Fisherman Frank, watching the same old Irish movies in front of the TV, then driving him to the poker rooms Downtown.

Frank's life had been deteriorating. He suffered from worsening back and knee injuries that kept him sidelined for much of the fishing season. He had started adding regular doses of Vicodin to his maintenance drinking. C. D. sent him money so he could make the trip, but his Christmas visit to the new house didn't go very well. By chance, coming in late from work, C. D. heard an odd splattering noise. He discovered Frank standing in the doorway of the guest suite, drunk, peeing into the hall, doing this in his sleep. Mindful of an old wives' tale never to wake up a sleepwalker, C. D. stopped himself from intervening, thinking also that if Catherine knew, she might feel ashamed. Frank pulled up his boxer shorts—ragged black things with a pattern of bright red whales—and stumbled off to fall face first onto the bed.

C. D. shut the guest room door behind him. He went upstairs and changed out of his suit, careful not to wake Grace. He put on old weekend clothes. He got out the bucket and mop and Clorox, then cleaned those gorgeous marble tiles. The next morning, when he mentioned this "little accident" to Frank, out by the smoking area with its chair and cocktail table fixed up for him by the pool, Frank let out a brief snort and phlegmy cough that passed these days for his laugh. "Must have been dreaming I was on the boat, pissing over the rail," he said. "Wouldn't be the first time that's happened."

C. D. took this in with a forced, fraternal chuckle meant to reassure Frank that he understood, no big deal. But he didn't, thinking he'd have to rig some kind of bell or buzzer on the guest suite door loud enough to wake him so it wouldn't happen again.

Frank waited for him to say something more, his stooped, stocky body curving further into itself, elbows resting on his knees, his hands, with a beer in one and cigarette in the other, still raised, a bit like a threatened crab, C. D. thought. Frank sucked in smoke with a tension-induced grin, like a schoolboy anticipating a scolding. C. D. asked if he were sure he had enough money this trip. Frank fired back with his stock reply, "Let's hope for decent cards."

Late that night, after Catherine had dropped her dad off at the casino, C. D. walked in on her sitting at the kitchen table, her head in her hands, staring into a bowl of melting ice cream. What a tall, leggy girl she had grown into, her body everywhere full but still trim enough, he thought, if she could avoid gaining too much weight. She kept her dark straight hair cut short into a pageboy, only longer on one side than the other, as was the fashion then, a cut that showed off lines of tiny silver globes in her ears, new piercings she had had done her first semester in college over her mom's objections. The way she carried herself during her first year at UCLA, still feeling out her new adult freedom she had so long anticipated, Catherine seemed to be growing into a fresh confidence and sophistication, a newly mature quality in her voice implying experiences she would no longer share with her parents—her first serious boyfriends, all disappointments, so far; and, as with most young people, her natural discovery that her new freedom, and the world, might not be all that she had hoped. Like her mom, when she was troubled or frustrated, she took solace in food. She had been eating way too much this holiday. C. D. had mentioned this to her, gently, more than once.

As he observed her sitting with her bowl of ice cream, she sensed him in the doorway. "What am I going to do with him?" she asked.

"You're not the one who should do anything with him," he said.

"Have you seen his stomach? It's all swollen out, like a football. Mom's told him to go see a doctor. But he just won't. He won't..."

Grace had reviewed this situation with him more than once—that Frank showed signs of liver disease. A doctor would tell him to stop drinking, what he most feared.

"Your dad lives his life the way he wants. You're not going to change that."

"It's just so...so *sad*," she said. "Why does everything have to be so sad?"

"Catherine," he said, sharply. "He's not your responsibility. Do you hear me?"

"I know, I know..."

"Say it," he said.

"*See-Dee!*" She used that rising sing-song when annoyed at him. It struck him like a welcome echo of the little girl she had been.

He softened his tone. "Say it," he said. "Say it and believe it."

"Okay, okay. He' s not my responsibility. Okay?"

He moved closer behind her chair and squeezed her shoulders, then he reached around, picked up the ice cream dish and carried it over to the sink to rinse out what she hadn't finished. She said goodnight, adding her usual "Love you" tossed into the air before she vanished into the hallway. He listened to her journeying up the stairs, the sounds of her footsteps growing fainter, absorbed into the vastness of the new house, until he could no longer hear them.

After that visit, C. D. self-questioned again if the policy he had insisted upon years ago of encouraging such closeness with Frank O'Malley, hosting him in their home, might have been a mistake. Too late to change now. Fisherman Frank would find winter boat work and skip his visit that next Christmas. While attending college, Catherine began seeing less of him, too, preferring to visit her dad as she traditionally had while growing up, briefly in summer, at her grandparents' place. And she came home less and less, busy with her active campus life.

So of course Grace felt lonely in the new house. What did she expect?

"We've got each other," C. D. said, laying his cheek against hers, sliding his hand under her nightgown again, holding her closer. Grace murmured something affirmative. He felt her settling into sleep. After a moment, he turned his face the other way, gazing off again into the spectacular view of the city through the balcony doors. The little white lab mouse on its exercise wheel began racing once more in his head, *creak, creak, creak,* as he thought, his mind made up now, convinced Lady Luck would surely stick with him and his timing was right: *We're going to get really, really rich, you'll see*. . .

– 3 –

Monday morning at The Beach, fax machines in the executive wing all at once began making those wheezing and beeping sounds fax machines make, each spitting out a form letter on letterhead of the VP of HR at Oz Resorts addressed to the Pyramid Resorts vice presidents and on down to the directors and mid-level managers. After a few opening lines self-congratulating the Oz team for the biggest acquisition in the history of the industry, the letters asserted cold instructions: *You are requested to vacate your office and remove all personal belongings by September 1. After this date, admittance to your former office will be denied.*

So this is the way the guys at Oz wanted to do things? Not even a meet-and-greet at The Beach with the new executives assigned to replace them at their jobs? Every hotel had its unique culture, its special problems, its complex facilities and staffing issues, each its own story and idiosyncrasies, not to mention the 1,001 ongoing streams of communications with the retail managers, suppliers, contractors, convention salespeople, and all the rest, and to its important guests, including Whales. Did they really want to play it this way?

"Jeez," Kinkaid said, leaning against the birch wood frame of C.D.'s doorway, fax in hand after comparing it to C. D.'s. "It's like an eviction notice. Get out now, the A team's on its way. You know of any bad blood from the sale?"

"You'd know before I would," C. D. said.

"Have you ever seen anything like this?"

"Does Greta know something we don't?"

"Not about the sale," Kinkaid said. "Not that I know."

"She know anything about the new deal?"

"All I know is Greta says all she knows is Lehman's going to run the paper."

"How does she know that?" C. D. asked.

"Some girl thing, at the Malibu house. Consulting on PR for that Cuban dancer."

"Venezuelan."

"Same difference. Lehman's Gregory flew out with that shopaholic wife of his. Quite the party. Some L.A. art scene thing. Anybody who's anybody was there."

"Joe Gregory flew out? With his wife? When was that?"

"Last Friday night."

"Doesn't anybody tell me anything? When did you talk to Greta?"

"This morning. She just got her fax too. But you know Greta. She always knows a lot more than she says she knows. I bet she does know something."

"Fuck 'em," C. D. said. "They can take this place blind, if that's the way they want it. I'm not leaving them anything, not even the new data on our customer base. Fuck 'em all." He gazed off over his balcony into the leaves of a pineapple palm tree, like a ragged crown reaching up to his window. Cheerful sunlight from the fountain pool shimmered from below its green canopy. "I'll miss this office," he said. "Took a lot of years to get here. What next?"

"You know Sheperd. He'll go cheap for the development phase. Probably cram us into some new strip mall again. Dangle bonus checks at the back end so he can cut our salaries to less than a third. You know the drill."

"He's not going to keep this one all to himself," C. D. said. "Not this time."

"I don't know," Kinkaid said. "Have you talked to Slocum? To Chevron?"

"They're out. That much *I* know. They've both made their numbers."

"Have you talked to Sheperd?"

"You haven't talked to him?" C. D. had been under the impression all week that Kinkaid had met with Sheperd to review last-minute details. He had been anxious about this, fighting back a sick sensation that Kinkaid might be more valued now by Sheperd and so get closer to him—they might cut him out of the deal.

Kinkaid hovered in the doorway uneasily, patting the top of his head as if to check how much of his combed-over hair he had left. He cast wary sidewise glances into the hall like he suspected a spy might be listening from that direction.

"I'll talk to him then," C. D. said.

"Fuck you," Kinkaid said. "We'll *both* talk to him."

"Whichever one of us talks to him first, we'll let the other know."

"Right," Kinkaid said, his slight paunch sagging over his belt after he let loose the muscles holding it in. They had been friends for sixteen years. Whenever there was tension between them, his pudgy body contracted, pulling in layers of doughy flesh as if self-consciously competing with his friend's more toned appearance, as though that mattered. "Thanks," Kinkaid said. He touched the edge of the fax page to his forehead like a kind of salute then went off down the hall to his prime office suite that would soon no longer be his, muttering, "Unbelievable!"

After the big sale, Kinkaid and C. D. had played the "how much is the boss's net worth" game and calculated Sheperd must be topping $400 million. No wonder they had trouble booking an appointment with him. Except for a few random, unpredictable visits to meet with attorneys, Sheperd had mostly vanished from Pyramid Resorts and his penthouse in Las Vegas. They tried calls, texts, and hounding Sharon Greene, his secretary, without success. C. D. kept trying Greta Olsson every hour, every call sent to voicemail until she finally answered. She was in L.A., working a job for Sheperd to help the publicists for his girlfriend. Esperanza Milonga had been cast for a supporting role as the sex-interest Latina cop for the cast of a new TV series called *Vegas Crime Wave*, just green-lighted by NBC—Sheperd was a major investor and would also act as associate producer to arrange various casino and Strip locations. Greta assisted with staging publicity events around L.A. to pump up Esperanza's career. That evening, at a club called Snake, the photo that made it into a supermarket tabloid showed the ex-ballerina's dark beauty in a glittering dress with deep cleavage, her arm hooked around a superstar actor (he doesn't deserve to be named, his acting is so bad). The photo caught her haughtily sticking her tongue out at the camera, a stunned expression on the actor's face as if he'd been ambushed by a crocodile that had suddenly rushed him from the crowd.

Later that week, at their meeting at the Starbucks near the Hughes Center, C. D. slapped a copy of the tabloid on the table like an accusation. "Nice job," he said, his tone not so nice.

"A favor for Lance," Greta said. "Besides, who am I to turn down the work?"

"Who's the new guy?" C. D. asked, nodding his head toward

a sandy-haired young tough Greta had strolled into the Starbucks with, earbuds in his ears, biceps and pecs bulging in a camo T-shirt. Greta had posted him at a corner table with a whipped cream drink and his iPod.

"That's Paolo, from Brazil," she said. "I bought him in L.A." She paused an instant, then added sharply, "What? You don't approve?"

"It's nothing to me," he said. "But on everything else, you of all people should keep us in the loop. When have we ever cut *you* out? I'm disappointed. So is Kinkaid. . ."

"You guys can take care of yourselves," she said. She batted her eyes in that way she had when she pretended innocence. He caught a whiff of whiskey in her spiked coffee. "Look, you think this is easy for me? Hanging out in his house while she's draping that body of hers all over him? That's mostly what I'm doing." She reached under the table and put her hand on his inner thigh. "Get me out of this. Run away with me, C. D., just the two of us. Or make it the *three* of us. We'll take Grace along, I don't mind."

"What about Paolo over there?"

"Him too. Paolo's got his virtues, lemme tell you, and he doesn't cost much."

"Sorry. We both know you're too fucked up."

"Tell me which one of us is really fucked up, kiddo," she said. She reached for a napkin and wrote down Sheperd's new private cell phone number. "Don't tell him I gave it to you."

"Are you okay?" he asked. "Are you? Can I do anything?"

"I should make you a list," she said. "*Haa*-hah. . ."

Later that day, he phoned the private number. Ever one to double-task, Sheperd set up a quick Saturday meeting at an art gallery called Gemini in Los Angeles, where Sheperd—so deep into his art buying it had become an obsession—would be looking over new works on paper they represented. C. D. drove off early on the five-hour trip to beat the traffic.

"Tell me about Biscayne Bay LLC," C. D. said, standing next to Sheperd, both let in to the gallery's private, climate-controlled storage area where prints and lithographs were kept in rows of metal drawers. "We want in. Kinkaid and me. Greta too. Some of the other guys maybe, maybe not. I don't know. Definitely me and Kinkaid."

"Naw. I don't think so." Sheperd said this in a way that made it only half clear he was answering C. D. rather than voicing a snap judgment about a lithograph he was inspecting. He placed it back and closed the metal drawer. "You don't want to put in for that much risk."

"Shouldn't we decide that for ourselves?"

Sheperd opened another drawer, inside which shone one of the few prints with a little color, blocks of yellow and blue connected by threadlike black lines. "There are partners, guys from Houston. Assholes. Unreliable," he said. He slammed the drawer closed and pulled out another that contained a print by the same artist, this one in blocks of green. "The only reason they need me is for the gaming license. It's going to be a fight to be in bed with these gonifs and not get fucked."

"What the hell are you in it for then, Lance? I mean, you're rich enough, right?"

Sheperd stopped opening drawers. He focused his full attention on C. D. for the first time, as if weighing something in his character—intelligence, loyalty, trust? After all these years, what? Sheperd relaxed a little then, as though he had decided something. "Let's just say I have expensive tastes. *Very* expensive tastes," he said. "Plus, I'll be unemployed, right? Building hotels is what I do. Only the partners on this project really are assholes. That's why I haven't answered calls, from Kinkaid, the guys at Oz, from you or Greta—not from anybody I know who wants in on this. I've been thinking maybe not spread this one around, look to the big banks and funds, maybe a few private investors who can stand to take the hit, just in case. Don't get me wrong, I plan to sink half my own fortune into this thing, eyes wide open. But I know what I'm doing. The principal partners are guys who would screw their own mother to make it into the billionaires' club. Not that I wouldn't do the same if it were only my mother. I just don't want to take any friends down in case the whole thing goes to shit, which, believe me, this one could. That's it," he said. "End of story."

Something caught Sheperd's attention in one of the drawers. He pulled out a poster-sized print and held it up to the light—an image of a roughly round shape, like a ball of string, made from squiggles of black ink pressed into the paper under what must have been tons of pressure. It had no number in the corner, only a letter, *H*, indicating it was a "state" pressing from one of the test runs before the series was printed. Neither C. D. nor Sheperd could make out the signature of the artist—Duran? Donne?

"Don't we deserve at least a shot at it?" C. D. stated more than asked. "Get in with the guys who are going to build it with you? Or even just talk to the guys handling the paper?"

"Is this worth anything?" Sheperd asked, holding up the lithograph and gazing deeper into it. Under the light, the image took on a slight sepia tone. "What do you think?"

"I like it," C. D. said, and he did. Something about the ragged, round shape made by so many tangled string-like lines appealed to him. "I don't know much about this kind of art. Still, there's *something* there. . . ."

"What do you see?" Sheperd asked.

"What comes to mind is a . . . a planetary image . . . like a planet . . . seen through a dirty telescope on a cloudy night. Who knows? How much is it?"

"About $5,000, I'd guess," he said. "Only you don't want this."

"I don't? Why not, if I like it?"

"You don't want it because it's shit," he said. "You'll lose money."

"But I like it. I can afford it. If I like it, why not buy it?"

"You can't say I didn't warn you," Sheperd said.

He held out the lithograph, and C. D. felt he had no choice but to take that strange work on paper into his hands, not even sure how he should hold such a thing, gripping it carefully by the corners. He tried to imagine the place in the new house where it might belong and drew a blank—his study? The upstairs hall? The guest suite?

"I'll get you my discount on this," Sheperd said. "I'll do that much for you. About the other, I'll give them your number. That's it. Nothing to do with me. You got that? All clear?"

"We understand," C. D. said. "Thanks. This means a lot to us. It really does."

Sheperd raised a finger in the air. On cue, a gallery assistant appeared and stepped in beside them, a smart blonde in a black turtleneck, all business as her white gloved hands carefully took the work from C. D. by its ragged edges. She replaced it temporarily back in its drawer, then pulled out a small notebook and wrote down the number—sold.

Later, in the gallery office, another assistant brought in the "state" lithograph and he put up a credit card, relieved it would be hit for only $5K plus taxes—cheap enough as part of his deal with Sheperd, though he was still unsure how he had been talked into buying it. In brighter light, the image appeared even more like a representation of a dirty planet, not that art of this kind meant to represent anything but itself, but he did see something there. He noted the artist's name on the receipt: August Donne. He observed a staff person carefully wrap it in paper between pieces of stiff cardboard then place it in an art box. Out in the parking lot, he directed it to be propped up on the back seat floor of his BMW. He set off on the mostly night drive out of L. A. then over the mountains and across the Mojave Desert to Las Vegas, feeling the package ticking against the seat behind him every time he used the brakes. As he dodged, weaved, and halted through the heavy traffic leaving L.A., he wasn't sure if he were excited or a little queasy, or both sensations at once.

Finally free of traffic and heading north on the I-15, he phoned Kinkaid and told him all about the meeting. He phoned to tell him what he knew as soon as he knew it, as they had agreed, but really so he could feel high and happy again, as Kinkaid did, and fight off any doubts. Their celebratory chatter covered what they left unsaid, how they were both a little scared at how they would be *all in* now, chips on the table, when Sheperd's guy at Lehman Brothers rang C. D.'s phone first thing Monday morning. He finished his three cheers call to Kinkaid and a sudden rush ran through him—it felt like leaning over the railing of a very high balcony, that quick thrilling flip inside as he caught himself just before falling.

What followed over the next two months would be meetings with an attorney, a young guy named Keely in training under Tim Slocum. Slocum had set up his own law firm since the sale of Pyramid Resorts. C. D. and Kinkaid spent several intense sessions together in either one of their home offices, working out figures on their calculators, fax machines spitting out a sheaf of legal-size pages that piled up as thick as a phone book. Grace pored over the documents too, untangling complex relationships in dense webs of legalese and numbers. Strange side deals had made their way into the contracts, subsidiary investments in commercial properties, including a new medical office building and shopping center down in Houston, Texas, that neither

Grace nor Kinkaid fully understood. Their attorneys and the guy at Lehman's—a senior trader and account manager named Morris Glickstein who recalled how C. D. had hosted him one wild night in Vegas when they were both young newcomers starting out—assured them that this was the way it was done, everything tied up with everything else, wrapped together and "bundled." If they wanted in, they should sign. "Get in on this!" Glickstein cheered over the phone. "Geronimo!"

C. D. worked on Grace, a negotiation that reminded him of years ago convincing her to marry him. Grace asked the same question: "Aren't we happy enough the way we are?"

"Should we turn our backs on this chance? What's life all about without taking chances?"

"I'm doing this for you, just so you know," she said. "It's *your* decision."

"It's *our* decision," he said.

"In for a penny, in for a pound, as Mom always says. . ."

And so they signed—multiple sets of papers, then authorizations for the fund transfers that all but emptied out their many accounts. Some units for Biscayne Bay LLC would be tied up into their own separate agreement—the Reinharts, the Kinkaids, and Greta Olsson in partnership together, Greta in for a quarter, the guys splitting the rest down the middle, theirs the smallest investment package included in the massive financing deals. C. D. took Grace out to dinner at Alizé to celebrate over the kind of meal that always made her happy, five delectable courses created by André Rochat, revered artist among Las Vegas chefs, rich with truffles and sauces and paired wines. They took their time to savor each course, gazing at the dreamy view from the top floor of the Palms, looking out over a neon kingdom—*their* kingdom—under the stars.

– 4 –

C. D., Kinkaid, Greta Olsson, Brick Rico, Gary Luongo, and others from Sheperd's former team at Pyramid Resorts put in ten- and twelve-hour days for the next two years planning and building Biscayne Bay and its twin condominium towers. Midway through, they moved into offices in the first and still mostly unfinished condo tower. And what they started to build really would be something—the architect's model looked like a space-age colony filled with jungle gardens, a turquoise glass and steel resort like a vertical tropics growing sixty stories into the sky. Biscayne Bay would offer first-class nightclubs, designer-label shopping, and gourmet restaurants to rival anything in Miami's trendy South Beach. High tech too, its spacious rooms controlled by motion sensors that sectored off individualized comfort and entertainment zones, the air-conditioning, ambient music, and visual displays following guests around as they moved through the ultramodern rooms. The gorgeous design opened up big spaces. Sprawling lounges on every floor would feel like unique and thrilling tropical environments suspended in the air over spectacular city and mountain views.

The sixty stories of the resort would be topped off by rooftop swimming and spa attractions glowing up there in the stratosphere, including four "infinity pools" that created optical illusions of water flowing over breathtaking precipices into limitless space. Looking out through panels of turquoise glass would offer views as if from a luxurious spacecraft hovering in the desert skies; and gazing inward to the pools and spas would reveal a sensual feast of a fertile island jungle with clusters of suite-size cabañas waited on by a cool and youthful staff—waitresses and waiters dressed in "barely there" bikinis and bulging Speedos would provide the service. Washing over all this would be bass-heavy music arranged by visiting headliner DJs who would make the pool and spa complex at Biscayne Bay into the trendiest and most exclusive "day club" in the city. Everything at "The Bay" would be aimed at the expensive social tastes and unbounded hedonism of wealthy young people from all over the globe, rich international visitors one of the prime target markets. The experience would be branded *the Bay Life,* with "Live the Bay Life" as the banner and keystone jingle for the marketing campaigns C. D. and the team were preparing to unleash to the whole world.

The Biscayne Bay Casino would not be built following any tired-out gaming concepts with rows of slot machines and table games arranged into ever-shifting "labyrinths" and "traps" designed intentionally to delay and confuse players. No: the casino would offer players a "social design" of many generous, open spaces with choices of several kinds of relaxed environments in which they could sit facing each other at curving islands of games so that people could actually see and talk to each other as they played. Or players could retreat in groups of four to up to a dozen into more intimate cocoon-like spaces where they could sit around together and gamble at big glass circles glowing with table-mounted, touch screen–operated games. Gaming expert Jim Kirby—"the Vacuum Cleaner"—didn't like this new concept; he had "no numbers" to inform him if "social-space gaming" could succeed. C. D. worked with Kirby and wrote up an internet survey to help gather data, but it was never used—there was no point once Sheperd made up his mind. He insisted that Biscayne Bay be "new and different" in every way, "a resort casino for the new century."

Social media would play a crucial role. Front desk staff, pit bosses, bell persons, showroom attendants, casino floor managers, the hosts, the waiters, the maids, almost every kind of employee on up to the junior executives could be summoned to serve guest needs via Facebook, Instagram, texts and tweets. Just before Biscayne Bay started construction, an ebullient Steve Jobs had produced a global spectacle at the Consumer Electronics Show in Las Vegas that had rivaled any Broadway opening night to unveil Apple's new i-Phone that would transform the whole world, for better or worse. That revolutionary innovation had sent C. D. scurrying around finding subcontractors to design resort-specific applications, or "apps," for the new device at $250,000 each, so he had to up his IT budget overnight, to which Sheperd had said, "Just get it done." By riding the new smartphone revolution, Biscayne Bay meant in every way to appeal to the interests of the ever younger demographic who soon would be living their lives according to that new universal mantra: *Share with your friends.*

"It's all about the kids now," Sheperd said, talking up "the Bay Life" to his team, clear that by "kids" he meant that crucial twenty-one to thirty-five demographic. "Forget stage shows and lounge acts. Kids aren't interested. And no more Cirque du Soleil, give us a break. The kids are done with acrobats and men in tights. They're on to day clubs with table service, sex palace cabañas with disco around the pool, and after that, they want the hottest nightclubs anywhere. Biscayne Bay offers them a total fantasy world for hook-ups, complete with an in-house Facebook-type check-in system so they can network with other kids who'll be there the same time they will before they even get to town. Once here, the system will track their networking with regular updates to smartphones telling each other where the hottest guys and babes are hanging out and what they're doing. Look at it globally. In the twenty-first century, the market segment of young people we're going after will be the richest human beings ever to inhabit planet Earth, offspring of the 1 percent, spoiled and wealthy and not giving a damn. What they want to spend their money on most is getting laid. So we want the coolest, richest kids all over the world to get the message that this is what the Bay Life is all about. . ."

Sheperd kept speed-talking to anyone who would listen. Many of the marketing concepts he pitched were C. D.'s ideas—the social networking preregistration, the tuned-in staff, the software-dependent lifestyle with brand-new Apple i-Macs in all the rooms plus additional terminals spread out around the tropical spas and lounges with touch-screen technology for doing everything, all proposed, bid out, and contracted for by his hard work and years of experience and connections in the industry. C. D. flew off on six trips into the ice and snow of Vermont, had to invest in a down parka to keep from shivering so much on his hustles back and forth to plan and negotiate the deal for customized Springer-Miller software that would run Biscayne Bay operations and coordinate with Jim Kirby's casino software so that everything would interface seamlessly together, harmoniously singing away. (No more Timmy Chin, ancient history now.) Biscayne Bay promised more than five thousand new jobs. In preparation for the launch, C. D. set up training schedules with

Springer-Miller staff for the fifteen hundred future employees who would be most responsible for running the house.

Whatever it was, Biscayne Bay would use only the latest and the best, as Sheperd had planned. Combine these new multimillion-dollar integrated software systems plus all the social networking and cool architecture with such ultramodern designs so richly layered everywhere with jungle-beat sensuality, add in the demographics of superrich twenty- and thirty-somethings from all over the world, and "the Bay Life" couldn't miss. The three massive towers of steel I-beams and concrete slabs poured floor by floor and then wrapped in turquoise-colored glass kept steadily rising, trucks and heavy equipment and thousands of laborers filling the days and nights with relentless noise, never stopping, not even for holidays, no matter the overtime. Deep into the skeletal structures capped off with a busy crane, ironworkers labored away high overhead, balanced like acrobats against the desert sky.

During this newest Las Vegas boom phase, up and down The Strip, it seemed everywhere the same—Oz Resorts building its massive $7 billion project it called Metropolis with six new towers and such pressing infrastructure demands that central Harmon Avenue and Flamingo Boulevard had their hearts dug out under the asphalt for the laying down of all that new pipe for water mains and sewers and electrical systems that would back up traffic for nearly two straight years. And stretching north past the elegant towers of Bellagio, past Caesars and the Wynn with its new Encore Tower and the Venetian with its new Palazzo and all the rest in that spectacular dream show, three other new hotel casinos and two more condo towers also had started up construction, more than $32 billion of investment all at once combining into the greatest-ever building phase in the city's history. And as ever, people started asking, *Can Las Vegas support all this growth? Is there a chance of overbuilding?*

"Not a chance," Sheperd speed-talked to investors, mostly guys at the big investment banks and institutional funds, also the new guys running private capital markets and hedge funds. No casino hotel had ever lost money in the whole history of "recession-proof" Las Vegas, not one—not ever—for going on four generations. Kinkaid and his staff kept running the numbers weekly, construction costs increasing, the price of steel rebar hitting unprecedented highs. He factored in the latest demographics and marketing projections from C. D. and their consultants plus advance sales of the condo units, still hitting targets that made the numbers work. Toward the north end of The Las Vegas Strip, the turquoise blue towers of Biscayne Bay kept on rising, with all their promise of tropical splendor and aesthetic beauty. Everyone on Sheperd's team agreed: no resort experience anywhere in the world would offer anything that could compete.

—

During that unprecedented frenzied pace of new construction in Las Vegas, the multibillion-dollar general-contracting corporations with their legions of subcontractors set safety aside in pursuit of profits. Twelve workers were killed by preventable accidents, four times that many suffering serious injuries. At Biscayne Bay, no worker yet had been killed but three (so far) had suffered disabling injuries—the first a crushed spine after being buried during the foundation excavation; the next a brain injury after being struck by swinging steel; then, as the building began to reach higher floors, an ironworker slipped off an unguarded walkway and fell two stories, his left leg impaled on a spike of rebar up to his thigh, skewered that way for more than an hour until his fellow crew members could jackhammer concrete and then jerry-rig a harness to lift him free. An angry gang of ironworkers barged into Lance Sheperd's office and threatened to walk off the job. Sheperd called in favors from the leaders of Ironworkers Union Local 433 to avoid this, promising to address safety concerns.

Sheperd did not have full power over the project; the initial setup for the construction of Biscayne Bay and its condominium towers was overseen by the partners in Gravenstein LLC, real estate developers from Houston, who had gone for the lowest bid by Mancini Construction as general contractor over Sheperd's strong objections. (When C. D. learned about this, he heard echoing in his head the phrase he wished he had used with old J. B. Roland: *The problem is mistaking cost for value.*) What followed at Biscayne Bay spookily resembled building Pyramid World eighteen years before—inadequate or missing safety barriers, safety nets left balled up on the site instead of strung out as required under the upper floors, faulty warning alarms on machinery, building materials piled up everywhere in dangerously tottering stacks, and worse, short staffing on an ever-shifting roster of foremen who operated with at best patchy communications from one crew to another and with few if any safety reviews—a hazardous mess. C. D. saw this for himself the two times he had donned a hard hat and held on for his life riding the shaky precarious crew lift that crashed and banged its way to the upper floors on tours with investors, grateful this was no longer a regular part of his job. He found he had developed a new fear of heights, dizzy and nauseous whenever he looked down. The smiling picture of Lester "Red" Stahl filled his head, cradling the UNLV basketball, his hard hat tipped back, showing his curly red hair, and he felt a familiar sickening flip in his middle envisioning the long slide and fall through an air shaft followed by a wave of regrets that he hadn't done more. Sheperd and his new legal team flew down to Houston for meetings to demand safety reviews and changes. He did what he could.

All that year, the *Las Vegas Sun* ran a series of investigative reports exposing the scandalous lack of safety in high-rise construction all over town (about fifty articles, for which they would win the Pulitzer Prize for public service). Their reporting started up federal investigations that also opened past cases of deaths and injuries, including the one at Pyramid World years ago. Agents from OSHA and representatives from Congress began doing interviews up and down The Strip. C. D. heard from Greta that Sheperd's team from Pyramid World might be on their list. He spent hard nights thinking this through, even going for the bottle of scotch to help him sleep. At his desk at work, he felt sick, fighting back waves of nausea. Finally, he resolved that if he were called, he would tell the truth. Before he could set up a meeting with Sheperd to inform him of his decision, as if by a sixth sense, Sheperd unexpectedly dropped by his office. He stood in the doorway and said, "The guys down in Houston will handle this. They've got the connections" (implying with the Bush administration, the "guys" major contributors and fellow Texans). "You're on a list but they probably won't get to you. If they do, it's okay by me to tell them all you know. I mean, what do you really know? What do any of us know? You got that? Reinhart?"

"Got it," he said. "And I will. I'll tell them."

"Let's just get this over with and get it done," Sheperd said, nodding once, agreed, then he headed off briskly down the hall in the direction of Kinkaid's office in accounting.

In the end, though C. D. assumed Lance Sheperd and other higher-ups eventually did speak to investigators, no one at his level would be called for an interview. Federal investigations take years. Even with all the exposés by the *Las Vegas Sun* and increasing pressure from the unions, new safety regulations wouldn't find their ways into law for more than three years. Still, safety improved, at least somewhat. Mancini Construction and its many subcontractors agreed to add supervisory staff and weekly safety reviews, as well as to clean up some of the mess. There were no more serious injuries at Biscayne Bay. Everywhere one looked, high towers kept rising up and down The Strip and in all directions across the city, tall cranes like the masts of great sailing ships in the desert sky.

– 5 –

In college, for a class in Shakespeare's tragedies, one of C. D.'s assignments had been a close study of *King Lear*. At the end of the play, Lear carries his dead daughter Cordelia onto the stage, in torment that he will never know her alive again. He cries out pathetically: "Never, never, never, never, never." The professor started the class off by reading this scene at the end. Then he asked them to page back to the first act, when Lear asks Cordelia what she can say of her devotion to him that might justify his planned bequests. The king's most beloved daughter answers: "Nothing, my Lord." The word "nothing" is repeated four more times in their exchanges, closing with Lear saying: "Nothing can come from nothing. Speak again."

She does not. So the class learned how tragedy can happen in a conceptual space between *nothing* and *never*, everything in between becoming some otherworldly playing out of actions already doomed. Thinking back on the two chaotic, stress-filled years spent working on Biscayne Bay, C.D. would recall that class and how, as with so many life lessons, he only understood it too late.

Biscayne Bay managed to get two-thirds built before Lehman Brothers crashed and burned, the first catastrophe of the world financial crisis. That horrifying Sunday night in September 2008, Sheperd, backed up by C. D., designer Brick Rico, and Gary Luongo, were entertaining a handful of visiting investment bankers in for the weekend at Carnevino, a posh restaurant in the Sands group's new tower, Palazzo. At the table that evening, talk circled cynically around the question of if America would ever elect a black man to be president, especially one named Barack *Hussein* Obama—what were the Democrats thinking? Not in a million years, and especially not with that attractive new VP candidate, that "hot babe" McCain had chosen, surely to split the Hillary vote, what a game-changing move by the good ol' GOP. The mood at the table turned more upbeat, anticipating new rounds of tax breaks after the election.

BlackBerrys started going off, i-Phones ringing, one guy after the other leaping out of his seat to field calls about Lehman Brothers going down. The federal bailout the financial world had been assured would happen had collapsed (there went $600 billion, *poof*, the first domino in a Rube Goldberg–like structure of financial firms tipping over in a chain reaction *click-clicking* into a mess). Prime steaks were left to go cold. Before ten minutes had passed, Lance Sheperd hurried off to McCarran Airport to take the company jet first down to Houston to meet with the Gravenstein partners, then on to New York. The visiting bankers fled too, the ones who had flown in on commercial airlines begging for rides from the ones with private jets. They all rushed off like so many doctors on call, only no mere medical emergency could strike any physician with that degree of terror. It was a terror possible to taste as C. D., Luongo, and Rico were left to settle the humongous bill. They felt an electric charge all around them like a sudden overdose of ozone in the atmosphere. C. D.'s tongue contracted in his mouth, a reaction that made him recall times as a kid when he had licked the terminals of a nine-volt battery—that cringing sting, his mouth filling with saliva. He was witnessing a new kind of terror, and he felt it too—apocalyptic fear, a fear of everything erased, a fear of vast, desolate spaces filled with nothing. Financing for Biscayne Bay had been wiped out in a day.

He didn't know what he expected when he told Grace, which he didn't do until the next morning, not that he needed to, as she had come to her own conclusions from reading the news.

"We could lose everything," she said, staring at her piece of dry toast and half a grapefruit, her breakfast on her latest diet. She paused, thinking this over, then added stoically, "And maybe that's not such a bad thing. Maybe the country needs this to come to its senses."

"You can't mean that, Grace," he said.

"Do you really believe a rat race like this can go on forever?"

He drew in a deep breath and started to say something, but he didn't know what it could be. Later, he convinced himself she was only getting herself ready psychologically, a bitter fatalism preparing for the worst. And at his job, it proved difficult not to believe in the very worst, all financing brokered by Lehman Brothers to complete Biscayne Bay reduced to ashes.

Construction suddenly halted. Nothing anyone on Sheperd's team had ever witnessed compared to the tension in the office during the weeks that followed—it felt like a threat of nuclear war, everyone waiting for the missiles to launch, the entire planet in danger of a meltdown followed by a nuclear winter, businesses left radioactive for who knew how many half-lives into the future. In Project Development, lower-ranking staff started leaving, taking more permanent jobs elsewhere, so each day, they had to deal with a crisis to hire enough competent people to perform the tasks that remained. Lance Sheperd threatened to walk too, if the Gravenstein partners didn't agree to stay in Houston and not distract him from putting his fullest energies into all the pitching and financial contortions and good-buddy favor-collecting to replace the $800 million in vaporized financing Biscayne Bay still needed to complete construction.

Their team worked overtime, staging presentation after presentation for the duets and trios of prospects Sheperd's relentless calls brought to town from all over the world—bankers, hedge fund guys, hard-edged representatives of China's limitless government funds, Canadian oil guys, a half dozen Arab sheikhs fastidiously dressed in their Saville Row suits. Day after day into the nights, their team ran through their prepared scripts and tap dances in the conference room. C. D. showed off the HD digital animations of "the Bay Life" in all its youthful hedonism on the jumbo LCD-TV screen. Brick Rico stepped in to pitch his prize-winning interior designs that spared no luxury; then Greta Olsson talked up marketing campaigns, her voice and manner powered by her flirtatious charms; then C. D. took over from Greta to show off statistics on the promising projected growth of the wealthy youth demographic and the considerable work he had done already on IT penetration into potential sales by microtargeting; finally, Kinkaid ran over the actual costs versus projected revenues, which were changing by the hour. After their presentations, Sheperd hosted expensive dinners at Le Buchon or Picasso or Guy Savoy, then Gary Luongo picked up these potential new partners in a long blue Bay Life limousine stocked with boutique vodkas and single-malt scotches and gorgeous working girls holding out trays of cocaine. Luongo performed his hosting magic, nobody asking any questions when he turned in his sky-high expense reports. Doing all this, they began to feel more confident again—how could this *not* work, when it had always worked so well? All seemed to be going smoothly, except for a faint, tinny edge of desperation in their voices, C. D. thought, that made their hard-sell pitching sound too hard.

Six weeks later, Sheperd *had* pulled it all together, with help from his team, yes, but mostly on his own, untangling the mess of completion financing from the Lehman Brothers catastrophe. Representatives from two major players bellied up to Biscayne Bay to place their bets—earnest-seeming guys from Deutsche Staatsbank and the Bank of the Nation, that good ol' "B of N"—banks that would soon be flush not only with Bush administration bailout cash but able also to leverage all that near-zero-interest money being pumped into the economy from the Federal Reserve. Only now, government agencies watched over their shoulders to make sure they followed new, stricter rules—the banks couldn't just bet those tens of billions of taxpayer dollars on tricky financial paper and phony mortgages as easily as they had in the past, on those fancy "bundles" and "derivatives" they had grown so rich on from collecting fees. As one of the guys from the B of N put it: "Right now, we're looking for anything *solid* and *real* to keep the meter running."

Nothing more real, more solid-looking, than a sixty-story resort hotel in Las Vegas. So both banks signed on, adding no little pressure to Kinkaid's calculations because the banks held up Sheperd for a half point higher interest plus $20 million more in fees for up-front "capital costs" than the original financing. Could Biscayne Bay make it with these numbers? Kinkaid and his team kept ironing out the steadily falling gross revenue projections, squeezing them into shape. The day the banks signed on, relief blew through the office like a cooling breeze. And a feeling like divine deliverance lifted up the ranks of the four thousand construction workers who had been left idle and without pay for six straight weeks. By the end of October, after that near-death experience, construction on Biscayne Bay started up again, announced by banner headlines in the local press.

C. D.'s last one-on-one meeting with Lance Sheperd happened late on the Friday following the final signatures on the new completion financing, complex pieces of his salvage deals locked into place. News had spread through the office with high fives and cheers. None of the Project Development team had dropped any tasks during the crisis, not even when the crane had stopped moving over the unfinished construction. C. D. got in mock-ups of graphic displays for internet ads from his design team at SKR Partners. He needed to run them by Sheperd, along with his latest brainstorm to change the marketing plan to include discounted pricing for different "levels" of "the Bay Life"—deals and upgrade offers at prices that would rise and fall at irregular intervals six and seven times a day, with "shock discounts" that could be blasted out over email, Facebook, and Twitter alerts. Doing this should develop a customer base always on the watch, the "kids" he targeted afflicted with a Bay Life–induced ADHD, obsessively checking their new smartphones for the latest price alert that would last only thirty minutes, max, so they could snap up the most discounted package. Keep them tuned in, then hit them with flash offers they would have a hard time refusing.

He made his way through the two outer offices set up like barriers to the boss. His appointment was the last of Sheperd's day. Sharon Greene had already gathered up her things, ready to go home. As she let him into Sheperd's corner suite, she cautioned, "Don't keep him too long. He hasn't been out of the office all week."

That so many of his staff had hung in there with him through all the overtime hours during the crisis proved their devotion to Sheperd. Only now, crisis over, did they show the effects of the trauma of the past six weeks. Since that terrible night in Black September, the sour electric taste in their mouths had lingered. Everyone on the team moved through the hallways with exhaustion now, and a shocked, thousand-yard stare—they had glimpsed the apocalypse, worse than any nightmare. Well past 5 p.m., the lights of the Hilton parking garage glowed in the distance through the modest window behind Sheperd in his office. C. D. found him sitting in a slumped posture over the Donald Judd table he used as his desk, his ice-blue eyes staring off as if hypnotized into that spookily empty, swirling gray surface of his table. His telephone was the only object within reach, as ever a landline. Sheperd had never thought cell phones were secure enough for business calls, so he used a quaint black console phone that connected him via actual wires inside its spiraling cords.

Sheperd looked like he had aged ten years, eyelids so heavy with exhaustion that they pressed into a squint, the old white boxing scar over his left eyebrow standing out starkly whiter against his pale complexion spotted with small red blotches, like bruises. Holed up for weeks under siege in this stripped-down office, a roll of paunch now strained at his waistline since he had been too busy to work out. Random, wiry gray hairs stuck up from the top of his usually close-cut dome—he hadn't been out of the office long enough to visit his barber. C. D. had anticipated a mood of relief, and at least some renewed energy, the boss pumping up the Bay Life again in celebration. Not this, like he had just intruded on news of a death in the family.

"Hey, *he-ey!*" C. D. said, putting extra energy into his voice as he sat down. "We *got some* again, thanks to you, Lance. Congratulations!"

Sheperd didn't react. C. D. opened his laptop and turned it on, waiting for Sheperd to speak, but he only stared at him as if from the dark side of the moon. C. D. considered all that must have been running through his head—the many affairs of his empire, his properties on four continents, his hundreds of millions in assets, his busy shell games to come up with the tens of millions in payments to keep all that going, and he understood that for Sheperd, a lot more than Biscayne Bay must have been tottering at the brink. He wondered how much of his own wealth Sheperd had sunk into Biscayne Bay. Kinkaid kept guessing about half, but it might have been more, at least $200 million of his own money.

So no wonder he looked tired.

"Should we do this another time?" C. D. asked. "Lance? . . ."

"Naw. It's all right," Sheperd said. His cheeks puffed, weakly. C. D. clicked through to his sample presentation, loaded it into slideshow mode, set the laptop on the table, and swiveled the screen so Sheperd could see. The boss only glanced at it briefly then gazed off into the air over C. D.'s shoulder toward an upper edge of a black-and-white swirl on canvas, one of the fantastically expensive minimalist works he preferred. Sheperd had decorated his office with Spartan functionality—plain charcoal carpet, two large black lithographs on the walls like asphalt rolled onto paper by Richard Serra, the gray Judd table he used as a desk, and two black office chairs, all illuminated by stark white halogen lighting. This represented his aesthetic these days—everything reduced to a few functional objects in an absence of color: black and white only, gray tones in between.

The ad campaign Sheperd wanted for "the Bay Life" reflected a similar aesthetic—the anorectic girl models with half-dead eyes, like they had just shot up with heroin, their starved bodies bandaged in bikinis and their skinny legs spread out, straddling chaise lounges. Always at least two and in some ads as many as four buffed, unshaven, rough-looking guy models in bulging thongs were positioned on either side of the one lone anorectic girl. The shots were off balance in arrangement, the male models packed into a group, in postures of indifference, at the edge of the central image of the wasted-looking girl. This photo series had been shot in grainy, high-contrast black-and-white, the effect like the first shocking images after a gang bang; or, even darker than this, like the dead-eyed girl had just fulfilled some sick, abusive fantasy. C. D. meant to talk to Sheperd about this new campaign, not sure the images would read with any impact when reduced to fit a pop-up box on a computer screen. He preferred to use hollow-cheeked close-ups of the starved-looking girl and rough guy faces set against the ultra-contemporary background of the turquoise hotel to get at least some color into the shots. In general, C. D. didn't agree with this approach to marketing the Bay Life that suggested danger and sexual decadence, this selling of luxury by appealing to death wishing. Still, he understood why, recalling his studies of the German playwright Bertolt Brecht—his famous maxims on alienation and estrangement, the *Verfremdungseffekt*—how merry little tunes should accompany tragedy, how sad songs should promise joy. He understood what Sheperd wanted, and both he and Greta had delivered: disturb the guests first, then bring them in for happy sins.

"What do you think?"

"Grace all right?" Sheperd asked.

"Tense," C. D. said. "She's all right now, though, thanks to you. Thanks for asking. Are you all right? Are we all okay now?"

"No," Sheperd said. "We may be all right, as far as it goes *here*, for now. But nothing else is all right. And it's not going to be all right, either, *anywhere*," he said.

He coughed, his voice hoarse, no doubt from the hundreds of hours he had talked nonstop on the phone. He shifted his gaze to the laptop screen, not looking at it so much as through it as he kept talking on in a hoarse, deflated voice. "We really *did* something here. Not only here but in America," he said. "We created the greatest culture of wealth in human history. Nothing can compare to it, not anywhere, not anytime. We promised an ownership society. And people who never had the chance to own a house before bought houses. It was working, too, it really was, and we could still have *made* it work, we *could* have. . ."

He paused, unnaturally for him, as if to let his tired thoughts catch up to his words, then continued in an even weaker, hoarser voice. "We could have made it all work if the average guy could have just hung in there and kept believing in the system. And if he had had the *guts* to live up to his obligations, fucking *keep* his promises. He didn't. He just wasn't up to it. That's what happened. It's that simple. That guy let us down. . ."

Sheperd stopped, as if waiting for C. D. to say something. He knew from experience that Sheperd didn't expect him to—he wasn't a man who engaged much in conversations. He took in reports, then he asserted his thoughts and pitches, expecting others to listen. "The average guy out there's blaming Wall Street. He wants to form a lynch mob to go after the bankers and traders. He wants to string up the people who've put in more hard hours than they've ever even *thought* of working to keep this whole fucking economy running. Blame *them?*" He jerked up straighter, like he had been punched in the chest. He searched into C. D. with deep, wounded eyes. "Have they ever worked that fucking *hard?* As hard as me and you and Kinkaid and Greta and everybody here is working? *That* hard? And now that it's all gone to shit, how many guys out there do you suppose are man enough to look at themselves in the mirror and say, fuck *you,* asshole, *you* did this? How many will admit that *they're* the idiots who signed the damned papers without reading the fine print first? What did they *expect? What?* Now they're blaming *us* for selling them the dreams they wanted to buy."

A long, uncomfortable moment passed, Sheperd at the edge of tears.

"I don't know, Lance," C. D. said, gently. "We'll just have to get through this. . ."

As if all business again, Sheperd reached out and tilted the laptop screen to a better angle, the computer still cycling through its stark slide show of Bay Life images. He examined them, but only managed a few seconds of concentration before he lost focus again. He breathed out, his cheeks puffing, and gave up looking at the screen. With an effort, he lifted his stocky body out of his chair and started pacing behind his table.

"Money is an illusion," Sheperd said. "It's just another *idea*. . . scraps of paper, that's it, that's all it is. Two parties get together and say this is worth such and such, that's worth so and so. I'll do this for you and you'll do this for me. Or they both place a bet, chips on the table. Then it's done, all set, they both *get some* and they make their trade. What the *fuck* is so fucking difficult to understand in that? It's enough to make you laugh," he said. "You gotta laugh, or you'll end up killing somebody. Am I right?"

C. D. nodded. He watched Sheperd move out from behind his desk, some of his old energy returning, arms pumping at his sides. C. D. understood that he should get up too, that their meeting was over before it really began. "What a waste," Sheperd said. He tried to laugh but the sound caught in his throat as if in a knot. "A fucking *waste*. . ."

"The, ah. . .mock-ups?" C. D. asked. He closed the laptop and tucked it under his arm. "Are these all right? Or should we go with the face shots instead, the ones I've marked?"

"Whatever you think," Sheperd said, putting a hand on C. D.'s back, ushering him toward the door as if he had just remembered some sudden urgency. "You decide. Whatever you say."

"Let's just get this baby finished," C. D. said.

"Almost finished," Sheperd said, but with a bright, glad-handing tone that made C. D. stop moving. "Close to done, anyway," he said with less energy, and in that hoarse voice like a vinyl record when the needle scratches over grooves. C. D. sensed his boss didn't believe it anymore. Sheperd stepped in closer and said, "Just remember, Reinhart. When they talk about me. . .when they talk about us. . .about *us*. . .be sure to tell them that we built *real things* here. We took nothing for ourselves that we didn't plow straight back into these magnificent hotels and casinos most people never dreamed they could afford to experience. We really *did* something here. . .You'll tell them, right? You'll tell them we did something here? Reinhart?"

Sheperd's worn face tilted up at him, pleading.

"Lance, please," C. D. said. "It's none of my business, but you could use some rest. As your friend, I mean it. Take a week. Go to Malibu. Or France. Wherever you like to go. . .Take a trip with your daughters. Get on a plane and get away."

"Maybe I will," Sheperd said. "Get my girl to go with me," he added with a quick smirk of locker-room conspiracy. Then, all business once more, Sheperd turned abruptly and said over his shoulder, "Just get it done."

On his way out through the two barrier offices, C. D. passed Greta Olsson on her way in, smartly dressed in a Dior suit and revealing lace top, her makeup freshened, radiating a sharp sting of perfume. She let out a flustered breath and said, as if he'd asked, "It's just *dinner*. God!"

He smiled, falsely, and said nothing.

That would be C. D.'s last one-on-one meeting with Lance Sheperd. The boss didn't come to the office the next day. He took time off, more than a week, only slipping in quietly one morning to sit with attorneys to sign more papers. After that, he left more work to his team, all through that fall out of the office more than in it, slow to return phone calls, Sharon Greene not telling anyone where he was. Rumors ran that the Gravenstein partners were somehow forcing Sheperd out. Still, Sheperd's team continued working, sailing along on the dangerous currents, powered by the winds of new agreements with the banks to finish building Biscayne Bay. Through the winter and into early spring—that year when it seemed the whole world reached for hope in the inauguration of President Barack Hussein Obama—one quarter more of Biscayne Bay would be completed, the shimmering blue buildings continuing their rise over the city.

– 6 –

That autumn of such apocalyptic fear included four intense weeks when the new house filled with people for the first time—more than filled, overfilled—after Grace opened it up to volunteers for the "Barack Obama for President" campaign. Eager kids were bussed in from California to help bring in swing-state Nevada. Hosting the Obama kids had helped C. D. to make it through. What a high time that had been, ten to fifteen college students coming and going through their big house day and night, a rainbow coalition of young people all dressed in big "o" sunrise-logo T-shirts. They spread out with their packs and duffel bags in the guest suite, upstairs in Catherine's bedroom, on the pullout sofa in Grace's office, and on air mattresses in his exercise room. Nights, the Obama kids draped themselves all over in the great room and living room, tired out and sunburned from hiking around all day canvassing Las Vegas and Henderson neighborhoods, yet still so powered up by all that hope. So much hope that, during the worst weeks of the financial panic, even C. D. grew hopeful. Grace finished work early so she could join the campaign in the afternoons, manning the phone banks at the Dina Titus for Congress office in Green Valley. And she pulled out all the stops on food, setting up cases of organic juices, laying out sandwich makings in the dining room, a big kettle of her vegan chili simmering away and replenished 24/7 in the kitchen. She baked rafts of lasagna and tossed up tubs of salads that she ran down to the campaign offices to feed hungry volunteers every day. Even as C. D. grew tenser and more strained with the emergency at the office, Grace seemed ever more empowered and moved by all that hope.

They also gave money, seemingly endlessly clicking those online buttons marked "contribute" that kept popping up on email—that in addition to his usual (and obligatory) checks to both political parties and their candidates at his job. Then came Election Day, and the ebullient Election Night party that drew at least ten thousand people to the ballrooms at the Rio to watch on stadium-array screens that heart-stopping walk out onstage in Chicago by the president-elect with his three beautiful girls and then hear his acceptance speech, punctuated by cutaway shots to joyous multitudes all over the globe. Grace hosted a big after party for the Obama volunteers—the biggest party the Reinharts had ever thrown. That whooping, hollering throng of up to a hundred or so campaign kids kept the new house alive with music and dancing that lasted past dawn and well into the next day. C. D. had been a little miffed by this at the time, anticipating cleaning up crumpled napkins, plastic cups, and cigarette butts from the desert landscaping for weeks afterward. Still, he had to admit it—the new house had never felt so alive.

The Obama kids left behind a breeze of hope that cycled through the central heat exchangers for weeks afterward, hope humming up out of the vents all over the new house. Grace and C. D. kept breathing in this charged air to keep their spirits lifted through the tense months of the economic slide and into the following spring, when it felt as though some monstrous force were crushing out all the air in the city like the way he had pressed his knees on the air mattresses the Obama kids had slept on to flatten them, and later, when it felt as though almost everyone in Las Vegas went out to their garages or driveways eager to drive off to their jobs only to discover all four tires on their cars gone flat—nobody was going anywhere. He didn't tell Grace what he really thought of Obama, his conclusion taking shape gradually, after the inauguration: he knew a great actor when he saw one. What a masterful performance, one for the history books, the best candidate ever, until, once Obama was sworn in as president and tasked with governing the whole complex bureaucracy and anthill of lobbyists and special interests, C. D. would come to understand that, no matter how many happy slogans about hope and change, very little really changes, and that, in the end (and maybe not the man's fault), for C. D. and Grace, people like them, *it's all the same, the same, the same . . .*

– 7 –

That day came when the banks broke their contracts and pulled out of the whole deal: *game over*. No matter the contracts and promissory notes, both banks in legal actions refused to let loose the remainder of the $800 million to complete construction of Biscayne Bay. The banks couldn't have guaranteed a bankruptcy better if they had stage-managed it from the beginning. And maybe they had. Kinkaid swore the banks must have planned it this way, their trading arms all along buying credit default swaps, betting the project would fail so they could pocket tens of millions more in federal bailout money after their armies of lobbyists had made sure in Congress that their swaps would be covered. Add to this that both banks, along with their Arab partners, were ass-over-teakettle committed to pouring money into the mind-boggling construction costs of Oz Resorts' $7 billion Metropolis—the most ambitious and expensive resort project in human history at that time finally guaranteed by the arm-twisting of Nevada senator Harry Reid, the Majority Leader of the U.S. Senate. Kinkaid believed the banks had joined in a conspiracy with Oz Resorts to cut the throats of any competition. Either way, the $2 billion already invested was wasted, as Biscayne Bay stood unfinished, towering sixty stories into the air, silent and empty, like an ugly blue exclamation point for a ruined city.

Lance Sheperd had been driven out by then. Details emerged that the partners from Gravenstein LLC wrote conditions into the new financing deals that had wrested control away from him. That's why Sheperd had started disappearing so much from his office, heading out on trips as if on the excuse of needing to take more time off for the sake of his health. He turned up or checked in just enough to give his team a sense of security, casual about his absences, trading on the team's solid faith that if this were any real crisis, the boss would never leave the office. Through the last weeks of the final fall of Biscayne Bay, one or another of the Gravenstein partners would appear (rarely the same one) to look over their shoulders and send out threatening memos about costs, then make upbeat statements for the business press either from Las Vegas or, toward the end, from their headquarters down in Houston. Manic headlines claimed that Gravenstein LLC had found new financing one day, then the next day, bankruptcy loomed. The orphaned employees still came in every morning to the offices, collecting their pay, working on their own, not knowing what would happen next. They felt as trapped in their offices as inmates in their cells. As long as the new hotel tower kept rising, the team would labor away, convinced that a miraculous reprieve would surely happen—hadn't it always?—only this time, Lance Sheperd had vanished for real, gradually then suddenly.

The day the final word came down, a hired specialist no one had ever seen before turned up exactly at noon and began distributing termination notices. She made her grim rounds with brown envelopes stamped "Confidential" in red ink, one for each employee, to be signed for on her clipboard. A half dozen security guards followed her into the offices to observe the packing up, hired by lawyers for the receivership.

Under watch by a guard, C. D. gathered up his few things—his nerf ball and mini-basketball net, his photo of Grace and Catherine in its silver frame, his old-fashioned electronic agenda that he still relied on, a silver pen set awarded to him by the mayor for excellence in the industry, the orange vest he had taken to wearing on site visits so crane operators might spot him before he got in the way of any swinging steel, his few office books, his aspirins. He unplugged the portable hard drive on which he had stored his new data files and placed that in a box too, ready for the guard to step in and say something about taking this but the guard said nothing. When he reached up to the wall and removed the dark, smudgy lithograph of an image like a dirty planet he had bought during that fateful gallery meeting with Lance Sheperd, the guard wasn't going to let him take it until C. D. showed him on the back of its boxlike, unmatted "float" frame that it still had the frame shop's receipt taped to it with his name. That filthy ball of galactic dust had stared down at him through all these tension-filled months. From time to time, at work at his desk, he had let his mind drift off into its dark textures, fearing this very moment he was now living.

Greta was away, off on sick leave to another rehab to address her drinking problem, or so she had said. C. D. found the receivership specialist in charge and explained, and she let him in to Greta's office. Greta had never cluttered up her office with many objects from her personal life, instead carrying everything with her on her laptop or on flash drives and in her big messy purses. Like a gypsy, Greta buzzed around, bubbling with chatter from task to task and place to place, so little remained in her office—a backup pair of nylons in a top desk drawer, an old makeup case in a mess of spilled powder, a half-smoked pack of cigarettes, a tin of chewing gum, a nearly empty bottle of perfume. C. D. recalled seeing a photo of her father in an oak frame, a rustic-looking old guy in a green-checked flannel shirt, sleeves rolled up over his thick wrists and workman's hands, but it wasn't there. He opened file drawers, disorganized and overstuffed with irrelevant memos and copies, crap to leave behind. Where were her other things? The signed books, most by politicians, on her shelves? The spare blouse and business suit always hanging behind her door? The backup shoes?

Gone. He searched the top of her filing cabinet. In whatever office Greta had occupied over the years, she had always placed her Cinderella crystal slipper on top of a filing cabinet or some other space high up where the glass facets could catch light, like a trophy—that practical joke and token of friendship he had sent to her after the first time he had covered for her, his reply to the gaudy ridiculous flower arrangement she had sent to let him know how much she had both appreciated and did not appreciate his stepping into her role for that soulless press release after Lester Stahl had fallen to his death and the sad errand that followed. C. D. recalled Greta's laugh when she had phoned him to acknowledge the gift of the glass slipper, that loud *haa*-hah, like a jarring, ding-donging bell, the same brash laugh she had used so differently with him later, that night in New York, after which nothing between them would be the same. The glass slipper was a reminder of the competitive charge they shared, and maybe of something else, too, something he didn't want to think about now. He examined the top of the filing cabinet where he remembered seeing it last. He noted a dust trail from where she must have snatched it away and stuffed it in her purse. It struck him then—Greta had known this day was upon them long before any of them. As ever, she hadn't let anyone know what she knew.

The day Greta left for rehab, she had dropped in at the office briefly. C. D. had walked her out to her car, trying to talk sense into her that she shouldn't be driving, not as shaky as she seemed after drinking her way through the past tense weeks. She was off to Hazelden this time, a real twelve-step rehab, not one of those spa-like spin-dries in California she had checked into last time. Drive all the way to Minnesota? All that way? Why not fly? Was she crazy?

"The long drive will do me good," she said. She climbed into her car, a silver BMW the same model as his own, but with scratches and dents she hadn't fixed. As he leaned through the window, a smoke stench rose up at him mixed with a woman's sour perfume. A tangle of clothes still on hangars filled the back seat, the back seat floor heaped with a jumble of what must be fifty pairs of shoes. What a mess, and Greta was too. He didn't mask his reaction. She noted this. She folded her arms over the steering wheel and slumped her forehead against them. "God, God, I'm *ruined,*" she said.

"It's going to be all right. Lance will get us through, you'll see," he said.

"Bad people. Bad decisions. Bad men. That's me. . ."

He thought of her last bad boyfriend, a commercial real estate salesman—another guy in gold chains and white shoes. It struck him how deeply she might have gone *all in* with that guy, hinting months ago that she might be sinking what remained of her nest egg into commercial real estate, that bubble now gone bust, too. Greta might be facing far worse than Biscayne Bay falling into receivership. C. D. still didn't believe it would.

"Come on. What is it they tell you in those places? This too will pass?"

He started to reach in through the window to give her a friendly squeeze, meaning to comfort her. She reacted like she'd been stung by a bee and slapped his hands away. "Fuck *you,*" she said. "What do *you* know? What did you *ever* know?"

She pressed a button and the window closed. With a bitter expression, she started the engine and pulled out of her parking space, tires shrieking, leaving him calling out after her to take care of herself, please, not to worry, his voice echoing in the concrete cavern of the garage.

He had believed his reassurances. Three weeks ago, he had still believed.

He should have known. And they really did know, all on the team, buried underneath their forced optimism as they kept on working through those last terrible weeks. Just before he disappeared from the office for good, Sheperd had called his team into the conference room one last time to pump them up with possibilities for last-minute financing deals that he and the Gravenstein partners were working on to pull them through, not to mention all the pressure by their attorneys to force the banks to honor their contracts—some of that fast-talking Sheperd energy reinforced by his rage at the injustice of it all, no way would he let the banks get away with this and end up so screwed. Afterward, the team headed back to their desks to keep slogging away, their inner voices still talking themselves into believing him.

Later that week, word ran through the offices that Sheperd had left town, cancelling all his appointments. Sharon Greene took an unplanned vacation. Kinkaid heard from custodial staff that the art in Sheperd's office had been removed in the middle of the night. Could this be true? C. D. doubted Lance would take off on them like this, without a word. Still, the door to his office and to Sharon Greene's office guarding it were locked. They could have found out for sure. They could have talked or even bribed their way in with cleaning staff or security. But deep down, they didn't want to know. Outside, at the nearby construction site on Las Vegas Boulevard, the tall crane still lifted its loads, workers still moved high above in the dizzying heights. Their paychecks still appeared in the mail room or by direct deposits into their accounts. How much self-deception is possible in a life?

After looking around Greta's office, more as a show for the security guard than any other reason, C. D. tossed a few items from her desk into a box: the nylons, the makeup pouch, the gum. Back in his own office, he filled three more boxes. He made four trips to his car, the last with his lithograph balanced under his chin, joining in a grim parade with forty-two other full-time employees still left in the executive offices, what remained of the almost two hundred who had started off with their team, all clutching boxes and personal items and filing out of that sterile temporary office floor into the elevator that would take them down the three stories to leave the building for the last time.

They gathered in a group like in a grim reception line at a makeshift guard station set up near the elevators so they could hand in their passkey cards and sign forms. The mood among them remained quiet, and stricken, as at a funeral. No security lockdowns. Nothing like he had heard about at other companies, where employees had shown up to find chains and padlocks on office doors. At Biscayne Bay, there was no need for this, so little left worth stealing in any case. With each trip down on the elevator, as they carried out their things, a security guard escorted them to the lobby, not so much to check them out as to complete yet one more formality of this sad universal ritual of bankruptcy in which they were all playing out their roles to the bitter end.

On the last ride down, C. D. stood shoulder to shoulder with Kinkaid and two of the office staff from accounting, Sarah and Katie. They tried not to knock into each other with their armloads of things. "No severance," Katie said, her suspicious gaze searching out the men for a reaction. "None."

Kinkaid didn't answer. Why make things worse? After a moment, he asked too cheerfully, "Anyone for drinks? McCormick and Schmicks? On me?"

The women from accounting gave him a death stare. Kinkaid shrugged and looked to C. D., who avoided eye contact, not able to acknowledge what was happening in any personal way yet, which is what Kinkaid wanted. Kinkaid was that congenial guy always ready to buddy up and get a group going no matter what, that guy ever on the hunt for friends. He had always operated in the workplace with the same set of social skills he had learned in high school. In an unprecedented situation like this, he'd need more than ever to find a group to hang out with so he could know how to respond and do just what they did. He was a first-rate accountant, nobody better at putting together a staff and managing the millions of numbers and tons of paper plus all the pressure of such a complicated machinery as building a new hotel. But in social skills, he was still that kid looking to others to know how to behave.

C. D. wanted nothing of Kinkaid right now. That would come later, when they were struck by the full shock that they really had lost everything. So yes, he needed to discuss and absorb these losses with Kinkaid. But he couldn't do this now. He wasn't in denial, just not up to any face time with Kinkaid that could lead to the question: which one of us got the other *into* this? That would have to wait for the weekend, when C. D. would pick up a bottle of Crown Royal Blue, Kinkaid's favorite, and bring it over to his place. They would hole up in his upstairs study, away from Pam and his demanding teenage boys. They would go over the numbers, make a few calls, see what might be salvaged, until they had downed enough drinks to be able to admit to each other that they would end up with zip, nada, nothing. He would do these honors as Kinkaid's friend, as well he should. Right now, though, he had to get down to the lobby and run away from him. He had to hurry up and make it to his car—one thing he still controlled—as fast as he could.

The elevator settled at the lobby floor, the doors whooshing open. Kinkaid pushed out first, everyone else making way, jostling and turning with boxes and bulky objects in their arms. Only then did Sarah from accounting let go a few tears she had been holding back with a hushed sob. Kinkaid stepped ahead of them through the doors onto the street. He looked up. C. D. and the women from accounting and a few of the others pushed out onto the sidewalk and gazed up too. Looming over them, the concrete superstructure and skeletal beams of Biscayne Bay stood imposingly, most of the lower floors already hung with brilliant turquoise glass. No workers were in sight anymore, not one. On top of the unfinished tower, mounted high up on its bare white spine, the tall crane had stopped moving.

"You see that?" asked Kinkaid.

Nobody answered. Construction had been stopped before, for six weeks, but this was different—no movement at all in the dark mouths of the unfinished floors, all vacant, all gaping now and empty, not one worker to be seen.

"Wow. Nothing," Kinkaid said. He glanced around as if hunting for support from among the milling group. No one knew what to say. He gazed up again, whistling under his breath. Then he said it once more: "Nothing."

– 8 –

Losing his job felt like an illness. Condemned to the limbo of unemployment, it grew harder to get out of bed, and it was all but impossible to sleep. Weeks passed, then months, then the months unbelievably became a year and more, almost two years, life swinging back and forth between a semi-conscious coma and insomnia. C. D. would lie there in bed trying to quiet his busy mind, the master bedroom in the new house suffused by a faint glow from the lights of Las Vegas through the balcony doors. He did his best not to disturb Grace, but half asleep, she still turned to him and asked, "What is it? Are you okay?"

"All okay," he would say. "Go back to sleep."

He rolled to his side and pressed close into the heat of her back, wrapping an arm around her familiar body, nesting his chin in her fragrant hair. He sensed her slowly slipping back into her dreams. And he thought how he had failed her, had carried her along on his crazy chasing after money, a chase as fevered as that of any compulsive gambler until it all went bust: *Game over*. Holding her in bed, anxiety turned inside like an icy corkscrew that she had been drifting away over these past hard months, and soon, she might even leave him. He would deserve it if she left him, he knew. And if she did, he wasn't sure how he would manage to go on living.

As he slid out from under the covers, he watched Grace slumbering, clutching an overstuffed feather pillow like a castaway clings to flotsam as a life preserver. It seemed that the more he suffered from insomnia, the deeper she retreated into sleep. He got up and pushed his feet into the worn-out moccasins he used as slippers. He padded out of the master bedroom and across the open loft space, lined floor to ceiling with his books, more than half as yet unread. All those books had started weighing on him, too—that magnificent library he had collected over the years with sincerest intentions to read all the books amid the busy-crazy rush of his life but somehow never got around to doing. These days, he had too much trouble concentrating. Still, what an impressive library. The whole house was impressive.

From the landing, the off-white walls in the living room reached high up—twenty-two feet. It took a hired miniature cherry picker to change light bulbs way up there so they rarely switched those lights on now because it cost so much to replace them. He gazed up at the vaulted ceiling with its skylight overhead, the effect to create subtle shades at the very edges of perception. What a house. What a tribute to his significance. The effect still thrilled him every time he descended the stairs: the opulence of the Florentine marble and how it transitioned to the warm birch floor in the living room, furnished with doe leather sofas and matching loungers, and far off at one end, the formal dining room with its glass and brushed steel table and chairs glimmering faintly in the predawn light, French doors left open to a low distant humming from Grace's state-of-the-art kitchen.

In the living room, he gazed for a moment at the painting over the fireplace. The early Charles Ellsworth he had acquired in a flash of extravagance glowed with a striking spectrum spread into the shape of a fan. He recalled the excitement of bidding on it at the silent auction, showing off how he belonged among the Las Vegas wealthy and elite. He loved that painting for its emphatic brilliance, for the clarity of its lines. Still, what had possessed him? Three middle-class families might live for a year or more on the price he had paid. He would never be sure Grace had gotten over what he had done, showing off like that, how she had disapproved of him admiring it, so self-satisfied, as if the painting were a mirror reflecting all he had achieved. And now? What was it worth? He didn't think it would be much longer before his prized painting would have to come down and be sold, possibly at a loss. Grace would be right, too, if she insisted on this—what would be the point of hanging onto it now?

As usual these past idle months, in the kitchen, he ground and made coffee, not even counting anymore the hours he had slept since he no longer really slept, could only doze off in fits and starts. This had bothered him at first—he thought he would go crazy from lack of sleep—but he barely thought of this now, accepting insomnia as a new condition of his existence. Coffee mug in hand, he slid open the patio door and stepped into the spacious yard, desert-landscaped with intricate runs of reddish stone and scattered cacti, a line of Italian cypresses planted along the back stone wall to shade the pool. He breathed in the sharp morning air and wished that, somehow, his life could fall into an order and symmetry that matched this careful landscaping. He made his way from the covered patio toward the spiral iron staircase at one end.

He climbed, circling, up to the balcony built off the master bedroom. He could just as easily have risen from bed and taken eight steps and gone out through the balcony door, but he had settled into this new morning routine so as not to wake up Grace. On the balcony, he pulled out a chair and sat down at the small glass table with his coffee. He took in the view that had finally sold him on building this house, the "wow factor" real estate agents had advertised and talked up, that glowing spectacle from the southeast slope of the Las Vegas Valley. He gazed out at the impressive lights fading against the dawn.

Las Vegas: city of second chances, boom town of improbable dreams. He had believed in it once as he had believed in his own second chance, had believed that nothing could ever stop Las Vegas, it would keep spreading out over its desert valley forever. There was nothing like Las Vegas viewed from the air at night—airline passengers cruised over little else but deep blackness below for hundreds of miles, then suddenly, glittering spills of lights appeared from so many new housing tracts and neighborhoods stretching off across the desert floor in celebratory display; and up ahead, in the rough shape of a brilliantly lit cross at its center, shone the multicolored lightshow of The Strip and the glitter of Downtown. Everything pitch black for miles and miles then there it was—all those sky-scraping casino resorts, tens of billions of dollars' worth of concrete, glass, and steel, their mammoth blinking signs promising adventures and fun. All this spread out below, a galaxy of starry lights set into the desert blackness with such deliberate celebration.

Hard to believe there wasn't a single hotel casino *not* at the edge of bankruptcy or already over the edge yet still afloat out there, somehow, still shipping more water, each like a foundering cruise ship that could easily tip over and sink into the desert sands, all that neon blinking off, light by light, into the deep. Sometimes, he wished they would break their backs and go under once and for all and just get it over with, and why not—why not hope they would all drown? After all, they'd set him adrift after almost nineteen years he had put into doing his part to build them. But he couldn't allow himself to think like this. Wishing it would all go to hell would be like giving up, not to mention failing to care about the tens of thousands of people still working whose lives would be ruined if the casino resorts sank back into their sandy foundations, little left but a mythic primeval slime of gangsters and Mob-run corruption layered over by a greasy patina from the Wall Street gang, the money and the power on which Las Vegas had been originally built, then desert winds could blow hauntingly over the emptiness forever. Every day, it was getting harder to will himself into a positive attitude. In his youth, studying to be an actor, he had trained to believe in almost anything—*Acting is believing,* as the saying goes. Lately, as he gazed out at this impressive view, he recalled a warm-up exercise for actors, whispering it, fast, feeling his tongue striking the edges of his top front teeth: *I believe I believe I believe . . .*

What must he believe? That today, his résumé would land on the desk of someone who mattered in this town and that same someone would pick up the phone to set up an interview? After all, he was not an unknown here, he had played his part to build this city into what it was—for almost nineteen years!—so someone in power *must* see this and remember him. He must believe that his nearly two decades of toil to help carry Las Vegas through at least three eras of growth into the new century had not been wasted. He must believe what the Las Vegas Convention Authority advertised in its new campaign, *Vegas is back, baby!* He must believe that its nearly 40 million visitors per year would come winging in once more from everywhere on earth, looking for an *experience,* to this most improbable of cities built on gambling and dreams.

Today, like yesterday, like the day before, after fixing breakfast for Grace and seeing her off to the accounting job doing taxes and filings for so many distressing bankruptcies, a task he knew she hated—the only paycheck left in their strapped household—and after dressing in jeans and a polo shirt as he used to do only on weekends, he would find himself stuck again, sitting in his study, no longer believing in much of anything. Sometimes, to pump up his spirits and keep himself company, he whistled, vague ditties from musicals he knew. Who was it who had written: *The wayfarer whistles in the dark to calm his fears but can't see any clearer*? He couldn't recall. At his computer, he did his daily search of job lists—nothing new.

He checked his LinkedIn—all the same. He sent out three more email queries to positions he had applied for that hadn't answered and never would. He had to work mentally to cool the heat rising inside at how disrespectful this was and rude they were, most of the new HR staffers underpaid kids who didn't know anything about hotels or casinos or even life—what miserable shits they were to leave him like this, ghosted. He fought off visions of strangling them, or better yet, their bosses—those guys at the top who now ruled this city through its three big mega-resort companies: he imagined the kingpins standing shoulder to shoulder in a police lineup from which they should be led off to years in prison for the crime of steering it all onto the rocks, ripping the bottom out of the whole damned boat, rescuing only themselves while watching others drown. But how hypocritical to blame them when, in his own reckless chasing after money, he would have done the same if given the chance.

He didn't want to let his mind spin off into self-recriminations and regret, reviewing his bad decisions and the misplaced trust he had put in others, especially Lance Sheperd. Still, there he would sit, staring into the shooting-star pattern of his screensaver, his inbox still empty of any message that might save him. Needle pricks ran up and down his arms. He fought off the waves of panic at losing everything, all he had invested, all he and Grace had been saving their entire lives. His friends—were they really friends?—had drifted away after he lost his job, his *position* in the world, as though he had contracted some contagious, ugly disease. Gradually, during that first year unemployed, the usual rounds of invitations from work colleagues and business associates to parties, fundraising galas, political dinners, and power lunches had slowed, then stopped entirely: the Slocums, the Chevrons, the upscale, arty crowd at the trendy home of Brick Rico and his partner, Rocky; the politico-filled fests put on by the Rogers and Greenspun families, and by the Adelsons for the right-wing Likud politicians in from Israel or fundraisers for their beloved GOP. Greta Olsson had fled to the icy north, to Minnesota, and had not been heard from since. The monthly lunches with his old work buddy Rick Rickstein had stopped, Rickstein rarely in town anymore since his promotion to the Sands International VP in Singapore. And one morning, C. D. suddenly understood it, like a man standing under a cloudburst with no raincoat or umbrella realizes he's getting soaked: his friends—if they ever had been friends—were avoiding him.

Some of Grace's friends remained—Lien Luu, her manicurist, came to dinner a few times, shocked at the collapse of her investments in old houses, and how, since the crash, her clients had dwindled to so few that she could hardly make a living (even Grace did her own nails about half the time now). She was considering leaving the country, retiring early to her native Vietnam. And Sam from Smith's Grocery, source for town gossip, would drop by for coffee, sometimes accompanied by her long-term partner, Rita, finally recovered from her treatment for breast cancer. Rita had just been laid off from teaching sixth grade by the Clark County Schools. Both were still making it, but only barely. Some Saturday afternoons, or by an impromptu invitation to a simple dinner, the three women would catch up on news of their kids, who had all gone to Green Valley High; then they engaged in nuance-filled girl talk, which to C. D. sounded like a foreign dialect whose drift he could never catch. Though he thought he did his best to be polite by sitting at the table an obligatory hour or so to trade pleasantries and listen to the women commiserate at how tough it was for most people to find jobs, any job, Grace noted his frigidity. She confronted him: "Who do you think you are? You sit there with your nose in the air? Or you glower and mumble like some kind of zombie? These are the only friends we've got left! What happened to *your* friends?"

Friends. Soon, he felt like the only friend he had left in the world was the one person he had least expected to act like a friend. What a gratifying surprise that this should be so, what an unexpected gift, that during those hardest times, Catherine would call him three or four times a month from Los Angeles when she was in her senior year in college; and the following year, after she had enrolled in law school, she called from Seattle. She sensed things weren't going very well, though he told her not to worry, reassured her that everything would come out fine in the end, to which she would ask in such a sincere, grown-up voice, truly wanting to know: "But how are *you?* How are *you* doing?"

They caught up with each other, he and his beloved stepdaughter, talking more and more like friends. That alone could keep him going. As for the rest, in his better moments, he talked himself into believing that his friends must be consumed by their own misfortunes and preferred hiding away. Like him, they drew drapes or plantation shutters closed over the tall windows of their magnificent unpaid-for, *underwater* homes, so they could sit inside unseen, alone and brooding in the dark. Month after month spent looking for work, sending out feelers, networking via hundreds of emails and LinkedIn messages, slamming out calls, shooting off résumés, it gets tougher and tougher to face each new day, pumping up the old belief that luck can change. Faith runs dry at the bottom of the well. Finally, it all reaches a point where the only thing left to do is pray—pray for what?—pray for *recovery*.

Some days, rather than sit there frustrated at his computer, reshaping letters and appeals, he sought renewal in physical workouts in his exercise room, pushing and pulling and pounding it out on his sleek Precor EFX 4.0 elliptical trainer, eager for the injection of mind-altering endorphins he felt sure would lift him into enough optimism to carry him through the rest of the day. Or he would alternate bench-press cycles on the good old BodyCraft KI, faithful pal of athletes, adding on weight in steps, challenging his strength until he felt if he added any more he might burst his lungs. He let loose a long outrushing of breath and sat up, dizzy, spent, and let his head drop between his knees. If he lifted his eyes, he could see himself in the mirrors of the sliding closet doors. He didn't like the sight of the diminishing shape he was in, his body so much leaner and tighter now, stringy and thinner with stress.

His regular routine for years had been one-hour sessions at the Las Vegas Athletic Club with the guys from work during lunch hours, hurried routines filled with competitive put-downs and snarky one-liners amid the clanging noise of the machines and humming voices of the TV set to graphic displays and droll commentaries from the market watch on CNBC. At home, evenings before his shower and bed, if he could fit it in, he would put in a quick half hour in his new exercise room, double that on weekends, just enough to keep his body tuned, at his age the challenge not to lose too quickly what he had made of his body in his youth. Since losing his job, his workouts weren't so much routines as obsessive-compulsive responses to fear. Overdoing it, he wrenched his back, for a week laid up with lumbar spasms like two hot blocks of pain radiating into his hips. He stretched a tendon in his shoulder, feeling a pop and sting under his left shoulder blade that left him unable to lift his arm over his head for a month. Still, he worked out, in fits and starts. Afterward, he would lie on his bed, fighting to cool down and steady his breathing. He thought of hanging himself, how the landing at the top of the staircase could serve as a gallows. He shook off these thoughts. He measured his breaths. He felt the pressure of his heartbeats in his ears.

The day came when "official" unemployment statistics were reported to be 14.6 percent in Nevada (and as high as 15 percent in Las Vegas). Though these "official" statistics would be revised downward years later, the "real" rate was much higher, as it always is. (Which of these measures of misery ever expresses the real reality?) Bottom line—Las Vegas passed Detroit for highest jobless figures in the nation. And Nevada passed all states, highest of the high in percentages for almost two years. Estimates in the press cited 190,000 unemployed workers statewide (the "real" ratio closer to one in five unemployed). And people were leaving, fleeing, as if a great hurricane had struck the city and driven out hundreds of thousands of refugees. The week this dismal headline led the news, C. D. received a threatening letter from the Nevada Department of Employment, Training, and Rehabilitation demanding that he make an appointment "within fourteen days" for an "eligibility review interview" for "verification of your work-search record." To extend his benefits, he would need to show evidence of his hunt for a job—hundreds of emails, letters, and calls over the past year. To collect unemployment, he had been attending dutifully to all the new online forms, a new form every week, it seemed, a bureaucracy transforming into threats, and for what? A piddling few hundred per week? That barely covered the utility bills on their big new house. After two other extensions over more than a year, why now?

He gave himself the news: time was running out on his paltry benefits.

Amid the crush of unemployment insurance claims filed via telephone and the internet in Nevada, C. D. understood that very few claimants were called in to verify work-search records. All sidelined workers usually had to do was register at one of the Nevada Job Connect offices to qualify for making a claim. He had done this after the collapse of Biscayne Bay. Who was it who had said that bankruptcy happens gradually then suddenly? In Las Vegas, there had been very little about it that was gradual—the whole economy had crashed in record time.

C. D. thought a lot about Lance Sheperd these days, too, how he had vanished on the eve of the bankruptcy, beating it out of town without leaving a forwarding address or phone number. His excuse—one left behind by Sharon Greene after she too was suddenly gone—was that he needed to hide out from the press hounding him for quotes. More probably, he was hiding out from process servers. Reporters tracked and wrote about the swift crash and burn of Biscayne Bay along with several other mega-billion-dollar ventures in the city. No one except a few select attorneys knew how to reach Sheperd, and there were rumors all over the business press that he was being hit with multiple legal actions and civil suits as well as investigations for alleged fraud. No reporter could get a comment from him. Sheperd flat out disappeared.

The half-finished hotel tower of Biscayne Bay stood abandoned, the top floors of its sixty stories still windowless, like rows of empty eye sockets gazing out over the southern reaches of The Strip, the unfinished condo towers on either side like two tall, blue glass tombstones. Four thousand workers lost their jobs. Those empty towers didn't stand alone. A messy expanse of heaped-up hulks of concrete crowned by tendrils of rusted rebar like sickly red hairs would be all that was left of the abandoned project called Echelon. One thousand more workers were sent packing, three thousand left without future jobs. Behind a sagging chain link fence, like a universal emblem of industrial decline, all that was left after the implosion of the storied Stardust Hotel & Casino would be a weed-choked, dust-blown field, its sixteen hundred former employees also now unemployed.

Other casino resort companies that had managed to avoid the perils of new construction fell into varying levels of litigation and receivership, or hovered close to bankruptcy. Mammoth Harrah's barely survived, going through a name change (like a vaudeville performer switching hats), ending up calling itself Caesars. With eight hotel casinos in Vegas, one in Laughlin, and four resorts in Atlantic City, Caesars began implementing desperate downsizing measures (laying off two thousand employees), still unclear if it would finally collapse. And Station Casinos, with its eighteen smaller "local" off-Strip stores, was still writhing through seasons of bankruptcy. During the boom years, Harrah's and Station had plunged recklessly into "private capitalization," pushing buyouts of publicly traded shares fueled by markers from investment banks plus all the private-investor capital they could find. Both companies were caught short, bleeding out tens of millions per quarter to service all that new "private" debt, so of course they laid off thousands more loyal workers even as whole squads of top executives responsible for this tangled mess resigned and waved bye-bye, sailing away on their golden parachutes.

None of this compared to the feeding frenzy at Oz Resorts, led by its new young Turk in from Wall Street as CFO, Bill Starling, and guided by its veteran CEO, Roger Terry—always a carpetbagger executive, commuting in and out of Vegas from his Brahmin lifestyle back east. Oz Resorts had bought out Pyramid Resorts; and before that, in its epic appetite for acquisitions, Oz had gobbled up the three oldest Wynn hotels, laying out a map resembling not so much expansion as an empire. Then, like some insatiable monster of the industry food chain, this biggest behemoth in the city went *all in* on its $7 billion Metropolis—the most expensive resort project in human history. Starling brought in financing with a finesse that outmatched any Lance Sheperd had achieved. His concept to build a futuristic, monumental casino resort megalopolis at the heart of The Strip would become a lumbering behemoth that he relentlessly (many said ruthlessly) pushed through to completion, managing this even during the economic collapse. That Bill Starling had pulled this off would be a wonder, though of success or folly, no one could say. As balance to the thousands laid off at other Oz properties, close to eight thousand construction workers eventually would find jobs, and thousands of employees would be hired if Metropolis hotels and casinos finally opened. Still, as an Arab immigrant cab driver C. D. rode with once had put it: "Why would people who come here from a big city want to stay in a metropolis?"

Little can stop a bad idea if it can become a big enough bad idea. The several towers of Metropolis rose all bunched together in the middle of The Strip, a disharmonious collection of glass and steel skyscrapers that looked like the spastic fingers of some monstrous robotic hand. Those ill-conceived ziggurats were packed into a challenged architecture comprised of four new hotels and two condo towers, all connected by a labyrinth of "upscale" shopping corridors boasting designer logos and prices like out of science fiction. The Metropolis towers soon formed their own skyline that reflected a silvery light like gigantic LCD screens stood on end then slammed together at odd angles. To C. D., it all appeared as if shoehorned into too little space, a strangely tilting architecture intended to invoke futuristic dreams now rising at the very heart of The Strip like a Fritz Lang nightmare.

All the other Oz Resorts properties suffered. To finish building "The Met" after the tourist economy had tanked, Oz starved the operating budgets of its other casino hotels, downsizing workforces (a thousand and more, and hundreds in management), the employees who remained pressured into increasing workloads and overstressed schedules. The older hotels were soon so strapped for cash that nothing was left for maintenance or upgrades, their rooms steadily more threadbare and rundown, the properties left to creak along as best they could with falling-apart facilities and antique computer systems, their frustrated, disillusioned employees continually reminded by management how "lucky" they were just to keep their jobs. Especially rankling to C. D. was what they did to The Beach and to Pyramid World—letting paint chip and fade, carpets get threadbare, their once gleaming public spaces growing dull and lackluster under layers of grime. Oz attempted to "unify" the different exotic concepts of their many hotels into similar stripped-down gaming warehouses with plain vanilla interiors, even painting over many of the hieroglyphs at Pyramid Word with a sickly yellowish hue; and at The Beach, once a luxurious Caribbean experience, walking along its corridors and across its vast casino floor now felt like being in any other Oz hotel, guest services hard to find.

Metropolis opened to underwhelming reviews, a major complaint its "lack of service" due to understaffing. Guests waited in long lines for checking in or checking out, and it was catch-as-catch-can for service. After the opening flop of Metropolis, the best Oz Resorts could do to fill rooms was offer discounts at far below its costs, and it started losing millions. Similar stories circulated all over town. Kinkaid crunched the numbers that Steve Wynn's new Wynn and Encore Resorts had to rake in $3 million a day from their casinos just to break even. And mogul Sheldon Adelson, once the third-richest billionaire in America, resorted to forking over billions of his own money to prop up Sands stock prices and keep the doors open on the Venetian and Palazzo in Las Vegas. Sands stock fell to a price per share a few cents lower than the cost of a subway fare in New York. With rising construction costs on a growing empire in Macau and Singapore, the tough old mogul's personal wealth ended up cut by about two-fifths at one point—not that anyone felt sorry for him, but still, that the third-richest man in America could see his wealth cut by that much seemed more proof that the city's economy was failing. Adelson's Sands and the Wynn Resorts both teetered on life support, kept alive by transfusions of money from deliriously profitable gaming ventures in Macau. Not long afterward, that the Sands would attract an SEC investigation for allegedly violating the Foreign Corrupt Practices Act from its ventures in Macau hit nobody in Vegas by surprise. What did the Feds expect? Chinese organized crime worked hand in glove with hundreds of superrich Chinese government officials to turn Macau casinos into the biggest, most lucrative money-laundering operation in human history. Did anyone expect that a shrewd casino mogul like Adelson, son of a cab driver who had clawed his way up from the mean streets of Boston (and outsmarting the Boston Mob to boot) would just sit on the sidelines? The Nevada Gaming Commission sure didn't, complete silence from them—the legal body responsible for auditing the books and enforcing laws against organized crime, even as far away as in China. After all, gangsters had built much of Las Vegas, all those "made" men and wise guys from the good ol' Chicago, Cleveland, and New York Mobs. Sheldon Adelson and his company would eventually (and many said brilliantly) quash and settle the case by paying a minimal fine. Las Vegas insiders could only wink and give each other high fives all the way to the bank—Chinese gangsters working junkets and the VIP rooms in Macau casinos might just save the entire industry.

Soon, the rush was on to set up in China. Oz Resorts would be the last to cut a deal, entering into partnership with family members of the legendary original godfather of Macau casinos, Stanley Ho, regardless of any alleged corruption. Mogul Steve Wynn, whose pioneering Mirage had set off the mega-resort boom three decades before, started talking up the idea of moving out of Vegas entirely, relocating his headquarters to Macau, where his newest hotel casinos had raked in more than $900 million in net revenue in the closing quarter of the year. And why not move to China? Why expect a casino mogul to express any loyalty except to his money? Why should any of them keep faith with the city, or even the nation, that had made him filthy rich? Wynn's talk about possibly leaving Las Vegas reinforced a sense that the city might be doomed. What was left here that anyone should stay?

In scarcely two years, Clark County hit number one in foreclosures in the nation. A quarter of a million people displaced—one-eighth of the population. Las Vegas hovered at the edge of total collapse, its citizens braced for the constant bad news they woke up to every day. The boom had gone bust, everywhere the waters rising, the dream city a washed-out ruin.

—

As usual, C. D. woke up before dawn from a fitful sleep. He quietly slipped out from under the covers so as not to disturb Grace, who slept curled up and turned away, her body wrapped around the big feather pillow she clutched to her chest. He noted a plate with crumbs on her nightstand. He had not felt her get up in the night or heard her snacking, taking solace in food she would kick herself for the next morning. He carried the plate downstairs. This morning, he must start work to prepare for his scheduled "eligibility review interview" for verification of his work-search record. He had said nothing to Grace about this. Why add to her worries? She had enough to do juggling their finances, and in that regard, he didn't want to think about what Grace must be sparing him.

Grace tilted toward the hypersensitive these days, after taking full charge of the household accounts plus everything else that had followed the bankruptcy of Biscayne Bay. She organized the bills and legal paperwork from the mess of court actions, everything spread out in growing piles in her upstairs office—all the demands for dates certain, the accounts paid, the accounts delayed, and those steadily thickening folders of what might be impossible to pay even from the frequent raids on their dwindling retirement funds. With the free fall of the stock market, Catherine's college fund had dwindled too, so he had had to limit out a Mastercard to cover tuition and fees for her senior year. But more than anything else, it was the new house that was sinking them.

This magnificent house didn't qualify for any emergency federal program, their mortgage too big, no sympathy at all in Congress to bail out multimillion-dollar homes. They had spent months trying to get adjustments out of the bank—was it really a "bank" anymore?—their loan with a "mortgage arm" of that same good ol' B of N that had pulled out of the deal for Biscayne Bay. They had started off doing it themselves, Grace compiling applications thick as encyclopedias on every aspect of their finances and daily lives down to the color of their socks. C. D. backed her up by talk, talk, talking to the clerks on the phone, rarely with the same person twice after he could get through the recorded loops. Nothing. Never any answer but vague legalese letters about *application pending*. He could never discover just who or which office should deliver an answer that never came.

It was the same story all across the city—piles of paperwork, notices, appeals to "the banks" stretching out, month after grinding month. Boxes of letters, applications, and other papers for the house were stacked in Grace's office along with the unpaid bills. A few evenings ago, he had stepped through the carved glass doors to her office and found her staring into space. "That bad, huh?" he had said.

"Why don't you try being nice to me for a change," she said flatly.

"What do you mean? I *am* being nice."

"Pointing out how bad things are is not nice."

He started to answer back, then stopped. They barely spoke two words to each other the rest of the evening. They were speaking less and less. And sex had become at best occasional, Grace making the excuse of "post-menopausal lack of desire." Then when they did make love, her body felt distant, or distracted. Most nights, she retreated into the sanctuary of their master bedroom, the shimmering LCD-TV tuned to soppy programs on the Lifetime Channel or Hallmark movies that, for some reason, he couldn't stand to be around. And how much time did *he* waste just lying there numbly on the great room couch, watching news on CNN until he understood it was all the same news, nothing had changed, so he quit watching news and zoned off into the monophonic sound tracks and black-and-white images on the classic movie channel. They rarely watched TV together as a couple anymore. Grace also raided the kitchen for whatever budget food she had bought—generic-brand ice cream she ate straight out of the carton, a whole block of budget cheese; she could put away a column of Ritz crackers or a bag of potato chips in minutes; and once, in the midst of his late-night wanderings, he walked in on her and discovered she kept a secret stash of fried pig's ears. "So what?" she said, as if he had asked, her mouth full, chewing. "Reminds me of my dad . . ."

This year marked fifty years since her dad's "accidental" death by carbon monoxide that Grace had blamed on her mom leaving him for another man. As if connected to this sad anniversary, her food binges accelerated. She ate things she would rarely have touched before: greasy sponge cakes; sticky caramel popcorn; all the leftover Halloween candy from so few kids coming to the door. Or if it wasn't processed sugar, it was canned fish, whole tins of oily sardines, salty anchovies, rank-smelling mackerel most people fed to cats. "Things my dad always liked," she said, as if she needed to explain.

As he was overdoing it working out, getting stringy and losing weight, she was overeating and gaining. Long ago, she had cancelled her expensive memberships at the Sage Valley Spa and the Las Vegas Athletic Club. They had the good home gym in the new house, but Grace rarely used it, called it *his* gym. She began to drape her body in plus-sized robes and nightgowns, in oversized towels getting out of the shower. Part of this self-consciousness about gaining weight no doubt contributed to her physical distance. She turned away from him in bed, clutching her big feather pillow like a barrier between them. What could he say?

Before dawn most mornings, he holed up in his study. That little white mouse still worked away on its rusty wheel inside the cage of his head, *creak, creak, creak,* as he ran through the numbers five different ways of what might have been, astonished at how the whole deal for Biscayne Bay really had come apart. Gradually decoded for them from stacks of legalese at meetings with their young attorney in Slocum's new law offices—another bill waiting to be paid—he and Grace finally understood how the whole project might have been deliberately torpedoed and betrayed. Six months after the public sacrifice of Lehman Brothers, the two banks had walked out on their completion financing contracts amid what must have been a sinister insider intrigue followed by a final, fatal backstabbing by Lance Sheperd's fellow Las Vegas power players. Rumor had it that top executives at Oz led by *wunderkind* Bill Starling had come up with this scheme, allegedly masterminding the total wipeout of Biscayne Bay to eliminate potential competition for Metropolis. They must have seen the Great Recession about to darken the economy like with a nuclear winter. They had probably run the dismal calculations on "overbuilt room inventories" against the projected drastic falloff in visitor numbers and an ever-sinking ADR—the average daily rate—needed to fight off their own bankruptcy. The banks had five times more bets on the line with Metropolis than with Biscayne Bay, not to mention all the back-room dealing they could do in insurance swaps, and let's not doubt for a second that those executives were also looking at buying swaps on their own enough to rake in a small fortune when the whole thing crashed, possibly making \$3 to \$4 million apiece on those side bets alone. Looking at the dismal projections, how long would it take for executives at Oz and the bank VPs to get together to map out that kind of scheme, no doubt at an upscale restaurant followed by cigars and night-crawling revels?

That was the speculation by "those in the know," as Kinkaid put it. C. D. doubted it at first—that alleged plot as nefarious as any the old Vegas Mob had pulled off, burying the bodies in the desert, a corporate whacking as final and bloody, in its way. But soon, he had to face it after Kinkaid had untangled the numbers.

"They ripped our faces off," Kinkaid said. "They've got blood on their teeth."

Still, C. D. didn't know *who* exactly to blame. He thought of his own small part in the bankruptcy proceedings, their little micro-partnership made of Reinhart, Kinkaid, and Olsson represented in the lawsuits against the banks. About twice a month, they received updates and more rafts of paperwork from the slow dumb show working its way through the state and federal courts. After each meeting, a new invoice would arrive from the attorneys, left unpaid now after exhausting the 100K they had set aside for legal expenses. As the attorneys had informed them, their little partnership would be among the last to get paid off from any settlements—*two and a half cents on the dollar,* and that much only if they were lucky.

Lance Sheperd faced far more in litigation, which they found out about mainly from the business press. Sheperd had filed a federal case against the banks, then suits and countersuits followed, plus multiple civil actions and at least one possible criminal investigation aimed at Sheperd and the Gravenstein partners not only for Biscayne Bay but also for a vast suburban shopping plaza and housing tracts in Houston that had crashed and burned. Even some of Sheperd's millions in art investments got tied up in legal proceedings, liens placed against them. No way to know how any of this would come out, except for the general rule that whichever party could pay law firms the most money to turn out the most paper and could last the longest might recover some small percentage of their losses.

The second year into this legal mess, the Kinkaids broke off all ties, turning their backs on nearly twenty years of friendship between their families. Pam didn't say anything directly to Grace. She just stopped returning her calls, or she would agree to meet then cancel with a three-word text message. Grace asked C. D. to find out what was wrong. At C. D.'s last meeting with Kinkaid, at his place, they sipped Crown Royals in his office den as usual while going over the latest papers from the attorneys and what, exactly, they might mean. As usual, Pam had left the house before C. D. arrived. C. D. asked what might be wrong.

"I think we've had enough of this, no offense," Mark said. "It's not me, really, it's Pam. She blames you. And sometimes, I'm not sure how I feel either. I mean, which one of us pushed Sheperd to get us *into* this mess? Who made the sale? Who? And who knows when it all might come apart so bad we'll end up getting sued ourselves or even suing each other? I mean, I've been okay with these . . . these *talks,* these *meetings* . . . Misery loves company, right? But Pam needs to cut loose from it all, and from you guys, just to keep going, and I've got to go along with that. I'm sorry. I really am. Tell Grace we're sorry. Tell her we just can't take it anymore. So let's just close the books and move on, okay? Time to go our own ways."

After delivering this speech, which rang to C. D.'s trained ear like something rehearsed, Kinkaid extended his hand. It was like he meant they should shake on it, like a man-to-man deal never to see each other again. C. D. swallowed back the *fuck you* on his tongue and the argument defending himself: like this was all *his* fault, really? Kinkaid hadn't stood in his office door begging for this? *He* hadn't pushed too for signing those *fuck*ing contracts? Wasn't it Pam who had popped the cork on a bottle of champagne? But what good would saying any of that do? Even so, he couldn't accept Kinkaid's hand, not like this, not this way. He stood there, staring at it, not quite believing what he was seeing and not saying anything—is silence really consent?—until the hand dropped away. He turned his back and let himself out of Kinkaid's foreclosed house. They would never speak again.

– 9 –

February, no matter that he couldn't afford it, C. D. took a quick trip to visit his parents, using the excuse of a job hunt at a regional hotel conference in Chicago held at the Conrad Hilton where he could spend a day passing out his résumé and talking himself up to mid-level managers and executives to see what he might shake loose. He rarely spoke to his parents, about once every two months to his father (perfunctory five-minute calls) and lately, why bother trying to talk to his mom since half the time she couldn't recognize his voice, kept confusing him for Desmond or Justin, and once even calling him Roger by some erroneous spark in the short-circuited wires of her senior dementia. His mother's mind was going, each day another line of its natural programming erased, her memories steadily deleting themselves.

He mainly kept in touch with how the folks were doing from Francis's reports once a month or so over the phone. The mostly Filipina staff at the nursing home Dad had been forced to put Mom in seemed kind enough, satisfied her needs, and practiced a wise tolerance toward her too impatient, explosive husband. His father would raise his voice as if shouting could force her to recall what day it was or if she had just eaten lunch, after which he would head back to his falling-apart print shop where he still insisted on working, the jobs fewer and fewer, most like charitable donations from loyal clients just to keep the old guy going.

C. D. regretted most that his parents had never visited him in Las Vegas. The times he had tried, offering first-class tickets, hoping to show them the town in style, sure, but mainly so they could experience close up his life with Grace and Catherine, his mother had dismissed him as sternly as if he had offered her a tour of the sinful seraglios of Casablanca: "Oh, no! Not Las Vegas! How could anybody go *there?*"

"Mom, please, we *live* here," he had said.

This became a routine exchange between them. He would go on with his standard pitch about how Las Vegas could be just like anywhere else and in some ways was a whole lot better, with its fine restaurants and shows, its colorful people, its nearby natural wonders of the Grand Canyon, the Valley of Fire, Zion National Park. And it offered some darned interesting churches, too, like the Guardian Angel Cathedral on The Strip where the collection plate filled with casino chips along with envelopes and cash. He talked up the town like a tourist commercial even though he knew she was no longer listening.

"I'm sure you'll do very well there, dear," Mom said. "We'll stay put right here."

As for his father, forget about it—he had never approved, his third son forever *that ungrateful son of a bitch,* like a final judgment he would carry to his grave. His parents had never once stepped foot in any of his homes. As for their home, no matter the increasing financial struggles, nothing could convince Mom to let go of that drafty old house where she had raised her family. She had spent her days as long as she still physically could trudging up and down its many stairs keeping it clean, beds made up in the six bedrooms, two refrigerators and the freezer in the basement kept stocked and full—Dad cleaned them out monthly and donated what wasn't spoiled to the food bank at St. Peter's—everything in her house kept as if her kids might come trooping in again that very evening. Selling the old house to transition into something more practical was an argument Dad had given up on years ago. He wouldn't take any financial help, either. The one time C. D. had tried sending him money, midway in his climb up the executive ladder, the check came back in a week, torn to bits inside an envelope from Dad's printing business, amid the blue confetti of the check a one-line note: *Who in hell do you think you are?*

Just after Christmas, he heard from Francis, in Washington, DC—after his extensive rehab, he had taken a desk position for the NSA with a two-step promotion. He told how Dad's life had been deteriorating, what a reduced existence he was living these days, all alone in their old house, the reverse mortgage he had taken out on it draining away and reaching near zero to pay for Mom's care. Little Francis had always been the closest to their parents, and this was especially true since he had lost his leg. He had spent weeks of his recuperation visiting them and letting Mom baby him, more to fill her needs than his own. Francis reasoned that *all* his sons leaning on Dad might persuade him finally to sell the house and make a move. Could C. D. at least try—the way Francis and Justin had tried—to talk some sense into him? "Dad never listens to me, so why would he now?" C. D. had said. "Me telling him might have the opposite effect." Francis pleaded, and so he agreed, using the excuse of the conference in Chicago. He booked a ticket with his frequent-flier miles. At the conference, he passed out his résumé and landed a few interviews. But he read in the eyes of those regional managers or executives of smaller hotel chains their instant responses: *too old, too overqualified,* and *can this guy be serious about Kenosha, Wisconsin?* From OTA representatives manning booths, he did come away with three follow-ups for possible IT positions whenever the job market might open up again. For some reason, all through making rounds at that icy gathering, he couldn't get a Stephen Sondheim song from the musical *Gypsy* out of his head, those rousing lyrics about how all will be swell and great, the world on a plate. . .

Nothing felt swell or great, no matter how often the song replayed involuntarily in his head either to pump up his spirits or mock him. Sunday morning, well before dawn, C. D. drove the icy interstate three hours down to Rockland, fighting winds that blew a horizontal sleet across the windshield, a reminder of why he had resolved never to live in the Midwest again. He arrived just in time to ride with Dad over to the Rockland Paradise Home, load Mom in the old Ford station wagon, and make it to St. Peter's for 9 a.m. Mass.

They found her sitting in a wheelchair in her room, more like a hospital room than a residence. He noted a too sweet odor of lilac air freshener to cover over what must be more unpleasant smells. The staff had fixed up Mom's white hair with barrettes, pinned a fresh yellow lily to the lapel of her heavy wool coat. Seeing her, C. D. thought what a gift it would be if she could just pass on this way, dressed up, waiting to be taken to Mass. She acted almost normal, only a bit shaky on her feet, so needing the wheelchair. Mentally, it seemed a good day for Mom. At least she recognized who he was, exclaiming both his first and middle names with a childlike joy as she thrust her arms out to pull him in for a kiss: "Curtis Daniel!"

In the car, she chattered away about the priests at St. Peter's now, an ever-shifting roster of newly arrived Mexicans and Filipinos, she maintained, who rarely stayed for more than a year before being replaced. "They don't speak good English," she complained. "I can hardly understand them! Since Father Brautigan died, it isn't the same. Is it, dear?"

"No," Dad said. "Nothing's the same."

"Oh, I wouldn't go that far," Mom said. "It's the same God. And at least they try!"

C. D. could sense his father holding back from what would have been their usual pattern to engage each other in a bickering disagreement, each contradicting what the other had said as though seeking a daily familiar conflict in their talk that would rise in pitch and then resolve, or not, like a music for their day. In the parking lot, C. D. helped with the wheelchair, his scarf wrapped tight against the merciless cold. Dad insisted on being the one who wheeled her into church. As C. D. followed them through the sparse, milling congregation, a few seniors he recognized stopped and thrust out their hands after Dad had grunted, "Our son, Curtis. The one from Las Vegas."

He noted a familiar mixture of curiosity and distaste in their expressions, these few seniors of his father's generation who, like him, were hanging on in this fading rustbelt town, Rockland, still a community these stoic midwestern natives rarely considered leaving, though most of their children had long since moved away. Part of their reactions to hearing "Las Vegas" seemed to mix with efforts to place just which son this *was* in the Reinhart clan from scant memories of those four unruly boys in their white shirts and clip-on ties at Mass. C. D. tried to explain himself—"I'm the son in *hotels*"—but that didn't help. He realized that his parents must not have talked much about what he did. Or the whole idea of *hotels,* in *Las Vegas,* brought to their minds scenes from violent gangster movies at which they recoiled. He shook their hands, said hello. He followed his dad as he wheeled Mom along a side aisle, relieved there weren't all that many faces he recognized, also struck by how few older, white faces had gathered at St. Peter's, most of the congregation brown people now, almost all younger families. Dad wheeled Mom past flickering votive candles at the feet of holy statuary to a front pew that had a space at one end for a wheelchair. C. D. slid into the pew beside them, noting the ranks of new missals printed in Spanish in the rack alongside a few worn prayer books in English like the ones he remembered, older and battered, as if they hadn't been replaced in forty years.

He sat through the Mass with dread. He remembered the church as bigger, more imposing, though so little about its soot-streaked interior seemed to have changed. As the voices of the priest and congregation started chanting out the rites and liturgy, he noted the struggling accent of the priest—he guessed Filipino-Tagalog by the open vowel sounds and sliced-up rhythms that he recognized from casino workers. The priest's jet black hair gleamed, shiny with gel. He gave the blessing, raising his hands over the altar draped with crisp green linens for the Sundays after Epiphany leading to Lent, that season of deprivations. C. D.'s mind drifted off into images and sensations remembered from childhood hours spent here thinking mainly of escape, or worse, creeped out by the fear that he would be punished for sins he never fully understood. A similar fear rose in him now—that he had done wrong, much wrong, all his life, including today, when his parents were so obviously in need. Because of difficulties and resentments with his dad, he would be the last of his brothers able to help them. Even Desmond still visited them, no matter that he played the role of Dad's verbal whipping boy more than the others. All right then, so be it: he wasn't even a Catholic anymore; on the irregular Sundays when he went to church, he reached for the more tolerant embrace of the Episcopalians, who had been so good to Catherine. How long had it been since he had stepped foot in a church? Yet he still prayed, more now than ever, not on his knees but sitting in his office chair or at the wheel of his car, and just before dawn, on the balcony of the new house, praying for recovery.

Kneeling in this church now brought discomforting memories of his mother, how all her life she had sought refuge here each Sunday after a grueling week enduring Dad's unhappiness. She had forced her kids to go to Mass, "Pray for your father" her repeated command. With an effort actually physical, he pushed back at a rise of resentment against his father. He did his best to expel negativity from his body. He willed himself to pray, an echo of a prayer from childhood: *Please, Lord, please relieve my father of his unhappiness and of his disappointment with life, if not for his sake, then for my mother, so she might find some peace. Amen.*

He opened his eyes, not sure he really meant his words or if he was just tossing them off out of a sense of obligation. So there he knelt, questioning his motives, letting his mind track off into doubts about praying for his dad, hearing in his head that line by Shakespeare, *Prayer without thought does not to heaven go,* until it struck him: it was all okay, even if God wouldn't hear him, and even if, in the end, there were no God—praying was the right thing to do because of his mother. Mom wanted her children to pray for Dad, as she prayed for him. Without sincere prayers of his own, he could honor her prayers. That felt right enough, and as he imagined he was achieving a genuine compassion for his father through the intermediary of his mom, the tension eased in his neck and shoulders, his breathing grew more relaxed.

The priest intoned the liturgy in imperfect English, then C. D. recited rote responses to the prayers. He moved his lips silently to phrases he had forgotten, acting as though he knew the lines, then stopped—why pretend like this when no one was watching? He let his attention wander, gazing off into the high ceiling vaults painted with fading gold stars, the stars lit by mixing colors from the stained glass windows of St. Peter's, just as he remembered. As a kid, how many hours had he spent gazing upward at Mass, distracted like this? He noted three cracked tiles up near the cupola, the same cracks he recalled, maybe blacker from the passing years. Then it was time to stand up again with the congregation. Voices rose in recitation of the creed, his mother's voice struggling, childlike, with the words. After the prayer for the Eucharist, Dad wheeled Mom to the rail to take Holy Communion. His father glanced in his direction as if expecting the three of them might go together, a look that quickly turned resigned, as if of course this son wouldn't, and he was right—no way would he take Communion in this church in which he no longer believed. As his father positioned her wheelchair at the rail, C. D. glimpsed his mother's face. For an instant, he saw exactly how she must have looked as a little girl.

After Mass, back at the Rockland Paradise Home, they sat with his mother as she picked at a bland lunch tray. C. D. noted a shift in her, a gradual dulling in her eyes. It seemed an effort to make sense of her food. More than once, she called her boiled beef chicken, and she mixed up the words for cabbage and carrots. Dad sat by, picking up then dropping his hat on his knee, marking time. One of the Filipina staff took Mom's tray and asked if she needed help in the bathroom. Mom gazed around, confused; it was clear she couldn't quite put together what this meant. Dad repeated the attendant's question in a too loud, too demanding voice: "She's asking if you need help in the bathroom! Can she help! Marion! Pay attention!"

His father turned to C. D., his frustrated expression communicating how no one could help. His loud commands had disoriented Mom even more. A flash of embarrassment crossed her features, and she reached out for C. D.'s hand, squeezing. With a nervous little laugh, she said: "Well, I don't know now, do I? I'm out of ideas!"

At dinner that night—cooked by a pleasant Mexican girl, her employment part of Dad's problem, since what little he earned at his shop paid for cooking and housekeeping plus everything else for that big empty house—C. D. did what Francis had asked. He explained to his father how all the brothers agreed he should sell the house before he ran out of money. He should move to a smaller place, or into assisted living. C. D. braced for his father's blast, his indignation that any son of his should question how he lived. But Dad just chewed on his pot roast for a moment, thoughtfully, then he washed it down with a swallow of wine. "Thank you, Curtis. I appreciate your concern," he said. "But the only way living in that place is bearable to your mother is if she believes she can still come home. Can you all understand that? Can you?" His father raised a hand, cutting him off as he started to answer that Mom wasn't capable anymore of knowing the difference, an eruption threatening. "Enough said. Go back to Las Vegas. I'm not moving until she dies."

On the flight home, C. D. recalled his last embrace of his mother, shocked at her fragile body, her knobby bones under his hands, and at how rapidly her mind had disintegrated into her dementia in the course of that one Sunday. By afternoon, she was no longer able to recognize his voice, fading in and out of an awareness that she ever even had children, a slow stripping away into a babbling blankness punctuated by the only words she could hang onto by then, two words she would remain cognizant of and cling to until the end—the name of her husband, and God.

– 10 –

The day C. D. returned from his trip to Illinois, while Grace was driving home that Monday night from picking up the weekend receipts for her job with ¡Lindo Mexico!, she felt a painful gripping in her chest and pulled over to the curb on Eastern Avenue, not able to breathe. She called C. D. and in a squeezed tight voice communicated her symptoms and where she was, then the phone went dead. He dialed 911.

He spent the next two days her side, trapped in an overcrowded purgatory of the emergency room at Desert Springs Hospital, no rooms in the actual building upstairs available to admit her. How strange that any hospital could be so overfilled in a city where many tens of thousands of people had given up and moved away.

Grace suffered in a cot-size rolling bed in a treatment space partitioned off by a flimsy curtain from the noises and pain of twenty other sick or dying patients hooked up to monitors, IV trees, and beeping machines. Nurses and doctors routinely came in to check on her but they kept changing shifts—it was hard to determine which doctor, if any, was in charge. C. D. held her hand through the bi-hourly enzyme tests and injections of blood-thinning and tranquilizing drugs, one doctor speculating that she might be getting worse by the way bad enzymes were ticking up, then the night shift physician assuring them just the opposite, that her blood tests were "inconclusive." After twenty-six hours straight, C. D. dozing fitfully in his chair by her bed, he followed as an orderly wheeled her out and they descended into a basement facility for the dangerous angiogram catheterization.

At the consultation afterward, on a big monitor, he watched her beating heart, the trunks and branches of her arterial tree appearing like a photographic negative of a wintry scene—white nets of branches against a charcoal snow. The hospital cardiologist pronounced, "No blockages. No permanent damage. She has the arteries of a teenager. She could lose some weight, but I'm sure she knows that." This doctor spoke of Grace in the third person right in front of her, then he said, too cheerily, "Mild heart attacks can be brought on by stress. We find this especially in women."

Prognosis: rest, follow-up appointments, avoid stress. Home, they went to bed. He held her as she wept, letting loose for the first time. "I'm so, so sorry," Grace cried. "Look at me. . . I *ate* myself into this! . . . Just *look* at me. . ." She cried and cried. He held her closer, saying how lucky they were this had only been a scare. "I can't *live* this way!" she sobbed. "We're *done* here! I can't *do this* anymore. . ."

She rolled to her side, clutching her pillow to her chest. Her crying slowly quieted.

C. D. got up, moved a chair near the bed, and sat with her a while as he had done in the hospital, watching her sleep, struck by the faint stress lines at the corners of her mouth as she breathed a little roughly. Grace had always had such a perfect complexion—smooth, clear skin of the lightest ivory—looking much younger than her age. He noted an unhealthy color in it now, a faint bluish gray like the shadows of two hands laid across her cheeks. He felt a stirring in his own chest, a grip of terrible sadness. He had done this to her, so deep into himself and his own selfish issues that he hadn't seen what she was suffering.

Later that night, in her office, he tried to make sense of the bills and files of legal papers Grace had arranged so neatly and stacked all around, thick folders with computer-coded labels filled with clipped-together sheaves of receipts and papers with Post-it notes: the paid in full, the partly paid with balance owed, the not yet paid and unpayable, the *action pending*. Not counting the jumbo mortgage on the house, which would stretch into six zeros for the next decades, he figured they must owe as much as $300,000 in overdue balances: on the home equity loan, the attorney bills, the all but maxed out credit cards Grace had been juggling payments on by swapping back and forth between accounts. He did a rough calculation of the medical bills from her heart attack soon to start flooding in—at least $15K in charges and "deductibles" not covered by their pitiful "catastrophic" policy they paid $900 a month for since he had lost his job and health insurance. And let's not forget the ambulance, also not covered—as much as $1.5K for that short, twelve-block ride. He sorted through the files, meaning to take over this mess and relieve Grace of some part of her hundreds of hours of stress, phoning creditors, massaging accounts, scheming to find ways to keep them going. But paging through the files, he understood he would never be able to do this—he didn't have a mind for accounting, never had, never any good with money except for spending what he earned and borrowed. And he had to admit it: Grace was right, they couldn't do this anymore.

What else could they do? For an instant, he fought off an impulse to box up the files of bills and papers and drive them out into the desert toward Alamo to set a big bonfire; or he could burn the whole damned house down, for that matter, why not? He envisioned everything around him going up in angry, purifying flames, then cashing a check in seven figures from the home owner's insurance. Hell, that could pay off almost everything they owed, all he needed was a good arsonist from the old Mob days. A wild fantasy—he was too honest, too responsible, too sane. He carefully put Grace's files back in order, arranged them in their places as though untouched. All the while he was doing this, he heard a voice in his head, his own voice from years ago, reciting from a play or a poem: *You must change your life.*

– 11 –

The morning of his "eligibility review interview," before dawn, Grace still sleeping, C. D. sat at his desk and switched on the computer to catch up on the news: markets down; more soldiers killed in Iraq and Afghanistan, many by IEDs like the one that had taken his brother's leg; in local news, the city cited again among cities in America in the grips of foreclosures and still keeping its place as *numero uno,* Las Vegas first of the worst; meanwhile, in Washington, the politicians sang their own praises as the global economy continued to sink under the waves—the same, the same, the same. He checked his email: nothing new except junk. He checked his LinkedIn: all the same as yesterday.

He logged out then moved his mouse to the folder for his "work-search" file, opened it, and began clicking through page after page of his letters, his logged phone calls, his copied emails and few replies so they could all begin cranking away through his ancient HP 1300 printer, old reliable. Only something had started squeaking inside, *creak, creak, creak,* as it spit out the pages. He muttered a prayer that it wouldn't break down, not today.

He organized the pages for the interview, which he had heard from his attorney should be little more than a formality. After obsessing about why for days, he had finally decided it was just bad luck that his number had come up, probably randomly selected. This would be his third extension, lucky his salary had been set up so he qualified, and that might have something to do with it. So he would have to make the long drive down out of Green Valley Heights into the city center to the state office. Over the past few mornings, he had reviewed the sparse notes he kept on his BlackBerry to account for his hundreds of job-hunting calls. He had weeded through his email backlog, copying into a separate file 347 inquiries and follow-ups over the past twenty-one months sent to HR managers and insiders at the casino hotels and OTAs. He sorted, reviewed, selected, made lists from his postings and one-liner exchanges with 141 "professional contacts" he had traded leads with on his LinkedIn page, many asking *him* for advice on where to apply for jobs. The few he did unearth were for jobs for which he would be "overqualified" or that required an MBA, which he didn't have, earning his BA in theater all those years ago and failing at that life. One or two other leads would require leaving Las Vegas, walking out on the new house in trade for about one-sixth (or less) of the salary he had earned before, if he were even lucky enough to be hired.

The one prospect he had put some hope in near his own level would have been reporting to Rick Rickstein at the Sands as director of IT marketing. Over three months, he had traded a half dozen emails with Rickstein about this position, which should open up just as soon as the Sands had weathered its capital flow crisis to fund its $7 billion more in new construction on Macau's Cotai Strip plus their new casino resort in Singapore. Then communications from Rickstein had turned mysteriously cold, C. D.'s many texts and emails left unanswered. He finally sent a large-font "?" in a message, repeating it five times in a day. In reply, Rickstein wrote him the death blow: *Sorry, Reinhart, nothing we can do. Tried hard. Corporate wants an MBA or an equivalent business degree for new hires, not like in past, when experience counted most. Why not get the very best?*

After C. D. had spent two hours trying to reach him, Rickstein finally answered his phone, in Singapore, then listened as C. D. yelled at him about that bullshit phrase—like he wasn't among the best? What the *fuck* was he saying?

"It's Biscayne Bay," Rickstein said, vibrations of sympathy in his Israeli accent. "No one wants near such a catastrophe." He waited for C. D. to say something, then added, "Take my advice. Cut Biscayne Bay off your résumé. Try anywhere else but Vegas companies. Sorry, I'm running here. Say hello to Grace for me. Wish her my best."

He hung up, C. D. left with that irritating beep sound of his phone from across the ocean that echoed in his head for days. That would be the last word from Rickstein. Still, Rickstein had been a help—the taint of Biscayne Bay had covered him, how stupid not to see this before. He deleted those two years off his profile and résumé. To fill in the missing space, he wrote in a new line: *marketing consultant*—not precisely true but not an outright lie, either. A few weeks later, he almost made it to the final interview for a local "hot" position in Vegas for the regional office at Zappo's, a company busy growing its marketing team. In the webcam interview—his first via video—the youthful crew manning the Zappo's ship preferred at least *some* previous experience with fashion and design, or in retail sales (and clearly, someone younger). That "web live" interview felt like he was talking himself up to a jerky screenshot full of kids with bad haircuts clustered around a high school cafeteria table beamed to him from the moon. And C. D. had to admit it: he knew little about shoes aside from wearing them. So it had gone, a precious few leads, then nothing. No one could recall anything like this dearth of jobs in the industry.

He didn't know what he expected to see at the offices of the Nevada Department of Employment, Training, and Rehabilitation—ragged, downtrodden souls lined up like at a soup kitchen, he supposed, or the same stressed-out people he had seen sitting in the battered plastic seats of the Nevada Job Connect office on Maryland Parkway. But once through the green metal gates of the state office building, which looked like some low-security prison, inside, the facility felt more like a modern airport waiting area than a place for the outcast and unemployed. He understood that his appearance might mean something, so he had dressed carefully in muted business attire—in his brown, windowpane-patterned jacket of buttery wool from Loro Piana, darker brown slacks, an ecru button-down shirt topped off by a green and red striped tie, and his best Gucci moccasins. He feared he might be overdressed until the security guard directed him into one of the side waiting rooms, long and narrow, like a shoebox, where he noted three dozen other, mostly smartly dressed people in two rows of padded chairs against the brick walls—women in good suits with leather utility bags at their feet; guys in designer polo shirts with jackets hung over them, briefcases or portfolios in their laps—seemingly white-collar folks, here and there maybe a construction foreman or two in jeans and sneakers and a billed team logo cap, but in clean jeans, crisp new caps. None of his fellow unemployed appeared in any way like the down-and-outers he had envisioned. The only oddness might be the unusual quiet, no one talking, newspapers and magazines held up in front of faces, or people just stared into space with a relaxed distraction into the inner privacy of their thoughts.

He gazed around as he took his seat, noting he was one of two guys wearing a tie, but other than this, he fit right in. They might be a group of patients of assorted ages and skin tones waiting stoically for follow-up appointments with a medical specialist, no outward signs of their distress. Then it struck him: he could easily imagine any one of these people working on the staff of a hotel or office or other professional setting—four years ago, he or any of the other VPs might have hired them—and that people such as these should find themselves among the long-term unemployed meant that conditions must be far worse than he had thought. He took his seat with them, perching his Tumi bag on his lap. He waited for his name to be called.

He didn't have to wait long. A pleasant-seeming clerk with a busy perm dyed an odd, unappealing shade of reddish blonde that contrasted with her indigenous features led him through a glass door to her office down a hall. Her office window framed a vista of an oddly empty parking lot, the asphalt slate-like, smooth and new, lines for the slots glowing with freshly painted yellow in a lake of pristine blackness. He thought: so this is what the federal stimulus funding had achieved, a massive paving over of the parking lots.

The brass nameplate on the woman's desk read: Marisa Gutiérrez. A picture in a silver frame stood angled to one side of her bulky antique computer monitor, set up so her petitioners could see it, too—a photo of three smiling brown boys sitting in a dull lineup together on a red sofa, hands in their laps, all the colors too saturated, as from a cheap home printer. On the only wall not crowded with filing cabinets hung a poster of the red, white, and blue–striped jets of the U.S. Air Force Thunderbirds, in formation like a rising bloom, messily signed in black marker by the pilots. By this, C. D. guessed Mrs. Gutiérrez must be connected to the Nellis Air Force Base—was she a military wife? Or was some family member in the air force?

He unpacked two thick folders of his emails, letters, and phone logs from his bag and passed them over her desk. He took a seat in the padded chair meant for her interviewees, or were they her suspects? She seemed barely interested in his documents, flipping through both folders in about a minute with a cursory formality, showing no sign at all of her reaction. She moved her mouse around, obviously pulling up his file from a list on the computer, then she started typing in a code composed of both letters and numbers, filling in a form.

"You are an executive?" she asked, dark eyes fixed on the light of her screen.

"That's right," C. D. said. "IT Marketing and Project Development. Some PR. . ."

She moved the mouse. She clicked once. "No education past the four-year degree?"

"Almost twenty years of industry experience," he said. "Does that count?"

She moved the mouse again, clicked again, without a twitch of her face. "I see you made it to vice president at Pyramid Resorts. Nice." She said this with what might have been a faint breath of being impressed. He kept catching a trace of a non-native speaker's accent, not in her pronunciation, which was perfect, rather in the rigid formality of her sentences. Her mouse moved and clicked again, filling in boxes of the online form. "You were laid off following the bankruptcy of Biscayne Bay," she said. "You have been collecting unemployment compensation for eighty-six weeks? Is this correct?"

"Believe me, it seems *way* longer than that, like *forever*. . ."

He meant this to come off as a sad joke of sorts, fishing for sympathy. Instead, her heavily ringed fingers froze over the keyboard. She aimed a sharp glance across the desk at him and he felt his heart thump, heavily, twice.

"Right. Eighty-six weeks," he said, almost adding, *Only thirteen more weeks to go!* with a cheery irony, but he choked this back with a quick little cough. He cleared his throat and said, "That's correct."

"Can you describe for me what is it that you do?"

"Pardon me?"

"When you are working, Mr. Reinhart. What is it that you *do?*"

"Ah. . .Marketing. . .PR. . .IT development. . .Doesn't it say so there?"

Not taking her eyes off the screen, Mrs. Gutiérrez brought a pinky finger up to her lips in an oddly impatient gesture, clicking a carefully filed nail against her very white, straight teeth. He guessed she must be deciding something important, but what? She said, "Perhaps you can describe for me your job. What you *do* when you are working?"

"I. . .ah. . .well. . .I suppose I'm an idea man. . .an idea *person*," he corrected himself, to which she didn't react. He wished he could turn the computer monitor so he could see what she was looking at—a drop list on an online form? A series of lit-up lines and spaces waiting for her to type into? What were the correct answers? He felt like a hot steaming rag had dropped over his brain. "Mostly, I went to meetings," he continued. "You know, with the boss, the president and CFO, and to more frequent meetings with the other vice presidents. And with the investors. Can't forget about them." He stifled a note of irony. "We presented proposals to investors, or to their representatives, who mostly flew in for the presentations. We also traveled to present to them. We constructed detailed plans of what work needed to be done, you know, various tasks that needed doing and how to address problems that came up. I'd go back to my staff and implement my part of the plan and assign tasks to the marketing directors at all the hotels. And I'd travel for new plans. . . there was a lot of travel, to consult with my counterparts at other companies, and to negotiate subcontractor contracts and decide how to do certain jobs and who would do them. I spent lots of time, hundreds of hours, on the phone with these people and on email, reviewing reports to me. Then I'd write reports for the bosses and the senior vice presidents. A lot of time was taken up writing these reports, five or six reports every week, to update the team on how *our* work was going. . . Is this what you want? Is this any help?"

"Would you say you were a supervisor?"

"Sure," he said. "At one point, including the travel website, I had a staff of fifty-some people working under me. . ."

She typed one long word—nine or ten keystrokes—was it *supervisor?*

"Listen. There was a lot more to it than that. . ."

She was already in motion, no stopping now. She quickly moved her mouse and clicked once, then moved it just a hair more and clicked again. That was it—all she wrote—before she scrolled up to the "save" function and closed out the form. Was that all?

"Do you mind telling me what you just did?" he asked.

"Thank you," she said, showing off her perfect teeth framed by her too bright coral lipstick—her official smile. "You will be hearing from our office." She picked up his heavy files and passed them back across her desk with a slightly exaggerated, girlish shrugging of her shoulders.

He relieved her of his files. "Am I all right?" he asked. "Did I pass?"

"Keep processing your claims as usual," she said. "You should receive a letter within three weeks." She stood up as he was still struggling to fit his papers back into his bag. He almost spilled them when a reflex of gentlemanly politeness jolted his body to stand up with her.

"Follow me," she said. He trailed after her into the hallway. "At the reception desk, we offer information about education and retraining," she intoned, her voice as dull and impersonal as a digitally recorded message. "We encourage you to take advantage of job-training programs."

He envisioned the form on her screen: Supervisor. Services. Nonessential. Obsolete. . .

Out in the parking lot, in his car, he leaned his head against the steering wheel, just breathing, until his head started to ache from the strong oily odor of fresh asphalt. He decided to take the streets rather than the freeway for the long drive out of the inner city. Along Charleston, he passed through a stretch of messy, Spanish-language signage, a rundown neighborhood of taco shops, discount and secondhand stores, storefront insurance and tax offices squeezed into crumbling cinder-block strip malls. He doubled east on Sahara, cruising past abandoned car dealerships with their towering vacant signs, the boarded-over windows of dark showrooms floating in the middle of their empty asphalt lagoons. He turned up McLeod past a closed Furr's Cafeteria tagged with tangles of spray-painted graffiti that must be gang symbols, then he drove more slowly along that once middle-class, busy residential street in Francisco Park where now almost every third or fourth house stood abandoned, the real estate placards tilting over dead brown lawns, roof shingles left to peel from the desert heat, here and there a garage door dented and sprung off its hinges, scattered trash and stuffing from ripped-up furniture in the driveways. In Winchester Park, homeless people sat gathered in the far corner under the picnic pavilion, shopping carts overflowing with filthy lumps that must be their possessions. Nearer the street, a squat Latina-looking woman with two brown kids struggled against the wind to hold down laundry strung from a tree to the open door of a van. At the corner of Desert Inn, a scruffy teen on a skateboard surfed over the curb and rocketed across the street after the light had changed—it seemed like a miracle he wasn't killed.

Along Pecos, vacant windows of half-empty commercial buildings gazed down over the traffic, urgent red-lettered *For Lease* banners luffing and straining in the wind. An empty lot with a sagging chain link fence spread out like a weed-choked urban wound at the corner of Flamingo. At the stoplight, a bearded crazy wearing what must have been five layers of filthy rags stood in the crosswalk, raving at the sky. Across from him, by the Shell station and car wash, a pudgy guy in a red chicken costume danced an awkward jig at passing cars while slicing a sign for El Pollo Loco through the air. Crossing Tropicana, just past the steady activity of a Wal-Mart Sam's Club, he caught sight of numerous wrecked or abandoned homes, their windows boarded over, yards heaped with junk blighting the streets that stretched off into surrounding neighborhoods. Everywhere the same: houses with empty windows, trash-blown yards gone to weeds, tilting real estate signs, shopping centers with dark storefronts like holes at their hearts; and everywhere forlorn people set loose to wander with what was left of their belongings along the sidewalks and through the parking lots; at the intersections, they lifted crude signs begging for money toward cars that mostly passed them by.

Even the guard-gated, grassy bowl of the once posh Legacy community, with its green golf course and upscale homes, seemed torn at its edges by untrimmed palm trees, sun-bleached paint, dying lawns. He drove up into Green Valley and across the I-215 freeway into the parklike district of Green Valley Ranch, then cruised even further up into his own luxury neighborhood of Green Valley Heights, whose magnificent views used to strike him pleasantly; he had always enjoyed the gradual transition from communities of the settled working class into such unrepentant prosperity. Now even these prosperous areas were being abandoned in a wave of "short sales" and "strategic defaults," many million-dollar-plus houses left empty, grass turned brown in the dying yards.

He turned into his own community, passing the guard house and waving as usual to a lone sentry in uniform who, these days, never seemed to be the same person. The big iron gates swung open automatically at the end of his car hood. He took the familiar left turn onto Deer Run, looked over by such magnificent mini-mansion homes—his neighborhood. Ahead, lining the street, he counted six new for-sale signs. At the corner, five houses down from his own, a large U-Haul van had backed up against the open doors of a three-car garage. The pretty wife of that family with two teenaged girls he had seen a few times but had never taken the time to introduce himself to was taking a break. Dressed in a green sweater and jeans and drinking an iced tea, she sat on a leather armchair between two dark wood end tables, atop each a brass lamp with a cut-glass Tiffany shade, all arranged in the driveway as if she had set up a portion of her living room just to show it off one last time before it would be loaded up and moved. Dust blew, swirling among the boxes. The woman sipped her tea, not bothered by the wind. He wondered if the wind would get strong enough to tip over the lamps. He tried to remember what Grace had told him about this family—the husband in a medical-related field, maybe a dentist or an orthodontist? The wife a teacher? He might have slowed his car and opened his window to wave; he might have stopped to talk to her, maybe even offered to lend a hand, but he didn't. Turning his gaze straight ahead, he sped up. What would be the point now? The city was dying, its people in flight. The sinking ship was pilotless, the passengers scrambling in confusion through the crowded passageways.

– 12 –

C. D. listened to the hum and clatter of his garage door closing. He sat for a moment in the gray darkness of his car. He closed his eyes, feeling his irregular breaths. His body felt tight all over. His neck ached. He gripped a handful of his hair on top of his skull, an old actor's trick to center the body, to will his neck to relax, the weight of his head hanging there, suspended by his hair, the bones of his spine slipping back into line as his breathing settled into a more regular pattern. He gradually let loose of his hair then climbed out into the faint new-tire smell of his garage. As he turned toward the door to the house, he saw it: on his tool bench, under the orderly ranks of his tools hanging on pegs, a coiled rope—thick hemp, not a cheap nylon or plastic rope, an old-fashioned rope.

He froze, staring at it, not able to remember when or where he had purchased it. But he must have, one of those impulse buys on his regular visits to Home Depot for light bulbs or a sprinkler repair, plucked up from a clearance bin by the cash registers. When had he done this? Not long ago, since it hadn't yet been freed from its green cardboard sleeve. He shook his head, shook off the thought, and kept on going into the house.

Inside, he found Grace in the kitchen, barefoot, still in her white terry cloth spa robe a bit ragged at the hem. It wasn't like her not to be dressed so close to noon. She was still recovering, and must have slept in this morning. His interview had been early; he hadn't fixed her breakfast. Come to think of it, he hadn't eaten anything himself—maybe that was why his head felt so fuzzy. With her phone pressed to her ear, she glanced his way. He raised his hand in a little wave. She returned his greeting with a quick nod then turned to face the window, absorbed by her call. Her voice was cheery, bright with the patronizing warmth she used when she talked to her mom.

He understood these calls to Janice could curve and bend through multiple topics for an hour or longer. This call might have started before Grace had dragged a brush through her hair, a brassier red recently, streaks of white near the roots, since they could no longer afford her beloved drag queen stylist, Matthew, who peppered his herbal color jobs with campy talk, so she had started coloring her hair out of a drugstore package. He imagined her jangled out of a coma-like sleep as she answered the phone, stumbling downstairs to pour a first cup of coffee from the pot he had left half full in the kitchen.

She had been home sick from work for four days. Her part-time accounting job had wound down to three days a week for the tax firm, mainly finishing up bankruptcies, and it wouldn't be long before the company would let her go. She might keep her extra side job on weekends, doing the books for a two-restaurant local mini-chain, ¡Lindo Mexico! At least working there cheered her up, and she brought home leftover specials they could heat up in the microwave. "The pay is barely better than pesos but at least they're honest. And hey, we can use the free enchiladas," she said, then laughed. "It's not like it's going to be forever, right?"

His bag heavy on his shoulder, C. D. stepped into the angled hallway toward his study, thinking he must have something to do in there but really not knowing what to do after his interview. He stopped in the hallway, listening for a moment to Grace's pleasant, musical voice. He heard the scrape of a chair as she settled in at the kitchen nook, then snatches of an upbeat chatter about fruits, what her mom had stored for the winter from the harvest of the Skagit Valley filling her talk these days. Due to illness and increasing frailty, she had been late last fall and was still into the winter with her canning. He imagined Janice singing away about how they had plenty of Northern Spies and how those with all the Jonathans were keeping Dewey busy at his cider press. "So glad he can still do all that, after his fall," Grace chimed in. C. D. could almost hear her mom's voice going on about what a relief those apples are after the berries were so disappointing last summer, not enough sun followed by too much rain so they had turned to mush on the vines and she couldn't make enough jam. But at least the blueberries had come in okay, and look out for those Bosc pears! She had loads of them for canning, if only she can keep finding the energy to get it done before she's laid up again. Grace said, "Don't push yourself, Mom, not this year, not for us. Take your time. At least until you get some help up there . . ."

He thought of the boxes of heavy mason jars Janice sent twice a year, each spring and before Thanksgiving, costing more in postage than if they had bought as many cases of canned fruit at a warehouse store if they added Grace shipping back the jars.

"Just go easy on the syrup, please," Grace said. She listened for a while. "No," she said, her voice darkening. "Mom, don't start that again. I'll be all right. Once we get this new house off our backs, we'll be just fine. . ."

The burden of the new house had become Grace's persistent theme with her mom. C. D. understood this was Grace's way of deflecting any comments about her husband, that son-in-law still without a job, and also now her health scare. He thought of his own mother, her mind melting away in the expensive Rockland Paradise Home, eroding his father's finances. At least it was clean, and she had a private room, despite the expense. He wished he could talk to his mother the way Grace talked to hers, wished they could have talked that way even once in their lives. He listened to Grace's voice echoing into the living room with that pleasant music of her endearments. It struck him that he might never speak to his mother again when she would be aware he was her son.

He stood there, dazed, not moving. He saw that he was standing in the living room, not the inner hallway, unable to recall just how or when he had made the turn in a different direction than usual into his study. Slowly, the room came into sharper focus. He gazed at his furniture, eerily unfamiliar somehow, breathing in the animal smell of the doe leather sofas, which neither he nor Grace nor anyone else had ever sat on much. He noted the coffee table with its neat fans of magazines spread out as if for show, *Harper's, New Yorker, Food & Wine, National Geographic,* and all the rest stopped in time at last year's dates, subscriptions expired when they could no longer afford them. He gazed at the gorgeous hearth and mantle, noting how the stone extended smoothly up and around the gas fireplace in richly veined textures exclusive to a ridge in Italy from which Michelangelo had selected the stone he had carved. He recalled the thrill of coming up with this design, the ivory tones set off by the blush-tinted accent walls, a contrast at the very edges of perception.

From over the fireplace, his treasured painting vibrated at him through a soft, rosy light—the bands of its vivid spectrum spreading out into the shape of a fan on a field of whitest white, all attention in the room drawn to its dominating presence, its bright optical illusion of a rainbow unfolding as if into limitless space. How he loved this painting, no matter his conflicted emotions about who he had purchased it from and the high price he had paid. For years, he had convinced himself that he had earned its expensive beauty. It struck him now like a harsh visual humming that set off a throbbing in his head.

The sweet pattern of Grace's voice finished singing goodbyes to her mom, then there was silence after she hung up the phone. C. D. became aware that he had been standing there a long time, in one place in his living room, not able to recall how or why, after coming in from the garage, he must have turned in this direction down the angled hall—going where? The strap of his bag dug into his shoulder with a sharp ache. He let it slip off and drop to the floor. Like his mother, he was out of ideas. Sunlight through the windows gradually shifted over that spectral painting, his mind going blanker, then *nothing, nothing, nothing, nothing*. . .

"Are you all right?" Grace asked. "Honey?"

"Fine." His voice didn't sound like his voice. "I'm fine."

"Oh, honey, come here. Come with me. Come on. That's it," she said. She took him by his arm and managed to turn him around. "Let's go lie down," she said. "Come on. . ."

Her voice kept singing at him brightly as she led him up the stairs with that cheerful tune she had started to use when he began spending his first whole days at home, newly unemployed, Grace so upbeat about how they were free now and could take advantage of the time and do anything they pleased, even rumple up the sheets at noon. She willed him up the stairs, past the library on the landing, pushing him along. She moved him into their bedroom and pulled off his jacket. Then he felt her fingers plucking at his shirt buttons and his tie and peeling down his pants, meaning to pull him down with her onto the bed in a way they hadn't done for a long, long time—so like the old days, the way they had resolved every crisis in their marriage by making love. How long had it been? Weeks ago, or longer?

"I'm not sure I'm up to this," he said. "And what about you. . .your heart?"

"My heart's fine," she said. "Just relax. . ."

She pushed him onto the bed and fell in alongside him. He mumbled no, she didn't have to do this, but she insisted. He closed his eyes. It didn't seem possible that he could make any giving gesture in return right now, not even to stroke her hair as she moved over him, kissing, then down on him, then back again, with a determination he hadn't felt in her lovemaking since he couldn't recall when, and with something else, too, that felt unfamiliar, as if she meant to prove something. Afterward, she did everything to pamper him, tucking him into the bed. She pulled the covers over their bodies and held him from behind. He dozed, in and out of half dreams, then fell asleep. When he awoke, she was gone.

He found Grace in the kitchen, busy preparing an intimate dinner the way she used to, just finishing rinsing wild rice and putting it on the stovetop to simmer. She broke off the ends of fresh asparagus (out of season), setting the stalks upright in the steamer, then she pulled a troll-caught king salmon fillet out of the refrigerator—since when could they afford this? He didn't ask. He put on upbeat baroque music, selections from Bach and Vivaldi. He watched Grace chop the garlic and fresh dill then whip up a Kiev butter. She diced some smoked salmon then expertly laced it into neat slits she made into the fillet, then topped off the packed slits with the herb butter before laying the fillet in a baking dish. It was a salmon Joseph, one of her recipes from Seattle she hadn't made since he couldn't remember when. Her artful focus on the food transformed his view of the world. All seemed in place again.

He observed her a long while, her assured, graceful movements in the kitchen, absorbing her warmth and the lively music. At one point, he lifted her apron halter and kissed her on her bare neck, the way he used to, until she playfully ducked out from under his embrace on her way to the oven. At the dining room table they seldom used, she had set her good Spode china, the fine silver, cloth napkins, the Tiffany candlesticks, then she opened a bottle of reserve chardonnay, a wine that might have cost as much as all the other ingredients of the meal put together. When she served the food and poured the wine, they touched glasses. As was their habit at expensive restaurants, they sat close together at one end of the table so they could touch each other at intervals, no need to speak or break the spell. They let the food, wine, and music wash over their senses. He realized she must have planned this meal, maybe the whole day, for a while. Then it struck him why.

"So this is it," he said. "We're broke."

Grace nodded, her mouth full. She sipped and savored the wine. "We've hit the limit," she said. "We can salvage just about enough in the retirement account for a minimal existence, if we're careful. No way can we keep this house. We can't keep . . . well, *any* of this," she said, waving her fork in the air with a careless gesture, a cheer in her voice and manner that could only be her letting go into the relief of no longer having to fight anything or anyone. "I've researched an agent who specializes in short sales. That's the best way to go now, if the bank will make a deal. And if not, we'll have to let it go all the way."

"How minimal is minimal?" he asked.

"Mom and Dewey minimal?" She shrugged, smiling. "Not quite. But almost."

"How long?"

"Two months, three months? Hard to say," she said. She scooted her chair back a few inches so she could turn and face him more directly. "There's something else. While you were away on your trip, I had lunch with Diane and Marjorie, you remember?" He nodded his head yes, though he didn't recall her telling him. "Marjorie had too much to drink, as usual. She started talking about Greta, how she'd come back to town looking for a job. Did you know she'd come back? Interviewing at Caesars and who knows where else?" He shook his head. "Hmm, I thought she might have given you a call," Grace said.

"I haven't spoken to Greta in nearly two years," he said. "Not an email, either. I've only heard about her thorough our case, from the attorneys, same as you."

"I suppose not. Why would you?" Grace said. "Anyway, a total disaster, according to Marjorie. Greta fell on her face, literally, drunk, at the interview. That's the story. Marjorie raised her glass and said, 'Good riddance to that bitch who fucked our husbands.' Which I thought odd, since, you know, her husband probably *did* sleep with Greta like he screwed everyone else, but Big Jim Chevron? Him? Not likely. Only Diane didn't say a thing, she just raised her glass too, with this sad, sad look. And, well, what else could I do? I said I didn't think so, not you, not you and Greta, no *way* that happened, you're not that *stupid*, but here's a send-off to her anyway, she was never anything to me. So I raised my glass, too. They both gave me these pitying looks—do you know what it feels like to get that kind of look?—and we finished our lunch. I wasn't going to say anything about it, but I've been thinking ever since, and I can't help it. . . I'd like to know what you have to say. Not that it matters—we're way past that, right? But it does, somehow. . ."

"Grace, please," he said. He looked her directly in the eyes, not blinking. It took every inner reserve he could summon to keep his look steady, and cool—he would never tell her, never, no matter what she sensed or knew. "Marjorie Slocum? Do you really believe that? More gossip from the champagne trail?"

"I don't know what to believe," she said. "You wouldn't tell me even if it did happen."

"Probably not," he said. "Still, I'm sorry you did that, joined in that catty kind of trashing. Greta deserves better, no matter what happened, no matter what those wives think. She spent her whole life, sacrificed her *personal* life, all of it, trust me, *everything,* helping to make their husbands rich, and they talk about her like *that?* She deserves better from those women, and a lot better from the men who mainly fucked her over all her life then dumped her off with nothing."

Grace sat quietly for a moment, absorbing his words, and his calm, level gaze. "I never looked at it that way," she said. She scooted her chair to face the table again, took his hand and squeezed. "I'm sorry," she said.

"You're wrong that I'm not stupid," he said. "I've been so *fuck*ing stupid about everything. I think about how stupid I've been every day. . ."

"Not about everything," she said. "You keep trusting the wrong people, that's all."

"What do you want us to do? What now?"

"Well, there's something else. . . Mom's going into the hospital. Not serious, just a circulation problem in her leg, a stent to open up an artery. I'd been thinking she'd be okay with Dewey to take care of her, but he's not back up to speed either, after that fall. Anyway,

I've used your frequent-flier miles to book a flight. I'm leaving day after tomorrow. Not sure how long I'll have to stay—not that long, I don't think. My hours run out with McKinley on Friday anyway, all done there, and I've got the restaurant pretty well trained so they won't get too far behind," she said. "I'd have asked you to come with me. I mean, how long since we've taken a trip together? Not since Catherine's graduation, our last nice trip. But you wouldn't enjoy it much, and the way things are, your time can be better spent going through the house, you know . . . figuring out how we can sell some things? More than *some* things. I mean, almost everything?"

"Everything?"

"I'll leave that up to you." She reached over and massaged his shoulder, briefly, then dropped her hand back to her wineglass. She sipped, savoring the last of it, like saying goodbye. "Who knows if a little alone time now might do us both some good?"

He knew he should answer this. But he couldn't think of what he should say.

—

C. D. dropped Grace off at the airport on Saturday morning, hefting two big suitcases out of the trunk, understanding by their weight that she was taking far too much luggage, her excuse when he asked that she wanted "to transfer a few good things up to Mom's." This was part of Grace's answer to several attacks of his denial that there was still a "live" résumé or two out there in the world, that something might yet happen to save them. In reply, she presented him with two clipboards she had set up with neat check-off spreadsheets to fill in, one spreadsheet for each room of the new house: number, item, estimated value, price paid, a space for notes on where and how to sell, locally if possible or on craigslist, only as a last resort on e-Bay. After unloading her heavy bags, he told her to give his love to her mom. On the sidewalk, they embraced, too long, he thought, for any casual trip. They kissed goodbye. He held the kiss, not wanting to let go, until she broke away. Flushed, she said, "Well!"

She waved off his attempt to help her manage the big suitcases inside. He watched her dragging them through the automatic doors and she was gone.

Alone in the new house, he meant to start on the guest suite: the gray button bed from Formstelle, Danish modern, he had picked up at one-third price through Brick Rico from a hotel room remodel job that had changed in midstream. He had no idea what it was worth, and felt an urge to keep it somehow. He roamed around the suite that had seen so few guests, running his fingertips over the teak veneer bookshelves, mostly empty of books, and the Bosch satellite speakers, the very best, their newness not lost on him. The rose granite and stainless Kohler fixtures in the bathroom hadn't seen so much as a water spot in almost a year, only a few weekend overnights by Desmond, and that first summer, a visit from his sister Cathy and her teenaged kids. The new house had really been filled all the way just once, during the three weeks or so that Grace had opened the doors to volunteers for the Barack Obama for President campaign—those eager kids bussed in from California to help bring in swing-state Nevada. What a high time that had been, that brief season of hope.

So much for hope. C. D. couldn't begin with the inventories, not today. Instead, he went upstairs and changed into his sneakers and sweats to work out in the exercise room, pounding it out for at least ten miles on the elliptical trainer in between his usual five sets of ab crunches followed by five bench press cycles, from time to time gazing out the tall windows at a view toward the jagged black mountains lifting up to the south that gave the room a sense of expansion way beyond its walls. He stretched out on his back for sets of leg lifts on the foam mat he spread out on the carpet. Midway through, he tore off his sweatshirt. He dug in harder and kept on going, alternating sets on the floor and on the two machines, overdoing it until he had to break to catch his breath and guzzle down a bottle of water. He glanced at his body in the mirrored closet doors. Not bad, he thought. Or not bad *yet*—not bad for a guy his age, anyway. Then the thought struck home that all of this—his sleek machines on which he had trained his body, that most welcome habit of his life—these, too, were to be included on the inventories of "everything" that must be sold. He lost the will to push himself anymore, at least for today.

He went outside into the yard and cleaned the pool filter, though he had done this three weeks ago and it didn't really need cleaning. Then he puttered away with a rake, pulling out a few loose twigs and leaves from the desert gravel. He walked a general patrol, looking for things to do, screwing around with sprinkler heads to adjust their aim just right; and over the barbecue, he straightened out the plastic cover that was so sun dried it was rotting into bits. In the kitchen, he did a check of the refrigerator, only then noticing Grace had left a stack of plastic containers with precooked meals for him: leftover salmon and wild rice; linguine à la vodka; green curry tofu and rice; three red sauce enchilada specials from ¡Lindo Mexico! with who knew what fillings. When had she done all this? He checked the clock—5:30 already?

He heated the linguine in the microwave and ate it at the kitchen table without bothering to spoon it onto a plate. He washed the container and his fork, dried them, and put them away. The thought hit him that he should switch on the news, but he decided not to—the news could wait, the news would be the same. Still, he might watch something. He settled onto the soft leather cushions of the sectional in the great room and switched on the wide-screen LCD-TV that he still marveled at for its color fidelity. He hunted with the remote to find a movie. As he channel surfed from image to image, the screen flipped, shifted, jumped, switching with a fragmented digital scattering that made him think of bits of colored glass.

He stopped. On the screen, a very familiar-seeming Roman figure, in a toga and with tonsured hair, made a grandly languorous, sweeping gesture with his hand in direct counterpoint to the panicked rushing around of several servant characters through a large stone room decorated with pastoral tapestries and classical columns. He recalled watching this scene on television several times in his life, though not for many years. He recognized the actor, a great classical British actor, still young in this film. In this CinemaScope classic, he was cast in a much older role—the part of a sage, kindly Roman senator who had sided with the slave revolt so brutally chopped down by the empire's legions, a Technicolor spectacle with a cast of thousands in climactic battle scenes that stretched out over rocky plains and jagged hills for much of the movie. The senator's side in the war had lost, despite his best efforts, and now, befitting a noble Praetorian of his station, he must pay the ultimate price.

In this scene, with gentle dignity and no sign of regret, the senator bids goodbye to his beloved household servants and the personal body slaves he has just set free. The folds of his toga keep slipping off his shoulder, exposing a fleshy arm and part of his thick, stocky chest as he reaches out to the tearful servants, most of them women and girls, with such familiar, gentle physicality, giving out little touches to a head or chucks on a shoulder and a few quick, intimate, one-armed squeezes, even one playful little slap to a behind, all these meant in a fatherly way, incorporating into these movements the easy, casual lifting of the drape of his toga back into place over his shoulder three times, using that business with the costume in a brilliant actor's touch that shows off somehow the ease with his conscience he feels at the end of his life. The Roman senator tells them all to go now, to hurry before the guards arrive to arrest him, using a sharp slicing of his hand and arm to indicate finality. One last, matronly servant curtsies to him, then she flees in tears.

The Roman senator turns regally and strides off, the camera following him into an adjoining room, revealing a boat-size, steaming marble bath. Next to it, a young boy stands with a pitcher of perfume and a red cloth bundle. The boy is handsome, at an age not quite yet a man but it is clear he soon will be a man, his dark hair tonsured in a style that exactly matches the senator's. The boy bites his lip, fighting back his emotions. How determined he is to carry out this one last duty for a man he adores. The senator pauses, stretching out his hand to place it reverently, palm down, on the boy's head, as if giving a tender blessing, a faint flash of regret crossing his features that they have run out of time.

In a wash of steam, the Roman senator slips out of his toga and steps into the bath, his head and shoulders pushing backwards like some heavy aquatic beast, then he settles sitting up at one end. The boy holds out the red cloth bundle with a charged reverence, as if in a sacred ceremony. The senator takes it, and the boy pours perfume into the bath. Swiftly, the senator unfurls the red cloth. A gilt-handled knife rolls out into the palm of his hand. He waves the boy away with a commanding motion of his other hand and arm. He watches affectionately as the boy backs up slowly, takes three steps, then turns and runs. As the camera closes in on the bath and the music rises, too much brass, too many drums, into a discordant resolve that repeats as a theme through the whole movie, this masterful actor, playing now with a thoroughly convincing and lasting nobility, this performance worthy of nomination for an Academy Award, powerfully lifts his left wrist out of the water and raises the knife. . . .

C. D. switched off the TV. Outdoors, the sun had gone down, a faint glow in the charcoal sky through the windows, the only other light from a lone white bulb in the kitchen. In near darkness, he sat there, listening to the barely audible crackles of the TV shutting down, like a faint unwrapping of cellophane. He strained to hear other sounds: the two heat exchangers humming outside in the distance, their fans sending off light breaths of air along ducts in the ceilings and walls then out through the vents like exhaling lungs. He thought of the rope, the rope still there, in the garage. The staircase was just down the hall, its impressive high landing suspended in space, its solid oak balusters perfect anchors for a gallows. Grace would recover, he felt sure, in time, but what about Catherine? Hard to know. His heartbeat speeded up. He felt a pressure in his ears. He couldn't move. If he moved, he might do it, so he dared not move. For a long time, he sat there, not moving, listening in the growing dark. At some point, a loud switch clicked in a nearby wall followed by a distant clattering outdoors of metal blades kicking to a halt. The house settled, gradually, creaking, with a series of diminishing groans. Then all was quiet. Silence. Not another sound.

– 13 –

In mid-March, during one of western Washington's notorious black ice storms, after putting in a night in a tavern poker room, Fisherman Frank started off on his unsteady, bow-legged walk home from Mount Vernon to his old trailer in the woods along a two-lane county road. Either a car hit an ice patch and swerved onto the shoulder or he stumbled a few steps onto the road.

Catherine called at 3 in the morning from Skagit Valley Hospital to report the news that her dad had been declared brain dead. Doctors had asked for her signature to pull him off life support. As it happened, Grace was nearby, at her mom's place. Talking fast, C. D. told Catherine what he thought were the right things: how Frank would want it this way, he was never a guy for extreme measures, no sense making him go on breathing as a vegetable, how a time comes when the only compassionate choice is to let a loved one go. Catherine answered yes to his reassurances in a flat, emotionless voice. Her robotic tone suddenly frightened him. He choked up, then said, "Sweetheart, maybe don't do this all alone. At least wait until Mom gets there. . ."

"I haven't told Mom yet," she said. "I thought you'd call her for me."

"Me?"

"You cared about him more than she did."

Silence, except he heard them both breathing. He pictured where Catherine must be—on her cell phone, just outside the doors leading to the emergency room, not twenty feet away from Frank surrounded by wheezing, pulsing machines in a curtained-off space. Since she had started law school in Seattle, Catherine had been driving up to Mount Vernon almost every weekend to see her dad. She cleaned his trailer for him. She kept track of his pills. She filled his refrigerator with healthy foods, and she sat with him for hours watching old movies. She brought the two big dogs she was raising out to the country with her too—gorgeous German shepherds, a brother and sister pair she had named Griswold and Beaver, and she and Frank would take walks with them, setting them loose to run free in the woods. What else they did together, what they talked about, C. D. couldn't imagine. Grace had been arguing with Catherine about developing an unhealthy codependency with her dad. They argued a lot lately, about this and other things, causing a mother-daughter turbulence.

Frank's life had been deteriorating. In recent years, he had suffered from worsening back and knee injuries that kept him sidelined for much of the fishing seasons, and he had added regular doses of Vicodin and other painkillers to his maintenance drinking. Grace grew concerned for Catherine, for what might happen to her emotionally, not to mention her progress in law school, if she were drawn too deeply into her father's on top of her aging grandparents' needs—so easy to get stuck in the slick clay mud of the Skagit Valley. C. D. felt caught in the middle, but he took Catherine's side, admiring her mothering nature toward her dad just as he had long been moved by this in Grace. Still, that Catherine hadn't even called her mom yet seemed proof of what he had feared—Grace's efforts to protect her from her dad's failings had only driven her away.

"I'll . . . I'll call her then," he said. "She should be there in about an hour." Airline schedules scrolled through his mind. "We're *both* on our way. I can make it around noon or 1:00 at the latest. So just hold tight, your mom's coming. She'll want to be there. She *needs* to be there. We should do this together, as a family. Tell the doctors to keep Frank on life support, extreme measures, *everything* possible until we get there . . ."

"No," she said. "Dad wouldn't want all that trouble. Just tell Mom."

"Catherine. *Listen* to me. I'm sure of this. You *shouldn't* do this alone."

"I'm doing it," she said coldly. "I'm signing the papers right now."

After a heavy silence, he said he was proud of her—what else could he say?

He flew up the next morning, so he and Grace could help Catherine grieve. Together, they made the calls for funeral arrangements. In spring, when the weather broke, a handful of Frank's fishing buddies would take the family out on a boat to spread his ashes in the straits off Orcas Island that used to be prime salmon grounds before the fishery collapsed, or as Frank put it, quoting an old Irish saying, had "gone the way of everything else." Catherine would pick the readings for the service from the Oxford Bible and the Book of Common Prayer. An old retired skipper would act as minister, reciting the liturgy for a burial at sea: *The first shall come last and the last shall come first.* All this would be set in motion during the following days.

That Sunday, C. D. helped Catherine clean out her dad's trailer, which she inherited. Her grandmother had already lined up another bachelor tenant to rent it, and she could use the income to help with law school. C. D. regretted that she had to pay for law school, one more troubling issue among so many that kept him awake nights with those "if only" reviews in his head of his bad choices in life, the vast sums he had lost in the Biscayne Bay catastrophe, and the sordid taint of his associations with Biscayne Bay that followed him now. He would never reveal these to Catherine, nor the bankruptcy he and Grace were getting ready to file to protect them from lawsuits. He couldn't afford to help her pay for law school now. Sensing this, Catherine kept reassuring them how she had planned to pay her own way anyway, with loans and part-time waitressing, "To be *independent*, finally," she insisted, an extra barb in her voice aimed at her mom, though C. D. felt the sting more.

C. D. had urged Grace to help clear out Frank's trailer, envisioning it as a way that mother and daughter might grow closer. "I swore I'd never step foot in that trailer again no matter what, and I'm sticking to that," Grace said. "Besides, what makes you think she wants *me* there? We'd only bicker. She wants you with her, or she'll do it all alone, just so you know."

They met at Janice and Dewey's, then he rode with Catherine down to Frank's double-wide in her used, beat-up Subaru wagon, her gorgeous pair of German shepherds poking their intelligent grinning faces over the front seats and panting steamily into his ears. When they got there, what a wonder to watch those big athletic dogs spring out of the car like forces of nature and go loping off into the trees. In a few minutes, a high, joyous barking rose up, breaking the damp silence of the woods. "Running deer again," Catherine said, with a faint trace of pride. "Bad doggies. I could get fined, but they love it too much. Too many deer out here anyway, they're killing off the orchards. They never catch any, so no harm done."

That day, as C. D. worked alongside Catherine, he sensed something different in her, more of an intelligent *centeredness* she had been growing into all along. And what a tall, leggy woman she had grown to be, her body everywhere full but trim enough, he thought, recalling the hours and hours he and Grace (mainly Grace) had spent driving her back and forth to practices and attending her swim team meets in junior high and high school, encouraging her to keep fit and trim, her solid, rounded shoulders evidence of this. During her teenage years, he had missed too much of her life, his management positions ever more demanding and stressful the higher he rose at Pyramid Resorts. Soon it had become only Grace who had chauffeured Catherine and her friends all over the Las Vegas Valley. Grace would sit in the parked Volvo, watching out for the girls as they walked the neighborhoods, knocking on doors for donations—first for the Girl Scouts, selling cookies; then the Clark County Humane Society, for dog and cat rescue; in her sophomore year, for Amnesty International—Catherine grew to be an overly serious teenager who devoted herself to causes, a new cause every season, or so it seemed, he would hear about at breakfast or on weekends.

As they worked together, sorting through Frank's outside sheds, C. D. noted again how Catherine kept her dark straight hair cut short in a pageboy, a style she had worn since her junior year in college, longer on one side, as was the fashion, and as if all the better to show off the rows of tiny silver globes in her ears, piercings she had had done against her mom's objections. Still, he recalled Grace so often saying how lucky they were that Catherine had grown up to be such a "whole person" even in Las Vegas, where children were exposed to almost everything, sheltering them so tough to do. One might think that growing up in Las Vegas, so close to mass-marketed vice and sin and to the underbelly of human existence attracted to its darker side, kids would be more at risk of falling at young ages into hedonism, drugs, and dishonesty. But just the opposite proved more generally true: children raised in Las Vegas realized early on how most people—rich and poor—are only two bad choices from ruining their lives. Most children raised in Vegas, especially the smart, sensitive kids like Catherine, developed an ethical sense of right and wrong and what is healthy much earlier in their lives than almost anywhere else.

Both he and Grace had made it clear to Catherine that they trusted her, and this had helped. Growing up in Las Vegas, her own good sense had guided her through her teens. What an outgoing, socially active person she had become, and a compassionate voice for causes she believed in—she was studying to become a lawyer for causes—both generous qualities she had inherited from her mom. What a beauty, too, C. D. thought, full-figured in all the right places, combining the best physical qualities of both her natural parents. Her last name had come from Frank—Catherine O'Malley—along with her dark hair and eyes, and her quirky sense of humor. But her ambitions and her drive, and her gifts with people—her smart way of reading and persuading them—he felt sure she got from him. Who was it who wrote that our children sum our count and make our excuse? He believed it to be true. And maybe, just maybe, this was one thing in his life he had done right, or so he hoped.

Together, they sorted through a few things of her dad's Catherine wanted to keep: a dented gold watch from Alaska; a small cedar chest containing seventeen tarnished silver dollars; two framed posters of Irish landscapes and one of a Dublin pub crowded with burly men all merrily raising pints; and a much-thumbed-through photo album that started with pictures of Grace, Frank, and the baby right after she was born. The subsequent pages were filled with shots of little Catherine growing up that C. D. had routinely sent to Frank, letting Catherine pick the shots until she had turned about ten, when she started sending her dad photos on her own.

Frank kept his trailer surprisingly neat—worn old furniture but clean, the pots and pans stowed in order as in a galley, electric cords coiled by appliances like lines on a deck. C. D. noted a folding poker table leaned up against a wall near a glass case filled with chips, decks of cards, junky casino souvenirs. After they had been working a few minutes, the stench inside the trailer became nearly unbearable. A lifetime of cigarette smoke had soaked into the carpet and the yellow-tinged walls, mixed in with a tar-like stink of creosote from an old wood-burning stove.

Catherine lit incense—sweet, piney-smelling. "Copal helps best for the smoke smell," she said.

He wondered how and where she had ever learned that. Steadily, with a solemn quietness, they worked together loading boxes, clearing out Frank's souvenirs and other things. They carried most boxes outside to the burn barrel, a few they set aside to donate to the Salvation Army, two or three they loaded in Catherine's car. While she finished in the kitchen, C. D. started in on Frank's tiny bedroom. In that dank, closed-in space, one whole wall was taken up by a big chest of drawers with an old TV and a combination DVD-VHS player set up on its top.

C. D. started with the top drawer. Instead of the socks and underwear he expected, he discovered Frank O'Malley's unspeakably explicit porn collection. He opened other drawers and found all were packed with VHS tapes, DVDs, and XXX magazines dating back years—a visual Babel of slutty cover photos, shockingly obscene contortions, grotesque anatomies. Somehow, he'd thought he possessed a complete knowledge of human sexuality, but he couldn't believe what he was seeing: double-bottomed anal, multiple-partner oral paloozas, she-males, even combos with animals. Catherine walked in on him, carrying empty boxes. He slammed the middle drawer closed, shrinking back as guiltily as if the smut collection were his own.

"Dad sure loved his cum shots!" she called out with an ironic brightness.

He just stood there, speechless that she could even know such a phrase.

"*See-Dee!*" she said with a familiar sing-song. "Who do you think's been cleaning this smelly place!"

She started over to the chest of drawers to unpack them. He drew a line right there: of course she was a grown-up now, her life was her own business, but *no way* would he let her go through such a porn collection and ever after have to think of her with those obscene images in her mind. He insisted on being the one who packed it up. Catherine laughed—her first real laugh in days. And he could tell she would make a funny little one-liner out of this incident, something light to say when people asked about her father's death to fend off the harder emotions: "My dad didn't leave much except a porn collection . . . and he left that for my stepdad!"

Out in the gravel driveway, as a kind of truce, C. D. asked what Catherine wanted done with the boxes of porn. She teased him a moment, pretending to think this over, in her expression a flash of the little girl clutching one of her story books to her chest as if to keep it from him, like hide and seek, until, with mock reluctance, she would hand it over to him to read to her. This brief game passed between them. With a grim smile, she jerked her thumb in the direction of the burn barrel.

He carried the first box over and dumped it in on top of a heap of papers, old clothes, other trash. A chilly, misting rain that fell over the Skagit Valley all winter, rarely ceasing, had started up again. The dogs came loping back from the woods, wet and shivering, and huddled together under the old wooden porch of the trailer. A rainy quietness settled over them as C. D. and Catherine continued working. The day had slid into evening by the time they finished. In the deepening, starless dark, they stood by the fire hissing hotly in the barrel, quietly watching Frank O'Malley's earthly belongings burn to embers. With a stick, Catherine stirred the last of the glowing ashes. She stepped back a ways from the smoke. He put his arm over her shoulders to warm them both against the chill of the north woods. She nestled against him. No need to say anything, and no need to rush, not now. His daughter could take all the time she needed to say goodbye.

Exodos

– 1 –

Grace called that winter and spring spent selling out and moving "the season of our happy divorce." Getting out from under the new house in Las Vegas—foreclosure capital of America—on which they owed almost twice what it could be sold for now, required them to play roles in a soulless dumb show called a "short sale." Short selling seemed the best option. If they played their cards right, at least one of them might keep a passable credit rating and emerge free and clear from their debts. To do this, a "strategic divorce" became part of the plan.

The decision to take this step only gradually emerged. At first, with Grace prolonging her trip to her mom's so she and C. D. had to rely on daily phone calls and faxed documents, they set out honestly to meet their commitments. But in the short-sale process, they discovered they would be thrown in with a sordid ugly cast not unlike a sinister mime troupe made up of slick attorneys and real estate agents and weird representatives of "the banks"—not really banks anymore but more like tag teams of fly-by-night traders and clerks at the "mortgage-servicing company" with ever-changing names yet oddly identical-looking handwriting for their signatures. Their mortgage had been loaned originally by the same Bank of the Nation—that nefarious B of N—that had violated its contract and pulled the plug on Biscayne Bay. The mortgage had been sold off, their jumbo loan split up into pieces and "bundled." Who actually owned the pieces of it now no one seemed able to say. Not long into the short-sale process, C. D. and Grace lost all trust, not sure they would *not* be held legally responsible and maybe get sued even after they finally did receive those coveted documents promising "release" from any "deficiency judgment" on the small fortune they would still owe plus the hefty fees (and some taxes) to secure their freedom.

The "mortgage-servicing company" represented itself as located in an actual building in Simi Valley, California. But when C. D. tried them, none of the phone numbers were answered with anything except recorded loops of robot voices instructing him to press numbers then the pound key, which led to other talking robot loops, on and on, until at the end of about six minutes of this, the system returned him to the very same robot voice where he had started. So it wasn't long before he began to believe rumors he read on the internet that the company supposed to be untangling the mess of those "bundled mortgage securities," or CDOs, or whatever the fuck they were, and so manage the release of his chopped-up debt to "the negotiator" for the short sale didn't actually exist in any *physical* sense at all. The company wasn't housed in any actual building anywhere but instead consisted of what must be hundreds of individual cyber-linked computers spread out across the globe from Simi Valley to Indianapolis to Santiago to Mumbai and even to a lone Sikh genius and graduate of MIT who worked from a disposable laptop via an unsecured Wi-Fi hub in the international departures lounge at Heathrow Airport, outside London, so his transactions could never be traced.

Every few weeks, at some odd hour—why 4 a.m.?—the latest confusing fax with a different return fax number came *creak, creak, creak*ing out of his fax machine; and every few weeks, a new email with a "no reply" address popped up in his inbox with a complex .pdf document attached that appeared to contradict in its fine print another recent legal document Grace and C. D. had received. Whenever he phoned his Las Vegas real estate attorney to ask questions—a guy named Simms (add his considerable bill to what they owed)—his secretary took a message. After C. D. charmed her and pressed, she finally admitted that shyster was either off playing golf or out to lunch with real estate agents to drum up new business. At least someone is getting rich these days, he thought—the same players who had piloted the world into the mortgage catastrophe in the first place were now huckstering at the other end of it, collecting enormous fees. The whole system exactly resembled organized crime. C. D. envisioned high-tech versions of the smoky back rooms of old-time Mafia sports betting operations, with officers of "the banks" like bookies taking bets over the phone. The odds of getting a final approval of his short sale seemed about the same as winning a trifecta at the track. Weeks passed. Legal bills piled up. Before long, like tens upon tens of thousands of distressed homeowners in Las Vegas, before their "negotiation" could be completed—by then driven so crazy C. D. would fantasize about committing multiple homicides, only just *who,* exactly, should he kill?—he and Grace threw up their hands and made plans to run away and leave the whole mess behind. If they had to, they would flee Las Vegas with all the "legal" (but truly criminal) process still pending.

Along with their frustration trying to get out from under the new house, they faced court actions tied to Biscayne Bay, for the first round of which they were plaintiffs trying to collect at best *two and a half cents* on the dollar from the massive bankruptcy. Then the latest news hit with a shock—the same "banks" that had broken contracts and delivered the final blow filed a countersuit, meaning to collect damages from former CEO Lance Sheperd along with Gravenstein LLC for "accounting irregularities" that "the banks" claimed amounted to fraud. Clearly, this must be a maneuver in legal proceedings that would take years to resolve, still, could the executives on Sheperd's team also end up in court? Could C. D. Reinhart be sued?

"Deep pockets," Tim Slocum told him at the lunch C. D. invited him to at Spago's to ask his advice. "None of your team should be targeted in this litigation. Except maybe Kinkaid. He must have known a great deal, isn't that so? Sure as Grandma's mouse, he'll be subpoenaed, and he'll have to testify." With a bemused expression, Slocum busied himself with fastidiously picking bread crumbs off the tablecloth, dropping them into his napkin like each was another coin added to his fortune. "It's that double bookkeeping, a standard in the industry. One messy set for the construction costs, a cleaner set for the banks. They never agree, those two accounts," he said. "Just a technicality, all balances get reconciled in the end, but those two sets of books can differ by several millions. And it takes one hell of an attorney to explain that to a judge."

"What about Sheperd? Where *is* he?"

"Word is he's in France, but damned if I know," Slocum said with a dismissive shrug. "Fitch and Marcus handle his business now. I want nothing to do with him. Or let's just say I'd rather be on the other side than defending him."

"That bad?"

"Don't worry about Sheperd. Lance always takes care of himself," Slocum said. "He'll just be tied up in court for the next ten years." With a grim satisfaction, he folded his napkin full of crumbs into a neat square and pushed it to one side on the table. As C. D. paid the check—in cash—Slocum added, "Not to worry. You and Grace should come out just fine. They won't come after you. No offense meant, but what could they expect to get?"

Slocum's parting words made C. D. worry even more. He had learned that whenever a Las Vegas attorney assured him of anything, especially involving "the banks," he must prepare for exactly the opposite to happen. With more advice from yet another attorney Grace retained in Seattle, after anxious nights spent talking over their options, they decided, reluctantly, that their best move would be to file for a "strategic divorce" to protect what few assets they had left and before they listed the new house for a short sale. After that, C. D. would file for bankruptcy. He flew back and forth to Seattle, eating up years of his frequent-flier miles, astonished he still had plenty, to help Grace get settled back into the same old house on Queen Anne Hill where she had started out decades ago and then sit together through meetings with yet another attorney. He also flew up for what they started calling "conjugal visits" before he returned to Las Vegas as if to a sentence at hard labor to take care of clearing out the new house and seeing to all the details of the move. So they began to live what became, in effect, a kind of commuter marriage, C. D. in Las Vegas most of the time, slowly selling off almost everything they possessed.

—

Grace would be treated most generously in the "strategic divorce," allowed to keep the mostly paid-for house on Queen Anne Hill and what little remained in their retirement accounts. C. D. would "keep" the new house until it short sold, and he would be the sole responsible party for almost all their debts and any outstanding judgments. Grace would be protected behind a fortress of isolating property-separation agreements and an ironclad decree woven carefully into the contradictory laws of two states to discourage any legal actions that might be contemplated by "the banks" over the next seven years. So C. D. handed over to his beloved wife almost all his remaining assets with a provision in the settlement that, since Grace was now the main income earner, if he could not provide for himself within the year, he could request that she write out a modest check to him each month for alimony.

After this "no-contest" divorce passed muster and the judge's gavel came down, one glorious, sunny, emerald-green day in Seattle—ideal weather, so unlike the rainy day when they had married—he filed for a Chapter 7 bankruptcy as protection from possible litigations. Kinkaid had been named already in one countersuit from "the banks." In another pending litigation, it appeared possible their little partnership of Kinkaid, Reinhart, and Olsson might be partly liable for actions involving a bankrupt shopping center project down in Houston since their contracts somehow tied them in with another possibly fraudulent investment group with Gravenstein LLC at the helm. "Don't sweat it," Slocum said, which made C. D. sweat even more. "Judges there know the drill. Those Texas lawsuits never amount to anything."

He couldn't wait to go bankrupt. For weeks, Grace handled the niggling details, the schedules of assets and losses. C. D. tensed up as she went over lists of what personal property he had left, arranged in general categories with only *value unknown* after so many items. When he mentioned this, she brushed him off by saying that, according to their attorneys, it was best to let a court appraiser figure out values. He did not mention the Charles Ellsworth painting. He understood that its value, even sold at a loss, must be included somewhere underneath her calculations, but she didn't say a word. He wondered when she would before the final filings.

He grew concerned about Grace's stress level, so busy on the phone with attorneys and with her printer and fax machine, handling it all. On top of that, she was starting a part-time accounting business in the front office she had made out of the parlor of her house. That old house still needed constant repairs, but with a new coat of paint and its floors refinished, it seemed not that bad, really, its best feature a big bay window she could gaze through into the rainy street as she worked. A rose garden she had planted across the front had started feathering into lush green life. She had lost weight, he noted a youthful color returning to her cheeks, and even her Vegas Valley allergies had gone away. She seemed happy—happier *without* him, he thought. And she seemed not unhappy that, after twenty years of so much hard work and striving in Las Vegas, she had landed right back where she had started out before they had married.

The day the judge's gavel came down for their divorce, granting them their "fresh start"—as Her Honor so cheerily called it—they sat in mismatched antique chairs at an old oak table Janice and Dewey had salvaged from a farm auction that somehow complemented the chipped crown moldings in the cramped dining room. With a pile of legal documents, including their signed, sealed decree as a centerpiece, Grace held up her wineglass for a toast: "Here's to our happy divorce!"

They agreed they wouldn't let slip one word to anyone about the divorce, especially not to Catherine, not after what she had just gone through with Frank's death. She rejoined the mainstream of her busy university life, studying hard, as ever, and taking care of her two rambunctious dogs. She also worked a job waiting tables at a popular campus music club to support herself and keep from borrowing so much in student loans. She kept her own apartment, with roommates, even though Grace had offered her free rent on Queen Anne Hill, but Catherine was too independent now to accept this. C. D. agreed with her decision to make it on her own, proud of her for it, but at the same time sick that he had lost the money he had set aside for her graduate school. He also wasn't sure that Catherine adopting a pair of German shepherds hadn't been in part to guarantee she could never be talked into moving back in with her mom, given Grace's allergies to dogs.

His other main regret was her life decision to study law. He just couldn't see it, no way, not even with her idealistic motives to specialize in labor relations and human rights. Selfishly, he hoped she might hit a wall in law school and turn to something else. Or that her new boyfriend might spirit her away down to South America. Catherine had started dating a Brazilian musician named João Ribiero, a semiprofessional conga drum player from Bahía (the "black Rome"). She had brought João over a few times for dinner, from which Grace concluded he might be too flighty, possibly a womanizer, too, and she didn't trust him. "You sure this isn't a race thing?" C. D. pressed. Grace insisted it wasn't, that her concern was only for Catherine, how João could end up breaking her heart. C. D. disagreed. He thought Catherine needed exactly João's kind of fun, carefree personality to balance her tendency to be too serious. "Besides," he said, "who's to say Catherine won't be the heartbreaker?"

He half hoped João might sweep her away enough so she would

drop out of law school, even that Catherine with her dogs might pitch a tent with him on a Bahía beach to play music and sell trinkets to tourists—anything seemed better than becoming a lawyer. Not his business to say this, but with five attorneys—count them!—now meddling in their lives, his daughter becoming a lawyer felt like too much. They wouldn't say anything to Catherine about their legal purgatory, much less that they had just divorced. They wouldn't tell Janice and Dewey, either. Why add to their worries? They agreed never to remove their wedding rings.

Late that night, unable to sleep, uncomfortable in the damp chill of the drafty bedroom in Seattle, C. D. couldn't help but marvel at the astonishing condition society had reached: some people so rich they lived sham marriages so as not to divest themselves of their mega-wealth; others so poor they couldn't afford but to continue to subsist together in rancor and misery even if what they most wanted was to split up and get on with their lives; then here *they* were—a couple still in love, surely, after all these years, now *not* married to protect what they could salvage and still own from their hard-working lives. Or really, as he had to admit it, as of today, to protect what little *she* still owned.

He gazed over at her side of the bed, where Grace lay on her back, her mouth open, arms spread wide, breathing easily through her unstuffed-up nose, her big feather pillow fallen to the floor. She was five years older, and lately, he had noted the stretch marks at her midriff and the cellulite on her thighs, all this visible on her body he still desired. After her diminished interest in sex in Las Vegas, here, her passion had renewed. They were making love again more like their younger selves, or even better, with a settled comfort in their familiar, satisfying moves.

Recently, like an emblem of a resolute shift in self-image to come to terms with her "natural" age, Grace had decided to cut her hair short and quit dyeing it, letting it grow out in mixed shades of muted auburn and steel-wool gray. She no longer minded that her age showed, although he—or so he thought—appeared younger than his age, only a few silver threads in his hair. When they were out together, he sensed people noticed the difference, not only because of the gap in years but the social injustice in the way people viewed women and men aging. Without him realizing when, she had adjusted to growing old. For his part, some women still checked him out, moving his way and showing off their feminine equipment. Grace must have noted this, as she always had.

Even so, she had come to trust him enough to divorce him. She had put it just that way: "Do I trust you enough for this divorce?" She had decided yes. And did he trust her? Yes: he trusted Grace, always would. Did he trust himself? Less clear: except for that one night with Greta that had cooled to a glowing ember in his heart, he had been faithful. Still, he couldn't promise himself he would never repeat what had happened. He loved Grace. Falling in love with her had changed his life. And Grace? After her bad first marriage, without her knowing it yet, she had been looking to find another man to build a life with, a man also happy to be a real father to her daughter before it was too late. He had fulfilled those roles the best he could, or so he believed.

And why had they never had a biological child of their own? At first, neither of them had pushed for this, reassuring each other one child was enough, "at least until we can get ahead a little and afford it," as Grace, ever so practical in money matters, kept saying in their early years. When the time came for her gynecologist to fit her for a new IUD, Grace let C. D. know she might be ready for a baby, suggesting that it should be now or maybe never, given their differences in age. At the time, C. D. had been so caught up in the ten- and twelve-hour days he was putting in building the IT and marketing for The Beach that he couldn't properly take in the full weight of her suggestion or the way it came at him via shy inquiries in bed when topmost in his mind was how he needed to hurry up and sleep. With his brothers and sister, there would always be plenty of Reinharts in the world. Besides, weren't they happy enough with just the three of them? Wasn't it Grace who insisted real fathering had little to do with who supplies the seed? And then think about little Catherine, when she became aware that some of her friends had much bigger families—in third or fourth grade?—she had kept saying, "I *like* being an only child."

Years later, if he had only paused long enough from a life spent counting up his money and achievements, he might have pushed for a child—a son—responding to some primeval urge to replicate the spiraling ladders of his DNA like further proof of his success. By then, Grace's age would have caused difficulties. The right moment, delayed too long, passed. And the way things had turned out, praise be he wouldn't have to face the shame of seeing any earnest child of his gazing into his father's eyes, hoping to look up to his example, not knowing he carried inside that most twisted of genes that would mark him forever as what he surely would be, too—like father, like son—a stupid *loser*. Maybe better to leave the future to the winners, let the losers fade away. In the end, he should feel relieved that he only had to make his amends to Catherine. And to Grace, too, however he could. Look what she had ended up with: Las Vegas and their twenty years together in a city that, after he had devoted decades of his life to building it, had treated him hardly differently than it did any other loser. But he couldn't blame the city. He had failed his wife. His choices—or, better put, his *responses* to life—had failed her, so no wonder she seemed so happy now in Seattle, so at home with their "happy divorce."

Did the divorce change things for him? He decided that it did. He didn't know just how yet, but yes—it did. He felt the chill in the room, not used to the damp of Seattle nights since his blood had turned "desert thin," as they say in Las Vegas, uncomfortable except in warm climates. He pulled the down comforter over his shoulders and squirmed his body closer against her familiar warmth in bed, not sure he felt he deserved her body in the same way now that she was his *ex*-wife. But what really *had* changed? He wondered, shivering. It struck him then: that they were no longer legally married, as of today, as of just this afternoon, made him feel even colder. And let's face it: *lonely*.

– 2 –

He spent his last day in Las Vegas loading up a few basic things and items of furniture he hadn't sold or given away—the $42,000 from fire-sold possessions paid off a big chunk of what they owed the attorneys, and what he couldn't sell he had donated to Catholic Charities. He loaded a midsize U-Haul truck with the Danish-design bed with matching end tables and lamps from the guest suite, where he had been sleeping; two boxes of linens, no more; a careful selection from his wardrobe, two full garment boxes, including his five best suits; four boxes of kitchen items; his cherry wood desk and the comfortable office chair from his study along with his obsolete computer, scanner-fax machine, and creaky old printer; five boxes of legal files; six boxes of his most prized books, which had taken him several weeks to mull over and choose; his tools; and, finally, some selected photographs and artworks he took down from the walls.

The packing and loading took most of the day into midafternoon. He loaded boxes toward the front of the truck bed first, then labored away methodically with his power tools to take the furniture apart as much as possible, loading it in pieces. He proved strong enough to wrestle the bed onto a rolling dolly, wheeling it out the front door then muscling it up the ramp of the truck, where he slid it into place and tied it down. He ate lunch sitting on the diving board of the pool, staring into the shifting whirlpools as the pump motor churned around in the sparkling water. He wasn't hungry. He tossed most of his sandwich into the desert landscaping for the sparrows and went back inside to finish up.

Last, he packed what remained of his art, three pieces—careful to place each into its own sturdy art box and not scatter too many annoying Styrofoam peanuts as he poured them into the empty spaces. First, his treasured eleven-by-fourteen matted and framed photograph showing him with his arms around "my girls" taken on a rare outing one weekend into the Valley of Fire: Catherine in the third grade then, her face red from the sun and bursting with a gap-toothed laugh after he had just squeezed her around her ribs; Grace with her naturally red hair windblown into an attractive mess as she leaned into him with a serene, thankful-seeming gaze directed as if far off over the horizon but really at a German tourist who had offered to snap the photo as they stood against a background of red-orange sandstone rocks with patterns of spiraling squiggles, snakes, horned figures, and starlike designs of Stone Age petroglyphs, all the color tones and separations in that photograph in perfect balance. How he loved this photograph from a time when all seemed in place in their lives, settled in after the big move to Las Vegas, all three dressed in their hiking gear like happy explorers who had just stumbled onto signs of an ancient and as yet undiscovered civilization. He poured in peanuts, settled the photo into its box, taped the box closed.

On his knees in his study, he packed the weird lithograph Lance Sheperd had placed in his hands, like a challenge, the day he had pleaded to get in on the deal for Biscayne Bay—that messy black-and-white image that struck him like a dirty planet with a few loose strings sticking out, any one of which could be tugged on and the whole thing might come unraveled. Like the new house, when he had last checked, the book value of the lithograph had dropped to less than half what he had paid for it, so he had decided to keep it, planning to hang it in a future office space he might inhabit so it could serve as a cautionary sign, like a warning there could be no turning back, not now, not ever again. He shook the heavy art box to make sure the work would travel properly then taped it closed. He carried both boxes out to the truck and secured them to one side of the load.

In the driveway, he keyed in the code for the garage door opener and the steel panels rattled up over his head about halfway, where he stopped it, then he ducked under it into the garage. He turned on the lights. He pulled back tarps heaped in a pile against the back wall. There it was, that spectrum of fanned-out colors, his rainbow—what he had kept to secure at least some portion of a future, no matter the possible crime.

He had been nervous about damaging the painting by hiding it in the garage. A month ago, the day the court-appointed appraiser phoned to announce he was on his way, on impulse, he had pulled it down from over the fireplace, quickly rigged plastic-wrapped pot-holders and towels at the corners and along the edges, then carefully covered it with plastic lawn bags stretched tight so they made no contact with the painted surface. He carried the painting into the garage and heaped tarps over it, arranging them to look like a casual mess. Not that it was likely any bank agent would know what it was, still, he had done this. All winter and into the spring, on balance sheets of their assets, losses, and property inventories for the bankruptcy court, he had left the painting off the lists. Grace had been complicit. It had taken her weeks to decide, then she finally brought it up: "Just make sure to leave it on the wall when the appraiser comes. The way I'm told these things go, he probably won't ask, and if you're careful, you'll be in the clear. And don't mention it in a text or an email," she said. "That way, nobody can prove I know anything about it. Whatever you do with it, I don't want to know."

This surprised him, as Grace all her life had been meticulously honest until this one significant omission. She had instructed him to list the painting along with everything else as *various wall art and miscellaneous household items*. Still, at the last minute, he hid the painting in the garage. Grace had no idea he had done this, and he would never tell her, so when the judge's gavel came down in bankruptcy court and he was set free (or presumably set free), if he afterward sold the painting and the money turned up in an IRS audit or by any other legal scrutiny, it would be *his* crime—his and his alone.

With only a day's notice by phone call, the appraiser for the bankruptcy court he had been fearing for weeks arrived, accompanied by Tom Haley, their real estate agent for the short sale. The appraiser turned out to be a young Chinese guy barely off the plane from Taiwan. As C. D. learned later, there were so many new bankruptcies that appraisal firms were importing professionals from abroad, rushing them through their certifications and H1 visas so they could handle the unprecedented volume of cases clogging the courts. Saying little aside from a few pleasantries in his accented English, the appraiser politely and efficiently hurried through the big house, room to room, checking off boxes on forms and on the lists of what they were keeping submitted to the court, all routine. He spent less than fifteen minutes going over spreadsheets of items sold and where the money had gone, asking only a question or two: what is the disposition of the washer and dryer? Why is the refrigerator remaining with the house? He spent less than an hour, total, in an apparent rush to finish and get on to his next job. In the garage, he didn't seem to notice the messy pile of blue tarps. The appraiser spent less than a minute in there, a quick glance or two around. C. D. suspected it wouldn't have made any difference if he had left his Charles Ellsworth painting on the wall, so quick and summary this walk-through seemed, a mere paperwork formality. After the appraiser had finished and left, how petty and ridiculous he felt that he had hidden the painting at all, and how contemptuous of the banks. He texted Grace: *Court appraiser just left. No issues. All lists accepted as submitted. Love you—*

In the garage, he followed steps of a diagram he had downloaded from the internet, setting up panels of cardboard against Styrofoam corner pads to make an inner box for the big painting; then he started with a drill and screws to assemble precut boards to build a strong outer structure to protect it for the move, a chore that should take about an hour to complete. As he worked, he felt like a burglar, stealing glances over his shoulder, apprehensive that his real estate agent might drop by earlier than expected. Not that the agent would likely suspect anything. Still, Tom Haley had been a Henderson cop once. After a decade, he had quit the police force, discouraged by its insider politics and the night shifts that took time away from his kids, so he had turned to selling real estate during the boom. When the crash hit, after his commissions dropped to almost nothing and he had to fight his way to get out from under his "underwater" home in Summerlin, he also got caught up as a player in that sad dumb show called the "short sale." He had suffered through the same frustrating mess with "the banks," so Tom had learned the system and become a specialist, recommended to C. D. by Tim Slocum. If any flimflams or bullying by the banks might happen—such as a future lawsuit to recover money he still owed—who could be better to have on his side than an ex-cop? On the other hand, he had no idea what this ex-cop might do if he figured out what he was up to—is there even such a criminal charge as *accessory to fraudulent concealment of assets?* If there were such a thing, he imagined half the guys on Wall Street could be tossed into handcuffs and marched in a massive perp walk down to White Street and the Tombs—what a happy thought! No matter any possible felony, he sensed Tom Haley would say nothing; still, best to hurry up and get it all crated before he came by.

As C. D. worked, his mind drifted off into satisfaction at his revenge—*fuck* the banks! If he were careful, not one of the anonymous processors located in Simi Valley or Indianapolis or Buenos Aires or Mumbai or even that allegedly lone Sikh genius at Heathrow would ever know.

During the darkest days of the crash, when the mega-rich weren't buying much of anything, he still might have sold the Charles Ellsworth for enough—even at a loss—to pay off a fifth of what they still owed on the house, or other debts, Grace's medical costs, some of the tens of thousands on credit cards. But paying any more on the house would have made no sense. No manager or executive at the banks would have made such a stupid move with their finances, no way in hell. All across the globe, the rich were the first to lawyer up so they could welsh on their bad bets as fast as they could. This proved especially so in Las Vegas—the prince of Brunei in a fire sale of his $20 million estate complete with air-conditioned horse barns; and several bankrupt or nearly so movie stars, athletes, and politicians, too, had dumped their Vegas real estate at breath-catching losses. Millionaires were fleeing in droves. A mega-rich businessman named Petersen had summed it up as he and his family cut their losses on a $15 million mansion before they beat it out of town: "There's no future left here that we can see."

The art market, though, functioned to a different rhythm. Two years into the crisis, prices began gradually rising again, sure to rise even more. Once freed up by the bankruptcy court, he only had to worry about how the record of any sale reported to the IRS might surface in any possible legal action taken by the banks or by any other party that might name him in litigations. What else was a guy like him supposed to do? In the tangled web of the various ways to report any meager capital gains or possibly even write up the sum from the sale as consultancy income (another crime), he only needed to be careful not to raise "red flags" (as the tax attorneys called them). And how likely was he to be audited? What was the risk? Minimal, at worst. A phrase from Alfred E. Neuman in the old *Mad Magazine* sounded in his head: *What, me worry?*

But he did worry. Not so much that he would get caught, which would be unlikely; and in truth, it wouldn't be the banks that would come up short even one thin dime by what he planned to do—no way the banks would ever lose in the vast pyramid scheme of the global economy. No. It would be the poor suckers at the other end of his mortgage, the well-meaning fools who still held onto the chopped-up pieces of his debt all split up and bundled—some fire fighters' pension fund, some college endowment, the sovereign wealth fund of some African nation, the struggling widow who had taken bum steer advice from a sleazy broker to buy crap paper—real people, somewhere, were going to lose. But he had also lost plenty, hadn't he? One of these days, he *had* to wise up, didn't he? Like in a game of musical chairs, wouldn't he be stupid *not* to take a seat when the music stopped? Why should *he* be the loser left standing?

He thought what his father would do, the story he would tell—how his mother, Augusta Reinhart, had spent twenty years paying off bad stock market margin bets old Otto Reinhart had made before the crash that had set off the Great Depression. After Opa Otto had dropped dead from a heart attack, Oma Augusta had worked as a nurse, dutifully paying a percentage of what she earned each month, raising her four kids with parsimony close to poverty until her husband's debts had been repaid. Plenty of people in similar circumstances had declared bankruptcy, got out from under, then picked themselves up and trudged on to build new lives. Not the Reinharts, no, never—*those Germans*—always duty bound, choosing the path with the most sacrifice and suffering, little more culturally sacred in their Germanic code than keeping a promise even if it killed them. As far as his father was concerned, a bankrupt deserved about the same level of contempt as a murderer. For C. D., this alone could move him to embrace bankruptcy with a passion. Let's face it: the whole system is built to privilege trick-and-trap scammers marauding and pillaging like a gang of highway robbers in a culture of piracy. How could his own peccadillo compare? This Reinhart had resolved to be proud of his bankruptcy, to hold his head high, and more: *fuck* the banks!

With its trends, fads, capricious fashions, its gallery owners like carnival barkers pumping up prices, the art world turned out to be at least as corrupt (or more so) as the business world. He had already pitched and negotiated the sale through a gallery in L.A., a branch of a major international firm with headquarters in New York and London. Exploiting his urgency, the gallery would buy the painting at a price close to a steal. All he had to do was drive to L.A. and present the painting to their curator to verify its authenticity and the deal would be done. He had explained his situation, his need for a "discreet sale" paid one-third up front, the rest in yearly installments stretched out "for tax reasons" for as long as the gallery agreed, which turned out to be four years (he took an additional price cut for their trouble). He did not ask them to invoice the sale as anything other than a sale (no telling how much that would have dropped the price), all left up to him how he would list the annual payments. That way, he could sell the painting and leave little trace (unless he were audited) and so rob the banks and commit, if not the perfect crime, then a messier kind of crime, one of those "gray areas" (as Kinkaid would say) on the scale of financial crimes. Wasn't everybody who was *any*body doing something worse, similar, or exactly the same? And Lance Sheperd had been right about the painting, how he would make out in the end. After the gallery took its standard percentage plus all the other cuts to get their price close to a steal, he would still recover a few thousand more than he had paid. He planned to use a lot of the first payment for what remained of his legal bills plus the costs of the move, with a little left over to contribute to Catherine's humongous law school tuition. Whatever modest sum he kept would buy him time to look around for whatever came next, time to settle into the new post-marriage with Grace, time to find himself again.

Bolting the last brace board into place, he finished the crate for the painting, satisfied by the stable way the contraption stood on its own, sheltering its fragile "gray area" contents. He swept up the bits of sawdust and dust balls on the garage floor, going over it twice with a broom. He would leave the house immaculate, the ovens gleaming, the holes and scrapes in the walls meticulously filled, all patched and touched up for any new owner who wished to stick with their color scheme, not that any new *resident* owner would likely turn up soon. It was more probable that a predatory investor flush from the oil sands of Alberta, Canada, or some newly rich, short-seller stock investor from Santa Fe or San Diego, or a Chinese investor group looking to hide all that money raked off the top of government corruption, would swoop in to make an offer within twenty-four hours of the house being listed. A private investor or real estate fund would surely gamble on an expected 20 to 30 percent "pop" plus the pressure of inflation when the market finally recovered to *flip that house* in about five years. When the title finally did change hands, their house would no doubt sit empty or be left to transient renters until it could be profitably sold. One out of every seven houses in Las Vegas were similarly distressed.

As he'd suspected, about a half hour early, he heard the rumble of the big SUV his real estate agent drove pulling into the driveway. With the crated painting standing behind him, C. D. opened the garage door the rest of the way. He met Tom Haley at the end of the drive. Over the hills to the west, the sky was turning into the orange and pink hues of a spectacular desert sunset. His agent would place a set of keys in a lock box hanging on the front door, then all would be ready for the short-sale listing to go up on the multiples at midnight, complete with a set of photographs he had taken of the house when it still had furniture, best "to stage" the home in this way, as Tom had said.

"All set?" Tom asked, taking the keys.

"Almost," C. D. said. "Just the trailer to hitch to the U-Haul, load the car, and she's done."

Tom Haley was an earnest, quick-moving guy, with even quicker eyes that took in everything in a few glances. He couldn't shake the hypervigilance of his training as a cop, that sense entering a house that he could instantly tell what waited around corners or upstairs. His head pivoted on his muscular neck a bit robotically; he looked like a cyborg with that Bluetooth device plugged into his ear. C. D. noted his fast appraisal into the depths of the garage, nothing unusual registering save approval he had left the garage so clean. Tom's wife dressed him in Hawaiian shirts or in colorful Mexican guayaberas. C. D. had never seen him wearing so much as a jacket over these even in chilly weather. This added to a sense of unaffected surface he projected, easy to read, little hidden in what he saw, which is what C. D. liked about him—his straight talk, his cool appraisal of situations placed before him. Today, Tom wore a dark green shirt with a pattern of scarlet parrots printed on it, and this struck C. D. as exactly right—like a flamboyant emblem of the marketplace itself, repeating back at the world whatever it heard.

The agent set up a lock box on the front door in only a minute, punching in his coded numbers. At the door, they shook hands, sealing the deal. Then Tom said something not at all a part of his usual manner, which would have been to say nothing. "I'm sorry people like you and Grace are moving on," he said. "What a shame."

"Win a few, lose a few," C. D. said. "Way it goes."

"I remember when they were building this development. We cops used to drive around up here saying to each other, 'Man, if we could only be lucky enough to *get in* on some of this.' Now the Wards, the Baxters down the street, the DiContinis on the cul-de-sac . . . all the others . . . Who would have thought this could happen here?"

"It'll be back," C. D. said. "Las Vegas always comes back, right?"

"I dunno," Tom said. "What they're doing to the schools now . . . I mean, I like to think of myself as a *conservative*. I don't like taxes. But now they're cutting so much, what family with kids would ever consider moving here? It's crazy . . ."

"It's always been crazy here," C. D. said.

"Naw. Not like this," Tom said. "Say, you need help loading that crate?"

C. D. swallowed, hoping the sudden jolt inside his chest didn't show. He nodded, mumbling "Thanks," and lifted the dolly down out of the truck. In the garage, the two of them balanced the big crate on it, more awkwardly sized than heavy. Stepping along the driveway on either side, arms spread against the crate, they kept it from tipping as they wheeled it into the U-Haul then slid it into a space C. D. had left on one side of the load. Tom didn't ask what was inside the crate, only remarked that the truck wasn't even half filled. In cop mode, he inspected the load as if checking for safety issues and found none.

In the street, Tom helped C. D. hitch up the two-wheeled auto trailer—its orange tongue bright with yellow caution warnings: *Do not back up trailer while loaded!* And *Danger! Do not back up!*—that one over a cartoonish diagram of a trailer doubling on its tongue and the loaded auto crashing into the truck with lightning bolt shocks. C. D. wondered how he could plan his drive so he could manage only straight pulls in and out of gas stations. Tom directed him like a cop, helping him straighten out the front tires of the new black Hyundai Elantra he had paid cash for after selling off his nearly thirteen-year-old BMW for a halfway decent price. He had decided on this cheap car over any other because it should be good on gas, came with a hundred-thousand-mile warranty, and hey, the dealer "threw in" the leather seats. What did it matter that it felt way too underpowered, and when he revved it up, the engine clattered like the lid on a tea kettle? What more did he need?

C. D. invited Tom in for a beer by way of thanks but he said no, he had to pick up one of his boys from a soccer game. They shook hands once more. Before he drove off, all business again, Tom called out the car window: "Should have offers in a day on this beauty! We'll get most and best written up and take it to the banks!"

– 3 –

All set, all done. Goodbye to Tom, so long to the neighborhood, cheerio to all, thanks for the memories. The sun dropped over the jagged black lines of the distant hills, darkness falling fast over the desert. C. D. closed the garage door, made sure it locked, then let himself back into his empty, dark, immaculate house. He had planned to eat a sandwich with a beer or a glass of wine and go to sleep early, stretched out with a pillow on the carpet of the guest suite, so he could get a start on the long drive before dawn, avoiding traffic. He aimed himself down the hallway that would avoid the sight of the high, suspended staircase landing, those balusters like a gallows. He shook off a thought of the rope, still in the garage.

How empty the new house was. The squeak of his sneakers along the marble floors echoed through emptiness into the kitchen. Even the faint sound of opening the refrigerator resonated from the high ceilings and bare walls. He pulled out the bag with its Subway sandwich, but he wasn't hungry. He set the sandwich on the counter and reached for a mostly full bottle of Two-Buck Chuck—some nondescript, sour-tasting red. On impulse, he carried the bottle through the sliding glass doors out into the yard and climbed the circling iron staircase to the balcony.

He hadn't ventured upstairs in two days. But if there were any sight to leave imprinted in his memory, it should be the spectacular view from the balcony, that promontory that had become, somehow, *his* space, all those mornings before dawn when he had sat gazing out over the inspiring lights spread out across the valley below. Not even a chair out there now. He sat down on the stone decking and leaned back against the rough stucco of the house, gazing out through the iron balcony rails. He uncorked and raised the cheap wine at the view. He took a small swig straight from the bottle. His mouth recoiled, his cheeks shivered. Spread out below, as the night deepened, the lights of the city sharpened.

Las Vegas: city of second chances, city of real estate and dreams, city where life could change in a blink, this city he had worked so hard to build with all his hope. What he could see through the iron bars all stewed and shimmered in a colorful blur of a thermal mirage in the desert night, lights mixing into a single humming glow beneath a slate gray sky. Red warning lights blinked from the mostly empty hotels and condominium towers of Metropolis, from the Oz, The Beach, from Caesars and Bellagio, the neon cross of Downtown, and from the tall black ziggurats of the unfinished towers of Biscayne Bay. How he wished some company would come along to buy it up at a steal and finally finish that tallest of the tall Las Vegas hotel towers, somehow, someday. All their work, partly *his* work, too, at least would come to something. He hoped for the day that visionary concept would be completed, decked out and filled with happy guests. He felt sure that would happen, the only question when—five years, ten years, more? The other possibility would be to tear it down, what a shame, all but impossibly expensive to do—too close to the surrounding buildings to be imploded, a salvage company would need to take all sixty stories apart, piece by piece, selling off the salvageable glass and steel, all the rest hammered to bits and hauled away. Would that happen? He thought not—it would be finished, surely, if there were any predictable future. Like the The Strip and the whole city surrounding it, it would rise up and be reborn again into a yet more exponentially spectacular form. Nothing could keep Las Vegas down for long. He felt certain of this. He would not be here to see that happen or be a part of that new triumph when it did.

He took another swallow of the sour wine. Every few minutes, the gliding, trembling lights of an aircraft slowly descended from the east or rose up from the west with a steady rhythm over the airport, located in the city's lit-up belly—jets coming in, then out, like rumbling breaths. Along the interstates, lines of car lights tracked in from the south and west then blended into the glittering wheel of the valley's display. Even in these hard times, millions were still arriving, leaving, teeming up and down The Strip, mixing into that vibrating rose of the multicolored lights of Downtown. That his own small destiny now lay elsewhere mattered little in the end. Las Vegas was still here, with all its show of celebration, all its hedonism and despair, its luxury and excess—this city where every man and woman for a day or two or even a week could live like a king or queen, and where every woman and man could be just as easily stripped to rags and cast out into the elements, this city that took in everyone at once in nobility and sin.

People came here to be amazed and dazzled. He worried about the way the casino hotels were letting their properties get so worn out and threadbare under pressure of so much cost cutting, so leveraged under massive debts. He could only hope the many millions of visitors wouldn't notice and keep coming. Would they? Yes—he believed they would. In any case, the city would remain, would cycle through its perpetual births and rebirths until the water ran out, he supposed, his brother Justin's pedantic engineer's updates about the drought still lighting up his email from time to time, pictures of the drying-up basin of Lake Mead ever more concerning, its levels dropping every year until eventually it would be a mere puddle of what it had been, the basin lined with chalk-white rings. Years from now, the city might dry up and be abandoned, as Justin had predicted, left to the desert sands. Who could say? The answer would be left to Catherine's generation. Surely, this city—the Las Vegas he loved—would be here for as long as he lived.

He searched for the beacon of the laser beam that shone from the peak of the old Pyramid World hotel casino, dimmed for aircraft safety years ago, and there it was, a white beam into the sky, but it was hard to make out the glass pyramid with its smiling Sphinx that had once defined the south end of The Strip, so crowded in and dwarfed now by skyscraper mega-resorts and condo towers on all sides. He recalled the death of Lester "Red" Stahl, that horrifying slide and fall, the grieving widow and children, his own complicity in saying nothing. There had been times when he believed his current circumstances might be a kind of karmic repayment for his silence, also for his other ethical compromises over the years, his loyalty to Lance Sheperd and the company. What for? Years later, The Pyramid had become at best a low-end property. He understood that some future development plan halted by the economic crash no doubt had it slated one day for an implosion. So it went in this city—nothing was built to last in this desert empire.

At the very heart of The Strip, almost center, the bluish glow of Caesars Palace rose up against the night. He thought of the hundreds of homeless who had discovered the vast drainage tunnel system that ran under the city and Las Vegas Boulevard, how they had set up complete alternative lives beneath the neon. Battalions of veteran vagrants now mixed in with the recently cast out and unemployed. The homeless and dispossessed had smuggled in salvaged beds and furniture into that dark labyrinth of the Las Vegas underground, those miles of tunnels running under The Strip, each big enough to drive a truck through—the president or a billionaire could order a single-malt scotch or a bottle of champagne to a High Roller suite at Caesars while thirty floors plus a few yards further below their feet, huddled in a drainage tunnel, the transient poor passed a bottle of screw-cap wine or heated up a pot of tea. What made the difference between these people? Hard work? Intelligence? Education? Talent? These qualities mattered, surely, as they must; but through the booms and busts of this city, what counted far more was *luck*—Lady Luck. All were drawn along in her gaudy parade. *Luck*. . .

As in a dream, he could hear a faint music approaching—bits from squeaky flutes, pan pipes, a smattering of staccato drumbeats out of time—like the distant sounds of a medieval parade, raucous and out of tune, or like the production number of a musical. The music rose in volume inside his head, adding off-key pipes, tinny trumpets, blasting trombones, a snappy patter of drums. He squeezed his eyes shut to hear it more clearly, and then he could see it, too: hordes of people dressed in motley and rags mixing in with the ones in suits and ties and smart dresses, the desert dust blowing up in whirls all around their long column, all singing and dancing along Las Vegas Boulevard. And there she was—Lady Luck in her parade, the goddess giving out her prizes to those who least deserve them.

C. D. thought of the lives that had touched him here and he might have touched, where they were now, who he would leave behind. The Kinkaids, gone after New Year's, dumping their big house into foreclosure, suddenly packing up in less than a week without telling anyone, not even goodbye phone calls to say they were off to Denver, where Kinkaid took a job paying a bare fraction of his former salary as the comptroller of a chain of restaurants specializing in buffalo burgers and barbecued ribs. The Kinkaids might do all right, but at another level entirely, with no more pretentions of pursuing wealth, maybe recovering just enough that Mark and Pam could retire one day without needing help from their kids. Pam blamed C. D. for their losses and the lawsuits, though Kinkaid knew better, knew that, like almost every other Vegas loser, he had gone bust chasing greed. Greed is a goddess always alluring and stark naked, like the most exotic skin show—and there she is now, her float drawn along at the head of Lady Luck's parade. She lies back obscenely on a mound of gold and silver coins, heaps of green paper money, gleaming jewels. Writhing in a sexual frenzy, she rubs her body with handfuls of money and precious objects of her treasure. She spreads her legs, humping up and down on her bed of cash and gold. Who knew why so many chased this masturbatory fantasy? C. D. had chased after her too, the same as Kinkaid, to his own undoing.

Not everyone had lost, those who got out years ago faring best. Rick Rickstein had played it all just right, still with the Sands, off in Singapore now, almost all the way up the corporate ladder. But what a precarious and uncertain world gambling in Asia had become—the lawsuits were boiling up from that smuggler's den of Macau lately, the most lucrative gaming destination on the planet. The VIP rooms of the astoundingly profitable baccarat games in Macau were allegedly controlled by Chinese organized crime, murderous *triad* and *tong* gangs running fat junkets full of cash-rich players brought in from the mainland. Macau had become the biggest and most lucrative money-laundering operation in human history. Corrupt business managers, factory directors, central party functionaries—almost any big shot in China in a position to skim cash off the top—all packed suitcases full of paper *yuan* and hustled down to Macau casinos to convert their illicit cash into chips then into Hong Kong dollars or other hard currencies, also to gamble like there was no tomorrow. A catastrophe would happen there, and soon. He hoped Rickstein and his beautiful wife Josefina and their kids could get out before it was too late. He hoped Rickstein would not be seduced by greed, and that he had enough street-smart, Israeli good sense to duck any prosecutions.

Many other people C. D. knew would stay on here, moving along in Lady Luck's parade, following her gaudy banner of a harp and tower, her raucous music with its beating drums. Tim Slocum—what an intelligent man, such a crafty attorney too, who "made his numbers" long ago. But Slocum's chasing woman after woman in the casinos and in his social whirls around the city, taking them off for quickie grinds in the rooms he kept at Caesars, that shimmering blue hotel, would make him ever more restless, ever on the move, never finding peace. How could his wife and children not turn their backs on him? Here, he thought of himself as happy, when his cynical view of life and fastidious lust made him among the most miserable people in the city. And that class of rich moguls, bankers, and politicians Tim Slocum served—C. D. could see them clearly now—were like a beastly cavalry riding the backs of everyone else, wielding their whips.

He saw Frank Ratchette now as one of these, once such a competent, concerned VP of Human Resources, setting up long-term relationships with his workers. In hard times, he had been fair with layoffs and schedules for rehiring; in fat times, he had rewarded his staff and thousands of employees, at corporate meetings talking up the value of a stable workforce. Ratchette had risen through the ranks at Pyramid Resorts and then he too had joined Sheperd's team at Biscayne Bay. He was the only executive laid off from the bankruptcy able to muscle himself into the upper ranks at the new Metropolis—that packed-together monstrosity of mega-hotels glowing with such a plasma-TV sheen at the center of The Strip. Ratchette had landed his new VP position by coming straight at the stressed-out executive team at Oz with a software-generated scheme to compress and reorganize work "credits" of the housekeeping staffs along with new "quotas" and "monthly production goals" of every other worker until they soon reached physical and time-pressure demands almost beyond human limits. With so many layoffs, the unions had little choice but to swallow Ratchette's punishing schedules he termed "new cost efficiencies." His scheme set off a competitive industrial speedup at all The Strip hotels until the bodies of the housekeepers and maintenance workers and front desk clerks and sales forces and all the rest were strained and some broken, employee morale reaching an all-time low. When union officials complained about "worker burnout," Ratchette answered with a notorious memo that stated: "In this job market, any employee who 'burns out' can be replaced in a day."

This became a trend throughout the industry—cut costs while increasing pressure on the workers even as the executives upped their bonus checks. Las Vegas had once offered such ebullient working atmospheres in which every employee could feel like a privileged part of a brilliant concept, a valued member of the team, primed and eager to serve up an exciting *experience* to customers. Now, more and more, the jobs were becoming like hell on earth. Still, workers hung on, with little other choice. And in the meanest dog days of such a dog-eat-dog business, who could blame Ratchette for acting like the other Big Bosses, seizing his new job by taking up a whip?

Gary Luongo would stay on also—where else could a guy like Luongo ever go? That sleazy host to Whales, as puffed up and ugly as a toad, fingers heavy with gold rings—why was his kind always so favored here? After Biscayne Bay crashed, Luongo branched off on his own as a paid consultant and host to the nightclub scene and high-end "bottle service" disco joints, also working the latest craze of orgiastic "day club" pool parties aimed at rich young revelers in the expensive waters of the resorts. On the side, Luongo also specialized in "facilitating" and "setting up" available girls. He rented swank cabañas to wealthy, mainly younger clients wanting to "blow it all out" for tens of thousands per day. Or he set up richer, older lust-monkeys (mostly Wall Street guys) who paid him even more. For a while, it had looked as though Luongo might easily rise to the very top of these fleshpot clubs and orgies of waterworlds, then a story hit the papers that he had been named in lawsuits by two groups of cocktail waitresses for forcing them to "engage in sexual acts with clients" to keep their jobs. Could that stop a guy like Luongo? His notoriety for pimping only upped his stock with Whales who demanded his kind of "full-service" experience. The lawsuits would be settled out of court. Luongo would carry on as before and charge even higher fees. Luck smiled on guys like Luongo, who in hell knew why. On the other hand, what would Sin City be without sleazeballs like him selling its wares?

And what of the tens of thousands of other people who would stay on here, mostly solid, hard-working folks who had learned long ago not to chase money at the tables? C. D. thought of Dominick Bodolotto, his old-fashioned barber Downtown. Dominick would keep clipping away and talking, although at far fewer executive heads now than before, his style never changing, nor the shop he owned—he and his wife were well into their seventies but would never think of retiring. Old-timers like Dominick would stay on here for as long as they lived. They would be among the last to keep the city's memory, and history, until the time came when even they would be gone.

C. D. recalled his last haircut, how Dominick expressed his views of the crash: "Whata shame what dey done to dis town. In de old days, I tell yuz, dem bankers woulda gotta visit from Shorty da Cleaner. Dey woulda nevah got away wid it," he said. "Bettah yet, Rocco from Reno woulda took care o' dem. Nevah a tougher guy den him, dat's for sure. Ain't dat right, Angie?"

His wife echoed him, "Dat's right, Dom!"

"In de old days, dey took care o' da people, ya get what I'm sayin'?" Dominick whipped the barber's cloth off his lap and said, "I'm gonna miss yuz. Smart guy!"

So many people C. D. knew were leaving. Brick Rico—that brilliant interior designer who had decked out five major hotels with his postmodern visions of luxury. Rico had been undone by the bankruptcy of Biscayne Bay, having invested considerable resources and two years of work for which he would never be paid. Other casino resorts had also stiffed him—paying Rico's firm small fees up front, then when he completed work, they "renegotiated" on paying his bills. It was as if a whole new short-paying ethos had become standard throughout the industry, the stock answer to contractor invoices for honest work completed now *Go ahead and sue us, let's see how long you last.* After two years of this, Rico closed up shop and took a faculty position in design at an art institute in California, where he and his husband for two decades finally legally married, a wedding C. D. and Grace had felt too broke to attend.

So many people they knew had left town: his mechanic at the BMW dealership; his handyman; his pool guy; most of the guards at his neighborhood's gate. At least a half dozen of Catherine's former teachers had pulled up stakes after Nevada politicians cut education funding so radically that hundreds of teachers had been laid off, class sizes swelled beyond anything seen before, per-pupil spending dropped to 45th place in the country. Add to this the closing of so many public museums, cultural venues and programs—gems like the Guggenheim Hermitage and Vegas Valley Art Museum the first to close, then the glitzy Liberace Museum had gone dark, that flashy emblem of a past Las Vegas era. Going fast, too, were other earnest efforts to build a high culture in the desert, all shuttered, lost, gone. Would any of this come back? He hoped so. New projects stirred: ambitious efforts to transform the warehouse wasteland of the inner city into an arts district; and plans for a first-rate performing arts center to be built Downtown. Still, at least for now, state-funded youth programs, community health clinics, the new Nevada Cancer Center, once such a civic achievement, even many treatment centers for gambling addiction—all had gone the way of everything else. No wonder so many people were leaving, peeling off from the city's parade.

As the night deepened under an egg-shaped moon, C. D. opened his eyes again, gazing out from his balcony through its wrought iron bars. Spreading off from the colorful glow at the city's center, spills of starry lights from vast residential neighborhoods still shone like a million tiny beads tossed out over a black cloth, but they twinkled more dimly than before. Smears of shadows marked whole areas of abandoned, lightless homes. So many people were gone already, a lot of them driven out, others smart enough to leave before it was too late, and more were still leaving. He wished them all well. He hoped they would make it, wherever they had gone.

And where was Lance Sheperd? How had he vanished so completely?

Rumors ran that he was in hiding out in his vineyard in France, as walled off on its two hundred hectares as a medieval castle. Others said Sheperd had fled to California, holing up in his fortress in Malibu, rarely going out so he wouldn't be seen; or he drifted around to various properties he had been buying up for years in far-flung places: California, France, Australia, Japan, even a remote wilderness in a corner of Idaho. No one who answered calls or manned any of the gates at these places admitted he lived there or accepted papers from process servers for his many litigations, which, as Slocum had said, would be hounding him for years.

What a fall, among the many who had fallen. His wife had finally divorced him, among the first of the legions suing him to salvage what remained of his empire. He had sold off his interest in Las Vegas Data Solutions. He sold his penthouse. He gradually sold the art from his diminishing collection. C. D. believed Sheperd had fallen, though some people claimed the exact opposite, Rick Rickstein and Brick Rico reporting tales of how Sheperd had hedged his losses, recovering great portions of the $200 million he had pumped into Biscayne Bay. As with all the mega-rich, when so much buoyant wealth is accumulated the ship becomes unsinkable even if it keeps taking on water and listing, powerless with the tides. Still, no matter what he had left, Sheperd would never rise to a position of power in any major company again. And this, for him—to become a *has-been*—would be far worse than any other fate. C. D. believed he had been effectively beaten—pistol-whipped, humiliated to the point he would no longer show a public face. No matter what, he had not deserved that. Sheperd had been the best of them, had pursued a dream to *make art* of this crazy city, art in a culture that valued only money, money and nothing else. Unlike the vastly richer Las Vegas moguls who survived him, famous CEOs like Steve Wynn, Sheldon Adelson, Rick Starling, and the others—men who lived surrounded by more bodyguards than any old-time Mafia boss—soon, most people in this city would forget him, if they had ever thought of him at all. And for those who had known him—known who he had been in Las Vegas once—the echo of his failure would follow him to his grave.

Sad, sad, sad—too many sad stories in that stew of simmering lights, in that out-of-tune music he could hear growing louder in his head. Flutes and pipes, drums and cymbals, blasting trumpets, farting trombones, all clashed together now into a steady din, not sad music, really, but more like the *oompah-pah* noise from some cheap, chaotic carnival. Whatever music was playing out there in the streets below, the tunes would soon start drawing people in again. Las Vegas would slowly begin to recover, ever so gradually filling up once more with tourists, conventioneers, vacationers, guys and girls looking to *blow it all out,* looking for the *experience,* plus the many hucksters, grifters, and vamps always a part of the scene. The dream city would recover amid the rise and fall, rise and fall rhythms of the greater casino economy—give it five years, ten years at the most, and all would be sailing along at a new peak speed again toward yet another era of economic boom. Yes—the dream city would recover, as would the country, then all would rush toward the next cycle of boom and bust, rise and fall, rewarding the few winners and casting out the many losers once more, Lady Luck riding high above them in her parade.

And there she is: Lady Luck—what a striking figure, dressed in her gorgeous green gown with a pointy crown on her head like the Statue of Liberty, carried along in her parade along Las Vegas

Boulevard. How strange, how odd (but then again, maybe not so strange) that the face of Lady Liberty on the U.S. postage stamp that year was *not* copied from the original iconic statue in New York Harbor but rather from its replica on The Las Vegas Strip—3 billion USPS stamps printed with the face of the faux sculptural foam version lifting her torch in front of the New York-New York casino hotel (representation more real than the real now, how fitting).

Lady Luck rides high over her parade along the boulevard. She smiles all around. She waves in all directions, her feet in golden sandals planted firmly on a big globe, a perfect replica of the blue marble of planet Earth. Over her shoulders, on a strap made of snakeskin, she carries a large golden cornucopia spilling out an abundance of colorful vegetables and fruits. As she turns and waves, fruits and vegetables keep falling from her woven gold basket, carelessly spilling out over her red, white, and blue float, bouncing off it into the crowd. One out of nine will end up big winners. Four or five out of nine will break even, more or less. As for the rest, Lady Luck smiles and waves. She tosses up her hands, blowing kisses. She reaches into her golden, horn-shaped basket as if to dispense her boundless favors to the crowd. Then she tosses her hands out into the air, empty, over their heads. People shout louder, mouths open wide, shoving more roughly, clamoring to get closer. What a delirium in the way they seek her out, so full of hope. How they raise their voices so in hope. She keeps reaching in and throwing her hands out, reaching in again then thrusting up and opening her hands, tossing to this crowd her handfuls of nothing. And the crowd—what a crowd!—they teem and squeeze in closer, fighting each other for her bounty that scatters so capriciously here and there as in that old Las Vegas truth: *No one in the house of fortune gets what he deserves*. Her music quickens with a bright, trilling melody of a fife and drums. Lady Luck passes by in her parade that moves on into the distance, tuneless melodies diminishing to a last high squeak of a flute, a final clatter of a tinny cymbal dropped flat onto the street, then her parade is gone, leaving in its dust the limping wounded and a few lonely, starved-looking stragglers following far behind.

—

C. D. sent out his most intense well-wishes to Greta Olsson, mixed with a pang of *what if*—what if he had been a better friend? What if, in some other destiny, she had permitted them to be steady, passionate lovers? It had been entirely her choice to leave him some integrity (if he had any left) and his marriage undamaged (he hoped), for which he felt grateful now. What a smart, dynamic, charismatic talent Greta had been in her prime, when she was sober. For years, she kept bouncing in and out of rehab to quit drinking and taking little blue pills. She had quit trying to quit after the fall of Biscayne Bay. Never prudent with money, she too had been wiped out—her total losses she would never say—by millions in their worthless partnership on top of what everyone guessed were unwise real estate investments with her last bad boyfriend. The last he heard, she had been reduced to living on borrowed money from her family.

He recalled the happy teamwork he and Greta put in together pitching projects, zinging out the press releases, strategizing and designing the marketing campaigns and websites, how Greta stood up so effectively to present these to the higher-ups, the investors, the sales forces, all the while projecting such girl-next-door wholesomeness and sincerity to which almost no one could ever say no—what a performance, every time. From the last news he had about Greta—the incident Marjorie Slocum had gossiped about to Grace—she had flown to town to interview for a position at Caesars. A former mayor of Las Vegas had arranged a lunch meeting with top executives to toss her a lifeline for at least a mid-level job. She arrived late to the meeting. At lunch—her excuse that she didn't think it "would look right" if she turned down a glass of wine, just one, then two, four, and more—Greta ended up thick-tongued, weaving around, falling all over herself in the booth at Spago's. At some point, rummaging through her purse for a pen, she knocked her purse off the table. Its contents flew out, scattering. Tough enough to land a job these days but even tougher when the VP of HR gets down on his hands and knees to pick up a mess for an applicant, no matter who she once was, or whose old friend. C. D. heard a confirmation of the details from Tim Slocum. He might have phoned Greta afterward—but what good would that have done? Even if she had answered his call, she would have put the best face on things and told him how "great" the interview had gone. He had heard Greta hadn't been sober since. She would never climb back up from this, he felt sure.

Less than a year later, after he had left Las Vegas, he would get a call from Big Jim Chevron: Greta had died of liver failure—so like her, always, without telling anyone what she knew, what her doctors had told her weeks before. Big Jim invited C. D. to a memorial in Las Vegas—some honor, at least, must be paid to the woman who had made it as high as a VP in the men's club of their industry. A funeral and burial had already happened, presided over by her family in the small town in Minnesota where she had been born. C. D. flew to Las Vegas from Seattle to attend. The gathering took place in a rented conference room at Caesars Palace, where a few PR professionals, journalists, politicians, and her former bosses raised a glass and spoke kind words, standing at a podium beside a big blow-up photo of Greta at her ebullient best from her glory days in marketing and as a flak for campaigns. Big Jim Chevron spoke first, then Tim Slocum and Frank Ratchette, followed by a former U.S. senator, a former congressman, several county commissioners, and others, all men except for a former mayor and one of the anchors from the local evening news. Mark Kinkaid didn't attend. Brick Rico sent flowers. Lance Sheperd was the most conspicuously absent.

C. D. had meant all along to step up next to Greta's big grinning photo and read remarks about what a friend she had been, the best workmate ever, then tell funny stories about times she had saved him. But listening to and watching those men in suits, his insides started churning as he picked out the men he knew or guessed Greta had slept with, stricken by how these men had failed her, and how he too had failed her, and he choked, he couldn't say anything. No tears were shed. The mood felt more like a send-off for a drinking buddy than a memorial service.

Afterward, very few of the guests hung around for long. Tim Slocum approached C. D. at the bar and remarked, "I expected you of all people would have said something."

He held back his urge to grab Slocum by his suit lapels and shake him. He took in several controlling breaths, then looked Slocum directly in the eyes and said, "You wouldn't like what I have to say. None of you would. Nobody would."

He would have said what had filled his mind that last night in

Las Vegas as he gazed out at the lights of the city and thought of Greta, how she had chased after both people and things she could never possess. She had learned too late (if she had ever learned) that a life spent in service to fame could be so thankless, and so lonely. What else is marketing but a lackey to fame, always for something or someone else? Serving fame often means self-destruction. Fame never gives back, she only takes away, or at most she sings her praises in a loud, buzzing noise. People throng all around her to touch and feel her gown, only look closely enough at her jeweled hands waving over the crowd and her fingers transform into a blur of wagging tongues. To this, Greta had given everything. She had split herself into pieces. She had carried out the many corporate orders and tasks demanded by these men to near exhaustion, then had stepped straight from those into the pressure and crush of political campaigns, all these jobs at once—when did she ever sleep? She had worked harder than anyone he knew to help make these men rich. And in playing her role as "just one of the guys" for them (and for him too, yes, for him), she would never be loved the way she desired. These men had used her up—Lance Sheperd worst of all—then, when she was no longer useful to them, they had dumped her off into Lady Luck's parade. Greta had sacrificed her heart. She deserved far better, at the very least to be properly mourned.

On the flight home, C. D. turned his face toward the window and wept.

—

Years later, in a dentist's waiting room in Seattle, C. D. Reinhart would pick up a *Forbes Magazine* and chance on a list of the nation's newest billionaires. He would note a name with no photograph, only two words for sources: *Lance Sheperd—hedge funds.*

—

The wind picked up and began to blow, lifting up a dust that darkened the night, dimming the lights below. C. D. shivered. He gazed out at the dust-dulled shimmer of the distant lights, the leaves of the palms in his yard moving overhead like feathery arms. How he had embraced Las Vegas for all its hope. How he still thrilled at this city and always would. He prayed Lady Luck would smile on all who stayed here and all who would come here in the future, as he had once, looking for a second chance. For him, it was time to leave. He couldn't stay longer, not even one more night as he had planned.

He lifted himself to his feet, hurried down the circling stairs, slipped inside to the guest room, and grabbed up the pillow and one small duffel full of his gear. In the kitchen, he took his sandwich for the road, also stuffing all that was left in the refrigerator into a bag. He checked around, feeling his way along the dark hallway, making sure all the lights were off, then he closed the door of the big house behind him. He lifted the heavy lock box and let it fall against the door, hearing the faint clanking of his keys inside.

C. D. climbed in behind the wheel of the U-Haul truck. He started the engine. He lumbered out into the street, pressed the accelerator, and rounded the corner, not looking back. He breezed through the gates, not waving at the sleepy guard—not one he knew anyway. Down the hill and into the flats, catching green lights all the way, he took the ramp onto the I-15, merged into the slow lane, and he was off, heading south. He rumbled along, gathering speed. The further he drove, the freer he felt, his doubts dropping away behind him.

As he crossed into California at Stateline, the thought struck him that for all his work to get the house so immaculate and spotless, he had left a half-empty bottle of wine sitting on the balcony! For some reason, he laughed at this, and for a while, every time he thought of it again, he laughed, feeling that old beater of a truck under him pulling its trailer, straining up the steep grade into the San Bernardino Mountains. Weight from the last twenty years steadily fell away, peeling off in layers as he drove, his rainbow tucked safely behind him in the load. He would beat traffic into L.A., drop the painting off at the gallery as soon as it opened, sign papers for the sale, then turn north and be on his way. He breathed in deeply, thought of the wine bottle again, and let loose a big Greta Olsson laugh out the open truck window: *Haa*-hah! *Haa*-hah . . .

In Seattle, Grace had prepared the house for him, making him an office space of the upstairs guest room. On Friday, the day he was due to arrive, they were invited to a party hosted by her old friend from college who worked for city government, well placed in its intimate circles. A tourism and events marketing position for the city would open up soon, and Grace thought he might have a shot at it with the right introductions. The following day, Saturday, would be his birthday, and Grace would bake a cake—the fluffy yellow cake she knew he liked, with sherry-raspberry filling between the layers. Catherine and João would join them for dinner and to watch him blow out the candles on that cake Grace would decorate with the words *Happy Birthday to Your Next New Life!*

It would be halfway through the year 2011. He would turn fifty-two years old.

He believed he would make it this time. Not that he was fooling himself—he figured this third chance carried odds similar to rolling a 5 or 9 at craps (about three to two), so he might very well fail. Hadn't he already failed twice? Still, he planned to seize this third chance and never let go, not for as many years as he had left in his passage on this Earth. Lady Luck would be waiting for him with open arms, he felt sure, and he would fall into her fickle embrace. Into the wind through the open window, he laughed: *Haa*-hah! He wasn't sure if he actually shouted into the rushing air or if it were all in his head, but he would ever afterward recall shouting out the window as he drove: *Good luck!* Calling out his blessings for the city he had left behind and for whatever lay ahead: *Good luck! Good luck, everybody! And good luck to me! Haa-hah! Haa-hah . . .*

Acknowledgments

Many people must be thanked for *Dream City*. Thank you to Irene Vilar, whose enthusiastic support kept the writing going; to the late wondrous writer Christopher Towne Leland for an early reading of a too-long draft and his advice; and to writer-editor Joseph Olshan for giving this book a try. I salute and honor the members of Iron-workers Local 433, with whom I stand in solidarity. A big embrace to the gang of hotel casino scholars, the "breakfast bunch" from the UNLV Hospitality College who let me listen in on tales from the industry (and in memoriam to friends who are gone): Pat Moreo, John Stefanelli, Karl Mayer, Bob Woods, Tom Jones, Gary Waters, Jim Kilby, Bernie Fried, Al Izzolo, Patti Shock, and my dear wife, Carola Raab, to whom this book is dedicated. A shout-out to Curtis Love and especially Bret Shannon for his many reports from the front lines. Thank you to interior designer extraordinaire Lee Cagley for sharing his insider stories plus my gratitude forever for his sponsor-ship, which kept me alive. To editor magnifico Gary Fisketjon for reading an umpteenth draft and taking time to write a detailed letter that gave me the keys to this final version, thank you more than I can say. Abrazos to poet Shaun Griffin, fellow Nevada activist, who always signed off to me with *ten fe* from his heart. Thanks to Curtis Vickers, JoAnne Banducci, and the cool new editors at the University of Nevada Press. And to so many former students (you know who you are) with whom I shared too much about the difficulties, trials, and self-doubt in writing this novel, thanks to you all for putting up with me when faith waned, then dissolved, and I needed your hopeful energy and spirit to keep believing. Books cycle through many lives, deaths, and rebirths. They are helped by many people. This story, this fiction, this dream, owes them all: *magnas gratias*.

About the Author

DOUGLAS UNGER is the author of four novels, including *Leaving the Land* (a finalist for the Pulitzer and Robert F. Kennedy Awards), *Voices from Silence* (a year-end choice by the *Washington Post Book World*) and, most recently, *Looking for War and Other Stories*. He has contributed to the *Nevada Independent* as well as stories and essays to *Narrative, Boulevard*, the *Brooklyn Rail*, and other journals and publications. He teaches in the Department of English at the University of Nevada, Las Vegas, and co-founded the MFA in Creative Writing International Program and the PhD with Creative Dissertation. He is affiliated faculty with the Black Mountain Institute, an important literary center and think tank in the American West. In 2007, he was inducted into the Nevada Writers Hall of Fame.